I0705957

SOUL

Published by Graveside Press
graveside-press.com

Editing: Kelley York and Hannah Graves
Cover Design: Sleepy Fox Studio – sleepyfoxstudio.net
Interior Formatting: Sleepy Fox Studio – sleepyfoxstudio.net
Interior art: Sleepy Fox Studio – sleepyfoxstudio.net
Interior art (ink drawings): Yusuf Astriyanto – @yusufastriyanto

eBook 978-1-964952-16-1
Print (KDP Paperback) 978-1-964952-24-6
Print (Paperback) 978-1-964952-18-5
Print (Hardcover) 978-1-964952-15-4

No part of this book has been created using Generative AI.

SOUL
A PARANORMAL ANTHOLOGY

CONTENT WARNING

For a list of potential trigger warnings,
please turn to page 385 or visit our website:
graveside-press.com/cw/soul

BAREFOOT IN THE BLEACH WATER
Christopher Bond

THE HALLWAY IS immaculate despite the crumbling building that it resides within. No wadded-up newspapers or bent, rusted soda cans tossed into the corners. No blankets of questionable origin or ripped-up mattresses hiding in the shadows. No dust, no dirt, no cigarette ash. Every bloodstain has been scrubbed clean. The light fixtures that once illuminated this vast space have been dead for decades, and now they hang dark and silent like the bodies of criminals left swinging at the gallows long after the crows have taken their eyes. There are no cobwebs clinging from their chains; spiders have too strong a sense of self-preservation to stay here long.

There is a faint odor of bleach that lingers like ghosts with unfinished business.

A large, ornate grate on the wall near the hallway floor shifts slightly. It has always been a grate, but now it is more than that. It is a door, an entrance, the ductwork inside no longer carrying the warmed air from the dead furnace in the basement but something more, something almost alive.

The grate shifts again, becomes unstuck. Bone-thin fingers so white they almost glow in the darkness reach through the cross-hatched metal. They curl and lift, and the grate is lowered as gently as a baby being placed into a wicker basket on a river. The floor is pristine, but there is a small, thin scar in the porcelain tile, one made not by intent but by repetition, and the edge of the grate fits smoothly into it. The bone-thin arm connected to the bone-thin fingers reaches out of the deeper darkness to lean the grate against the wall, its top edge also finding a well-worn scar to nestle into.

Nothing has broken the silence.

This pleases the thing in the vent.

This hallway, this building, they were not always this way. They were once a place of learning, of study. A sanctuary. Now, a tomb. Countless black-shoed feet once walked these tiles. Important feet connected to important people, en route to performing important tasks. Now, only one pair of feet walk these halls, and they are decidedly not black-shoed. They don't wear any shoes at all. There are still important tasks to be performed here, though. The coldness, while shocking, is a small penance.

If this space was filled with blindfolded people, they would not notice the presence of the old man as he walks down the center of the hallway, so light are his footfalls. Skin calloused and worn and as soft as the bottom of well-oiled moccasins, decorated with twisting scar tissue that wraps his feet and ankles and calves in a fine filigree, an intricate geometry. There are no windows here. Instead, there are paintings. Portraits. Some of those important people who performed important tasks. They watch the man who was once a boy with their eternal gazes. There is no judgment painted in the brushstrokes of their eyes, but the man who was once a boy still believes he is being weighed and measured with every step. His naked, slumped shoulders can hardly bear the weight of it, but he does not slow.

A man stands in a nook of a wall built of shadow. He is not a tall man. He wears coveralls the color of dust. Black was for the others. Black, to show the seriousness of their work. Black, to hide the unsightly blemishes that are produced from the seriousness of their work. But gray was meant to conceal, to blend in. The left side of the man in gray's face has caved in on itself.

"You can't do this any longer," he hisses at the pale man that roams the hallway. "In fact, I forbid it."

The man who was once a boy ignores him. Tries to, anyway. He doesn't have to look at the man in the gray suit to know that they share the same crooked nose, the same lime green eyes.

At the end of the hallway, the heavy wooden door to the operating theater stands open. An angled doorstop of cast bronze wedges it against the wall. The man who was once a boy has not located the key to this particular door, so the door stays open, despite that an open door mars the orderly nature of this space. It is a small infraction but one he never fails to notice. Yet another thing for those old masters on the wall to weigh and judge and ponder over. The man who was once a boy sighs through the doorway.

The operating theater was once the heart of this place, nestled deep within the now crumbling structure. Every empty hallway led here, the place where knowledge was created and curated and examined and decided upon, and then that knowledge went back out like blood being pumped into the arteries of this once-great institution. It was always a secret place, a sacred place, but now time has lain across it as thick as a heavy snowfall, covering it, concealing it, and it has become more secret and more sacred with every layer, with every year.

The man who was once a boy has also been concealed in this way. The weight of it has bent his back, has pressed on his spine until he must look up to look forward. He does not mind. He wears it like a mantle of the finest silk.

A heavy oak table sits in the center of the circular room, another silent light fixture hanging just above it. Rows and rows of elevated wooden chairs all face this table. The table is old, like everything else in this place, but its craftsmanship is remarkable, and it has not lost a sliver of its original conceit. The top has been worn smooth from years and years of learning, of teaching, of *finding*. The man who was once a boy has polished it to a fine sheen, identical to the one it had when it was first brought here.

Unlike the floor of this room and the hallway, the ancient wood has refused to give up its stains. They spread across its surface like the galaxy in miniature; a swirling constellation here, a battered dwarf star there. Every dark brown speck a story, a person, an idea. Every miniscule stain a bloody step on the road toward enlightenment. These, too, have been judged, have been weighed. They were important once. They had *purpose*. They were battered mile markers. They were tattered prayer flags. They showed progress.

Once, but not now.

Now they read like ancient histories, telling a story to those who have learned to read the dialects of this forgotten place. *Almost* forgotten.

The man who was once a boy runs his fingers along the tabletop and reads each stain like they were braille, and he does not feel shame or horror or pity or bitterness at the story they tell. Loss, maybe. *What could have been*. It was never *his* story, anyway, not entirely. He is just the curator.

"You are not allowed in here," a voice calls from near the top of the rows of chairs. This man wears a black suit, but his suit jacket has been draped over the chair beside him. A canvas apron hangs from his neck, swirling stains akin to those on the wooden table spattered across the fabric. His mustache is graying, though he is not as old as the gray would indicate. His eyes burn from behind his spectacles. He has one hand over his neck as if he is trying to choke himself. "When I call for you, *that* is when you are allowed to enter. You desecrate the sanctity of this place with your presence."

The man who was once a boy ignores this, too. The Director leers at him, drops his hand from his throat. The pallid flesh beneath splits horizontally, exactly along the path of a straight razor. He says no more.

The man who was once a boy continues through the surgical theater to the wooden door on the other side. It is smaller than the door in the hallway though built of the same construction. It was built smaller, the man thinks, because it was not meant for an audience to walk through it. It was meant only for those few important men. The ones who stare down from their painted perches in the hallway.

The creators of knowledge. The disseminators.

The Directors.

The man who was once a boy would have never been allowed in this room, not while the others were alive. But the harshest lessons have a way of sticking to you, to your bones, your guts, even long after those who taught them have gone away and turned to ash. The man who was once a boy slopes across the small chamber, shoulders tense, waiting for someone to reprimand him for this transgression. No one does. No one ever does. Still, he does not relax until he has grabbed the metal key from the loop beside the desk and made his way back into the theater.

The man with the blazing eyes and the severed throat is gone now, but others have taken up their posts around the table in the theater. They murmur to each other, a low, thudding sound like coal tumbling down a chute into the furnace room. Some are dressed in those peculiar black suits, others in white shirts and corduroy pants. They have the look of students, though they appear much older, more refined. They watch the man who was once a boy with keen interest, but whatever comments they have are shared among themselves, not deeming the subject of their dialog worthy of such direct communication.

The man who was once a boy does not mind. He has nothing to say to them, either.

The work done at this secret place was not well-known outside of its walls. There are facets of knowledge that the world turns away from, no matter how important that knowledge is. How vital the work is. The men who walked these halls did not seek approval from the masses, nor fame, nor accolades. The truest seekers of wisdom never do. Every experiment performed here in the shadows was meant to bring the light of discovery to civilization. To forward the understanding of what it is to be human. Every idea was nurtured, every whim given fresh soil to be planted, to grow, to blossom. Not every experiment was a success. The furnaces in the bowels of this crumbling building were not designed to burn just coal or wood. Fire, like bleach, could be cleansing. The man who was once a boy knows all about the purifying nature of fire. He has not had to go to the basement for a long, long time. Still, he shudders when he thinks of it.

There is another door off of the pristine hallway. It is a small door. Compared to those doors that lead to and from the surgical theater, it appears as an afterthought to the original construction. Square-framed and unpainted, just a thin layer of stain applied infrequently. A small placard has been mounted to the front. *Custodial Works,* it reads. Beneath it, in even smaller letters: *Douglas White, Head Custodian.* The man who was once a boy sighs, runs his finger over the name. It's like trailing his hand over the cool, chiseled rock of a headstone. His father never received a proper burial. And since the man who was once a boy refuses to go deeper, to allow the shadows of those hulking furnaces in the basement to cross his own, this is as close as he can get to paying his respects. His lips move in a silent prayer, but he has long ago forgotten who exactly he is praying to. God cannot see him here, he knows. God was never allowed within these walls of learning.

He fits the key into the door and pushes it open.

Inside the small room, the man who was once a boy does not need a light to find what he needs. He's grown so accustomed to the dark that light would be a detriment. He finds the familiar shape of the wooden mop bucket in the corner. He wheels it to the faucet of the floor sink and begins to fill the bucket with brown water. The pipes are ancient; they sound like someone trying to breathe through a hole in their throat. They've had no maintenance done since the building above collapsed into disrepair. It takes a long, long time to fill the bucket even halfway. A mop hangs beside the sink. The wood handle is worn smooth, nicked all over with the scars of heavy use. The mop head itself disintegrated long ago. Like his small, gray uniform. Like his socks. His shoes. Strips of old bedding have been torn and fashioned into long strands, secured at the end with a frayed bit of rope. The man who was once a boy plunks the mop into the bucket of brown water and wheels it over to the shelves that line two-thirds of the room.

The nature of the work done here in this sacred, secret place required a special type of person. Someone who could see past the obvious, someone not cruelly oblivious but religiously discerning. Someone who was not blind to the injustices and the atrocities, but rather recognized them as necessary steps toward the greater good. In this way, the sacrifices made here were given their proper respect. This type of person was not limited to just the doctors, the researchers, the disseminators. The engine drives, but the cogs keep the wheels spinning. The general public would have no concern with wolfing down a T-Bone steak, but most would balk at the heavy smell of blood that permeates the butcher's workshop. The man who was once a boy does not balk. He knows the heavy smell of blood. He knows how to be rid of it.

Bleach is as cleansing as holy water, his father used to tell him. Bleach is strong enough to clean sin. As the man who was once a boy grabs a glass gallon jar of his profession's holy water, he wonders for the thousandth time what changed his father's opinion of the work done here over the years. What made him finally believe that some sins couldn't be justified. That some sins couldn't be forgiven, be wiped clean.

The screaming had been horrific; even the heavy wooden door to the surgical theater couldn't muffle them all. The screaming of the children was always hard, particularly. What remained on that well-built table in the center of the room after all the well-dressed men had departed was worse. But for years, Douglas White and his son had bent to their tasks as earnestly as any of the important men that wore the black suits. They worked diligently, fervently. Cleanliness was next to godliness, and this place was their church.

But something changed. The man who was once a boy named Timothy White does not know exactly why. But he remembers when.

The former Timothy White, now just another ghost that walks these halls, wheels the bucket of bleach water down the hallway and back into the surgical theater and begins to clean.

The water stings at first, the bleach finding those small pockets of skin that have yet to be covered in scar tissue. The stinging, like the shocking coldness of the floor, is just another form of atonement. He does not mind. Others have paid much larger costs in this place. He pauses outside of the door to the Director's office. It was here, when he was much smaller, when he first knew that things were about to change. He didn't know then—*couldn't* have known then—how *much* they would change. Change this place, the work done. Himself.

His father had gone through that door and shut it behind himself. As a rule, neither one of the Whites were allowed inside the office unless called for. The surgical theater itself, too, was off limits, at least until the doctors and observers had left and things needed to be cleaned, to be burned, to be purified. Young Timothy White had waited at the door to the Director's office, feeling unsure of what to do. He'd placed his ear to the keyhole. Some words couldn't penetrate the thick wood he'd heard most of them.

"What are you doing in here?" a man's voice said.

"I…I need to talk to you. *We* need to talk."

"When I call for you, *that* is when you are allowed to enter. You desecrate the sanctity of this place with your presence."

"You must stop. *This* must stop It…it cannot go on," Douglas White said in a low voice, no doubt knowing his son was just outside the doorway.

"I *must* stop? Stop what, exactly, Mr. White?"

"All of it. This…this isn't right. What happens here."

"And who decides what is right, in your opinion? We are state-sanctioned, after all. What we do is important."

"But at what cost?"

"And yet you have had no issue taking your check every week, have you?"

Timothy White didn't know for certain, but he was sure that his father glanced to where he stood on the other side of the door. He coughed, cleared his throat.

"You can't do this any longer. In fact, I forbid it."

The first man was silent for a long time, and when he finally made a sound, they were not words that the boy heard behind the door but laughter. Harsh, cackling laughter. Only after a few long moments did he finally speak. His voice was closer now; he had risen from behind his desk.

"And who are you, Mr. White?" he asked.

Then there was a loud, dull thump. The sound of something solid cracking, breaking. Then a gasp. Then silence.

The boy, Timothy White, stood beside the wooden door for what seemed like an eternity. His mind blanked. His father had never shielded him from the truth. He was only ten, but he knew what sort of things happened here. What kind of sounds were made behind closed doors, and what he would find if he opened them. Even now, though, he dared not open this door. He did not want to see.

Eventually, the door opened anyway.

The Director stared down at the scared little boy, skin already the blinding pale of someone who had scarcely seen the sun. The man took off his spectacles and wiped the small spatters of blood from the glass before returning them to his face. He did not show surprise or concern to find the boy there. There were fresh drops of red beside the older, darker ones on his canvas apron. He turned and nodded toward the slumped shape lying on the floor of the office, a pool of blood circling the ruined head in a grisly halo.

"Another one for the furnace, boy." And when the boy said nothing, he added, "Make it quick or I daresay your father will have a companion in the fire before the day is out."

Timothy White was young he was not stupid. There was no protection here, not for him. He could not say anything. In fact, he would never speak a single word ever again, though he did not know that then. Instead, he nodded. It was hard work bringing such a heavy load to the basement without the help of his father, but he managed. Those he passed in the hallway as he pushed the wheelbarrow averted their eyes. It was the first time the boy felt what it was like to be a ghost.

The man who was once a boy named Timothy White mops the surgical theater. He starts with the top row of seats and works his way down to the floor in a methodical pattern. He does not ask the men sitting in the chairs to move their legs. He doesn't have to; the mop moves freely through them. They stare at him with their bulging, bleeding eyes, hissing mangled words through their swollen throats and ravaged lungs.

Timothy White does his work, and he pays them no mind. After all, they never paid him any mind when they were alive.

Douglas White taught his only son many things in the last decade of his life, and Timothy White had always been a faithful student. The elder White showed his son where to keep the tools of their job, and how to keep them orderly and in working condition. He showed him where the various keys to all the doors in the hallway were, and how to perform their duties and at the proper time. He showed him the chemical shelves and explained what each glass bottle contained and what they were used for. Lye could break down biological material and help to sanitize the smell. Vinegar could clean glass. Ammonia was a fertilizer, but it could also break down fats and oils rendered and spilled from a human body. Bleach could cleanse the blood.

"Never," his father once told him, "mix the bleach and the ammonia, Timothy. Especially in the industrial concentrates we work with. They make a terribly caustic gas. It can kill you if you're not careful."

The man who was Timothy White was a faithful student.

He remembered *everything* his father had taught him.

Locking all the doors in the hallway had been a simple thing. Spilling gallons of ammonia and bleach from their glass bottles across the floor while the others were preoccupied in the surgical theater had been easy as well. They were surprised, to be sure, when the heavy wooden door had been thrust open during their work, but once the gas entered the theater, panic blinded those inside. No one thought to kick away the bronze doorstop wedged at the bottom while their eyes and lungs bled and their throats closed up.

Timothy White slipped through the grate in the hallway, and he did not return for a long, long time.

When he did, there was only one man left breathing among the dead piled at the doorways. The Director had locked himself away inside his office, but he had not been able to escape all the effects of the poisonous gas. Timothy White found the proper key and pushed the door open, and when he came upon the Director, the straight razor from the man's own shaving kit had finished the job that the gas had started.

The furnaces ran nonstop for four days before the halls were clear again.

Others came into this holy place after a while. They searched the empty hallway, the immaculate surgical theater. They did not peer through the grate in the hallway. They did not think to search the vents. They *did* search the furnaces, but all they found were tiny silver dental fillings and bits of bone hidden amongst the ash. The clerical staff in the offices above were relocated. The surgical equipment was inventoried and removed. The patients, those few who remained, were likewise inventoried and removed; one last day of black smoke from the chimneys. Eventually, those in charge of the investigation left, locking the doors above and trying to forget about whatever might have happened there. The still-scared-but-not-quite-alone boy watched them leave from the shadows.

He did not forget. He did not make a sound. Silence had become a sacrament.

Bleach can clean anything. The man who was once a boy named Timothy White knows that better than most. It can clean blood. It can clean ash. It can *almost* clean sin, if you scrub hard enough. If you're diligent enough.

As he dumps the dirty water back down into the floor sink in the custodial closet, he wonders if this time he was able to clean every sin. Every transgression. He wonders if he scrubbed enough to wash away all the things that occurred here in this secret place. He wonders if he has been forgiven yet. He nods to the specter of his father still standing in one corner of the hallway before he crawls back into the vent and replaces the grate.

Almost, he thinks as he disappears back into the darkness.

Almost.

DESIRE & SONS

DESIRE & SONS

Nicola Lombardi

Translated by J. Weintraub

THE SMALL YELLOW sign displayed in the window draws my attention as if someone were repeatedly tapping his knuckles against the glass as I pass by. Instinctively, I slow to a halt and take a few steps back. So, I had read it correctly…

Leaning against an old suitcase and surrounded by a collection of the most varied of objects (silverware in an antiquated style, alarm clocks, massive photo albums, dolls, small boxes of inlaid wood), a lemon-colored poster the size of a business letter announces in words precisely traced with a red marker: "GHOSTS—BOUGHT & SOLD."

It's clearly the shop of a dealer in curios, second-hand antiques, or something of that sort. I had never noticed it before, but it's also true that I rarely pass through that part of town. I lift my eyes to the store's sign. A string of characters in wrought iron, simulating an elegant cursive script, informs me I am standing in front of "Desire & Sons."

I take a quick look at my watch, although I'm not in any particular hurry. Even before I decide to enter, curiosity drives my palm down onto the door handle.

At the ringing of the small bell hanging above the door, the noises of the traffic along the main street seem to be sucked into a vortex that removes them instantly from my hearing. The piercing, heightened sound of a siren is lost in the distance, along with the honking of horns, the voices of passers-by, the annoying musical buzz streaming from cellphones. Quite an evocative effect, also due to the second ringing—the one set off by the closure of the glass door—that proclaims the descent of a silence that I instinctively associate with the inside of a church.

Looking around, I venture an, "Excuse me?"

The space is not very large, and that it is extraordinarily cluttered with items on display makes it appear narrow and almost cramped. From the shop window, the late afternoon light illuminates everything with a powdery golden sheen, and I can't help but lose myself gazing among the shelves packed with inscrutable rummage, the dusty cabinets, a pair of bleak grandfather clocks, a barrel piano, a cumbersome globe, and the endless supply of books occupying almost every empty section of the walls as they compete for space with the already pitch-dark paintings made even darker by the shadows. Lingering in the air, a faint floral aroma, perhaps calycanthus, hovers over the scent of closure.

I try again, "Good evening," and then behind the counter, from a blue curtain that I hadn't noticed before, appears a man, slight and bald, with a pair of old-fashioned pince-nez glasses fixed to his nose. I catch myself thinking that such a character would not have been out of place in a Harry Potter movie.

"Good evening, sir," he says, greeting me with a broad and calming smile. He looks to be about sixty, but he could also be a good deal older or even younger.

"Hello," I begin. "I…"

"You want to take a look around?" he asks, anticipating me.

"Well, to tell you the truth… I was intrigued by that sign in the window. 'Ghosts—bought and sold.'"

He lays his hands on the counter and nods. "Are you interested in buying one?"

"No, good heavens, no!" I smile in turn, my palms raised upward. "It's just that I amuse myself by writing tales of the macabre, ghost stories, things of that sort, and so as soon as I read… What is it, a joke?"

"Oh, no, sir! Certainly not a joke!" He looks me straight in the eye. "Do you want to know how it works?"

"Nothing would please me more!"

The little man strokes his perfectly clean-shaven chin. "So, if someone needs some ready cash, a hefty loan, say, he only has to make a deal, a very special one. We, Desire and Sons—my grandfather, way back, and then my father, and so on—we give him the money and, in exchange, he pledges, once dead, to consign his ghost over to us. And that's it."

I remain speechless for some moments, my face having assumed, I fear, a vaguely idiotic expression.

"And that's it, you say? Well, that's really very nice, but then what do you do with…?"

"With a ghost? My dear sir, you have no idea how many very rich people are ready and willing to spend a bundle of dough to get their hands on one to haunt their mansion or their hotel or even their castle. Have you ever heard of Supernatural Tourism? There are millions behind it, believe me. Wealthy people inclined to visit or stay in dwellings that turn out to be truly haunted… And we, of Desire and Sons, are among the biggest suppliers in that regard."

I cannot wipe the smile off my face. The entire affair is utter madness, and quite a good story could come out of it. "But how does it work?" I ask, having decided, enthusiastically, to play along.

"Very simple. Clients deposit with us objects that belong to them, a kind of surety or bond, something to which they are attached, something like a ring, or a watch, or whatever else, after having first marked it with a drop of their blood." The little man mimics the act of piercing a finger with a needle. "We store it for an indefinite period, that is to say, until the day of our client's death, at which point…we receive what we are owed."

A few seconds of silence are enough to shake me out of the spell that his delirious tale has ignited in my imagination. "Then… I suppose you have some sort of safe storage where you keep…"

"The sureties, of course. Are you interested in seeing some of them?"

I was hoping he would ask me that. "Very much so."

"One moment, then." Stepping from behind the counter, this odd junk merchant crosses in front of me, leaving behind a faint scent of camphor and soap. Arriving at the front door, he gives a sharp twist to the key already inserted in the lock, after which he rotates the laminated rectangle hanging with a chain and suction pads to the glass, presenting to the outside world the notice "Be Right Back."

"There, that's done. Please, this way."

I mumble a thank you and, zigzagging behind, I follow him as we wedge past the counter. The little man pushes aside the blue curtain from where he had appeared a few moments before and thus I wind up in a short, open hallway poorly lit by a naked bulb hooked up to the wall.

"Here we are," my companion says in a soft voice as we stop in front of a small door. From a pocket, he produces a key with which—after lowering our heads a bit—we enter a room where a shadowy darkness makes its dimensions entirely indefinable.

The odor that greets me is the kind that stagnates in basements, in enclosed spaces lacking ventilation. Given that the little man flips no switches, the yellowish beam penetrating from the hallway is the only source of light, and I open my eyes wide so as not to miss a single detail. The thought that I have stepped into a potentially dangerous situation does not even cross my mind. It is all far too astonishing, far too above the ordinary, for me to allow myself to feel any real concern.

Against the wall, illuminated by the slant of light, sits a piece of furniture consisting of numerous shelves in raw wood, packed with small boxes or little glass cases similar to miniature coffins.

"Inside here, for example," the little man informs me, grabbing the first container in front of him and placing it before my watchful eyes, "there's a silver locket." Through the small transparent lid I admire the floral oval, its engraved flower obscured by a brown stain. "It's dried blood," he explains. "It belongs to the woman who gave me this as a bond. Whereas this…" He sets the locket aside and points to another box, small and flat, "…is a silk handkerchief with lace trim. And yes, that dark stain is…"

"Blood, of course," I conclude, nodding and letting my eyes wander over that crazy collection. Really, I don't know what to think. My head is full of questions. I choose the first that springs to mind. "So, what do you do then? Resell these things or what? In short, how do you…?"

The little man retains his angelic smile. "Still very simple. Once the owner of the surety dies, he or she comes back here and waits for me to find someone to purchase that very same object. And when a buyer for the item is found, the ghost follows it."

"And goes to haunt the home of the buyer?"

"Exactly."

I fail to hold back a small laugh, even if in this circumstance it sounds rather out of place.

"Excuse me, but this is all so…"

"Peculiar?"

"Sort of." It's not really the adjective I had in mind, but it will do. This man is the very essence of the most clear-headed kind of insanity. For me, always on the lookout for the most incredible tales, he is pure gold. "But I'm curious about something else. From the moment the owners of these sureties die, until you find an arrangement for them, so to speak… The ghosts, where are they?"

The man stares at me for a few moments from above those old-fashioned glasses of his. Maybe he hasn't yet decided if I believe his words or if I am simply making fun of him. Slowly he turns toward the far end of the room opposite us, an increasingly dense gulf of shadow, gradually lost in impenetrable darkness.

"They are here," he replies in a quiet tone. "And they wait."

Those words sear every square inch of my body. Instinctively, I follow his gaze, and I realize that the power of suggestion can play some weird tricks. I barely suppress a shiver as I am seized by the feeling that there, in the thickest of the darkness, are persons, motionless, silent. I see nothing, naturally, but the eyes of my imagination set my brain on fire, making me feel that I am under the scrutiny of invisible presences. Coughing nervously, I am suddenly very uneasy.

"What is it, Nicola? Some sort of problem?"

My breath is cut short. "How… how did you know my name?"

The little man extends a hand out toward the shelf and, his fingers hovering over several objects, he finally picks up a small box, long and thin.

"I've got a good memory," he replies calmly. "And then here, on the metal clip, your name is engraved. See? Do you recognize that spot of blood?"

I feel a chill all over as if somewhere a window had been thrown wide open.

"But I…" I stammer, and fail to say anything else.

"Unfortunately, yes, my friend," comments the owner of Desire & Sons, feigning a look of despair. "You died a short while ago. A drunken driver drove straight into you as you were walking along a sidewalk not too far from here."

The room seems to rotate slowly, and I recall the distant wail of a siren. I look at the stained fountain pen that has, in the meantime, been returned to the shelf, and I sense the onset of tears stinging my eyes.

"I know," the man continues, "at first, it's always hard to remember. I helped you get out of that mess you'd gotten into with that ugly loansharking crew about six years ago. And now, as per our agreement, here you are. You could not have gone anywhere else."

I want to cry out from all the horror that is wrenching my heart, but not even a breath escapes from my throat.

"Now calm down. I know it's a painful reality to accept, but there's nothing we can do about it. A deal is a deal. Now, stay here, settle down, and wait, along with the others. I trust I'll find good buyers within a few weeks, or a few months…"

I stare at him as he withdraws into the corridor. The faint cone of light contracts, disappears. The door closes with the strident sound of a key turning. I stay there, enveloped in a darkness becoming ever colder, still convinced I have a body that can shiver.

And then I turn around, or am under the illusion of doing it, to go meet my new companions.

KIN

Ken Farrell

THE MAN UPRIGHT in the saddle was dead, yet the weary horse continued heading home through the swamp in half moonlight. From where he watched hunkered in cypress knees, Arlon Wilkins' first thought was biblical, that the man approaching on the slow horse was a spirit come for him for running off from the battle. Arlon shook his head free of the notion, deciding his fever accounted for this fear. Even in the scant moonlight, Arlon could tell by the rider's boots and saber that he was a Yankee officer. Probably a deserter like him. *No other reason an officer'd be out here alone on the slow ride west.*

The battle two weeks before was a rout. Most on his side had died; the smoke and confusion had been so thick, he was able to just walk away, and as a conscript pulled from a work gang just a month earlier, he doubted he'd be missed. Hiding during daylight, Arlon picked his way home many miles each night, avoiding everyone lest he end up back on the front lines or back in the chains.

This stranger was the first man he'd seen in days.

The Yankee listed: *Asleep in the saddle*, Arlon guessed. Arlon looked from the Yankee's boots to his own cut-up, blackened feet; he appreciated the horse, the finest of its kind he'd ever seen, and he eyed the beast's rippling flanks. Arlon's belly ached for meat.

That man's got too many gifts, he decided.

Arlon drew his folding knife and crept onto the swamp-edge trail. The horse perked its ears, but kept an easy gait. Arlon shuffled three steps closer, and the horse spun. Arlon had raised the knife, thinking he'd stick the Yankee under the ribs, but instead caught the horse in the right eye. The horse shrieked and reared, throwing the rider, its bellow echoing over the water. Arlon lost the knife into the swamp and grasped at the reins, trying to put the roiling beast between him and the rider, but the horse shook and shrugged, yanked Arlon off his feet, whipping him side to side. Arlon climbed up the reins, hand over hand, and hooked one arm around the horse's neck and settled the creature enough to locate the rider.

The Yankee lay flat on his back, mouth and eyes awed open like he stargazed. Arlon saw he was dead—gut-shot—and ashamed of his folly, said aloud, "Broke his neck on the fall," as if the crowd of cypresses were judging him.

Arlon hobbled the horse with a length of rope and then worked over the Yankee. First, he spit on the dead man, and then tugged off his boots: too big, but workable. As he rummaged through the dead man's pockets, the nearest cypress knees shuddered, resonating like drums, the great gnarled trees swaying like they meant to uproot themselves, while hoofbeats echoed across the swamp. Arlon couldn't mark from which direction the riders came: it was as if they charged from all sides. He rolled the body into the water, un-hobbled the eye-stuck horse and swung himself up into the saddle. He'd ride the brute fast and far until it dropped…and then he'd have his supper.

Terence Wilgus, the caretaker of the defunct weekly newspaper, *The Culverton Star*, slammed the office's oak door, a feat for the slight eighty-five-year-old. He stood at the antique slant-top desk in the small room and watched the young man outside babble to himself as he climbed into his Jeep and tear up the street, scraping the blue mailbox as he cut the corner onto Route 12. Terence shuffled to the rotary phone on the back wall and dialed Sheriff Truitt to say, "I have a problem."

Sheriff Truitt said he'd be over directly.

When Sheriff Truitt pulled up and saw Terence, he was worried. Like every other day, Terence sat in front of the *Star* office in his rocker, but unlike every other day, Terence wore his Marine Corps piss cutter, a bandolier askew on his chest, and a shotgun across his lap.

The sheriff climbed out of his cruiser.

"Mornin' Terry," he said, tapping his Stetson.

"Sheriff," Terence replied.

"Haven't seen you in that get-up since those boys broke out of the state pen. You have a spot of worry?"

"It's that fella who come over from Baltimore."

"Who bought the Sampson place?"

"Yup. He come in, hollerin', askin' for records I just don't got. He went on and on about 'breathin' in the house, how the house is 'breathin' so loud at night he can't sleep. Crazy fool."

"Breathing, eh? What records was he after?"

"He got it in his head that somethin' awful happened at the Sampson place. The fool thinks the house is *haunted*."

Sheriff Truitt, always professional and temperate, chuckled. Surprised, Terence thought the sheriff laughed at him.

"Well damn, Sheriff! He made a mess of the office—" he poked the shotgun over his shoulder— "and I don't want him comin' 'round again. If he does, he just might be able to talk to them ghosts up close and personal!"

"Take it easy, Terry."

"*I'm* the Editor-in-Chief, not no one else," Terence said, his jowls tensed.

"Did you find anything that might fit what he's looking for?"

"Sherriff, when he stopped by last week, he was lookin' for information on the house and the Sampson family going back as far as the war." His eyes narrowed. "The War of Northern Aggression."

"I gathered that's what you meant."

"I figured he was just curious, tryin' to get a feel for the history of the place." The more Terence spoke, the quicker he rocked. "So, I spent two days in the boxes and files, and I even checked at the Assessor's office for anything that maybe'd been overlooked, and she searched in her computer. It was all nothin', just plain news—marriages, obits, records from when they built the house—nothin' about what I come to find he suspected, like somebody hacked somebody up and buried 'em under the floorboards! I gave him copies of everything. He was none too pleased, but he thanked me and went on his way. Then he come back in today tossin' everythin' everywhere and hollerin' about *breathin'!*" Terence stopped rocking and gritted his dentures, tightening his grip on the shotgun: "Hollerin' how I'm lyin', how I'm keepin' somethin' from him. *I'm* the Editor-in-Chief!"

"Yes, you are, Terry. I'll get to the bottom of it. You take that shotgun inside and lock up. If he comes back, give a call and we'll be over. The fella just might be in trouble, and our way is to help out those in trouble?"

Terrence eventually nodded yes.

"Did he say where he was heading?"

"He's collectin' family bibles now. He went to see Ava Davenport."

The sheriff thought a moment: "What's the fella's name again?"

"Wilkins. Eric Wilkins."

Just after midday, Arlon hefted the last of the hogs off the two-wheeled cart and threw it into the fire pit atop the other carcasses. He'd lost the entire passel to the flu, and despite two years of fatiguing work since he'd come home from the war, he was once again without prospects. He clicked his tongue at the horse, yanking the noosed lead rope.

"Git, Cy!"

But a shadow of the once mighty, scar-backed, one-eyed horse was sluggish to respond, the now empty cart it dragged still a burden. Arlon limped along the root-broken path and through the woods to the house, occasionally jerking the lead rope, chatting at the horse.

"We're in a hitch now. Them hogs was gonna set us for the winter." Arlon patted his belly, leaning close to the horse. "Your reprieve might soon expire."

The horse swung around, glaring with its hollow eye, snatching the rope from Arlon with its teeth.

"Goddamn trickster." Arlon grabbed the dangling rope and yanked hard. "You're a vicious bastard."

When he came through the trees, Arlon saw his sister Loretta's boy, Buddy, on his back in the mud, one arm tied to the hitching post in front of Arlon's tumbledown hut. Two men, one big and tall, one rail-thin, stood near the boy with rifles. Buddy had been worked over, his shirt collar torn, lip split, bleeding from a gashed forehead.

Arlon flushed from anger and from guilt. Loretta was the only kind person he'd ever known, and before she'd died, he'd promised to look after the boy. Arlon hadn't done much on that account, he knew, mostly leaving Buddy to fend for himself. Arlon limped forward but tried to stand a little taller.

The skinny man was about to speak, but Arlon cut him off.

"I can't tie off my horse if you're gonna use my post for that whelp."

The two men in their wool suit-jackets and starched collars looked at one another.

The big one grumbled through his thick mustache, "You blind or ignorant? Don't you see we're armed?"

"Oh, yessir. I see it all."

Arlon pressed forward, bumping into the skinny one, then the big one. The big one cracked Arlon's mouth with his rifle butt. Buddy whimpered, and Arlon stumbled and spit, blood splashing the men's boots, and then he laughed.

"Is one of you fellas gonna hold Cy's rope?" he asked. "Scrawny, but this beast's a hellion. I ain't never gonna catch it if it runs off on account of you sonsofbitches."

Arlon snickered again, wedging himself between the two men, bumping each. The big man reared back with his rifle. Arlon snatched the skinny man by his coat's lapels, hauling him between himself and the big man. With his right hand, Arlon swung around the skinny man and stuck the big man over and over in the belly and ribs with the grass-thin filet knife he'd snuck from his pocket. The big man sputtered and fell, the skinny man trying to shake Arlon. Arlon jumped around, hand fisted in the man's suit, dodging the flailing blows and sticking the skinny man wherever he could. They tripped over the big man who was on his back, gurgling.

The skinny man went limp. Arlon dropped him on his friend.

Arlon pushed himself up, wheezing. "Whoooey. Ain't tussled like that in quite a spell." He scooped the horse's rope. Cy hadn't budged but was attentive to the ruckus. Arlon walked Cy around, drawing the cart up alongside the dead. The air thickened with rust, and Buddy looked nauseous.

"I done the hard part," Arlon said. "You're buryin' 'em."

With this, Arlon cut the rope that held Buddy to the post and grabbed his wrist, yanking him to his feet, before lifting a pocket watch and some coins and bank notes off the dead men.

Buddy trembled and stared at the bodies. "I just—"

"Shut up, Buddy. Don't matter what you did. Kin is a debt you can't never repay. Let's load 'em. We'll take 'em out to Culver Creek. Won't no one find 'em in a forever."

They each grabbed an arm and a leg and swung the skinny man into the cart. They struggled but eventually hefted the big man in. Then Buddy threw up. Arlon forced a laugh to ease his gut's impulse to throw up as well. The horse stepped on Arlon's foot: the sharp pain tipped him and he heaved. Arlon punched the horse's rump to set it moving.

Sheriff Truitt pulled up at Ava Davenport's and tried to make sense of the scene: a jagged hole gaped in the front wall of her house, and Eric Wilkins' Jeep idled in her living room. Ava sat on her porch in a floral robe, smoking a cigarette. The sheriff called for an ambulance. Ava waved as he stepped from his cruiser and then cupped her gray curls as if to adjust them.

"You okay, Ava?"

She shrugged, wincing. "Right as rain, though I would like to report a theft."

"Just a theft?" the sheriff asked, cocking his head at the run-over rose bushes, the rubble, the idling Jeep where the coffee table used to be.

"All this isn't quite what it seems," she said, her eyes sweeping the horizon.

"You don't say?"

"Oh, I do." She ground out her cigarette nub on the hardened sole of her slipper and struggled to get up, waving off the sheriff as he leaned to help. They entered the house through the front door and stood next to the still-running Jeep. Truitt peered around, his hand on his revolver.

"You won't need to shoot anyone, Sheriff. He ran off."

"What did he take?"

"My great grandad's Bible," she said, grinning at him as if it was a big hoot. "He drove up while I was out front and said he was doing ancestral research and asked to see my family Bible." She lit another cigarette. "He looked a little desperate. I didn't care one way or the other, so I fetched it for him. He looked over my family tree inside the cover and said, 'We're cousins'."

"Cousins."

"That's what the man said."

Ava groaned, trying a deep breath.

"You sure you're okay, Ava?"

"The air's so thin," she said, caressing her lower back. "I guess the mirror clipped me when he gunned it."

Truitt threw aside a cracked asbestos shingle and batted chalky dust off the haircloth footstool, cupping Ava's elbow to ease her down.

"Did he say anything else?"

Ava responded to a question not asked, gazing somewhere behind the sheriff: "He said we were cousins, but I can't be responsible for every third cousin thrice removed. Some of the fruit on the tree is gonna be rotten," she added between pained breaths, swaying back and forth, back and forth. "The Bible settled it for him. It eventually settles all things." She snapped back to attention and looked again at Truitt. "Well, I was about to ask him to tell me how he knew we were kin when he looked in his mirror and screamed, *He's here! He's here!*' That's when he floored it past me. Didn't try to turn or break. Just—in!" She dusted her hands once: the hard clap startled the sheriff.

"Who'd he see that set him off?"

Ava stopped swaying and pulled another deep breath through her cigarette, never seeming to exhale. "That is the question, isn't it, Sheriff?"

Truitt sighed at Ava's cageyness.

"Ava, did you see the man he was running from?"

"I didn't see." Ava bounced a little as she continued. "Might have been. Under that big crabapple tree by the pasture fence." She pointed with two fingers, cigarette erect between them. She gazed at the tree through the jagged hole in her house, her face suddenly slack. She whimpered, then blurted, "Then he got out and ran off with the Bible."

"Okay." The sheriff patted her shoulder. "You're okay."

She adjusted herself to ease her discomforted back while Truitt reached into the Jeep and pulled the key from the ignition, dropping it in his pocket.

"I'm gonna look around a bit," he said, heading toward the gash where the picture window had been. "Looks like the lintel is okay," he said as he scrutinized the mess. "No pipes or wires busted. If you're gonna have a car drive through your house, this isn't a bad spot."

Ava laughed too enthusiastically, then stopped. She stared at the crabapple tree and the pasture beyond it.

"I lived in this house all my life," she said, speaking to no one, "and when I was a girl, many an afternoon, I'd reach fallen crabapples to the horses through that split-rail fence. It's not fair. All those kind memories, trampled."

Truitt stepped through the hole to the porch, kicking glass aside, stepping over splinters of white porch railing, and crossed the lawn to the crabapple tree. The tufted grass was wrecked like someone had been milling around. The disturbance swirled a few feet toward the house.

His walkie chirped:

"*Sheriff, we got a disturbance at the Sampson place. Had two calls on it. Angie's already there.*"

"Copy. I'll head over."

An ambulance turned up Ava's long gravel drive and sprinted toward the house. The sheriff climbed into his cruiser. As the ambulance pulled up, he called over to the two paramedics.

"Sixty-year-old woman, possible hit-and-run. She's conscious and talking. I don't think the wall is gonna come down, but there's glass, split two-by-fours and fiberglass and shingles everywhere, so be careful."

The paramedics stood still, looked at each other, looked toward the house, perplexed.

The sheriff saw Ava in the hole, eating an apple.

"I think she took a blow to the head," he added.

"Okay, Sheriff."

Truitt turned on his lights and siren and sped to the Sampson place on the hill overlooking the reservoir.

THOUGH WORN THROUGH from the day's planting, Buddy barely slept. He stretched himself on his straw pallet, watching a few stars that shone through the neglected roof disappear as clouds slipped by. He held his breath, waiting for them to peek in again. Wind battered the shack, rattling loose boards and whistling through the gaps.

He'd not slept through the night in a long time. He mostly lay awake, praying. Waiting for the men to come for him and for Uncle Arlon, for all the wrongs they'd done over the years. He lay awake because ghosts would wander in from the woods to surround the shack, dancing and singing, and they'd whisper to him to come outside. It was a sinister invitation, and on the nights when they came calling, Buddy prayed aloud.

The stars reappeared, and he breathed again. He wondered if he could squeeze through the splintery hole, grab onto those stars, and pull himself through the sky to another world where men didn't hurt other men, didn't steal from them, didn't lie to them and kill all at once, didn't kill them slowly, one bushel at a time. Buddy believed there was such a world, but to enter it, he needed to be clean, and although he'd never killed anyone directly, his hands were bloody just the same.

The wind died down. Clouds suspended over the hole, obscuring the stars, and Buddy again held his breath. All sound stopped: the boards didn't rattle, the wheezing ceased, and even the tree frogs no longer chirped. Buddy knew the hungry ghosts were near and he was about to pray, then Cy nickered. A voice soothed the spooked animal, and the horse quieted. Buddy wasn't sure if ghosts talked to Cy or if it was a human voice. He eyed the gaps for shadow moving on shadow, searching for a living shape where only the dead should be.

A hushed conversation trickled from behind the shack, and then footsteps fell all around. They splashed the roof and walls. Slick and pungent kerosene dripped in, gumming up the dirt where the walls met the floor. Then someone hollered and flames scaled the walls, blinding Buddy.

Buddy finally got his prayer started.

"Our Father, who art in Heaven—"

Arlon crawled to his side. "No help comin' from on-high, Buddy. They mean to burn us alive!"

The gruff voice of old man Truitt bellowed through the flames: "Took me three years, you bastards, but I got you! You killed my boys! You murderin' cowards are gonna be carried to hell in a chariot of flames!"

The others whooped and cursed them, and then a half-dozen horses thundered off, the commotion fading as the flames wailed.

Arlon kneeled over Buddy. "You want to live, boy?"

Buddy couldn't say. He didn't deserve to, he thought. He just wanted peace. The heat pressed against them, the thick smoke acrid.

Arlon screamed, "You want to live!" then heaved backward, snatching Buddy to his feet, and running them into the flaming wall. They crashed through the burning boards and into the rain barrel. Arlon dragged a hacking Buddy toward the horse. Cy just looked at Arlon, nonplussed by the whipping flames. Arlon hoisted Buddy into the saddle and yanked the horse by the mane into the woods, where they'd stay for as long as needed to keep Buddy safe.

"I can't do it no more, Uncle Arlon."

"What?"

"I can't be wicked. I want to be saved. I want to go to church again, like I used to with Momma."

"Right now, we save our bodies. After, we look to your soul."

Arlon dragged the horse and rider deeper and deeper through the thick underbrush, sometimes pushing the placid horse through brambles, keeping it motivated with frequent blows to its flanks. The humbled horse clicked forward on worn joints, its spine bowed. They forged on until the flames disappeared at their backs.

By the fall, old man Truitt had died of natural causes, and no one came looking for Arlon and Buddy. Beyond ever-trailing whispers, they were left alone. They rebuilt the shack and planted when the soil would take it and felled trees for timber when life was leanest. Arlon went into town each Sunday with Buddy and left him at the church while he and Cy delivered wood if they had it, or sometimes he'd gather scrap from whatever the townspeople discarded. Arlon had a knack for finding things with hidden value, and he felt a Sunday was well spent if he brought Buddy home safe and maybe had a little money or the horse hauled a little junk. Some days he'd let himself be rubbed the wrong way while haggling, but he only sliced ears or busted legs…for Buddy's sake.

THE ROAD TO the Sampson house traced the reservoir where a troupe of dinghies idled, their tiny sails slack, as girls and boys chattered, swimming between the stalled crafts. The sheriff recalled when they'd dammed the creek when he was a boy. His father brought him home a tin mug full of arrowheads from the worksite. In excavating, they'd also found potsherds, a Civil War twelve-pound mortar, even a pair of human skulls. After the reservoir filled, he'd spent many a sunny day fishing and swimming, just down the hill from the Sampson property.

On the final turn toward the house, the sun hit the reservoir and roared, blinding him. Dazed, he pulled up to the house, still rubbing spots from his eyes.

He found himself parked between his deputy's cruiser and Eric Wilkins' Jeep.

Truitt regarded the Jeep through the pulsing spots and galloped his fingers on his steering wheel. After a few moments, he climbed out of his cruiser and laid his hand on the Jeep's hood: cold. He scooped everything out of his jeans pockets and fished through the tinking coins for the Jeep key, but he couldn't grasp it as it fell under and under the coins and then was gone. He scattered the coins on the gravel and checked the ground around him. There was no key.

Mystified, he walked to the house where a jaggedly-toothed mouth yawned, a hole cracked open from the inside, burst out of the living room. Angie, his deputy, waited just inside the hole.

Angie was pale and seemed more withdrawn than she'd always been.

"I ain't seen nothing like this."

"I thought I just did at Ava Davenport's."

"Sherriff?"

Sheriff Truitt stepped over the debris through the hole, following his deputy, but not really listening to what she said. The hole was only the beginning of the destruction: wherever the sheriff looked, the wallboard and plaster had seemingly exploded from the studs, the chalky, fibrous discard everywhere, a layer of grayish dust coating everything. He followed Angie. Every wall was a hole exposing skeletal two-by-fours and wiring and discolored copper pipes and gray ducts, the neighboring rooms visible beyond, and the walls in the further rooms were portals to the next. Except for the gaping wound in the front, the house's outside walls had held but were little more than a cracked shell strained and fractured trying to keep the madness inside from spilling out into the world. The house creaked and gasped like a breeze whinnying through.

They turned a landing and entered the main bedroom. Truitt almost walked over the body, but Angie held him back.

"Sheriff?"

The sheriff looked at the man, flattened dead at his feet. He was no more than the suggestion of a human form: he was mercilessly compressed, his shirt and jeans burgundy with blood. Ava's Bible lay open on the floor near the body.

At the top of the family tree, a name written in faded ink: Johnathan "Buddy" Wilkins.

"I think this is Eric Wilkins, the fella that bought the place," the deputy said, not looking at the body.

"Him. His Jeep, outside," Truitt said.

"Yes it is, Sheriff," Angie replied, thinking the sheriff had asked her a question.

The sheriff squatted and opened the dead man's hand: Wilkins clutched a chunk of plaster with many coarse hairs mixed in to strengthen it. He crumbled the plaster chunk, pincered out the hairs, and twirled them between his thumb and forefinger. With each twist they brayed, snorted, each of the half-dozen hairs a crying throat.

"I called State and they're sending over some troopers to help out."

"Good. Good Angie," the sheriff said, rapt with the choir he twisted.

The sheriff's walkie chirped: "*Sheriff, Doc Evans is at Ava Davenport's and needs you A-S-A-P.*"

"Copy. What's going on?"

"*He's peeved you left the body with the paramedics.*"

The sheriff looked through the wall of no wall to his right, and felt gripped, as if being pulled between the timbers into the bathroom, and further, through the guest room, until he was rushed to where that cracked membrane of the outer wall trembled and barely kept him from lurching out into an awfulness, awesomeness, he couldn't name. He thought he was about to be lost. He had to leave.

"Copy," he said, flinging away the dusty hairs. "Angie, wait outside for the troopers."

"Sheriff?"

Truitt hustled down and out to his cruiser, and he sped back along the glaring reservoir where he saw no sails, only the white-shining belly of a single overturned sailboat, two tiny sailors atop it, motionless like lizards on a rock. He drove faster and faster, racing away from the Sampson house, away from the corrupted present, pretending if he went fast enough, he'd find a Jeep in a living room and Ava alive on her porch, smoking a cigarette.

His need found no purchase. Ava's house was unblemished. There was no hole. The paramedics leaned on their ambulance, and it was Doc Evans, bespectacled in his white linen suit, who sat on the porch where Ava once had. Doc jumped up and started hollering as soon as the sheriff pulled up.

"Why in Sam Hill did you leave the scene?" He jabbed a finger at the house. "Why'd you leave this poor woman alone?"

The sheriff said nothing, pushing past Doc through the open front door. The living room was spotless, but Ava laid face down, long and straight, in front of the footstool, where she once sat while chatting at Truitt about a Bible and a family tree. Like Eric Wilkins, she was trampled. Not as severely, but not too far off. The sheriff noted the body bluing, the blood already dry. She'd been dead for some time.

Doc Evans dropped to a knee and pulled her blouse partway up, revealing her bruised back.

"I'm not yet sure what did it, but she took just a vicious beating with something heavy and curved—see the focal points of the blows here, here, here," he said, drawing his fingers in near-closed arcs over Ava's back.

Sheriff Truitt nodded and walked absent-mindedly to the front window, looking out at the crabapple tree Ava had so loved. A few of its branches hung just over the fence, and a mangy, battered horse yearned upward, trying to reach an apple.

"Sheriff!" Doc Evans yelled. "Are we gonna see to this?"

The sheriff didn't respond. He exited through the hole and crossed the yard to the tree. As he neared, he saw the horse wasn't battered at all. He was a large, kingly animal, very fine. His nostrils flared, and as he shuffled in place, the ground shook. His ears turned to the sheriff, who pulled a hefty apple from the tree with a snap. The horse shook its mane and pawed the ground as Truitt reached the apple over the fence toward the quivering lips.

THE TWO MEN haggled in front of the livery in a steady flow of those just out of church.

"Maybe once, ten years ago, that was a fifty-dollar horse," said the man in the fray-brimmed bowler from his perch on an empty milk-can. The horse was almost toothless and scarred heavily about its nose and shoulders and rump. Its ribs bulged through its mange, and a tumor grew on the bone in the socket where the right eye used to be. "It's only good for glue and plaster. I ain't givin' you nowhere near fifty dollars."

Arlon's hand gripped his knife handle as heat simmered in his gut, but he rode out the long, long silence, the potbellied man eyeing him, wondering what Arlon was going to do.

Arlon had thus far kept his promise to Buddy and hadn't killed a man in six years, not since the Truitt brothers, and he'd told Buddy he'd sell the horse to buy train tickets west. *No one is s'posed to escape Hell, but Buddy's got a chance,* Arlon thought, *unless I kill this fat man on this street in front of all these people in their Sunday best…*

"Well, my fine sir, what will you pay for the wretched sack?"

"I'll give you five dollars," the man said flatly, spitting tobacco juice into the dust.

Arlon pulled his blade, an eight-inch bone-handled gutter he'd lifted off a tosspot a few weeks before.

Trying not to swallow his chaw, the man watched Arlon's blade rise.

"How much will you give me for the knife?" Arlon asked, leaving no doubt that the man would be taking the knife one way or the other, either by the handle or by the blade.

"I-I'll give you fifteen," he said. "Five for the horse, fifteen for the knife."

Arlon's flush passed. "Twenty dollars. All right."

Arlon handed over the knife and lead rope and pocketed the money. Cy kept his hollow, tumored eye on Arlon throughout the exchange. He kept his eye on Arlon as he was led away. Cy would always keep an eye out.

Arlon felt something novel, a quiver in his gut, a light buzz. He strolled, window shopping with the regular folk, mulling this oddity brimming in him, a feeling he might call excitement, or *pride*, but not the kind of pride he'd gorged on so often, not the screaming-kettle pride that had compelled him to strike men down.

Arlon found Buddy on a bench across from the church, his hat twisted in his hands. Buddy looked up oddly at Arlon, and then unclenched his hat and smiled. Arlon hadn't yet said a word, but Buddy knew Arlon had gotten the money to go to Denver. He hopped up and whooped and rushed over.

"The train pulls out in 'bout fifteen minutes, Uncle Arlon. We need to get our tickets."

Arlon hadn't realized he'd been smiling until he stopped.

Buddy was his mirror, his smile tapering as Arlon's did, his excitement reined in.

Arlon handed Buddy the money.

"With this, and the little we already got, it's enough for a ticket and some pocket money," Arlon said, leaving no doubt that it was always only Buddy who was taking the train west. Buddy threw his arms around his uncle. Arlon embraced him. It was the first time they'd ever hugged.

"Come inside and say a prayer with me," Buddy said. He'd made this request many times over the years.

Arlon looked at the simple spire and cross yearning atop the bright white church. He hadn't been inside a church since he was a boy. The closest was when Loretta invited him to Buddy's baptism so many years before, and he hadn't said a prayer in so long he couldn't remember how. Then he felt a little tickle, a tingle, that if he allowed himself to think the word, he might call *hope*. He looked at Buddy and scrunched his face, trying to tear the tickling feeling out by the root.

"There's only so much forgiveness to go 'round, Buddy."

Buddy embraced him again.

"You best get to the station," Arlon said, pulling away.

"Thank you, Uncle Arlon. Thank you! I'll see you. I'll come back and see you."

Buddy sprinted to the station, the burlap sack stuffed with his personals strung over his shoulder bouncing as he ran. He glanced back just once, waving his ticket as he crossed through the gate to the platform.

Arlon knew Buddy meant it, that he'd come back.

But Arlon didn't want him to, not ever.

And through the years, right up until Arlon died at seventy, he made sure each time he replied—often months or years late—to one of Buddy's letters, in his near illegible, near illiterate text, to let Buddy know how his prospects kept him moving, that he didn't know where he'd be in the fall, or that Christmas wouldn't work, because he'd met a true lady, and they were going to visit her parents in Vermont. Arlon let Buddy know about all of his romances and all of his successes. All invented in the shack where Arlon lived alone and where every night he laid awake cursing to a god he was sure had long ago forsaken him and crying prayers to drown out the screams of dying soldiers, the gurgles of murdered men, and the unearthly beating of hooves.

EVERYDAY IS THURSDAY

Felicia Ann Lee

NIGHTS ARE THE worst. That's when I most fear that the children do, indeed, remember. No, not fear—*know*. That look in Lucy's and Merrill's eyes when they awaken from their dreams—how could I witness that and believe they don't remember?

Orville, of course, says I'm being ridiculous.

"Really, Mavis. They are mere babes. How on earth do you think they can remember anything? Trust me, my dear, they're just dreaming the dreams of childhood." But from the way he averts his gaze when he says this, I can tell he doesn't really believe it.

What is most curious are the late nights when the others are least active, and we have our house to ourselves once again. One would think that this would be the very time little children would feel most comfortable and secure but no. Soon after their prayers and bedtime stories and repeated requests for kisses and more stories, followed by fitful slumber, their screams begin. And always, I rush in and rock them in my arms, reassuring them everything is all right, it's just a bad dream, and hours later we fall asleep, tangled together atop one of our beds.

When the red-birds begin their singing the next morning, it's as if it never happened. Lucy and Merrill are sound asleep in their bedroom, and I awake in mine.

Every morning is that Thursday morning, a clear, cool day in early spring, with the tender leaves of the dogwoods just beginning to emerge from their gray branches. I clean up at the washbasin, dress, and make my way to the kitchen to stoke the fire and have breakfast ready for Orville and the children when they awaken. Of course, our Bridget would normally have already taken care of this, but she hasn't come around for a bit. Not since *it* happened. I look by the stove and make a mental note to remind Henry that we need more firewood, then remember that we'll never get any.

I try not to think about Henry.

On good mornings, I enter a still and silent kitchen, the newly polished black stove awaiting the day's meals. I pride myself on keeping a respectable home, and I'm pleased that even without Bridget's help, everything is tidy and in order. When the fire is hot, I put on the water for coffee, measure out the oatmeal, and pull half a dozen eggs—two each for Orville and me, one for each of the children—from the icebox. I truly love this time of day and this routine and the scent of wood smoke and coffee. Right here and now, life feels normal and real again. How pitiful it is that I took all this for utterly for granted before! Truly, if there were a heaven, this would be it.

But now I know there's no heaven, and not all mornings are good mornings. Some days, I catch myself reminiscing on how the rest of a happy, productive day used to be: chatting with the children's tutor, a morning meeting of the Women's Club, perhaps a visit with some of the DAR ladies and a little embroidery in the afternoon before Orville returned from City Hall. Then I remember that today, there would be none of that. Just us, alone in this house.

But not always alone. On some days—there seems to be no pattern to it—the others are here, too. I know this when I hear their odd, grating voices, then smell their strange coffee and food. I can't remember when they started to appear, and I have no explanation for who they are or what they want. Sometimes, there are many of them, plodding through the house together, muttering softly. Talking about us—our courtship, my charity work, Orville's purchase of the railroad before running for mayor. How respected and beloved we were in this town.

Then they'd talk about Henry. Our Henry, the hardest working, most God-fearing freedman one could hope to employ.

And how he killed us all in cold blood.

I can't bear to listen to this.

Oddly, Orville says he has never noticed them. And thankfully, the children have not, either—and, as I have been telling Orville, they must hear none of this. They were so little and innocent when it happened, and little and innocent they shall remain—they cannot yet understand their fate, and being, as Orville likes to say, "blessed with eternal childhood," I hope with all my heart they never will.

Yet, at night, I fear they remember.

But Orville remains unconcerned. I asked him how he and the children manage to sleep through *their* talking, and he says women have more tender ears than men and children, and I need not worry about them.

Worst of all, if I dare step into the kitchen on one of the bad days, they are standing right beside me. Even though I can't see them, I can smell them and feel their movement the way one feels a storm coming in. On some days, I can hear bits of their conversation, coarse and vulgar, as if they were standing right beside me: *Another day of hometown hagiography!—Well, it brings the tourists in.*

This was horrid enough. But as of late, their conversation has gone from vulgar banter to heated whispers: *People need to know the real story. How much longer are we going to keep lying to everybody?*

I hoped this didn't mean what I thought.

And when I woke up today, I knew in my bones it would be yet another bad morning. Every morning would, if their whispers meant what I feared. Already, those dreadful people were here, with their muffled footsteps and strange voices shattering the still of the morning.

The children simply could not know about this.

And in a few minutes, they would awaken.

I took a deep breath and tried to calm myself before climbing the stairs to the nursery. Already, Merrill was stirring under his quilt. Lucy, dear little Lucy, was still curled up like a kitten, her thumb in her mouth despite the wormwood I put on it the night before to break her of the habit.

I stroked Merrill's head first. "Darling, it's past daybreak. It's time to get dressed."

He opened his round blue eyes and stared at me, my words slowly sinking into his sleepy mind. "Yes, Mother." Pushing back the covers, he crawled out of bed and toddled to the washbasin on the dresser. I poured in fresh water from the big white pitcher, which Merrill was still too little to do by himself. Soon after, Lucy too was awake. By the time I had washed her face, helped her into her pinafore, and tied back her hair, Merrill had already dressed himself.

"Mother, have we any more sausage for breakfast?"

"No, darling, we ate it all yesterday, remember? But today, you get another treat—you get to play outside before breakfast!"

Small children are far more perceptive than one thinks. Merrill looked at me with doubtful eyes. "Yes, Mother."

"Come, then." I took each child by the hand and hurried them down the stairs, planning to rush them quickly past the kitchen, out the back door and into the healthy spring air.

"But Mother, I'm hungry!" Lucy mewed. "Why can't we eat now?"

Why, indeed?

"You need some fresh air first. It'll be good for your health; you've been looking a bit sallow."

"But Mother!"

"Don't argue with me, Lucy. Come along now, it's a beautiful day out."

I saw Lucy shoot a look of concern at Merrill, who loosed my hand and ran toward the kitchen.

"Merrill! Dear God, no!" I rushed to catch him, my heart already in my throat, as he scrambled down the stairs.

"Mother! Why is there no food? The stove is cold!"

What, were they gone already? I turned to Lucy. "Stay put for a minute, will you?" She nodded, putting her thumb in her mouth, and this time, I didn't stop her. "I will be back in a minute. Be good."

"Mother!" Merrill was already seated at the kitchen table. Through the lace curtains, I could see it was another cool spring day. Across the street, the magnolias in the park—*our* park, the one I had urged Orville to build for the townspeople—were already blooming. "Why is there no breakfast?"

"Fire's not started yet? Has Henry forgotten the firewood again?" Now Orville was standing in the doorway, Lucy in his arms.

"No, dear." I went to the stove to look for kindling. Orville liked having his coffee as soon as he was up, and the children did not like waiting for their meals.

"Are you all right, Mavis? You look a bit flustered this morning." Orville set Lucy down and stroked my cheek. "Did you not sleep properly last night?"

"We need to talk," I whispered so the children couldn't hear. From the look on his face—a mixture of knowing and irritation—I could tell he knew what I wanted to talk about.

"In good time, my dear. Now, how about some breakfast? The children are surely hungry."

"Yes, dear." I lit the fire and took the eggs from the icebox. "But it will be a bit before the fire is hot. Shall we all go outside for some fresh air while we're waiting?"

Orville gave me a quizzical look.

"Children, go play outside until breakfast is ready," he said. "Your mother and I need to talk."

"But Father!"

"Merrill, do as I say."

He nodded and, taking Lucy's hand, headed for the back door.

"Very well. What is it?" Orville asked. "Did you see those phantoms of yours again?"

"You know very well they are not phantoms, Orville. You said you've heard them yourself."

"I said I heard something. Whether it was those creatures you keep talking about is debatable."

"They were here again this morning. They were talking in the kitchen. Lately, they've been saying some disturbing things, Orville. *People need to know the real story. How much longer are we going to keep lying?* They know, Orville! They know everything!"

Orville stiffened for a moment, then reached across the table and held my hand. "I know you are frightened. But are you sure you're really hearing what you think you are hearing? You've been a bit nervous as of late. Could it not be one of your episodes again?"

"It's not an episode, Orville!" I worked to hold back my tears. "I heard them, clear as day. They were right here."

"Perhaps a touch of laudanum—"

"It's not nerves! They were right here. Right where you are now."

"Well, are they here now?"

I sighed. "No, they're gone."

"And do you have any idea who they are?"

"No."

"So, why do you think they were talking about us?"

"Because of what they said: *The truth must be told.* Who else could they be talking about?"

"Just about anyone, Mavis. Really, five words out of context mean nothing. And those words could apply to almost any situation. If they were indeed said at all." He stroked my hand again—the same gesture that used to give me butterflies back when we were courting. I pulled it away. Orville folded his arms.

"I believe the stove is hot. Let's have breakfast before the children and I starve to death."

I turned to the stove and put on the water for coffee. Perhaps Orville would come to his senses after he'd had a cup or two. It always helped his mood.

Or not. More likely, mood brightened, he'd rush out to the door to catch the trolley to City Hall. After all, it would not do for our illustrious mayor to be late. Even if his own wife was alone with the children, shaking in terror.

"Mother! I'm hungry, and so's Lucy!" Merrill rushed in and dropped into a chair next to his father. Lucy followed close behind, her little thumb still in her mouth. I noticed a grass stain on her skirt.

I sighed. "Very soon, darling." Oh, to be a child again—so innocent, so fully present in every moment of one's existence.

But I, too, am fully present in my existence. I have no choice. Alas, I am no longer innocent.

On the stove, the coffee started to boil.

DO THE CHILDREN remember? Orville says it would be impossible. I say it would be impossible to forget. Of course, they never mention it as they go through their days, Lucy playing quietly with her dolls, Merrill attending his spelling lessons before rushing outside with his slingshot. It's as if the screams and cries of their late-night dreams never occurred.

But every day, I worry more and more. Today was Thursday again. I woke up before the others, as usual, and could already hear them downstairs. Louder this time.

"Everybody's already talking about it. It's time to tell the whole story."

"Not yet. The trustees still have to approve it."

Who were they? And how did they know?

Of one thing I was certain: they weren't a product of hysteria. Or, as Orville sometimes said, the voice of my conscience. Whoever they were, they were real. They were set upon ruining our good names, our legacy. And no matter what, the children must never hear them.

I peeked into the nursery. Both children were still sound asleep. Last night had been bad—worse than usual. Indeed, I was surprised when they stirred a few hours after their dreams and asked to be returned to their own beds. Nights like that, they usually wanted to stay with me. And I wanted to stay with them.

I love how peaceful they look when they're sleeping. What the townspeople always said is true; they really are beautiful children. As Orville always tells me, we have everything we'll ever need—a fine home, fine standing in the community, and each other. "You must stop fretting," he always reminds me. "You need not look far to see how very fortunate we are compared to many others. Indeed, we have blessed lives."

Or did. I looked at their innocent little faces, and my heart fell again.

I had no desire to wake them, and they needed some extra sleep after their long night. I heard Orville stirring in his room, so I knew it was time to start breakfast.

The voices seemed to have stopped, so I tiptoed downstairs and peered into the kitchen. They were gone. And as always, Henry had not yet brought in the kindling, but there was enough left to cook our meals for today.

I kneeled by the stove and opened the firebox. Then I heard them.

"We can't keep hiding the truth—people need to know."

"You know what that means, right? Everything here will change. Our whole image of ourselves will change. It's going to be damned ugly."

"Mavis, are you quite alright? Are you hurt?" Orville put a hand on my shoulder.

"Did you hear that?"

"I heard you cry out—I thought you burned yourself."

"They were right here, talking about us again. Clear as day. How could you not have heard it?"

"Mavis." He gently lifted me to my feet. "You've been worrying too much about nothing. I was right here and heard no voices but yours. If you did indeed hear anyone, perhaps it was just a peddler on the sidewalk."

"There are no peddlers out there, Orville. There's no one here but us."

"If that is the case, my dear, then why do you keep insisting that these invisible wraiths are gossiping about us?" He took my hands. "You look a bit piqued. Really, perhaps a little laudanum will help your nerves. You're only punishing yourself by carrying on like this."

"I know what I heard. They know what happened."

Orville sighed, sat back at the table, and picked up a section of yesterday's newspaper. "Of course. That story about Henry that you keep nattering on about. Damned pity, that."

"No, what *really* happened."

Orville set down his paper and glared, and I immediately regretted my words. Over the course of time, we had come to a silent agreement never to speak of this, nor Henry's fate, and this was the second time in two days I had brought it up. Yesterday, he pretended to ignore me. Today, he couldn't.

Instead, he took a deep breath, furrowing his brow, before turning to speak to me. Ever the politician—always planning just the proper words to say, whether or not he actually meant them.

"Please. For the sake of the children, calm down. You keep talking about protecting them. How are you protecting them with all your antics? All you're doing is making them nervous and worried, too."

"You don't believe me."

"I'm not saying you're lying, Mavis. But you know you have always been a bit fragile. Perhaps you are still recovering from your last episode. I think you should just rest today. Have Bridget clean up the breakfast dishes and look after the children when she comes in."

"There's nothing wrong with me. And Bridget is not coming in today. Or tomorrow, Or ever. You know that."

"Well, if you insist you are all right, then you should go check on the children. I hear them moving around upstairs."

When he gets like this, there's nothing to do. How could he possibly be so blind to what's happening in this very house?

I mounted the stairs. As I paused on the landing to catch my breath, something—no, *someone*—brushed against my skirts. I heard a clear gasp, then I gasped too.

"Huh. Crazy."

I spun around towards the strange voice. Nothing. And no one. Downstairs, Orville still sat at the kitchen table, back to reading his newspaper. Clearly, he hadn't heard a thing.

I continued up the stairs. Behind the nursery door, Lucy was protesting some tomfoolery of Merrill's. Most likely, he'd gotten it into his head to scare her with boogeyman stories or steal her doll again. Really, where do children get these outlandish ideas? "Boys will be boys," Orville always said.

Lucy yelped again. "Stop it, Merrill!"

I looked at the closed nursery door, then turned to my bedroom. I couldn't bear to look at the children now—not in my mood, and not with them riled up so. It all reminded me too much of the night it happened.

On the vanity sat my bottle of laudanum. I'd been quite proud to have gone without it for weeks now, maybe longer, but perhaps Orville was right. A little couldn't hurt. And it would calm my nerves.

The bitterness of the elixir startled me. How could I have forgotten that taste so quickly? But almost immediately, the cares of the morning faded, replaced by warmth and calm. How lovely it was to feel normal and healthy again!

I considered a second dose, but decided against it. Instead, I opened my armoire and found, behind my bottles of pomade and cologne, a bottle of pear *eau de vie* purchased in Paris by one of Orville's former business partners. Orville, after tasting it, said he preferred plain American whiskey and told me to dispose of it as I wished. So here it has stayed. Only a thimbleful or two would suffice to wash the bitterness from my mouth and the remaining troubles from my day. After that, I'd look in on the children and see that they were behaving.

The cordial went down faster than it should have. I'd forgotten how uncannily it smelled of fresh pears, or how very drowsy it made me. Lying back on my still-unmade bed as the room swirled around me, I drifted off into a happy slumber, dreaming of French orchards in springtime.

"MOTHER! NO! PLEASE stop!"

Good God, no, is it night again already?

Yes: Through the lace curtains, I could see it was dark and the gas lamps had long been turned off. I jumped from bed and ran to the nursery.

"Merrill? It's all right, sweetheart, it's just a bad dream." I tried to hug him, to comfort him, as I did every night, but tonight he pushed me away. Across the room, Lucy wept. "No Mother, no—don't hurt me."

"Lucy, darling, I would never hurt you."

"NOO!" She too drew away from me. "Go away!"

"So, the trustees approved it. The signage, the script—the whole tour. Trust me, a lot of people are going to be really upset."

Good God—they were right there. "Who are you? What do you want?"

"The important thing is, an innocent man's reputation will be restored."

"And the reputations of two people everyone loves will be ruined."

"Mother, no, please no!"

"Lucy, Merrill, be quiet! God, just be quiet for one minute—is that too much to ask of you?"

"It wasn't her fault, not really."

Who were they? I could feel and hear them right in the room, but even with the full moon shining through the window, they cast no shadows. "Who are you? Just stop, stop! Leave us alone!"

"Mother, who are you talking to? I'm scared!"

"Mavis! What is going on here?"

"Father! I'm scared!"

"They're here, Orville—and they know everything."

"What are you talking about? Will you stop riling up the children?" Orville strode into the room, still dressed. I thought at this hour he'd already be in his nightgown.

"But it was his fault. He was a murderer. Full stop."

"The father of our city. The one whom every freaking building in this town is named for."

"But people need to know."

"What in blazes?" Orville spun around, just as I had.

"Now do you believe me?"

"Must be someone outside. Has to be."

"Look outside, Orville—there's nobody there."

"He was having financial problems. Not uncommon after the railroad panic."

"How did they—" Orville looked at me. "What have you done?"

"Nothing, Orville, nothing—I—"

"And she had some mental issues."

"NOTHING? Killing our children is nothing to you, Mavis?"

"Father! Mother's trying to hurt me! Make her stop!"

"Can't believe this stayed covered up for so long."

"And what about you? How am I supposed to forgive you for what you did to me?"

"I was just trying to stop you. To protect the children. Alas, it was already too late for that. And yes, to put you—*us*—out of our misery. My God, I didn't want to see you put in an asylum or taken off to prison and hanged like a common thug. Or to watch the bank take our home and put us on the street with just the clothes on our back. I couldn't bear the thought of it. Could you imagine? It's better this way."

"After all these years, Henry Long will have his name cleared."

"Unfortunately, we can't un-hang him. And no apology to his descendants will be enough."

"BETTER? How is this better? Our good names are ruined—can you imagine what people will say? Can't you hear what they're saying now?"

Orville pulled me into a tight embrace, then stood back, tightly gripping my hands. "Mavis, think about it—it doesn't matter. We're in our own home. We can always be proud of everything we've done for this town, no matter what. And we're here forever. Nothing and no one can take our home or our children away from us."

"But—"

"They can talk all they want, but this will always be our home, and we'll always have everything we need. My dear, once you understand that, you will realize that we are, indeed, in heaven. I never really understood the appeal of harps and angels and all that, in any case."

"But—"

"My dear, my conscience is clear. As for the children, they don't remember a thing."

I glanced at them, still shadowy in the faint light of dawn—how was it morning so soon? I could hear Merrill yawning and hear the gentle slurp of Lucy sucking her thumb as she sniffled. Was it even fair that I could see and hear them acting like the innocents they were before?

"See? For them, this will be just another lovely spring day. And it should be for you, too."

"Your conscience may be clear, but mine is not. And you, how can you even look at me?"

He gave me an odd look. "You know, my dear, that after elections, I go back to treating even my cruelest opponents as honored colleagues. And I've always treated my business rivals like the gentlemen they think they are—though I still carry my pistol when I call on them. Contrary to what our esteemed reverend says every Sunday, one need not forgive to have peace. It's enough to simply ignore. Now, how about some breakfast?"

I headed downstairs. Outside, the red-birds were singing. As usual, the box of kindling was nearly empty, but there was plenty of coffee and food for the day.

There was nothing to do but marvel that Heaven and Hell were, indeed, the same place.

BLAME

Warren Benedetto

from: LinkedIn job-listings@linkedin.com
to: Kristie Griffin kristiegriffin99@gmail.com
date: Aug 20, 2021, 6:13 PM
subject: Today's job listings

Hi Kristie, Here are the latest job listings from the companies you follow:

AudioSnap.com

Software Engineer *(posted 2 weeks ago)*

For more listings like this, visit LinkedIn.com.

——

from: Mitchell Sanderson mitch@audiosnap.com
to: Kristie Breslin kristie@audiosnap.com
date: Aug 23, 2021, 12:06 PM
subject: Audio corruption

hey kristie, nice meeting you just now. sorry for the confusion … i didn't realize we had hired anyone for that role yet. anyway, welcome to the team! i hope you brought your bikini, because i'm going to throw you right into the deep end. Rob (CTO) is on my ass about an audio glitch that has been affecting our voice chats. we just pushed some codec updates … maybe one is borked? idk. anyway, please take a look when you get back from lunch.

Mitch

Mitchell Sanderson
Engineering Manager
AudioSnap.com

—

from: Kristie Breslin kristie@audiosnap.com
to: Mitchell Sanderson mitch@audiosnap.com
date: Aug 23, 2021, 12:42 PM
subject: Re: Audio corruption

Thanks, Mitch! Looking forward to getting my feet wet. Hopefully I'm not in over my head.:-) I created a JIRA issue (AUDIO-149). I'll let you know what I find.

Kristie Breslin
Software Engineer
AudioSnap.com

—

AudioSnap / AUDIO-149

AUDIOSNAP JIRA

DETAILS

Type: Bug
Priority: Urgent
Status: Open
Created by: Kristie Breslin kristie@audiosnap.com

DESCRIPTION

Customers are complaining about unusual background noise during voice chat. Variously described as droning, weeping, whispering, crosstalk, etc. Recent codec update may have introduced a bug.

—

from: Kristie Breslin kristie@audiosnap.com
to: Mitchell Sanderson mitch@audiosnap.com
date: Aug 23, 2021, 3:19 PM
subject: Re: Audio corruption

Hey Mitch, FYI, the codec was a dead end. No issues filed on their GitHub, so it's probably a bug in our stack somewhere. I'll keep you posted.

K.

—

AudioSnap / AUDIO-149

AUDIOSNAP JIRA

COMMENTS

Kristie Breslin (just now)

Attaching audio recordings from customer complaints for further analysis:

helpdesk-issue-39520.mp3: "Whispering in background of call."

helpdesk-issue-39566.mp3: "Weeping noise during group voice chat."

helpdesk-issue-39590.mp3: "Background droning sound."

helpdesk-issue-39621.mp3: "Sounds like someone is crying."

—

Mitchell Sanderson

This is the very beginning of your direct message history with @mitch

Kristie: hey, you around?

Mitch: for you? always. lol.

Kristie: so, i pinged angie in customer service and had her send me the recordings of the voice chats

Mitch: smart girl
Mitch: you, i mean
Mitch: not angie
Mitch: she dumb. ;-)

Kristie: i definitely can hear the problem

Mitch: that's … good?

Kristie: well it's easier to fix a bug that i can hear, so yeah
Kristie: anyway, what's weird is the noise is basically the same in all the recordings. if it was a compression artifact, it would be different for each call. but it's always the same no matter who's talking or what they're saying.

Mitch: what's it sound like

Kristie: listen
Kristie: *attached helpdesk-issue-39590.mp3*
Kristie: you hear it?

Mitch: it sounds like crying

Kristie: yep   Mitch: wtf

Kristie: don't know yet. will let you know when I do.

—

Angie Martinique

This is the very beginning of your direct message history with @angie

Angie: hey you. got another one of those complaints just now.
Angie: *attached helpdesk-issue-39633.mp3*
Angie: give that one a listen. it's a little different than the others.

Kristie: define different

Angie: it still has the crying or whatever, but there's also like this voice underneath

Kristie: listening …
Kristie: holy f

Angie: i know, right? it's creepy as hell

Kristie: what's it saying?
Kristie: sounds like "which will get it"

Angie: i heard "bitch i'll hit it"

Kristie: lol   Angie: hahahaha

Angie: it's like one of those audio illusions where people hear what they want to hear

Kristie: totally

Angie: you figure out the problem yet?

Kristie: meh. not really.

Angie: any clues?

Kristie: a few. still trying to connect the dots. every time i think i know what's happening i find some new detail that completely changes the picture
Kristie: like, i think i'm drawing a bird, and then i'm like "wait, maybe it's a frog"

Angie: wow sounds super fun /s

Kristie: that's why they pay me the big bucks

Angie: alright, well don't work too late
Angie: watch your six if you do

Kristie: my six?

Angie: your back

Kristie: … ok?

Angie: mitch can get a little handsy sometimes. dude watches too much Mad Men if you ask me.

Kristie: oh hell no
Kristie: i will cut him

Angie: hahahahaha that's my girl

—

Kristie-Breslin-PC ~/Desktop/AudioSnap/branch/AUDIO-149

```
$ git status
On branch AUDIO-149
Changes to be committed:
new file: RAPIST.txt
```

—

from: Kristie Breslin kristie@audiosnap.com
to: Security security@audiosnap.com
date: Aug 25, 2021, 9:09 AM
subject: Unauthorized PC access

I was just checking my git status, and I saw this (screenshot attached). See that RAPIST.txt file? I didn't create that. All my changes were committed before I left last night. Which means someone accessed my computer sometime between when I went home at 1 AM and now. What do I do?

Kristie

—

from: Security security@audiosnap.com
to: Kristie Breslin kristie@audiosnap.com
date: Aug 25, 2021, 9:42 AM
subject: Re: Unauthorized PC access

Looks like you were the last person to leave last night, based on the keycard logs. Nobody came in or out after that. You sure you didn't just forget that you created that file, babe? ;-)

Jasper
Infosec Lead
AudioSnap.com

—

from: Kristie Breslin kristie@audiosnap.com
to: Security security@audiosnap.com
date: Aug 25, 2021, 9:54 AM
subject: Re: Unauthorized PC access

No, I didn't just *forget* that I created that file, babe. Somebody accessed my computer last night, and it wasn't me. My name is Kristie, btw.

—

from: Security security@audiosnap.com
to: Kristie Breslin kristie@audiosnap.com
date: Aug 25, 2021, 10:01 AM
subject: Re: Unauthorized PC access

Fine KRISTIE. Bring your laptop down and we'll take a look.

Jasper

—

Kristie: what is it with the men in this company?

Angie: what did he do
Angie: did you cut him? lol

Kristie: no, not mitch. jasper from infosec. fucking weirdo.

Angie: oh HIM
Angie: the neckbeard is strong with that one

Kristie: that fedora has seen better days, lemme tell ya
Kristie: i can smell it from here

Angie: hahahaha
Angie: be careful or he will try to make you his waifu

Kristie: /giphy barf
Kristie: this is why i'm gay

Angie: lololol
Angie: so what happened?

Kristie: somebody accessed my PC after i left last night
Kristie: created a new file in the branch where i'm working on that audio
  bug. RAPIST.txt

Angie: holy shit

Kristie: i know, right?

Angie: what was in it?

Kristie: nothing. it was empty. which makes it even weirder.

Angie: you sure it wasn't him?

Kristie: him who? jasper?

Angie: i mean, he does have root access to every computer in the company, so…
Angie: he can basically do whatever he wants

Kristie: why though? just to mess with me?

Angie: maybe it's his weird way of getting you to talk to him?

Kristie: oh god. kill me.

—

```
// Add new audio channel, up to MAX_CHANNELS
   addNewChannel: function(newChannel){
   if (this.numChannels <= MAX_CHANNELS){
   return AudioSnapLib.addChannel(newChannel);
   } else {
   throw new Error(TOO_MANY_CHANNELS)
   }
   // He lies.
}
```

—

Kristie-Breslin-PC ~/Desktop/AudioSnap/branch/AUDIO-149
   $ git blame AudioSnapLib.js

—

Kristie: i'm freaking out right now

Angie: oh no. why   Kristie: so i just got back from lunch and my computer was already logged in
Angie: uh oh. senpai strikes again.

Kristie: i noticed a file had been modified, so i did a git blame. check it out.

Kristie: *800a806f (Greta Griffin 2021-08-25 13:23:10 266) // He lies*

Angie: what's a git blame

Kristie: sorry. git blame is a command that shows who was the last person to edit each line of a file
Kristie: someone edited the file at 1:23 PM while I was at lunch
Kristie: and added a comment that says "He lies"

Angie: the hell?

Kristie: who is Greta Griffin

Angie: she was the programmer on the project before you started

Kristie: well she obviously still has access

Angie: i don't think so

Kristie: she has to. she's the one who edited the file. like literally 10 mins ago.

Angie: that's not possible

Kristie: why?

Angie: because she's dead

Kristie: omg
Kristie: what happened

Angie: killed herself

Kristie jfc are you serious

Angie: we should talk. meet me outside?

—

from: Kristie Breslin kristie@audiosnap.com
to: Mitchell Sanderson mitch@audiosnap.com
date: Aug 25, 2021, 2:35 PM
subject: Harassment

Hey Mitch,

I hate to be the squeaky wheel, but I'm having some problems and I need your advice. Somebody has been changing files on my machine without my knowledge. Last night, they created a file called RAPIST.txt that I found this morning when I came in. Now, I just got back from lunch and another file was changed while I was gone. I feel like someone might be messing with me.

Do you have time to chat sometime today? Thanks.

Kristie

—

Mitch: saw your email. got a sec to chat now?

Kristie: yep

Mitch: great. okay if I record our call for HR?

Kristie: of course

Mitch: *is calling you*

—

Audio transcription between Mitchell Sanderson (@mitch) and Kristie Breslin (@ kristie)

Mitchell Sanderson
Hey, Kristie. Thanks for hopping on. You okay?

Kristie Breslin
Yeah, I'm all right. I mean, I'm a little freaked out, but—

Mitchell Sanderson
Sure, of course. I would be too.

Kristie Breslin

So, what do you think I should do?

Mitchell Sanderson

Well, first, let me say that I'm really sorry this is happening to you. Whatever it is, we'll get to the bottom of it. You have my full support. And anything we discuss is confidential. Cool?

Kristie Breslin

I appreciate that.

Mitchell Sanderson

Great. So, I'll be honest. This isn't the first time we've heard concerns about Jasper.

Kristie Breslin

I didn't say anything about Jasper.

Mitchell Sanderson

No, right. I know. I'm just saying. He can definitely come on too strong sometimes. He's just, you know, he's kind of awkward. Big guy, hasn't been around women too much. But I promise, he's harmless.

Kristie Breslin

Okay…

Mitchell Sanderson

I think the main thing I want you to know is that it's okay to take it easy a little bit. Give yourself a rest. I appreciate you staying late to figure out that audio bug, but it's not worth sacrificing your health for it. I can have someone else look into it.

Kristie Breslin

My health is fine.

Mitchell Sanderson

Sure, I get it. You're a trooper. I just don't want you to get too burned out in your first week.

Kristie Breslin

Really, I'm fine. I can handle the hours. But I'm not sure what that has to do with what I emailed you about.

Mitchell Sanderson

Well, I talked to Jasper—

Kristie Breslin

You did?

Mitchell Sanderson

Not about your email! No, no, sorry. Let me be clear. Not about your email. Just about the unauthorized access to your computer. He brought it up to me.

Kristie Breslin

Uh-huh.

Mitchell Sanderson

Anyway, he mentioned that, you know, there wasn't really anybody else who accessed your computer at the times you said. He checked the security footage and everything.

Kristie Breslin

And you're just going to take his word for it?

Mitchell Sanderson

He's worked here for, what? Thirteen years? So, yeah. I trust him.

Kristie Breslin

Oh. Okay. So, what...? I just dreamed it? Maybe I sleepwalked into the office and started editing files?

Mitchell Sanderson

I'm not saying that.

Kristie Breslin

Maybe that's what happened to Greta Griffin, too? She just sleepwalked off the roof?

[Silence. 00:11]

Kristie Breslin
Mitch? You still there?

Mitchell Sanderson
—hear … *[unintelligible]* … driving—

Kristie Breslin
Hello? Mitch?

[Call disconnected]

—

Are you sure you want to delete "mitch-kristie-20210825.mp3"?

This item will be deleted immediately. You can't undo this action.

CANCEL | **DELETE**

—

Kristie: that motherfucker

Angie: what did he say?

Kristie: oh, nothing. just tried to blame me. told me to take a break, that I was working too hard

Angie: well, are you?

Kristie: oh no. not you too.

Angie: I'm just saying, it has been a long week. maybe you should take off a little early.

Kristie: why is everyone treating me like i'm made of glass
Kristie: i'm fine

—

```
// Add new audio channel, up to MAX_CHANNELS
addNewChannel: function(newChannel){
    // HIS FAULT
    // HIS FAULT
    // HIS FAULT
    // HIS FAULT
    // HIS FAULT
}
```

—

Kristie-Breslin-PC ~/Desktop/AudioSnap/branch/AUDIO-149

```
$ git blame AudioSnapLib.js

862s446d (Greta Griffin 2021-08-26 02:07:10 258) // HIS FAULT

862s446d (Greta Griffin 2021-08-26 02:07:10 259) // HIS FAULT

862s446d (Greta Griffin 2021-08-26 02:07:10 260) // HIS FAULT

862s446d (Greta Griffin 2021-08-26 02:07:10 261) // HIS FAULT

862s446d (Greta Griffin 2021-08-26 02:07:10 262) // HIS FAULT
```

—

Kristie: is there anyone else in infosec besides Jasper?

Angie: yeah, there's a whole team
Angie: they all report to him though, so …

Kristie: /giphy goddamnit

Angie: still having computer problems?

Kristie: you were friends with Greta Griffin, right?

Angie: work friends, yeah

Kristie: what was she like?

Angie: hella smart. ballsy. kinda hot, it a nerdy sort of way.
Kristie: did she seem depressed at all? before

Angie: no, that's what made it so surprising. she was totally fine.
Angie: just got a new puppy
Angie: just moved in with her girlfriend in park slope
Angie: she was happy
Angie: at least she seemed like it
Angie: obviously she wasn't

Kristie: if I tell you something, do you swear not to tell anyone?

Angie: of course

Kristie: let's go for a walk

—

from: Amazon.com auto-confirm@amazon.com
to: Kristie Breslin kristie@audiosnap.com
date: Aug 26, 2021, 3:44 PM
subject: Your Amazon.com order # 111-8508406-3189834

Hello Kristie,

Thank you for shopping with us. We'll send a confirmation when your item ships.

DETAILS

Xiomi Micro Security Camera w/High Sensitivity Microphone

Arriving: Tomorrow, August 27
Order Total: $23.57

We hope to see you again soon.

Amazon.com

—

from: Willis Cole mailroom@audiosnap.com
to: Kristie Breslin kristie@audiosnap.com
date: Aug 27, 2021, 9:10 AM
subject: Amazon Package

Hi Kristie,

Your Amazon package has arrived.

Willis

—

Jasper: did you see what she installed at her desk?

Mitch: no, what?

Jasper: security camera

Mitch: seriously?
Mitch: /giphy facepalm

Jasper: dude. literally *nobody* touched her computer.
Jasper: i swear, she changed those files herself
Jasper: where did you find her anyway?

Mitch: i didn't

Jasper: well, she's nuts
Jasper: bat
Jasper: shit Jasper: crazy

Mitch: i know i know

—

from: Angie Martinique angie@audiosnap.com
to: Mitchell Sanderson mitch@audiosnap.com
date: Aug 27, 2021, 11:25 AM
subject: Kristie

Hey Mitch,

I'm a little worried about Kristie's mental health. She has been working crazy hours trying to figure out that audio bug, and I think she's starting to crack a little under the strain. She told me yesterday that she thinks the bug is actually being caused by the ghost of Greta Griffin. Like, literally, a ghost is changing her code. That's not normal.

I just thought you should know.

Angie

—

from: Mitchell Sanderson mitch@audiosnap.com
to: Angie Martinique angie@audiosnap.com
date: Aug 27, 2021, 11:38 AM
subject: Re: Kristie

oh man, that's bad. thanks for the heads up. i'll talk to HR and see what they think we should do. i hate to let her go, but we obviously can't have that kind of crazy around here.

mitch

—

r/AudioProcessing *Posted by u/kristiegriffin99*

Can somebody help me extract and analyze a specific background noise from a series of audio and video recordings?

I have a couple of voice chat mp3 files, as well as a couple of security camera mp4 video files. To my ear, it sounds like they all have the exact same sound in the background, despite being recorded at different times in different places on different devices by different people. That's impossible though, right? Bonus points to anyone who can actually figure out what the voice in the background is saying.

audiodoc *1 min ago*
DM me. I can probably help.

—

kristiegriffin99: any luck

audiodoc: yeah, that's definitely crying, and it does seem to be the same person on all the recordings

kristiegriffin99: even on the security camera footage?

audiodoc: yep

kristiegriffin99: and you're sure it's the same sound as on the voice chat recordings

audiodoc: absolutely
audiodoc: maybe it's the girl

kristiegriffin99: what girl?

audiodoc: in the video

kristiegriffin99: there's no girl in the video. it's just my empty desk the whole time.

audiodoc: look again audiodoc: in the reflection on the office window

kristiegriffin99: hang on

audiodoc: you see her? standing next to the desk?

kristiegriffin99: oh my god

audiodoc: weird, right? audiodoc: could be someone behind the camera.

hard to tell.
audiodoc: or could be a ghost lol audiodoc: anyway
audiodoc: you still there?
audiodoc: hello?
audiodoc: all right, well… speaking of ghosting hahaha
audiodoc: btw i'm pretty sure i know what the background voice is saying audiodoc: it's clearer in the video than the voice chats audiodoc: sounds to me like it's saying "mitchell did it"

—

Mitch: i'm running out to get food. want anything?

Jasper: nah im good thanks

Mitch: you sure? i can expense it since we're working late

Jasper: say no more fam

Mitch: i'm thinking mexican. the usual?

Jasper: si
Jasper: swing by my office when you get back
Jasper: i found something interesting about that kristie girl

Mitch: like what

Jasper: more red flags than a chinese pep rally

Mitch: /giphy kill me
Mitch: who hired her anyway

Jasper: um Jasper: you?

Mitch: not me

Jasper: who did then?

Mitch: probably Rob? idk

Jasper: well he should have done a background check
Jasper: the girl has issues

Mitch: she has been asking about greta

Jasper: yeah i heard
Jasper: did she know her?

Mitch: dunno

Mitch: i hope not

Jasper: so what are you going to do?

Mitch: gotta run
Mitch: let's talk when i get back

—

WALMART
Save money. Live better.
ST# 01453 OP# 567890 TE# 23 TR# 03111

Product: Camillus Carnivore X Machete
Serial #: CM778976
Subtotal: $26.82
Tax 8.000%: $2.14
Total: $28.96

Account #: XXXX XXXX XXXX 9983
Change Due: $0.00

08/27/2021 8:42 PM

—

AUDIOSNAP.COM KEY CARD ACCESS LOG

Fri Aug 27, 2021 8:54 PM: Kristie Breslin [ENTER] Main Lobby

Fri Aug 27, 2021 8:55 PM: Kristie Breslin [ENTER] Elevator 1 [UP TO] Floor 4

Fri Aug 27, 2021 8:55 PM: Kristie Breslin [ENTER] 4th Floor West

Fri Aug 27, 2021 8:55 PM: Mitchell Sanderson [ENTER] Main Lobby

Fri Aug 27, 2021 8:56 PM: Mitchell Sanderson [ENTER] Elevator 1 [UP TO] Floor 4

Fri Aug 27, 2021 8:56 PM: Mitchell Sanderson [ENTER] 4th Floor West

—

AudioSnap Tower Security
Date: 2021-08-27 9:01 PM

Caller: Mitchell Sanderson | 212-555-4932 | 4th Floor West

Front Desk
Security. This is Nick.

Mitchell Sanderson
[unintelligible]

Front Desk
I'm sorry, can you repeat that?

Mitchell Sanderson
[unintelligible]

Front Desk
I'm having a hard time hearing—

Mitchell Sanderson
[whispering] Mitchell did it.

END OF CALL

—

Jasper: yo you back with the food yet?
Jasper: im starving Jasper: holy fuck
Jasper: did you hear that?
Jasper: sounded like screaming J
asper: you there?
Jasper: hello?

—

AUDIOSNAP.COM KEY CARD ACCESS LOG

Fri Aug 27, 2021 9:03 PM: Jasper Heinz [EXIT] 4th Floor East

Fri Aug 27, 2021 9:03 PM: Jasper Heinz [ENTER] 4th Floor West

—

911 CALL
Q=911 Dispatcher
A=CALLER

Q: 911, where is your emergency?

A: Yes, hello? 911?

Q: Yes, sir. Where is your emergency?

A: AudioSnap tower. The address is, um…

Q: It's okay, I've got it. Tell me what's going on there.

A: I don't know. There's so much blood.

Q: Are you injured?

A: No, it's not mine. Oh, god. I'm going to— *[vomiting noises]* I'm sorry. *[vomiting noises]*

Q: It's okay, just try to remain calm. I've got a unit en route. What floor are you on?

A: Fourth floor. West.

Q: And how many people are injured?

A: I don't know. There's no body.

Q: There's no body?

A: No. Just blood.

Q: Okay. And what's your name?

A: Jasper Heinz.

Q: Are you an employee there?

A: Yeah. Oh my god. Mitch. *[weeping]*

Q: Who's that? Mitch, you said?

A: Yeah. Mitchell Sanderson. I'm in his office.

Q: All right. Is there anyone else there with you?

A: Just me and him. We were working late.

Q: I mean, is there anyone else with you right now? Are you sure you're safe?

A: I… I don't know.

Q: Okay. I want you to go ahead and lock the door to the office until officers arrive. Can you do that for me?

A: *[unintelligible]*

Q: Say again? … Sir? … Sir, are you there?

CALL ENDED

—

AudioSnap / AUDIO-149
AUDIOSNAP JIRA
  DETAILS
Type: Bug
Priority: Urgent
Status: Resolved
Resolved by: Kristie Breslin kristie@audiosnap.com

—

AUDIOSNAP.COM KEY CARD ACCESS LOG

Fri Aug 27, 2021 9:09 PM: Kristie Breslin [EXIT] 4th Floor West

Fri Aug 27, 2021 9:09 PM: Kristie Breslin [ENTER] Elevator 1 [DOWN TO] Floor 1

Fri Aug 27, 2021 9:10 PM: Kristie Breslin [EXIT] Main Lobby

—

NEW YORK POLICE DEPARTMENT

Incident Report

Case #: 12-0386

Incident #: 75240

Date Reported: Friday 08/27/2021 21:04

Date Occurred: Friday 08/27/2021 21:00 (approx.)

Incident Type: Homicide

Date Written: Monday 08/30/2021 14:21

Officer Name & Rank: KELSEY, JONATHAN (PO)

Narrative: PO Kelsey responded to the AudioSnap Tower (4th Floor West) after being dispatched to investigate a 911 emergency. Upon arrival, PO Kelsey secured the scene, then began his investigation. No bodies were found, nor was the 911 caller present. Based on the volume of blood at the scene, PO Kelsey concluded that multiple homicides had likely occurred.

Upon reviewing security footage from the scene, PO Kelsey noted several audio anomalies that warrant further investigation: the sound of weeping, as well as the repeated whispering of a phrase sounding like "witch will get it." Expert analysis is pending.

Keycard logs indicate the presence of an individual named Kristie Breslin at the time of the murders. However, there are conflicting reports about whether anyone by that name was ever employed by AudioSnap. CTO Rob Davenport maintains that no such employee exists; others interviewed by PO Kelsey insist a woman calling herself Kristie has been working in the office for at least a week. Residential records indicate a Kristie *née* Breslin living in Park Slope, Brooklyn, but attempts to contact her have been unsuccessful.

An item believed to be the murder weapon, identified as an 18-inch Camillus Carnivore X Machete, was retrieved by PO Kelsey from a dumpster in the South alley behind the building. A Walmart receipt for said weapon was also found in the dumpster. Credit card records indicate the weapon was purchased using a card belonging to Greta Griffin, a former employee of AudioSnap.

PO Kelsey noted that the South alley was the scene of an incident to which he had responded three weeks prior: the death of Greta Griffin (Case # 12-0299 Incident # 68323), who fell from the AudioSnap Tower roof. Although the death of Ms. Griffin was initially ruled a suicide, additional forensic analysis now indicates the presence of semen in her genital area, raising the possibility that she may have been sexually assaulted before her death. Given the relationship between Ms. Griffin and the suspected victims in this case, and the use of Ms. Griffin's credit card to purchase the murder weapon, the Griffin case is now being reclassified as a possible homicide.

—

from: LinkedIn job-listings@linkedin.com
to: Kristie Griffin kristiegriffin99@gmail.com
date: Aug 30, 2021, 6:10 PM
subject: Today's job listings

Hi Kristie, Here are the latest job listings from the companies you follow:

AudioSnap.com

- Software Engineer *(posted 3 weeks ago)*
- [NEW] Engineering Manager *(posted today)*
- [NEW] Infosec Lead *(posted today)*

For more listings like this, visit LinkedIn.com.

FROM DARKNESS TO PROMOTE ME

Pablo Lacalle Castillo

The following chronicle was cobbled together from a patchwork of archival documentation, medical records, and letters related to the life of the once-celebrated Commander Jean-Jacques Auguste. I would like to thank Monsieur Auguste's estate for graciously providing access to the late Commander's private journal.

I will reluctantly admit that I cannot provide any comments as to whether the events recounted here are credible or not. History, mendacity, and superstition shape this epistolary puzzle: I leave it to my trusty readers to be judges, juries, and (dare I say it?) executioners of time's sordid legacy. But enough from me—it is time for the living to hold their tongues, and for the dead to speak.

Report drafted by Garrison Commander Jean-Jacques Auguste, Second Franco-Mexican War, 2nd of August 1865

Frightful business with a spot of local unrest. Juárez loyalists took up arms to storm the munitions arsenal. Attack was quickly thwarted. Minimal French casualties sustained. Loyalists apprehended. One civilian death reported, a young native girl. Unable to properly ascertain the culprit. Most likely an accident. Family has been duly compensated for the cost of the burial. Men are in high spirits after the victory. There seems to be no indication of further violence.

Glory to the Emperor, and may God have mercy on our souls.

Private correspondence of Garrison Commander Jean-Jacques Auguste to Madame Madelaine Auguste, 3rd of August 1865

They hanged the brigands today in the courtyard, as the sun was setting. Oh, my dove, what a beastly hour to take the life of a man! A condemned man should be permitted to leave this earth beneath a clear sky. Instead, they shuffled onto the gallows, stained blood-red by the dying light of the evening. They cast great shadows for men so small.

I hope these words I write are not too displeasing. I appreciate your desire to be informed of my doings overseas, but I can make no promises as to the content of these letters. The work of a soldier is grim business, and our duties here in Mexico are a far cry from the parades in honour of the emperor back home. I still remember the blush on your cheeks as I strutted in that silly dress uniform. Good heavens, I looked like a wedding cake!

I would rather you hold on to that image of this proud fool who loves you too much for his own good, than that of the battered, tired man who writes this now.

The crowd did not cheer when the brigands swung. I am not sure if it would have been better if they did. I simply wish for this confounded war to end. One can only hope that braggart Juárez sees sense and forfeits the debt these Mexicans refuse to pay to the Crown! My palate is more refined for our evening treats at the Boulangerie Viennoise than these base offerings of blood from a gaggle of Cains. Oh darling, that I could once more see fields of dew-slick grass, feel the grey mist of an evening rain! I struggle to put it into words, but this country's soil does not agree with me.

Excerpt from the personal journal of Garrison Commander Jean-Jacques Auguste, 3rd of August 1865

I watched as they buried the young girl, though I knew I was not welcome. Nevertheless, I felt compelled to see it with my own eyes, as they lowered the coffin into the red clay. I think I buried the family dog in a similar fashion, stuffed inside a crate once used for storing milk. I could not tell Madelaine. I fear I have already upset her with my grisly talk of executions. Besides, women take the sufferance of children quite poorly. I cannot help but wonder whether they are more sensible for this. It is difficult not to ponder how I would have felt had it been a daughter of my own sepulchered beneath the dirt. Try as I might, I could not coax out any tears.

The natives said nothing of our presence there, but I feel that for the first time since our arrival we are seen. Before they simply stared, but did not *look*, those vacant, simple black eyes flitting over uniforms and flags, like a gentleman sighting a vagrant begging for alms on the side of the road. Acknowledging that he is there (as a stone in your path is) but not recognizing him as a thing that *lives*. I fear the natives see us clearly now, and anything that lives, one knows, must also bleed.

The searing winds have picked up, and they unearth a putrid smell. My only hope is that any threat of further violence is buried quietly alongside the coffin. It would be a terrible thing indeed for them to lose more daughters, now that they have no fathers left to raise them. The native girl's mother did not weep at all throughout the burial. Instead, she simply stared mutely at the earth.

Before I departed, she moved to toss a final clod of parched mud onto the mound, my shadow spreading out to mingle with hers. Native and Frenchman intertwined by an umbilical stretch of darkness, knotted over the remains of a murdered girl.

Private correspondence of Garrison Commander Jean-Jacques Auguste to Madame Madelaine Auguste, 9th of August 1865

…a most unusual occurrence was brought to my attention this morning, my darling. It appears that one of the men, Maxime Dupont, refuses to participate in drills as expected of him. I investigated further myself, as the lad in question has always been a most noble, patriotic, and proud fellow. I am sure that if you think back hard enough, you will remember Monsieur Dupont, darling, for he was present on our wedding day. A rather tall, brown-haired chap with crooked teeth, very polite. I recall you remarking that his gentlemanly manners quite impressed you, so you will also share my puzzlement.

Upon being questioned as to the nature of this bizarre attitude, Monsieur Dupont refused to explain himself properly. He appeared to be melancholic, and convinced that he was under severe risk of being harmed. Monsieur Dupont's condition was serious enough that he has been temporarily placed under the care of our physician. Most likely, this is the consequence of too much time spent beneath the sun. That, or there may be some thuggish behaviour carried out underneath my nose by scoundrels harassing Monsieur Dupont. Regretfully, it would not be the first time this has happened within the army, though I pray such shameful deeds are not the cause of his distress.

I do hope you are taking care of yourself, my dove. The French heat is often as merciless as the brands of Mexico. It heartens me that you took my last letter so well, though I feel I must apologize for indulging in gory details. Do try out the new hat I have sent if it has arrived already. I am certain it will be the envy of all your reading society. I tried to look over the Baudelaire you enclosed for me, but I confess I do not really understand it. It will fall to you to help me through it when we are in each other's arms once more.

Your love and faithful servant, Jean-Jacques.

Report drafted by Garrison Commander Jean-Jacques Auguste, Second Franco-Mexican War, 11th of August 1865

…Dupont's case continues to worsen. Has been isolated away from the rest of the men for his own safety, and theirs. Have ordered him to be physically restrained. He insists on inflicting grievous wounds upon his own person. Ordered his quarters to be lit constantly.

He is at his most demented in the presence of darkness. No certain diagnosis has emerged as of yet. Cause of madness is still unexplained. Private Dupont is physically in perfect health and has yet to see battle.

Have instructed for the old well to be inspected, and a new well to be dug. Contamination in the water may explain Dupont's behaviour. Have also issued an investigation following frequent reports of whoring and men soliciting the services of native girls. I would not be surprised to discover that the diseased is hiding the initial symptoms of syphilis.

This unfortunate circumstance has taken a toll on morale. However, I am confident order will be reinstated soon. Have personally attempted to interview Dupont, but there is nothing of value to report in his testimony.

Entry from the personal journal of Garrison Commander Jean-Jacques Auguste, 14th of August 1865

Monsieur Dupont passed away this evening. The poor man resorted to chewing out his own tongue to end his life. There is little in this world more pitiful than suicide, but even this defies belief. The physician found him drowned in his own blood, the pink stump of flesh a bulging mass inside his throat. It was wedged so firmly in the poor devil's gullet that they had to slit it open for removal. This is not the handiwork of a syphilitic lunatic, and I confess, to my great disgrace, I have not been entirely honest in my reports of Dupont's behaviour. Yet, in my defense, there are certain happenings so outlandish that to relay them to my superiors would, at best, question my authority and, at worst, my own sanity.

The day before he bit out his own tongue, Monsieur Dupont fainted, screaming in fear of a little girl.

A widespread search was conducted as to whether any of the native population had managed to infiltrate the barracks. No foreign presence, never mind a little girl, was located. I would be remiss not to mark the unsettling echoes of the Mexican child buried two weeks ago, but it would be preposterous to fall into the waiting jaws of superstition. It is a ravenous beast that gluts itself on paranoid delusions and self-fulfilling prophecies.

That being said, I find it hard not to attach any importance to Dupont's words the night before he expired. All the while, he shrieked the same three words over. Even when fatigue overcame him, he moaned them in a stupor, droning them out with the manic repetition of a schoolboy reciting passages in the exam hall: *Solid. Dark. Shadow. Solid. Dark. Shadow.* The nature of its meaning has kept me from reporting the tragedy further to my superiors. After all, the words make so little sense.

Emergency message delivered to Garrison Commander Jean-Jacques Auguste by Chasseur Hugo Verne, 17th of August of 1865.

...whilst on sentry duty this evening, Garnier and I spotted movement from up on the garrison. The watchword was asked for. No answer was given.

No reply or any more movement was noted. Later, around midnight, movement again. Garnier and I observed a solid, dark shadow on the Eastern wall. I noted solid, Commander Auguste, begging your pardon, as this wasn't a trick, and Garnier can back up my statement. Lost sight of the intruder before we could get any closer. No evidence of the stranger's presence could be found, no footprints or anything of the kind.

I believe it is for the best, if you don't mind my speaking out of turn, Commander Auguste, to perhaps consider more security along the walls. The ease with which this intruder fooled both me and Garnier is…troubling, as on my honour as a Christian, I swear that neither of us were neglecting our post or sneaking a drink that night and were on the highest of alerts.

From the personal journal of Garrison Commander Jean-Jacques Auguste, 17th of August 1865

I do not know what to make of Monsieur Verne's report. Recent circumstances leave me shaken to my core. I have prayed to God for assistance in this matter and asked Him to dissuade these fancies that threaten to plunge me into the raving world of witches and lunatics. He remains silent as the crowd that saw those brigands hang, a mute disgust that watches me with sable eyes and quietly measures out a noose to circle my neck.

It was those words again, in Monsieur Verne's tale. Words said in sequence, that he could not have possibly heard from the departed Monsieur Dupont, who howled them out only to a physician and to me. Solid. Dark. Shadow. Solid. Dark. Shadow. What on earth does it mean? Is this a code or cipher, a motto whose significance I am simply too slow to understand? Yet there again it appears, creeping through the flow of his speech like mold slowly spreading from beneath its dank abode, *solid, dark shadow, solid, dark, shadow*, a redundancy made manifest that, nevertheless, I find myself repeating as I would my nightly prayers.

How can I not peer into the folds of night and imagine, hidden in them, a *shape*, biding its time, observing me in silence, waiting for my back to be completely turned to lunge at me in fury? The longer that I squint into the shadows, the more they seem like slippery coils of matter coalescing and drifting apart-but no, no, they do not yet appear to me dark, or solid, though shadows they may well be. The candlelight strikes at their questing tendrils and whips them back. What fear is there for a soldier of the Empire that quelled this dry and savage land when faced with goblins, ghouls, and childish inventions? Ours is an age of reason, and to reason I must pledge myself as servant and crusader.

Private correspondence of Garrison Commander Jean-Jacques Auguste to Madame Madelaine Auguste, 24th of August 1865

Though it pains me to admit it, Madelaine, I exhumed the child's corpse yesterday, alone, under the cover of darkness. Of late these days, I have been more than a little dishonest both to you and to my superiors. I understand this must confuse you, but all I ask of you is to try to understand.

It was my bullet that ended the poor thing's life, a terrible accident. I would never have committed such an atrocity in good conscience. You know how much I love children, oh Madelaine, how can I make you see it? The smoke, the shouts, the haze of gunpowder…a stray bullet, but nevertheless, one from my own gun. It was dismissed as a tragedy. You are the only soul that knows of this, the only soul that I can trust to lead me with your perfumed hand through this field of thorns. Please, if the holy bonds that join us as man and wife could ever be called upon for a matter such as this, let me call upon them now.

Should I have come clean, admitted the murder to be my fault? Would my superiors have even cared? We all knew the bullet that the physician removed from her heart was of French make. Yet no uproar was raised, no guilt doled out—we all witnessed it, but only I *saw*. Madelaine, my love, the world will never know it was my rifle. The world does not *want* to know, but I will always bear that memory upon my shoulders, splinters, and all. And now with all this talk of specters and shapes and death, it is choking me, Madelaine.

Even now I question the decision, but it is for the best neither the Mexicans nor my men know of my momentary lapse of good conscience. I had to *know*, had to ensure that shame and rumour did not run amok any longer through my garrison. The chaos would be unimaginable. I rest easy with mud beneath my fingertips rather than innocent French blood staining my palms. Some doubts are best put to rest expeditiously and without fanfare. The fire that burnt what remained of the native girl left nothing solid indeed. Though try as I might, no matter how high I fanned the flames, I could not quite dispel those infernal shadows.

Report taken from the medical journal of Garrison physician Jean-Baptiste Rochefort, 26th of August 1865

Deceased have been identified as Chasseurs Hugo Verne and Charles Garnier. Monsieur Verne's wounds point to a shattered skull and broken neck. Body was found at the bottom of the stairs leading to the watchtower. Little blood found on the stairs themselves, indicating Monsieur Verne threw himself, or was thrown, impacting beside the final steps with tremendous force. Vertebrae in the neck completely pulverized. Serious lacerations on Verne's hands, torso, and feet. Bitemarks and scratches from a human hand, other deeper injuries, certainly from a knife of some kind. Unable to accurately identify marks as those of an attacker or self-inflicted.

Monsieur Garnier found impaled through the jaw on the bayonet of his service-issued rifle. Blade lodged firmly in the top of the cranium. Gunpowder burns on Garnier's hands and face are evidence of an attempt at discharging his weapon. Angle of entry of the blade proves that Monsieur Garnier was aided by gravity. Monsieur Garnier's torso and extremities bear signs of grievous corporal punishment.

Presence of unusual blemishes on the eyes of both deceased. Cloudy bruises on the surface of the pupil are reminiscent of a solid, dark shadow.

Private correspondence of Garrison Commander Jean-Jacques Auguste to Madame Madelaine Auguste, 5th of September 1865

"This will be the last letter I send to Paris, my darling, not because my love for you has dimmed in any way, but because I believe it is best you separate yourself from a wretch such as me before it is too late. You may weep when you read these words, you may call me cruel, but it is the necessary cruelty of the monk who shreds his back to ribbons in the pursuit of salvation. As it is, I have resigned myself to the knowledge that even in death, we will not be reunited. I will still remember you fondly, though my eyes be blinded with hot blood from the boiling lakes of Hell. I sleep next to the fire now, for its blazing light is infinitely preferred to the cold, the teeming, wet womb of shadows that slide themselves over my skin, seeking to pour into my ear, thrice blasted and thrice infected for the purpose of my ruin. Yet I confess myself a coward, for still I wince and turn away when the edges of the fire's tongues lick at my cheeks and fingers. If I cannot even stomach these flames, what will I endure in the dungeons of Tartarus?

I did not mean to kill that little girl. It was an accident; *I could not have seen her!*

I saw her the other night, in the hallway outside my quarters. Scoff at my words, denounce them as the fevered delirium of a madman driven insane by guilt. I know what I saw. It just…*stood* there, the silver mist of moonlight hovering like a miasma behind it. Before I had dismissed the reports of my men of the "solid, dark shadow" but now I know what they meant. That slight figure did not move, but even surrounded as it was by its brethren, the shadow of the girl hung in space, a rip in the fabric of the world.

Perhaps the worst thing about it was its weight. The thick, heavy feel of its shape that belied it as something tangible, something set in its place and its purpose. Not an airy, vapid specter that could be passed through, but a creature whose hands could touch and grasp and feel and hurt and choke and scratch…its footsteps leaden thuds advancing onwards at the call of twilight, fingers smudging their blackened grime on doorknobs forced open, sabers shattered, rifles broken.

Even then I understood that though it could be touched, it could not be killed. Any round discharged at that chest would be devoured by the hungering dark. Within the shape of that thing there dwelled the entrails of midnight, a gloom of mortal oblivion, a corruption unlike any other, that had leeched its shadows from our hearts and minds and gorged itself on it to coalesce and multiply. Had it been lying in wait, spreading like gangrenous rot ever since the winds blew that rancid stench from within the murdered girl's coffin? Or maybe, like a seed, like grain, it was we who had carried it. Packed it in straw, sealed in crates, stuffed tight alongside the cannon, the rifles, the swords, the mortars, the grapeshot, and gunpowder sent over in droves on the emperor's boats to germinate in this world of unspoken, bloodied truths. I had stared at similar shadows on the prow of my ship as it crossed the Atlantic, dripping from the folds of the *tricolore*, I had glimpsed it crawling inside shell-casings and lurking behind my shaving-mirror, wearing my face as a carnival mask. It had helped me dig up the girl. The task had seemed faster that night, as if some being was scrabbling at the wood of the coffin from below, eager to be free.

I ran. Why bother denying it? I ran, tearing down the corridor, bolting back towards the fire, towards the light that could beat back the shadows. It did me little good. It never will. This terror that stalks us all is not a foe to be vanquished by any means of reason, for we have always been endarkened.

I can feel it within me now, from where it peeled off and slipped into my own shade. The filth is a second skin sewn onto my back. It hovers over my head, stretching and dancing on the walls as it catches the light, doubling my every move like a mime, a clown, an ape with a thousand forms. How could I possibly return to France, nestling this parasite in my bosom, a prodigal son of lies returned to the place of its birth? It would flit from host to host, trailing the putrescent blossoms of its tarnish in its wake, curdling the souls that already hide within themselves the kernels of that self-same umbral seed.

I will not be the father to a legacy of shadows.

I love you Madelaine, though you wish I never had. Remember the gilded uniform, remember the walks by the Seine, the pastries shared by lamp light. Please remember my face, one last time, before its features run and melt into a pall.

Section of medical records obtained from Charenton Asylum, Charenton-Saint-Maurice, 28th of October 1865

Monsieur Auguste's mental state has not shown any significant indications of improvement. Almost a month has passed since his internment and transportation from Mexico, and he continues to be stricken with active and severe attacks of melancholia.

Recently discharged from the infirmary after a case of self-mutilation, Monsieur Auguste flayed chunks of his own feet with a stolen kitchen knife. Claims it was to cut away his shadow. Fear of the night has repeatedly been observed being his most obvious and frantic concern. Monsieur Auguste has been moved into solitary quarters for his own safety.

Admittance today of a new lunatic. Assaulted several prostitutes due to bouts of psychosis likely triggered by a prolonged abuse of absinthe. Request for further medical examinations for possible venereal diseases carried by the patient: his body is covered in unusual blemishes, like solid, dark shadows.

KID SISTER

Anastasia Dziekan

I CAN DO NOTHING but tell the story to myself again.

It starts in the house.

It starts in the bedroom.

It starts in the car.

Yes, in the car, it has to start in the car if I want to tell it right. In Todd's car. That baby blue Volkswagen that used to be our dad's, handed down to him. It'll be mine next, once he gets sick of it. He claims he's gonna hold on to it forever; it's sentimental and vintage and cool, but I know eventually he's gonna want something better and faster, something modern that he can really take places, and then the car will be all mine.

It's four of us packed inside. Todd is driving, and in the passenger seat sits his new girlfriend. Some blonde that's taller than me named Angie. She wears her hair straightened, down almost to her waist. A college t-shirt a size too small for her over a pair of jeans that look painted on.

And in the back: me and Jacob, Todd's old friend-turned-frat buddy. It would have been five of us had Jacob's girl not dumped him two days prior. Before we pick him up, driving from our house to his, where I will be ushered from my sibling-secured shotgun seat to the back to make room for Angie, I'm told to "go easy on him," because "he's going through it in the heartbreak department."

That's how the deal goes: Todd, tough guy back from college for spring break, gets Mom and Dad's permission to go where he likes with friends as long as he brings his kid sister with him. No one, they figure, can get into any kind of real trouble with their annoying little sister, still in high school, cramping the style of the college cool kids.

"Hey, are you eighteen yet?" Jacob asks, lazily turning his head to face me.

I weigh the pros and cons of lying, knowing I can still pass for seventeen, sixteen if I push it. I don't like the way he's looking at me, the way he shifts his body a little closer, recently dumped and desperate. I have to consider if being sixteen would save me, and maybe it would since he asked, but maybe it wouldn't, since I've been sixteen before and he's been around before, and it didn't stop him from leering back then. Maybe he remembers, waiting to call me on it, but I bet on the joint in his hand stinking up the whole car doing enough of the thinking for him.

I do not get to make my choice. Todd speaks for me.

"Yeah, she turned eighteen a couple months ago."

"Lucky," Jacob says, and I don't know if he means him or me.

We ride in silence save for the music for a while before Jacob lights another joint and offers it out to me.

"Isn't she a little young for that, Jake?" Angie speaks up.

"She's literally eighteen. That's legal."

"There's no legal age for weed, dipshit," Todd calls back.

"Because marijuana *isn't* legal," I helpfully contribute.

There is an awful quiet that falls over the car.

"Come on, you're not gonna rat us out, are you, Kit? Gonna make me stop so you can use a payphone and call Mom and Dad and call the whole trip off?" He makes eye contact with me in the rearview mirror.

"You know I'm not gonna," I say in a huff.

Jacob laughs even though nothing is funny, and half-casually drops his hand onto my thigh, right where the hem of my shorts ends. The car is quiet, full of nothing but Todd's preferred radio station. Jacob doesn't move his hand; it just sits there for a second too long. I tell myself he didn't mean it, just a friendly touch, an accident on a burst of laughter. But I'm dumbstruck and still until he removes it.

The car stops in front of an old house. It's massive, more like a Victorian style mansion than a house, but its age shows in its disrepair, rotted shutters close to falling off of windows and paint long discolored with age.

"I thought you said you rented us a place," I say over the sound of the old brakes bringing the car to a halt. We were supposed to be out by the lake, where there are campgrounds and cabins and nearby little summer homes that mainly just sit out there to be rented to scam spring breakers out of their cash.

Todd is aware of the manipulation tactic; you have to be when you live so close to it.

"Yeah, I know what I said. But, look, I did the research, okay? No one's lived here in years, and no one checks up on it. We stay here for the weekend, we leave it like we found it. No one gets hurt, and we save money."

"There are better ways to save money, Todd, holy crap."

I glance around the rest of the car to see if anyone is on my side, but they won't even meet my eyes. He must have told them and not me.

"Come on, Katherine." He uses my full name just to pick at me. "It's not a big deal. Victimless crime."

And I am outnumbered. There is no version of events where I say, "This place is creeping me out, and I don't like that you lied, and I'm not going along with this plan," and they let that slide, and we all pile back into the Volkswagen and drive back home, Todd tells our parents the truth, and spring break is canceled.

I am the little sister, the sign of goodwill to the parents, held hostage. There is nowhere for me to go—there's only one car and it's his, just like everything else.

We unpack. Suitcases and sixpacks.

Things get fuzzier when we set foot inside. It's harder to recall the sequence of events.

It doesn't take them long to break into the beer. Jacob tries to offer me one, gangly arm outstretched like some sleazy door-to-door salesman, but Todd laughs off the prospect of his "baby sister" committing a crime as heinous as underage drinking.

I remember a Todd that would have noticed Jacob's behavior and called him on it genuinely. I remember a Todd who used to give bullies hell when they pushed me over in the sandbox, a Todd that sat with me when I bawled my eyes out about my middle school boyfriend dumping me in homeroom.

But now Todd's got his arm around Angie's waist and a beer in his free hand, and nothing matters to him now but playing macho and cool.

"Why is this place even here?" I ask, just to break the awkward silence. "None of the other houses looked this old."

"It's a historical site," Angie chirps.

"Yeah," Todd adds. "Angie found it, actually. Some girl died here. She was the daughter of the owner, right?"

"The sister," she corrects. "Little sister."

"Well, I heard it was the guy's cousin, and they just said it was his sister for, like, societal reasons," Jacob says.

"Well, that could have been it." Angie sounds less sure now.

"And it was the old times or whatever, so like, you know, cousins and stuff… all kinds of things were going on. And it was allowed then. So." He smirks.

"What do you know, anyway?" she huffs. "You failed your last history class."

"Only because I slept through the final."

Todd waves us down a hallway to look for bedrooms for the night, and we follow behind him like the Scooby-Doo gang.

"Well, if you're too stupid to set an alarm, you're too stupid to get a good grade in that level of class, anyway. It's supposed to test your intelligence, and regardless, you failed."

"How did she die?" I ask, voice coming out with a quiet crack.

"Suicide."

"Murder."

Angie and Jacob answer at the same time.

"She was murdered," Jake makes his case first. "The guy who lived here, they called him the lord of the house or something like that, he was mad at her for not being married, or for trying to have her own money, or … It was some kind of thing that was important for women of that time. He was so angry that he killed her over it."

"Jake, come on. Don't tell her your weird conspiracy theories. She committed suicide." Angie imparts this information to me like the world's most morbid preschool teacher. "She *did* feel stifled by the limitations of the time, and she felt like the only way out was to take her own life. She left a note and everything."

"Notes can be forged."

"Jacob, actually shut up forever, oh my god."

We're halfway down one of the long hallways when we see the painting hanging on the wall: a portrait of a young girl, sitting with her back straight and looking directly ahead. Her face is largely emotionless, in that way that all people in paintings are, barely frowning, eyes dark and judgmental.

"That's probably her," Angie says.

It feels a little too real then. She actually existed. None of them even know what her name was. They're arguing over her death like they're trying to recall movie trivia. Within the details of her picture, her brows are just slightly furrowed.

Well, if she's angry, I think, *she has every right to be. I would be angry, too.*

Todd must notice me staring because he clears his throat awkwardly and says, "Both of you guys need to stop making up stories just to freak out Kit. I bet no one even died here at all."

And he and Angie walk ahead while she mumbles something about,

"No, it's true, I read…" and Jacob rolls his eyes at me as if to signal to ignore Todd.

We eventually find enough usable rooms and take off in different directions. Todd and Angie take what was once the main bedroom, Jacob takes a room downstairs, and I am banished to the other end of the upstairs hall in what seems like it might have been a young girl's room based on the untouched decorations and smaller bed. "Other end" is a misnomer; the hall wraps around itself. There are multiple directions to walk, to run.

Goodnights are said, and we separate. It's a struggle to get to sleep. The room is massive, the bed is unfamiliar. The early spring heat, compounded by the sleeping bag over scratchy untouched sheets, makes the room feel hellishly humid and disgusting. There is no way to place my body that feels right, feels comfortable. I think about the others, unbothered, already asleep, half drunk and dreaming with freedom and ambition. My brother and Angie curled up like the cover of a romance novel, and Jacob, alone, doing God only knows what. I imagine leaving the room, walking out, getting in the Volkswagen and driving away. I imagine claiming the vehicle as my own, finder's keepers. I imagine leaving them as stranded as they have me now.

But I know I won't. I know I can't ever.

I lay there tortured by the fantasy of escape. My only solace is knowing that eventually exhaustion will win, my body will give up fighting, and force me to sleep. I'm on the edge of a dream. I'm falling, plummeting, and just before I hit the ground, instinct tells me to snap my eyes open, but I don't. I wait. The feeling of movement drifts into a pause.

And then I feel her.

She drifts over me, settles on top of me like a sheet. She feels like a fog, murky and amorphous. What I imagine is her hand clenches around my throat, the weight of what must be her body presses down on my chest, bearing down on my lungs. I gasp; I breathe her in like secondhand smoke. I'm falling again; she falls in reverse, into me. My heart beats at a rate I didn't know it was capable of, my body making jerky motions that aren't mine. My thoughts are clouded, out of order—there is no way to make sense of things, to see it all pass linearly. At some point, I open my eyes and screw them shut again. I try to breathe desperately, air flooding in and out of my lungs. I am fighting, I think, I must be, I am fighting her, or my body is, spasming, trying to reject the intruder.

All too soon, I'm still. My body is still. I'm awake.

And she is inside of me.

There are three things I must keep track of now to tell the story. Me, her, and my body. I am, as near as I can tell, the same as I have been. I am awake in here. I am aware. I feel pain. I feel fear. I have already tried screaming enough times to know it does nothing.

But I do cry. She cries too; we cry in tandem, connected. She sobs inside of my body, wails and hungers. I can feel the tears leak out of my eyes, thick and black like they've run through mascara. The tears are hot when they streak down my cheeks. When she speaks, my throat aches, hoarse. She uses my voice to speak out loud, but inside of my head, I hear her as she really is. She taunts me. She questions me. She's in my thoughts, in my memories. Looking around, finding the best ways to draw out my emotions to match hers. She speaks with an anger that verges on madness, a hungry, smiling anger characterized by the feeling of wanting. And there is my body, which we share now. Which she pilots and I struggle against. If she can feel my efforts to struggle against her, she doesn't seem bothered by them.

It's my body that rises slowly from the bed, back straight, movements stiff. She takes a while to get used to me, to moving my limbs. Maybe I'm too gawky, even for a ghost. Maybe she'd like someone prettier, more graceful.

"Jealous?" an unfamiliar voice asks from inside my head, and I try to control my wandering thoughts.

She finds her footing eventually. One leg stepping first, and the other dragging behind in a limping parody of a walk. We stumble like that for a few steps before a rhythm is struck, and then it's almost as natural as if I were doing it myself. There is no time to waste on questioning the *hows* and *whys*; my body is moving and no matter how I try to fight it, I can do nothing to stop it. It's like being frozen in place, like being trapped in drying concrete.

She walks my body up to the mirror, makes me look at my own face. My eyes are glazed over, half-fogged up. My hair sticks out at odd angles. It's just bedhead, but it makes me look inhuman in the darkness of the room. She smiles; I smile. A shaky grin that stretches horribly across my face. She brings up one of my hands, touches my cheek. It's warm, delicate when she drags the soft pads of my fingers down the skin of my face. We cry together, her tears from my eyes. She uses my hand to wipe them away, refusing to break eye contact with the mirror.

"So pretty," she says, and it kills me when she sounds so genuine. *"Thank you for this."*

I try to scream at her to get out. I try to hold on to being someone, being *me*, not just a loose collection of thoughts and feelings, abstractly fear and disgust.

We walk out of the bedroom with plodding steps. I try to speak to her; I can do nothing else.

"Why are you doing this?"

"Angry." The answer comes, and it burns under my skin. *I have been here for so long. Just me. Just thinking. Going in circles. Losing myself in the infinite nothingness. Now I have a body. I don't know how long it's been since I had one. But I have one now. You made space for me."*

"I didn't." I feel like a petulant child trying to argue, not knowing what good it's going to do.

"You did. I am here. Now we must do something. Something for both of us. We will not be made to sit and accept anymore. I am going to indulge my need for action.

And for you, I will try not to have you suffer. "

"I'm suffering already. You're using my body. It hurts." It doesn't quite hurt really, but I cannot find the words to describe the sensation of being alive without feeling yourself breathe.

"It is our *body now. We will learn to share."* She's in my thoughts, playing them back as if she were flipping through a photo album. *"You're not alone here."*

We keep walking, stalking down the stairs shakily, until we reach the kitchen. She knows where everything is. My hand opens the drawer, reaches in, grabs a knife. It's old, untouched by anything but the years, for I don't know how long. It fits naturally in my hand when she curls my fingers around the handle. We turn. We walk.

"You hate him."

I know immediately that she means Jacob; we're walking toward his room.

"I don't."

"He touched you, and you didn't want it."

"It's not like that—"

"He put his hand on you like this." She mimics the action with my own hand. *"You were scared of him. Scared of his appetite. Of his power. You feel powerless with him."*

"Stop."

"You can feel powerful now. I can give this to you. Do you want to feel in control? Do you want to know that he will be harmless forever?"

"I don't."

"Don't lie. It's unbecoming."

"I don't!"

But though I fight, we make it to his room. He's asleep in bed. Idiot didn't even consider that the sheets must be filthy. She laughs at my mean little thought. We stand over him. We watch him breathe. He kicks in his sleep like a dog. My head tilts. She's studying him. She's looking for an entryway.

My fingers clench around the knife. I feel my arm raise. Time stops.

With a swing, she slams the blade into his chest.

He wakes instantly, screaming in high-pitched panic that turns to gurgling from blood rising in his throat.

"You scream like a girl," I say. It's her speaking. (But it *is* my thought.)

He throws his body around wildly, limbs flailing. She leans our full weight. The knife sinks further; he lets out a strangled yowl. My free hand holds him down. We make eye contact. Confusion enters his face. I smile. I sneer. I growl.

Eventually, he stops moving. He falls backward, flat and still. My body heaves breaths. I try to move. I try to ground myself like an anchor. I try to fall to my knees and cry. I try to look at my blood covered hands.

"Did you like it?"

"No."

"You did. You felt strong."

"I fucking didn't. I can't feel anything when it's you in control of me."

She doesn't answer.

We move.

Todd and Angie are down the hall. As we get closer, I can hear their voices. Must have been woken up by all the noise. They're frantic. He's trying to calm her down. She won't listen.

We fling the door open with a slam. We stand there, backlit by the hallway lights. It must be quite a sight: little sister, covered in blood, just standing still. Smiling.

"Kit?" Todd tries.

Silence. I brandish the knife. Within a second, they both take off out the door on the other side of the room. I follow, they go in different directions.

"Which one?"

"Neither. Get out of me."

"You're jealous of the girl. You think she's pretty. You think she gets more attention. Do you want her gone?"

"I don't. She's just some girl."

Angie is easy enough to follow. She runs clumsily.

"It is alright. You do not have to protect her. You can want her to go away."

This hallway is a dead end. I don't know when Angie is going to realize it.

"I don't want to kill her. I don't want any of this."

"You are angry. You should be free to express it. You should take what you like. Act in large and beautiful ways. Make the world around you bend to your desires. You have been passive. You can act now; admit you want it."

Angie finds the end of the hallway when her shoulder collides with the wall. She lets out high-pitched wail like some kind of movie scream queen. I lunge. We struggle. She doesn't go down easily. She kicks her skinny little legs, claws with her painted nails. She begs as she thrashes.

"Please don't, Kit, I'm sorry——" She doesn't know what she's apologizing for. I don't know what she's apologizing for. But sweetness got her far enough in life. It can't save her here.

"Persistence. You will receive if you do not stop."

We are not so careful with the knife this time, not so calculated. We slash erratically. We stab repeatedly. I become accustomed to the pattern of feeling the blade breach skin and sink into the flesh, and then the yank, which sets it free with a squelching sound. She dies with her eyes open.

My body turns. We walk.

Downstairs, I hear a scream. I can only assume Todd's found Jacob's body.

"And what of the brother?" she asks.

"Don't hurt him."

"He doesn't listen to you."

We keep walking. I keep fighting.

"He's my brother."

That's enough on its own, isn't it? He doesn't have to listen, doesn't have to be perfect. We're family and that's that, right? We're supposed to know who we'd choose if it came to that.

"There's something you hate about him. Something you want."

"There's nothing."

He changed, sure, but that's not a crime. I know he's still Todd, the Todd I know from hazy memories and home movies. And with some sick joy I think that it's his friends' faults he changed at all and now they're gone.

In the end, it's just me and him.

I can tell this gets to her. The inside of my body feels cold. She's bitter. We don't stop moving. The grip on the knife becomes white knuckled. My brother's footsteps echo, and we follow like a predator stalking a deer through the forest.

"There must be something you want.*"* Her tone now is frantic, delirious. I try to struggle against her, I try to hold her back. We follow Todd, and we retrace our steps at the same time, the path leads to the kitchen.

"What else do you want? I can give it to you. What do you want?" She's in my head again, in my thoughts. It hurts, like she's digging through my skull like hands digging through mud, tearing it and throwing aside what she doesn't like.

I see Todd then. He's digging through a drawer, and he turns, cornered and frantic like a feral animal, holding a knife to match mine. He's bloody now, too. It must be Jacob's blood. He must have touched his friend's corpse and mourned.

The beast inside me taunts: *"What do you want? What do you want?"*

And my brother screams at the verge of madness at her, through me, tears streaming, shaking and terrified like I have never seen him: "WHAT DO YOU WANT FROM ME?"

I cannot move, but I do freeze. She is still buried in my thoughts, dragging out any desperate semblance of a memory that could expose a desire. I stay still. I let it happen. My only act of control is to give up. My hand goes slack. I barely hear the clatter of the knife on the floor, too busy watching his movements.

When he stabs me, it's my voice that screams.

She rips out of me, like the sound, and I almost expect to see her in the air, the way you can see your breath on the exhale when it's cold enough outside.

He draws back in an instant, almost cowering, as if afraid of what he's done. The blade aches in my shoulder, and I can't look at him. I breathe then, slow, heavy breaths, like I'm trying to teach myself how to do it. The gulps of air catch themselves in my throat, and I shudder, and then sob. I can't decide whether I should smile to be myself again or just keep crying, tense hands clenching like they're holding a weapon that isn't there. Phantom pain and rapidly developed muscle memory.

I am the only person who knows the true story, I realize. Yet even now, my own brother, physically larger than me, more powerful, sits a ways away and shrinks himself, half-trembling.

I look up at him, and he must see pain in me, because he reaches forward and yanks the knife out from where it was lodged.

I let out a sound not unlike a hiss. "You're supposed to leave it in."

Horrible first words, actually. What a little sister buzzkill thing to say when people are dead, and this is the first time since it started that I've been able to use my own voice.

"What?"

"The knife," I say, because it's too late to back out of this now. "You're supposed to leave it in. It stops the bleeding."

Sure enough, blood pours down my arm like a waterfall, and Todd snaps to attention, looking around for a rag. He stands up then, scrounges around, settles on a washcloth, and somehow feels safe enough to get close to me and hold it against my wound.

"Kit," he says, like it's some kind of ancient magic word, half in a whisper and almost like he's afraid to pronounce it. "Kit, what happened?"

And now I'm forced to consider: is there a version of the story where I tell the truth and my brother believes me? He knows Jacob is dead, must know Angie is dead, or at least assumes it. Can see his little sister looking feral and bloodied.

What happens if I lie? What happens if I'm caught in a lie? What are the consequences of crying wolf when I'm the one who killed the sheep?

What happens if I plead insanity? How far can "I don't know" get me?

What's the point?

"It wasn't me." And that feels like a confession, too. "It wasn't me, Todd, you have to believe me. It wasn't— I wouldn't—" Desperation wins out over every other option, and suddenly I'm crying again, spilling hot, useless tears in a body that feels too big and too empty and every kind of wrong.

Todd stares at me.

I don't think he sees a murderer. I don't say the word ghost; I don't say the word possession; I don't have the words for the horrible and impossible thing that happened to me. I only have awful choked, snotty sobs and the silent face of my big brother. And I can't say for sure, but I think what he sees is his kid sister on the floor of an unfamiliar house, crying and covered in blood. I think he sees me scared and sorry.

All he says is, "Okay."

I have conversations that night with my brother that I wouldn't wish on anyone. There are plans made, arrangements. There are two bodies in the house—they must be dealt with. I recount the story of what happened to him, and I can't tell if he believes me. He concocts the story that we'll stick to, and we run it over and over again like we're rehearsing lines backstage at a school play.

I don't know if he will hold to it, or if he'll call me insane and sell me out, to hell with protecting family.

I don't know if *they* will believe it, if they will pick at us until one of us breaks. (It would be me.)

I don't know if someday I'll believe the fake version myself. I try to commit the truth to memory, because someone has to know what happened. An event like this can't just be painted over with false memories, half-remembered lies, vague truths. Someone has to carry the weight of knowing what happened.

In the morning, when the sun is up and the house is nearly empty and as freshly cleaned as sun-bleached bones, and all that's done is done, Todd sits numbly in one of the kitchen chairs, head in his hands.

"Give me the keys," I say. "I'm driving."

He passes them to me without resistance.

And at the very least, I know the way home.

FUDAKAESHI

Marshall J. Moore

SHIKOKU, JAPAN, 1577

"YOU MUST BE very polite to Minoru-sama," Goro said. "She receives few visitors and is eager for your company."

Yukiko smiled slightly as she followed the elderly servant up the winding trail. The wind blew strongly from the sea, and she pulled her ragged kimono more tightly about her shoulders.

"Courtesy is one of the seven tenets of the warrior," she told him. "I will strive to exhibit it to my host."

"That is good," Goro said, glancing over his shoulder at her. "My lord and lady have need of a capable bushi[1]."

"Even a ronin[2]?"

The old man paused at the top of the slope and gave her an appraising look.

"It is not for me to say," he said at last. "But if you are the same Okabe Yukiko that we have heard of, I think my masters will be glad of your service."

KAGAWA MINORU KNEELED at the top of the hill, bent over a long scroll, its four corners weighted down with round stones. She ran her

---

1   **bushi:** warrior
2   **ronin:** a masterless samurai

brush carefully across the scroll in long, elegant strokes, humming quietly to herself. The sea breeze tugged at the few strands of dark hair that had fallen loose from her bun.

Her back was to Yukiko and Goro as they approached. The old servant slowly lowered himself to his knees, beckoning Yukiko to do the same. He placed his hands flat on the ground and bent so low that his brow nearly touched the grass. Yukiko kneeled as well, though she did not bow nearly so low.

"Minoru-sama," Goro said, loudly enough to draw her attention. "I have the honor of introducing you to Okabe Yukiko."

Minoru stood and turned around, hiding her ink-stained hands in the sleeves of her kimono. She bowed from the waist, though her eyes never left Yukiko.

The ronin was a striking woman: tall and long-limbed with the lean features of one acquainted with hardship and hunger. Her kimono with its cherry blossom patterning was well-worn, and the two swords tucked into the sash about her waist looked as though they had been drawn often.

"Good afternoon, Okabe-san," Minoru greeted her. "Have you had rice today?"

"Thank you, Minoru-sama," Yukiko replied, straightening to look her in the eye. Minoru's breath caught. Yukiko's eyes were as gray as the sea. "I have eaten."

"Good." Minoru nodded. "Come and sit with me. You may go, Goro-chan."

The old servant bowed once more, then turned and set off slowly back down the hill. Yukiko rose and walked over to Minoru. She pulled both her swords from her sash, still sheathed in their saya[3] used for Japanese swords, typically made from laquered wood, and set them down on her right side as she kneeled. This was a gesture of trust and respect; if she meant Minoru violence, it would be difficult to draw her blades

---

3   **saya:** a scabbard

from this angle.

"Thank you, Yukiko-san," Minoru said, returning to her brushwork. "I appreciate you meeting with me."

"The pleasure is mine." Yukiko's gaze fell to the scroll in front of her host. Minoru was painting the seascape before them: the broad sweep of the rolling hills to either side giving way to the wide gray plain of the Seto Sea dividing the island of Shikoku from its larger neighbor, Honshu. The day was overcast, and Yukiko could just make out the distant shoreline on the horizon.

"You paint well," she said.

"Thank you." Minoru flushed. "Are you a painter?"

"No." Yukiko shook her head. She glanced down at the swords beside her. "But one artist recognizes another's skill."

"I suppose that is so." Minoru drew a long, winding brushstroke near the top of the scroll, representing the far horizon. "Did Goro tell you why I wished to meet with you?"

"No." Yukiko shifted slightly. "But in my experience, there is only one reason a noble lady seeks out a ronin."

Minoru dipped her brush once again. "You speak bluntly, Okabe Yukiko."

"Some have told me so." Yukiko shrugged. "I prefer to think of it as candor. Is it a tongue you require, or a blade?"

That earned her a faint smile. "Neither, I hope. It is your keen gray eyes I need."

"Ah." Yukiko gazed out at the roiling sea. "You need me to banish a ghost."

The salt wind blew cold. Yukiko's long black hair fluttered in the breeze, and Minoru felt the chill bite at her exposed hands.

"Let us speak directly, Yukiko-san. My family is being haunted. I believe this yūrei[4] seeks to kill my husband." Her dark brown eyes met Yukiko's sea-gray ones. "And I believe that someone is helping it."

____

4   **yūrei:** figures in Japanese folklore analogous to the Western concept of ghosts

"IT APPEARED ON the last full moon," Minoru explained, steam rising from the teapot as she poured into Yukiko's cup. "It wailed and moaned for three nights while trying to break into our home."

Nodding her thanks, Yukiko raised the porcelain cup to her mouth with both hands. She breathed deeply, savoring the grassy aroma. It had been many seasons since she had tasted good matcha.

"I trust the ofuda[5] kept it out?" she asked.

A look passed between her hosts—Minoru and her husband, Kagawa Ryo, daimyo[6] of this stretch of Shikoku's northern coast. They kneeled on woven tatami mats facing Yukiko in the tearoom of the family home. It was a small manor, nicer than any building Yukiko had been allowed inside of in the past year.

"Yes," Ryo said. He had a deep voice, one that was slightly at odds with his refined, birdlike features. Yukiko judged him to be at least a decade older than her own thirty years and twice the age of his young wife. "We keep three ofuda in our house. One hanging from the ceiling outside our bedroom. One mounted above the door to our home. And one outside the children's window."

Yukiko nodded. Ofuda were protective amulets, charms inscribed with the name of a kami on paper, wood, or metal. When placed throughout a home, they were meant to protect against invasion from hostile spirits or angry ghosts.

Like the one Yukiko had been hired to dispatch, for instance.

"And this happened last month," she said, taking a sip of tea.

"Yes." Minoru nodded. "The ofuda kept the yūrei out, though it wailed and howled something terrible. The children hardly slept those three nights."

---

5   **ofuda:** a protective charm or ward issued by a Shinto shrine, made from metal, cloth, or paper

6   **daimyo:** a Japanese feudal lord

"How many children do you have?"

"Two," Ryo said. "Sato and Kaede. Both are under the age of three."

"And they saw this yūrei?"

"Yes." Minoru shuddered, her face pale at the memory. "It appeared outside their window but could not get in because of the ofuda we had placed there."

"And now the ghost has appeared again?"

"It has." Ryo looked at Yukiko with a direct, unblinking gaze. "It appeared again last night, the first night of the full moon, just as it did a month ago."

"Did the ofuda still keep it out?"

"No," Minoru broke in before her husband could answer. "I awoke in the night to hear it screaming in the garden. I ran to see that the ofuda were holding it at bay, only to find the one outside our door had been torn down and trampled on. I raced to the children's room and hurried them from their beds just as the ghost tore in through the window. The ofuda there was gone, too."

Yukiko listened in silence, fingers tight around her porcelain teacup. Ryo watched his wife tell her story, his own face pained. Yukiko sympathized. She knew what it was to fear for the life of one's child.

Tea sloshed onto her shaking hands, painfully hot. But Minoru was so rapt in her retelling that she failed to notice.

"I took the children to the bedroom and locked them inside. Then I stood on the threshold, the last ofuda hanging over me. The ghost howled and raged, but she could not touch me while it was there." She shivered. "I stayed there until dawn, when the ghost left. Then I sent Goro to the village to see if any ronin there had dealt with ghosts before."

A wry smile touched Kagawa Ryo's lips. "Imagine our surprise when he returned with Okabe Yukiko, the Ghost Hunter herself."

"The Seven Lucky Gods have smiled upon us both," Yukiko said. "For I am in need of work, and you have a ghost in need of hunting."

"You will help us, then?" Minoru asked, leaning forward eagerly. Ryo's expression was more guarded.

"I will. All I ask in return is food and shelter through the winter." Yukiko met Kagawa Ryo's gaze directly. "You will have my aid and service until the spring thaws."

"Impertinent," came a voice from the corner of the tearoom. "Lord Ryo already has one bushi retainer. He does not need a second."

He leaned against the door, a gaunt, hard-featured man wearing the topknot of the samurai caste, both swords tucked into his obi. Yukiko's own swords were on the far side of the manor, resting in a sword rack provided for visitors.

"Peace, Hayate," Ryo said. "Okabe-san is our guest and deserves our courtesy."

He had not introduced his yojimbo[7] by family name. That and his hardened looks told Yukiko Hayate was a masterless ronin like herself. Until now, he had not spoken; he merely gazed at Yukiko with undisguised mistrust.

"It is no offense," Yukiko said, gazing levelly at the daimyo's bodyguard. "I am sure that Hayate-san and I will become fast friends, given time."

One corner of the yojimbo's mouth twitched, though his expression remained unfriendly. Yukiko turned back to the daimyo and his wife.

"What did the yūrei look like?"

Ryo's shoulder twitched in a shrug. "Like all ghosts look. A woman in a kimono with long hair. You could see through her, and she faded away at the legs."

Yukiko sipped her tea. Many ghosts looked like that, though not all. But for it to have sabotaged the protective charms around the house… no ghost could have torn them down without help.

---

7   **yojimbo:** bodyguard

Which meant she was dealing with a fudakaeshi[8].

"Your ofuda," she said at last, careful not to let her thoughts show on her face. "Have they been replaced yet?"

"Yes," Minoru spoke up. "The one outside our bedroom remains. The other two have been replaced with paper charms by Shichiro, the village priest."

"Excellent." Yukiko stood, and Minoru's fan once again fluttered in front of her face. Rising before one's host was highly rude.

Good. Yukiko wanted their full attention.

"I mean no disrespect, Kagawa-sama," she said, inclining her head, "but if you want this yūrei dealt with, you must do as I say. Do you agree?"

"Yes," Minoru said as her husband opened his mouth. "Of course."

Ryo frowned at his wife but nodded his assent.

"Good. Then here is what must be done. The children must sleep with you in your room, in case the ofuda above their window is tampered with again. How many servants do you have?"

"Goro and his wife, Nanako," Ryo answered. "They live in a servant's cottage on the grounds."

"Bar their door, then, when nightfall comes." Yukiko's gaze turned to Hayate. "You are Kagawa-sama's yojimbo, yes?"

"Yes," Hayate said, somehow making the affirmative a challenge.

"Then you must wait in the family's room with them. If the yūrei devours me, you will be all that stands between your lord and an angry ghost."

"And you?" Kagawa Ryo asked. "What will you do while we cower in our beds?"

Yukiko's eyes were as gray as the evening sky. "I will sit outside your room and wait for the ghost to reveal herself."

The ghost, she thought, and the one who serves it.

---

8   **fudakaeshi:** resembling a classic yūrei, spirits which remove the magical wards that protect from evil spirits

THE NIGHT WIND gusted quietly through the sliding shojia paper screen serving as a wall, partition, or sliding door screens. Yukiko kneeled in the center of the manor with her back to the Kagawas' bedroom door, resting her buttocks on her heels. It was an uncomfortable position, but she had maintained it for hours ever since night had fallen and the Kagawa family had retired to their bedroom. The discomfort helped sharpen her senses, keeping her awake and aware through the long hours of her watch.

Her swords lay sheathed on the floor beside her on her left. In one swift, practiced motion, she could stand, draw, and strike with either blade, should the need arise.

The ghost that haunted Kagawa Ryo and his family was a fudakaeshi, a charm-ripper. Yukiko was certain of that. No yūrei could touch an ofuda, but the fudakaeshi was a master deceiver, adept at tricking the living into tearing down their protective charms and letting them inside their homes.

Yukiko gazed at the screen before her, a watercolor painting of a kitsunea Japanese fox spirit darting between the trees of a lush forest. A fudakaeshi knew the inmost desires of the heart. It would promise, plead, threaten…whatever it thought would subvert the living into serving it.

Lies, always.

It must have been the Hour of the Tiger by then, the last stretch of night before gray dawn. Yukiko fought the urge to rub at her eyes. It was not the first time she had remained awake all through the night, but each time she did so she felt more tired the following day.

A wail split the silence, a piercing feminine cry. Yukiko's breath caught, the hairs on her neck standing on end. Still, she waited patiently, her eyes fixed on the shoji leading to the front of the house.

A sillhouette appeared on the screen, a dark shape with long hair. A woman stood on the other side—or at least, the shadow of a woman.

"Let me in," the shadow whispered. Yukiko heard its voice as plainly and clearly as though it had been sitting beside her. "Let me in, little onna-bugeisha[9]."

Yukiko said nothing. The shadow raised one hand and scratched a fingernail along the screen, leaving a trail like an ink stain.

"Let me in, Okabe Yukiko," the shadowed whispered again. Its voice was plaintive, pleading. "Let me into the room behind you. You need not even open the door. Merely take down that terrible charm above you."

Yukiko looked up at the ofuda dangling over her head; a single strip of thin metal hanging from the ceiling rafters.

"Take it down," the shadow pleaded.

"I will not," she said, her voice dry. Speaking to the fudakaeshi was a mistake, but she could not help herself.

"There is much I can give you." The shadow pressed its hand flat against the screen, fingers spread. "I can bring you to the home of the general with the oni[10] mask."

Yukiko's breath caught. The darkest corners of her memory summoned that mask to her mind: a war menpō[11], flames gleaming off its curling tusks.

"Tear down the charm, and I will lead you to where the oni dwells," the shadow promised. "I will dance in the flames as you burn his home to the ground. Surely, he deserves to have his own sins visited upon him, Yukiko-san."

Yukiko gazed down at her hands. She remembered how they had looked, covered in her husband's blood. She remembered the heat of the fire blistering her face.

"No," she said, her voice barely a whisper.

---

9   **onna-bugeisha:** a female samurai of the bushi (warrior) class
10 **oni:** demon
11 **menpō:** a type of mask or facial armor of demonic aspect

"The other charms are gone," the shadow said. "Only this last remains. Tear it down, and I will take you to where your daughter is."

Yukiko did not remember standing, but she was suddenly on her feet, her wakizashi[12] in hand.

"My daughter is dead."

"Is she?" the shadow whispered.

Yukiko stood there, her shaking hands tight around the sword.

"Tear the ofuda down, and I will tell you where little Izumi is."

"You lie," Yukiko hissed into the darkness.

"No," the shadow said softly. "Not about this. Remove the charm, Yukiko-san."

Yukiko shut her eyes as tightly as she could, her hand trembling on the wakizashi's grip.

"I will not," she whispered.

Distantly, a rooster crowed, heralding the approach of dawn.

When Yukiko opened her eyes, the shadow had vanished. Only its handprint remained—a dark smudge on the painted screen.

"I HAVE A question for you, Shichiro-san."

"Oh?" The rotund little priest turned, fixing Yukiko with an appraising gaze. "I may have an answer."

Yukiko gave him a tired smile. The night's vigil had left her weary.

"Is Minoru-sama the daimyo's first wife?"

Shichiro chuckled. "Noticed the difference in age, did you?"

"It is hard to miss."

The village priest, Shichiro, had arrived that afternoon bearing paper ofuda to replace those destroyed the night before.

The ghost had not lied about that, at least. Once the sun had cleared the horizon and she was certain the fudakaeshi was gone, Yukiko had

12 **wakizashi:** a traditional Japanese short sword typically used as a companion sword for a katana

patrolled the grounds. Sure enough, the protective charms over the front door and the children's window had been torn down and ripped into little pieces.

No yūrei could touch the ofuda or cross a threshold protected by one.

Which meant someone had been up and about, moving through the house on silent feet even as Yukiko had maintained her vigil.

"Well?" she prompted, returning her thoughts to the present. "Is she?"

"No," Shichiro admitted as they reached the front door of the manor house. Yukiko was most of a foot taller than him, so he handed her the paper ofuda. "He had another wife, Aiko. They were wed nearly ten years but had no children."

Sometimes it is easier not to be a mother, Yukiko thought, standing on tiptoe to tie the charm to the rafters. "How did she die?"

"Tragically," Shichiro said. The good-humored smile faded from his round face. "She and Ryo-sama took a walk along the cliffs one night. The moon was full, like tonight, and so bright that they could see every step. But even so, she slipped and fell into the waves."

"That is tragic," Yukiko agreed, tying the knot that kept the ofuda in place. She stepped back and admired her handiwork. "I've another question, Shichiro-san."

"And I may have another answer."

"When I—" she cleared her throat and started again, reminding herself to leave the past in the past. "Some daimyo have secret passageways in their castles for when they must escape an enemy invasion. Kagawa-sama has a fine house, but it is not a castle."

"You are asking if there is such an escape here?" Shichiro asked as they walked to the children's room.

"I am."

The priest chuckled. "You are a shrewd one, Yukiko-san. As it happens, there are two loose boards in the daimyo's bedroom. If things were dire enough, the family could be smuggled out that way."

"That is well." Yukiko nodded. "I hope it will not come to that, but it is good to know that they might flee while I hold off the yūrei."

They reached the children's room. This must have been where the ghost had entered the house last night. Claw marks scored the wooden exterior walls, and the shoji had been torn to little more than shreds.

All color drained from Shichiro's face. "Do you really think you can defeat such a ghost?"

Yukiko surveyed the wreckage grimly. "I can try."

But first, she reminded herself, *I must deal with the one who let it in.*

THE SECOND NIGHT of her vigil wore on much the same as the first. Again, Yukiko kneeled patiently outside the daimyo's bedroom, the single metal ofuda dangling from the ceiling directly above her. Her swords lay at her left side.

Yukiko waited as the hours passed, her eyes and ears alert to every breath of wind and rustle of the leaves. Once, toward midnight, she heard the soft, mournful hooting of an owl. A good omen, or so she hoped.

The rhythms of the night shifted, and she judged it must be near the Hour of the Tiger. The fudakaeshi would soon make its appearance. Its living collaborator would tear down the ofuda she and Shichiro had placed earlier that day, leaving the one directly above Yukiko as the only remaining ward protecting the daimyo's family from the ghost. It and its mortal servant would have to go through her to reach them.

And Yukiko would be ready for them.

THE HOUR OF the Tiger drew on. Still, the ghost did not appear. Slowly, Yukiko's eyes closed. Her head fell to her chest, shoulders slumping. Her breathing changed, coming slower and deeper, a slight snore whistling through her half-open mouth.

There was a subtle, nearly undetectable shift in the air around her. A slight change in pressure, gentle as the wings of a moth fluttering through the room.

It was enough.

Yukiko's eyes snapped open, two points of gray light in the blackness. In one fluid motion, she rose to her feet and turned around, raising her sheathed wakizashi in her left hand.

Her attacker's blade hummed as it cut through the air, only to bounce off the wakizashi's lacquered saya. Yukiko drew the sword, keeping its saya in her off-hand. She laid the scabbard along the flat of her blade, using both to parry the attacker's backswing. Steel clashed against steel, breaking the tranquil nighttime silence.

Yukiko swept her wakizashi in a horizontal cut, feeling resistance as the blade bit deeply across her enemy's stomach. She knew it to be a mortal wound, but that was not the end of the fight. An enemy wounded to death was still an enemy that could kill.

Her attacker grunted in surprise and pain and thrust his sword at her. Yukiko sidestepped, though not quickly enough. She let out a pained hiss as the tip of the blade pierced her side, drawing a long, shallow cut just above her left hip.

It had been a reckless attack, one that left him open to her counterstrike. She stepped forward, inside the reach of his blade, and drove her wakizashi into his middle. Hot blood washed over her hand, and her foe let out a startled gurgle. His sword clattered to the floor.

Only then, in the light of the full moon, did she see her attacker's face.

"Hayate-san," Yukiko breathed, her heartbeat pounding in her chest. The fight had been brief, but nothing set the heart to racing like battle.

The yojimbo's eyes were wide, his face draining swiftly of color. Blood seeped from one corner of his mouth.

"You fought well," he managed to gasp. He stumbled forward, clutching at her. Yukiko lowered him to the floor, kneeling over him. She heard the sound of commotion in the room behind her; Kagawa Ryo and his family must have been awakened by the struggle.

"Tell me why," she whispered to Hayate. "Why betray your lord?"

"Never," Hayate breathed. His eyes fixed on the metal ofuda dangling above Yukiko's head. "I tore down the charms at his command."

A shiver crawled down Yukiko's spine.

The ghost's low, mournful wail echoed through the house.

The screen behind Yukiko slid open.

She threw herself to the side, acting on sheer instinct. The long blade of a katana whipped through the air where her head had been only seconds before.

Yukiko rolled, grabbing her own katana from the floor and drawing it as she stood, assuming the classic fighter's pose: one foot forward, sword gripped in both hands, the blade pointing at her foe.

Kagawa Ryo stood opposite her, his stance mirroring hers. Awoken from sleep, he wore only his underclothes, his bare feet padding silently over the wooden floor as he and Yukiko circled one another.

"You," Yukiko said as the ghost's wailing drew closer. "You ordered Hayate to tear down the wards. You *wanted* the fudakaeshi to come inside."

"I did," Ryo said. A bead of sweat stood out on his forehead as he gripped his katana tighter. "And he obeyed, as a good samurai should."

The ghost let out another long, ghastly moan, even closer. It was inside the house by now.

Understanding dawned.

"Your wife," Yukiko breathed. "Your first wife, Aiko. She is the fudakaeshi."

"Yes," Ryo said. There was a strange gleam in his eyes. "I loved her, you know."

"Yet you killed her."

He did not deny it, only gave her a tired, sad smile. "Ten years we were together, Yukiko-san. Ten years, and not one child from the union. A daimyo must have heirs."

Kagawa Ryo's gaze shifted to the bedroom. Yukiko could see movement through the shoji; Minoru rousing her children from sleep.

"Why not take a concubine?" Yukiko asked—not out of curiosity, but hoping the longer she could keep Ryo talking, the more time Minoru might have to get her children safely away from their father.

Ryo barked out a joyless laugh. "You have seen the extent of my domain. A rocky strip of coastline whose income is barely sufficient to keep one noble lady, let alone two."

"So, you pushed Aiko into the sea." Yukiko advanced a step, the tip of her katana unwavering. Ryo took a corresponding step back, his own blade unsteady. "You found a new, young wife. A fertile wife."

A second shadow appeared beside the one Ryo cast on the shoji behind him. It had the outline of a woman with long hair and fingers like claws.

At the same time, Minoru appeared in the bedroom doorway, her eyes wide with fear. She held her two children against her sides, sheltering them in the folds of her kimono. Her face glanced from Yukiko and her husband standing with drawn swords to the fallen body of Hayate, then drifted up to the shadow on the screen behind Ryo. Her mouth fell open in a scream, but no sound came out.

"Stay back," Yukiko ordered her. "Do not cross the threshold."

Minoru swayed in place, paralyzed by fear.

"Minoru gave you what you sought," Yukiko said, advancing so that the ofuda hung directly over her head. Now she stood directly between Ryo and his living wife. "Children. And then the ghost appeared."

"The ghost of my wife!" Ryo shouted, his eyes wild. "Aiko, who I loved! She came back from death to be with me once again! She promised me we would be together once I disposed of her usurper!"

The blade of his katana suddenly pointed at Minoru. A stifled gasp escaped her lips, mirrored by the rising wail of the fudakaeshi behind the shoji screen.

"Be with her, then," Yukiko said, and cut down the last ofuda.

The katana was a longer blade than the wakizashi, meant for use outdoors on the battlefield, not within the confines of a home. But with its greater reach, Yukiko severed the cords of the protective charm in a single stroke.

The ofuda dropped to the floor with a dull thud.

The ghostly wail grew to a piercing shriek. Long-fingered claws ripped through the screen and seized Ryo around his neck and shoulders. The daimyo turned with a start as the translucent visage of his first wife burst through the tattered screen, her face twisted into a mask of hunger and hate.

Behind Yukiko, Minoru screamed.

The fudakaeshi that had once been Aiko wrapped its ghostly arms tight around Ryo. He flailed helplessly, katana forgotten, as the ghost's implacable strength hauled him off his feet, dragging him through the shoji.

Minoru stood horror-struck, rooted to the spot, her children clinging to her legs. Only once Ryo's screams had faded into the night did she sway like a tree in the wind. Her eyes rolled back into her head, and Yukiko barely caught her before she fell into a swoon.

"Shh," Yukiko murmured, cradling the other woman's head against her shoulder. "It's alright, Minoru-san. It's over. You're safe now."

Minoru did not open her eyes. "Truly?"

"Truly," Yukiko assured her. "The fudakaeshi wanted your husband, as you first told me. Now that it has him, you are safe."

"Are you certain?" Minoru's narrow shoulders shook. "Ryo… He said that the ghost loved him. That it promised to replace me."

"No. They are gone now, both of them."

Of that, Yukiko was certain. The fudakaeshi had dragged Ryo off in the direction of the very cliffs from whence he'd thrown his first wife into the hungry sea.

Minoru sobbed and buried her face against Yukiko's neck. Yukiko held Minoru tightly in her arms, comforting her as she would a young child. Minoru's own children, too small and frightened to understand what they had just witnessed, joined them, throwing their arms around their mother.

"I will tell you where your daughter is," the ghost murmured in Yukiko's memory.

Yukiko squeezed her eyes shut and shook her head.

"Ghosts always lie," she whispered.

MANIFESTATION

Hannah Birss

IT BEGAN AS it always does in those parts: on a long dark stretch of back country road, treacherous in its apparent emptiness. The rusted red F150 rocketed along the empty desert, the windows rolled down and a few tools rattling around the otherwise empty truck bed.

Inside, Robert bounced along with the sound of the tinny music coming from his battered speakers. His hands shook, and he reached for the flask that sat on his dashboard. It slid to the other side of the cab, and he swore. Beside him, his shepherd Goon panted, white teeth grinning underneath a lolling pink tongue; it had been a good run along the scrub brush, chasing roadrunners and growling at rattlers. The dog was tired and pleased. His owner was sauced.

She came out of the dark on the left, moving fast, her thumb raised.

Reaching one-handed for the leather flask, Robert swore and jerked the steering wheel. He meant to jerk it right, but his sodden nerves were cross-wired, and instead he jerked it to the left, toward her.

He didn't see her face, only the long dark hair that fanned out as she crumbled beneath the radiator grill with a wet thud. He swerved and lost control, Goon yelping as he slid over and crashed into Robert. The car rolled off the road and into the sunbaked sand. The headlights shone away into the desert, illuminating two cut pieces of the night. Robert sat there, shaking. Goon whimpered.

Nothing moved outside the truck. Robert sat there for a minute, staring, eyes wide. A jackrabbit leapt through one of the headlight beams, breaking the stillness. Goon whimpered again, and Robert ran a rough palm through his fur. The dog stilled.

"Stay," the man cautioned, and he opened the rusty door of the truck. There was no noise from outside the cab. He put one booted foot down, felt the ground give slightly beneath it. He stood, weaving slightly, and called out into the dark. He took one unsteady step, and then another.

"Hello?"

He found her twenty feet back, hunched at the side of the road like a dead animal. Her skin was dark, and she had long black hair which must have hung to her waist when she was standing. It covered her face. She wore black hiking boots, green khakis, and a light black sweater.

"Hello?" he said again. She was curled into the fetal position, one arm lying underneath her head as if she was sleeping. He reached down and touched her shoulder. There was still no response. Fresh scratches and bruises marred her skin. She wasn't bleeding that he could see, but she wasn't moving either.

He brushed some of her thick hair off of her neck. He placed two swollen fingers—calloused and gnarled after decades of less-than-careful construction work—on her neck. Her skin was warm and smooth to the touch. As he crouched there, her skin began to cool; the desert was quick to steal back any heat. He looked at her hands and noted that they were very small and smooth, flecked with what he thought might have been paint.

She was wearing a backpack—a red one, old and tattered, with a faded name in childish scrawl at the top. He averted his eyes. He did not need to know her name. She was his problem now, and the sooner he forgot her name, the sooner he could get on with his life.

He stood up. Runaway, probably. A hitchhiker looking to get away from home or heading to home? It didn't matter.

Goon whimpered from the truck again.

"Shut up," he said. The dog shut up.

He couldn't call the sheriff. He had too many DUI's, too many minor records attached to his name. He'd lose everything. He hadn't worked hard, spent his life baking underneath the hot sun, to have it end like this. She shouldn't have been hitchhiking at night—it wasn't his fault; it was just an accident.

Robert realized that he couldn't stay here along the side of the road when another person could come driving by at any moment. He couldn't leave her there, either. He remembered watching a documentary—they could find something on the body. Chips of flaking truck paint, a bit of rust from a radiator, tire prints. All things that could be traced back to him if he left the body there. It would have to come with him.

He steeled himself, and with trembling hands, he hefted her up into his arms. Her limbs dangled like a doll, chest pressing up against his. She was very young, and she was *very* dead.

Robert stumbled through the dark, stubbing his toes and nearly dropping her twice. Her head rolled, chin coming to rest against her collarbone. He heaved her once, up and over into the bed of the truck. It clanged as she dropped into it. He got into the cab, counted to ten, and started the engine. Goon looked at him with worried eyes.

"It's okay," he said to the dog. "No one will know. It was just an accident."

The truck started with no issues and lumbered back on to the road. Robert drove slowly, his eyes darting to the half-empty flask. He licked his lips, but he didn't reach for it. He had learned his lesson for the evening. It could wait until he was home. His shirt was sticky, and he brushed at it. The dog tried to sniff at him, but he pushed Goon away. When he made a turn, he could hear the slide of the body in the back, from one side to the other. He felt a sob rise up in his chest, and he fought it down.

When they pulled into the driveway of his dusty-bricked bungalow with its badly shingled roof, Robert finally allowed himself to reach for the flask. He took a deep gulp of it. The burning in his throat reassured him, and it warmed his chilled body. The evening was not turning out as planned.

He opened the passenger side door. The dog rocketed out and went around the house, tail between his legs. Robert took another swig and let the alcohol numb his unsteady thoughts. He followed the dog around the house to where an old shovel leaned against a rusted barbeque. He grabbed it, swearing as the handle splintered in his hands. He pulled a jagged piece of wood out of his palm and stuck it into the corner of his mouth and sucked on it. His blood was tangy. He picked up the shovel again, more gingerly this time.

There were a number of outbuildings on his property. One had been an old smoke-shed for curing meats with a pit in the floor that had once been filled with wood chips and was now filled with ash. He went out to it, the shovel clutched in his hands before him as if it were a cross warding off evil.

It was an accident.

He reached the old smoke shed with its door hanging off its hinges. It had been years since he had been out in this area of his property, and he knelt down and began to dig. More splinters drove into his hands with each frantic shovel. What remained of the rotten handle fell apart before he had gotten too far into the hole. He grasped the shovel's head and continued to dig.

The grave was shallow when he finished. He threw the tarp over her in the bed of the truck, tucking it around her body while she lay there. Robert did not want to directly touch her again. He moved slowly back out toward the shed, stood over the grave for a moment, before he rolled her into it. His eyes threatened to close with exhaustion, but he forced them open. Dirt trickled down from the edge of the hole, dirtying the tarp. Using his feet, he pushed the dirt back in until he couldn't see her anymore.

It was an accident, he said to himself again as he climbed into his own bed. His boots had tracked dirt and ash all over the house. *It was just an accident*, he repeated to himself until he fell asleep. *No one has to know.*

He realized as he pushed himself over the brink into unconsciousness that he had never looked at her face.

THREE BLURRY DAYS later, the sheriff came to knock at his door. Robert and Mac went way back; they had gone to Dusty Heights Elementary School together decades ago, though they had never been friendly when they were boys. They'd been cordial; a wave here, a small conversation there. Robert's history of minor brush-ins with the law had only cooled their already lukewarm relationship.

Mac was darkly tanned. His eyes, quick and intelligent, appraised Robert from within his wrinkled and leathery face, roaming over Robert's ragged pajama pants, the stained t-shirt, the red and sunken eyes. Robert's thinning hair fell to his shoulders in a tangled mess.

"Hey Rob," Mac said, glancing at Goon. The shepherd lay curled on the grimy linoleum of the kitchen floor. Goon stared back at him and gave a slow and friendly swish of his tail.

"Hullo Mac," Rob said. His voice was clear—it was still too early to start drinking. He'd been woken by Mac's insistent rapping at the door. His hand throbbed. Rob glanced down at it. The digging had done a number on it. He'd soaked the wounds from the shovel's splinters in alcohol and wrapped an old rag around it. Mac caught the glance and followed it.

"What happened there, Rob?" he asked.

Rob's mouth was dry. He licked his lips. "Thought I would try cleaning up some of the old buildings," he said, gesturing out past where the sheriff's new Chevrolet was parked. "Turns out some of those old boards have some bite."

"That's a hell of a bandage for a splinter," Mac said. "Sure you didn't get into a fight somewhere?"

Rob shook his head and unwound his makeshift bandage. The wound was red and angry. There were still large slivers of wood embedded in his hand, despite all of his attempts to remove them.

The sheriff frowned. "That looks bad. You should get someone to look at it. You don't want an infection."

"What do you want, Mac?" Rob said. He'd had enough of pleasantries.

"We have a missing girl from up on the reservation. Her parents reported her a few days ago."

"I'm not that kind of felon," Rob said.

Mac held his hands up. "I'm not implying anything," he said with a shrug, but his eyes searched Rob's with some intensity. He pulled a creased picture from his pocket. A young girl with raven hair, perhaps fourteen, grinned up at him. A school photo, by the looks of it. "Her name is Samantha. She was out in the desert several days ago and never came home. Her path home probably would have swung close by here. I was wondering if you had seen anything. Search efforts are underway."

Robert gingerly took the photo. He pretended to look at it, but looked past it, his eyes unfocusing. He didn't want to see her face.

"If she was out in the desert, she's probably dead," Rob offered, avoiding looking at the picture. He tried to hand it back to Mac, but the sheriff refused to take it. Robert's head hurt. There was a large bottle of rum sitting beside his bedside table. He didn't want to think about the little dead girl anymore.

"She had a camera with her," Mac said. "We're wondering if someone took it from her. She also had a sketchbook and some paints. Her parents swore she never went too far off the road. She hitched back a lot."

"Someone probably picked her up," Rob said. *And buried her back in the smokehouse.*

Mac listed off what the dead girl was wearing.

"I haven't seen her," Rob repeated. "I don't know why you're telling me this."

"Just keep an eye out," Mac said. "We sure would appreciate it."

Rob nodded.

Mac looked at him again, his dark eyes assessing him. Robert tried not to squirm. "Let me know if you see anything," Mac said, and he turned around and walked back to his truck. His boots caused little sandstorms in his wake.

Robert watched until the truck pulled back onto the main road before he went back inside and poured himself a drink. Mac had left the picture with him. He sat at the old, chipped Formica table and tried not to look at it. The girl's eyes seemed bright and accusatory. He mentally blurred her features and threw a blue tarp over her. His hand ached.

He drank his rum quickly. It numbed the pain and blurred the edges of his mind. It was good. Goon looked at him from the floor and whined.

Someone ran past his window.

Robert started, surprised, the alcohol slowing his senses again. Goon whined again, before the dog got up and went to the front door, scratching at it.

Someone was on the property. *Probably Mac*, Robert thought, a slow anger burning in him. Of course he hadn't believed Robert. He was back, snooping around, looking for that girl. The girl in the smokehouse. Fear swirled in his belly, fueling the anger. He got up, poured himself another drink, and knocked it back for liquid courage. He went into the bedroom and grabbed his Browning double-barreled shotgun from its place in the closet. Mac was trespassing, and Rob would put the fear of God into him, sheriff's badge or no sheriff's badge.

Goon continued to whine in the kitchen. Robert threw on his boots and went out, shotgun in hand. Goon slunk out behind him and stayed close on his heels.

Mac's truck wasn't there. He must've parked further down the road and walked back in the hopes of surprising Robert. Rob wouldn't give him the satisfaction.

He walked quietly around to the back of the house, stumbling only a bit. A small figure flashed in the corner of his eye, and he raised the shotgun. Two bangs echoed through the desert and part of an old outhouse erupted into splinters. A jackrabbit started and raced across the scrubland. Goon's ears pricked up, but he stayed still.

"I know you're here, Mac," Robert said, raising his voice. "And you're trespassing. I don't appreciate you sneaking around here like a thief. I don't know anything about that little girl."

He was met with silence.

He searched his property for a half hour and found nothing before he and Goon went back inside and he poured himself another drink.

RUNNING LOW ON food and booze, Robert had no choice but to go into town a few days later. Goon stayed behind. He stopped at the grocery store and liquor store, and after thinking about it, stopped at the pharmacy to pick up some antibacterial ointment and a real bandage. His whole hand was swollen now, and it throbbed in time with his head. He had not had a drink yet—he would not drink and drive again, not where Mac could catch him.

Once his errands had been run, Robert stopped for lunch and a coffee at the diner. He ate his scrambled eggs and sausage slowly. Above the milkshake bar, the TV displayed a silent news station, and he watched it as he ate.

The girl's face popped up on the screen. A red scrawling banner screamed at him: MISSING ONE WEEK. He averted his eyes and sipped at his coffee. He glanced back at the screen. She was still there. He asked for the check.

While he waited, he stared at his beer bottle, the thumb of his good hand picking at the corner of the damp label. The bell above the door rang, and he looked up to see a couple enter, their faces long and drawn. The woman had dark circles under her swollen eyes, and the man's face was blotchy and red, as if he had been crying. In their arms, they clutched wrinkled papers. They approached one of the booths closest to the doors, and he could hear them frantically talking to the people sitting there. The couple handed them a paper and moved on to the next table, repeating the process.

The waitress dropped his check, and he dug through his wallet and pockets in a hurry. He felt eyes on him just as his hand closed around the bills he needed, and he looked up to see the woman approaching him.

"Please," she said, holding out a paper in her trembling hand.

His heart skipped a beat, and he felt his coffee and eggs rise back up in his throat.

"What do you want?"

"Our daughter, have you seen her?" Her eyes were filled with an unfathomable sadness, spilling over in the shape of tears. "Her name is—"

"I don't know what you're doing asking good folks where your brat is at," he interrupted in a rush, his tongue tripping across his teeth in his anger. "You should leave them alone. What kind of parents let their child hitchhike, anyway?"

They recoiled as if they had been slapped. A paper floated down, a picture on it of a smiling girl with dark hair and a gap-toothed smile. It landed underneath his table.

"Sir, we're going to have to ask you to leave," the waitress said sternly from behind them.

"I'm going. Don't think I'll be back to this establishment, where you're willing to let your patrons be harassed," He tossed a bunch of change and small bills on the table. "You should all be ashamed of yourselves." He stormed out as people began to crowd around the bereaved parents, muttering apologies and shooting Rob nasty glares.

He went out to his truck and fumbled in his jeans pocket for his keys. The hairs on the back of his neck stood up, and he glanced into the driver's side-view mirror as the key slid into the lock and popped.

Dark eyes stared back at him from a small, tanned face that peered out from the glass. The features were smudged with ash and sand, and when it opened its mouth, dirt began to trickle out instead of words.

Robert made a small noise in the back of his throat and his hand fell from the keys still in the door of his truck. He backed away slowly. In the mirror, he saw the reflection of a MISSING poster from a nearby phone pole. His heart slowed in his chest, and he shakily got into his truck and started the engine. He didn't look in his side-view mirror until the poster was out of sight.

It was just an accident. I have nothing to feel guilty about.

As HE PULLED up to the house, Robert spotted Goon cowering out front under an old dead scrub brush. His ears were laid flat against his head and his tail tucked so far between his legs that, at first glance, Rob was sure that it had been removed.

"Get out here," he grumbled at the dog. Goon didn't listen. Rob approached him, and instead of running toward him, Goon began to bark at him. He reached under the bush to grab the dog by the scruff of the neck, but for the first time in his life, Goon lunged at Rob's exposed hand, snarling. Rob swore and yanked back.

"What in the damn hell is wrong with you?"

Goon growled deep in his chest, and when Rob tried to circle the bush, the dog's eyes followed him, black lips pulled back in an awful snarl. Goon's tail remained firmly in between his legs.

"Fine," he spat at the dog. "Rot in there."

They stood there at an impasse for a moment, and then Goon glanced off to the right of him. Without another sound, he bolted off into the desert. Rob watched him disappear from sight, weaving in and out of the rocks, buildings, and garbage that dotted his personal landscape.

"Damn dog," he muttered to himself.

His hand burned. He went inside and unwound his makeshift bandage. The throbbing skin was stretched tight, straining and shiny, and tendrils of red crept up past his wrist. Here and there, he could see dark pieces of wood still embedded, black, wormed so deeply into his skin that they barely peeked out.

He staggered to the medicine cabinet and threw it open. It was bare except for a few bottles. One was a bottle of aspirin, and the other was a blue prescription bottle, so old that the words were faded and inelible. He thought they might be antibiotics, so he tossed all four of them back in one go, and took several aspirin as well, chasing them with some cheap whiskey. He poured the whiskey on his hand and hissed as it burned.

Robert stomped toward the kitchen table, rattling around in the grimy drawers until he found a half-rusted pair of pliers. Sitting down heavily at the table, he took a deep breath and plunged the pliers in, grunting with agony as their needle-nose tips rooted around in his hand, grabbing at the splinters and digging them out with less-than-surgical precision. His eyes watered, further obscuring his view, but he kept at his gruesome task as he grunted with pain.

He stopped when the world began to spin. Beside him sat a pile of splinters, black, jagged, like small lightning bolts. The pile was big. Too big. There were pieces of all shapes and sizes and when he looked at his now-mangled hand, oozing pus and blood, he felt a little sick to his stomach. There seemed to be even more splinters left in his hand now than when he had begun.

It was an accident. I have nothing to feel guilty for.

He was coated in sweat, his clothes clinging to him, his chair damp with the efforts of his exertions in his attempts to remove the source of the infection that was now clearly coursing through his body. The smell of pus clung to him, and when he stood up, the old chair scraping along the cracked linoleum was a sharp bolt of pain in his temple.

A shower was the ticket. He would clean himself off and use that

Polysporin and fresh bandages he had picked up at the pharmacy. He drank the last of his whiskey and left the empty glass behind as he walked to the bathroom, shedding clothes along the way into the musty piles that already littered the hall. He gave the old knob a rough twist, and his pipes rattled to life as he clambered into the shower. It washed away the pain and his thoughts. He stood there, eyes closed, in the blast of hot water, and let the thoughts empty out of his head.

It took him a few minutes before he realized that the water wasn't draining. It had risen to his ankles, and he swore at the interruption, then bent down to see if he could do something about the clog.

He stuck his fingers in the shower drain. Something wet and soft brushed against his fingertips, and he stuck his fingers further down. His nail snagged on it, and he managed to pull it up enough to grab it. He slowly began to draw it out, the water finally draining as he removed the blockage.

It was a mass of hair, long and coarse and black. It just kept coming and coming, sliding out like a snake from its hole, smooth and easy. He gagged and gave a final yank as if he was starting one of his old gas mowers.

There was a moment of resistance, and the last bit of hair came up and out of the drain gate, with s a piece of bloody, rotting scalp attached to the end, dripping something thick and dark.

Robert dropped it, scrambling and slipping as he tried to get away. He dove out of the bathtub, tangled in the shower curtain. The curtain rod came down with him and hit him on the head. He lay on the ground, panicking, the world spinning. His hand throbbed, his head pounded, and the bathroom was filling with steam. He untangled himself as darkness began to creep in on his periphery. He barely had the wherewithal to turn off the shower as he struggled upright. In the foggy mirror, he could see another dark shape in the room with him, but he paid no heed as he slipped out of the bathroom, first-aid forgotten.

He barely made it to the bed before he collapsed into unconsciousness.

SOMEONE WAS KNOCKING on the door. Robert started to struggle into consciousness, but the dark yanked him back. He floated it in, hazy and feverish, drifting in and out of the void that threatened to overwhelm him. He could feel every sluggish heartbeat in his arm and hand.

The knock grew more insistent.

"Go away," he slurred. "Please go away."

They didn't. He wondered if someone had found Goon, and that brought him out of the dark. He wanted his dog. He missed his dog. His eyes opened, and if he could have recoiled, he would have. Instead, he pushed his body further down into the beat-up mattress, a whimper escaping his lips.

The girl in the smokehouse stood over him. Insects roiled in her, her ash-encrusted face rippling as they writhed beneath her skin. Her eye sockets were dark caverns inviting him in, the eyes eaten away, their outline ragged. Her lips were chapped, great pieces of their skin flaking away, her small white teeth exposed in a horrible rictus. Sand trickled down off of her burgeoning hourglass shape, and she leaned over further, head tilting as she regarded him. A maggot dripped onto his face, wet and slimy. It wriggled, tracing a cool path across his flaming cheek. Frozen with horror, he watched as she took one small, desiccated finger and brushed it off of him.

At her touch, he found himself able to move. He rolled himself off of the bed and scrambled to his feet. She regarded him from the other side of the bed as he stumbled for the front door.

He could hear the rustle of her clothes behind him as she followed. He threw open the door. Before it stood a surprised Mac, his fist still raised, his mouth open in surprise.

"Rob? Jesus Christ, man, look at you. You need a doctor."

"Out of my way," Rob slurred in his panic. "I need to get away."

"I'm going to call an ambulance," Mac said, stepping back. "I was just bringing Goon back. He's in the cab," he continued, jerking his thumb back over his shoulder in the direction of his truck, "but we need to get you to a doctor."

"Can't go now. She's coming, she's coming," Rob said frantically, pushing past Mac.

"Who's coming?" Mac pulled out his cellphone, his forehead creased in concern.

"The girl in the smokehouse," Rob said, and he began to half-run, half-tripped away. "It was an accident," he mumbled to himself. "It's not my fault. I have nothing to feel guilty about."

His eyes locked on the horizon, Rob ran into the street, where he was promptly struck out of nowhere by an old blue hatchback that came barreling down the road, a pair of dirt bikes strapped to the back. He didn't feel any pain, but there was a horrible ringing in his ears and a sickening crunch as he rolled over the top of the hood. He landed hard on the weathered concrete, sand blowing across it to fill his eyes and mouth with grit. The world was turned on its end, and it took him several moments to come back into his body.

He could hear Mac on his phone, begging for an ambulance. In the background, Goon howled. The driver in the old hatchback was hyperventilating, while their passenger sat on the ground beside Rob, wrapping Rob's leg in a makeshift tourniquet just above where bone jutted out. His blood mixed with the sand. A cold, icy feeling began to creep up his body, and he knew that their first aid would be for nothing.

From out in the desert, a dark shape approached. It stood on two legs, and as it came closer, he knew it was her—knew that she was there for him, and that there was no escape now. He wasn't sure that he even wanted to escape. The urge to do anything was gone, and as the black crept in from the corner of his eyes, he knew that this was it. It wasn't supposed to end like this.

It was only an accident.

As she came closer, her body began to stitch itself together. Her hair came back, thick and lustrous. The bugs vanished. Her lids blinked as her dark eyes reappeared. Her skin smoothed out. By the time she was ten feet away, she was back to the state she had been in the night when Rob had struck her with his truck, her red backpack slung over her small shoulders. She reached the edge of the road and fell to her knees. Her small hands scraped against the pavement as she crawled to him, her dark eyes beginning to glaze over with a white film. She curled up beside him, lying down, her eyes widening as if suddenly shocked, and then she was still.

The last thing Robert saw before the void took him was her face, the high cheekbones and long dark lashes, the small pert nose, and the mole above her left eyebrow

"Samantha," he said, the word escaping his lips as his soul fled his body. "Samantha."

GRAVES IN DIFFERENT PLACES

R. Wren

1 HIM

IKE A KNOCK, unexpected, on the lid of your coffin—the funerary drumming on the bathroom door. No shadows underneath, but the sound of voices. The low rumble nearly lost in the cacophonous beat. The foyer's hard concrete is awash in the escaping sounds of the concert. The metal handle twists up and stops. I hear the door rattling. The bass throbs like the beating of a monstrous heart.

A man's stern voice: "Sir, is everything alright in there?"

Moralistic. Middle-aged. Managerial.

Lenora's eyes move beneath her eyelids. She is not yet awake. Cold but starting to warm again in my arms. Everything in me is waiting for the colour to spread back into her face.

Three staccato beats, the hammering of his fist against the door. I wince at the high-pitched ring that screams in my ears. Casualty of the speakers. The sound of absence.

"Just open the door, please. Are you both alright? That's all we want to know."

"Can't you help?" I ask the empty room.

I feel my words in Her presence. She'd been behind Lenora's eyes only moments ago. She is still in the room with us. But no answer comes from Her, neither spoken nor planted in my head. She is a sullen mist in every inch of space. The mechanical crack of the door handle frightens me, the way the hunting-whip frightens the fox. I hear the whispering outside the door. The concerned young women who watched us, alert, when Lenora first collapsed. God bless them, I think. Any time but now.

But Lenora sleeps, and She is remote.

From outside the door, the man says, "Alright, get the key."

We'd known this was coming, Lenora and me. We felt Her raging against her limits. We travelled too far from the grave, left it too long since we fed Her body—and Her grasp on us began to slip. In those disconcerting moments of silence, Her presence became spotty, like a voice coming through an old coat-hanger antenna. A comparison for which, if She entered my mind at this moment, She would surely rend my synapses as punishment.

But She never enters my mind anymore. She will only inhabit Lenora— and how it pleases that ancient mind to be a young woman again, to immerse Herself in the banshee wails and burning coloured lights of the city, of music and dance, like the bacchanalias She remembers so vividly in ancient times.

"Lenora," I say. I stroke her hair with my shaking fingers. As gently as I can, I whisper, "Lenora, you're Lenora, remember?" And now, the inevitable mechanical crunch. The lock turns from the other side. I massage Lenora's temples and whisper into her ear, bending like to breathe air into a drowning victim's lungs. In this tiny space, the air is thick with Her presence. "Mistress," I whine.

The door cracks open. The flare of neon lights burns my eyes. Hard-set gawking faces emerge to peer in at us through the narrow doorframe. The rising thunder of the speakers like judgement coming down upon us. The calloused man's hand on the door handle. The luminous panelling of his coat. Swinging at the end of his string, the laminated card which reads, "Security."

"Sir," the security guard says, not taking his hand from the frame. "Could you not hear us from outside? Why didn't you open the door?" He looks at Lenora. "Madam, are you alright? Can you tell us what's happening?"

Behind the man, I see the passers-by peering at the scene. From the group of girls, whispers that sound like sharpening blades.

It had been a sudden and complete rending, amidst the spiralling control of the audience, when Lenora crumpled with an empty mind. I had to hold her limp body against mine, like propping up a corpse, every part of her cold as grave soil. And all around us the cries of upset, the flare of a phone torch picking us out from the gloom. The whispers as I carried her away from the crowd, the soles of her shoes dragging with rubber squeals.

The tongue inside my mouth is too dry, too thick with anxious anticipation to shape a sound.

Behind her eyelashes, thick with clumped mascara, there is a quick grey movement of the iris. I see the pit of her pupils shrinking against the buzzing overhead bulbs. In her expression, utter confusion—utterly lost. I whisper her name and, hearing my voice, her eyes turn slowly to mine. Her slack expression warms, just a little. But then the curtain comes down. A sneer of tired command fills her expression. Lenora's gentle doe-eyes grow very cold indeed, as Lenora is shoved down below. She is inside her now.

"Sir, can you tell us how you know this woman?"

And I, exulting in Her presence, tell him, "We worship together."

I hear the speculative whispers my answer set off.

I watch my Mistress through onlooker's eyes, this fragile, seemingly lost woman suddenly rising as if from the dead. The momentary unsteadiness of inhabiting a body again. The odd posture. The slight inward bend of shaking legs. Then, the lifting head, the ancient weight. The light-headed girl sobering in an instant.

"Are you alright?" calls a woman's voice from outside. "Do you know him?"

Her eyes fall on them. Somehow, they know to stay silent.

And then I cover my ears as I see Her prepare to walk.

The sweating security guard holds the door. Pale-faced women step back from a waiting taxi. The driver glances at us once in the mirror. Somehow, in some remote and animal way, they all sense what She is. They all know to cringe away, to quake at her presence as I do. My Mistress sits upright, like a high priestess in a gilded carriage. She is prepared to be triumphed down the sacred ways, to pass beneath festooned and blood-soaked arches, to be fanned with great wafting peacock feathers.

Sodium lamps burn through rain-spattered windows. She regards me with eyes that glow like amber.

"You will have to go back to the grave. You have let me grow weak."

"Yes, Mistress."

"You need to give more blood. Much more, this time."

"Yes, Mistress."

Turning back, She senses something in Her borrowed body. She lifts the hem of Lenora's beaded shirt and examines Lenora's ribs. There is no self-consciousness in the action. No shame in another's body, or in the wine-dark stain spreading beneath the skin. *"See to her bruises. I have not lived these ages to be in such discomfort."*

And with that, She is gone.

Lenora is left to hang on her seatbelt like a rag caught on a wire fence. The poor, sleeping girl will wake with a stiff neck. Then She would complain. And so, I take off my jacket and fold it into a pillow, which I gently place between her head and the widow. In the morning there will be pain. For now, Lenora sleeps with a mind submerged in oblivion, her breath light and untroubled.

2 HER

REACHING UP OUT of a deep and fetid slime. When you are pushed out of your own skull, you do not disappear. Nor are you sunk below. You go to another place. A place where the stench of rotting vegetation fills your nostrils. When She leaves, you do not come back. You have to crawl upwards through the treacly swill. You must plunge your fingers through the skin that has settled over your world. Pierce them through the back of your head, and, pulling aside your skin until the light comes in, split the scalp and crawl inside.

And I wake. She is gone.

He is here, packing clothes into a bag.

"Where are we?"

"Home," he says.

He means the flat. A tiny place, a locked box, a capsule. The place in the city where She puts away the toys when She's letting them rest. A stained couch and a sagging mattress. The curtains are always pulled so the room is cast in eternal night.

There is a scuffed gym bag open on the table. Our things are thrown in unfolded. My clothes that really are mine. They have not been washed since the last time I saw through my own eyes. How long has that been? Only Her clothes are pristine. Every stain is hand-washed, every crease is massaged out. Some of them are new. They are beautiful, expensive, scarlet and golden. They would fit me perfectly, but they are not mine. Mine are moth-eaten.

He alone can work, and only when She spares him to, and only for Her benefit.

Everything flows upwards towards her.

"Where is she?" I ask.

"Resting," he says. "We need to go back."

I sit on the edge of the bed, and the springs protest only a little. I wince at a pain behind my ribs. I resist looking. It will not do any good to see how She has been careless with me. She often forgets to feed this body. My bones are too close to the surface. They hurt easily.

So, She didn't loosen Her grip.

She *lost* it.

I know that resting is euphemistic. She is not in my head. Nor is She perching on my shoulder. Nor his. She can't sustain it. It is disquieting, at a time like this, to be alone. I can hear the faintest ringing in my ears. These are the only times I feel it—when our Mistress weakens, takes fright, flees from the icy winds of her mortality, so long put off. These long weeks, I have taken Her place in the grave.

I watch him. I feel for any trace of his hands on my skin.

"Kiss me," I say suddenly. "My lips are still numb."

He turns, pensive. I see myself as a small and distant reflection in his eyes, except that he won't keep them on me. The tension in his jaw. A guarded reticence, yes. The hunching of his shoulders against an expected impact. A guilt that keeps his eyes on the task before him, keeps his hands turning and folding clothes.

"You're allowed," I say.

"*She*'s the one who enjoys that," he says. "I don't want it."

"So we don't fuck." He flinches at the word. "I know the deal. Your blood keeps Her vivid. I keep Her walking. I give Her a body to scream in, to throw into walls, to press into crowds, and all the rest. It's not often She leaves us alone. Shouldn't I get to enjoy some of it, too?"

"Your lips go cold," he huffs. "It's like sleeping with a corpse. Did you know that?"

I lie back on the mattress. He clears out the medical bag. The scalpel and thread. The disposable syringe, rubber seal and plunger. His part of the deal. I stretch out until my joints feel a tug. To be back inside my body…it's like returning to your hometown. Retracing old steps. What has changed, and what has stayed the same? I wonder what they've done with me. I wonder when She will be back, and whether I will get to see the coastline with my own eyes this time.

We will take the ferry. She doesn't like to fly.

We leave that same day.

He handles the tickets; he finds our seats. A first-class armchair for me, but not for *me*. I will enjoy it, nonetheless. I feel Her in my head now and then. Fleetingly. Like a cat scratching its claws on the window, just to see whether it will open. There is something about a ferry. Cheap carpet rolled out by the square-mile. Rust around the railings. The froth of white waves churned up beneath the lazy propeller. A streak of torn water stretching back to the slim blue line of the horizon. The coastline just slipping out of view.

I feel a slight tug of Her. I'm not sure which of these are my own thoughts.

I find my way to the observation deck without really meaning to. A cluster of elderly tourists, their plastic raincoats snapping in the wind. The wind blowing out their cigarettes. I grasp the salt-eaten railing. The thoughts of vaulting over it are most certainly my own.

I wonder whether, if you jumped, you had any real chance of drowning. Either way, the water is not so far away. Maybe, if you tried it, you'd just be fished out, embarrassed, soggy, subject to the judgement and concern of pensioners. Over my shoulder, I see that he has followed me out.

I wonder whether She is whispering in his ear, telling him to keep an eye on me.

"I'm not going to," I said to him. "Just indulging."

He nods, somehow shamefaced. "I know. Do you want a cigarette?"

"She doesn't mind?"

He shrugs. "She's done worse."

A little touch of suicide. There was a time when I might have jumped. Just to try it. I had made more futile attempts than this. That was before, though. Now I get to taste death in small bites. Little stretches of oblivion. Like power naps. And it's hard, I suppose, to feel alone when you never are.

"Kiss me," I say again. And he shuffles forward. He means to this time. Only now the coastline is fading, and the burning scent of petrol is fading too. He comes because he is bid. She wants it this time. Whatever will follow will be at Her direction. I grip the railing to keep myself on my feet during the hand-over.

The Body. Abstracted.

Even without throwing myself over, I get to fall away.

3 SHE

WARM BREATH ON our lips. Air from his lungs. The cutting spray of sea-salt. The weight of a skull atop our neck, of arms hanging limp from shoulders. The stacked totem of vertebrae that makes a spine. His cold fingers on ours. The wet, squeezing cramp of intestines. The tedious inflating and deflating of lungs. Life. That dreadful thing. How it insists.

In olden times, I had devotees to tug by golden thread lashed around their wrists. By the light of bonfires, they would stumble forward onto their knees for me. Their eyes shining darkly, like the gems at my throat. The paint that daubed their body like animal marks. How they bowed before me. Mine to raise up. Mine to offer to my own glory. Mine to offer the gleaming bronze blade, to hold the gilded bowl, and to catch the blood, steaming black in the light of the night flames.

Now, I must hold his wrist like a parent leading a child.

I must brush shoulders with men in buttoned shirts. Must bow into foul-smelling rooms with turning locks. Must push his head down before he will drop to his knees. I am compelled to hear his shoes peel from the floor, where the fabric over his knees now adheres. I, too, am compelled to hold my voice.

I was dead before I ever crossed the water. Before then, there were worse things than drowning. Sinking to the seabed and yet failing to sleep. To become corpse and spirit with no shrine to sustain me. No offerings but the scraps thrown over by fishermen. No pilgrims but the fellow-drowned and the scuttling insects of the seabed. It could happen easily in those days of flimsy boats made of lashed branches and hollowed trunks. But this—this vessel, this ferry—is a palace. Great sheets of iron, held by bolts that pierce and bind like a brooch through a woollen cloak.

It was iron that scattered us. Iron axe heads that bit through our walls. Iron spearheads that cast down my devotees. Cold men from the east with blades that could shatter ours. To be carried back to my grave in such a thing. A monument to decay. This suffocating iron room, this foul casket, is a long way diminished from what I have known. My grave is on the headlands, bound in a ring of stone. It has endured. As have I.

I watch the crown of his head, where the greasy hair is thinning. There is no urgency in him. His fingers grip our hips without reverence. No devotion to the dull stroking of his tongue, flat and humourless like the blunt blade of a shovel. The barest sparks of pleasure. The numb striking of flint, never catching. Only the sightless eyes he is not even aware he has left open.

The pale hollow of his ribs. The jutting of his hips. The fading of a man, his flesh like a drum skin bound too tight over the frame. Such is the way when the devotee becomes merely a follower. I take his face in my hands. Lift it to look upon me.

"I will need more blood this time," I say.

"Yes, Mistress."

"Much more," I say. "Or I will not make this journey again."

"Yes, Mistress."

A hollow, too, behind his eyes. His mouth shining with drying blood. He waits for me to tell him what to do. To stop or to go on. I saw his panic when he thought he was alone. Where is that urgency now? He is like the dog that whines and fouls itself when left alone, but only sleeps when its owner is back.

I remember when I walked in him. He begged me to step into his mind back then. Now, he knows better than to beg. He knows there is nothing in him for me. He can serve, body and blood.

When I died, they built a pyre and threw themselves into it.

When there is no other service I can take, I will take life itself.

"Leave it," I say. "I tire of this. You can have her back."

And I let her drop.

There are winds in the air that the body cannot feel. A howling gale. It shakes me even within my grave. When I am sustained, I can stride through these winds like wildfire marches through trees. But I am weakening. I must be like a seabird and ride them, lest I am blown away and darkness take me. So I soar above, to where the ferry is but the head of a sailing arrow. The sea tracing its path in churning froth. It flies for me. Always for me.

4 HIM

ON THE DRIVE, I sometimes see Her on the side of the road. She will manifest at the edge of a ditch, or on the crest of a knoll, or I will find Her sitting like a pharaoh atop the crumbling slate roof of an abandoned farmhouse, surveying the landscape in the golden light of sunset. I wonder whether it makes Her nostalgic. Perhaps it makes Her feel powerful—to see how the landscape has changed while She, alone, has endured.

She rides with me in the car sometimes. I think She enjoys the speed. Sometimes She urges me to press my toes down on the pedal and hurtle us down bumpy, rattling country roads. Hanging branches whip our windows and slash at the paintwork. She grins, Her fingers sinking into my thigh like claws, hooting with almost animalistic joy. But not today.

"Go safely and slowly," She speaks through Lenora's lips. *"Blood spilled on the roadside will do me no good."*

I admit that I had been pushing it, allowing the speed to creep recklessly higher. Sometimes I try to pre-empt Her whims like this. To encourage them, even. When She is happy, when I am pleasing Her, then I am fulfilling a purpose which I never even intended to make for myself. There is a cavity that was left when She extracted herself from me. I feel Her pleasures as distant echoes.

I follow the line of old train tracks. There is no use in asking Her for directions. The roads are newborns to Her. I imagine how they must seem from Her perspective, these petty trails and tarmac ribbons spreading and receding over Her ancient slopes, like snakes writhing across Her skin.

At the end of this trail, where the soil turns wet and black, and blood-coloured heath is tugged by insistent winds, there is a ringfort clinging to the edge of the earth. Ancient stones, moss-covered on one side only. An eroded stub of headlands. Aeons on battering waves, tearing away clumps of earth bite by insistent bite. And at the centre, a grave. My blood to fill it. A gash in my arm, a slit into my vein. And Her waiting for me, arms wide, body warm, every part of Her grateful.

And why?

I saw how She looked upon me when She held my face on the ferry. Not as a slave, not as a pet, but as a mere object. A tool coming to the end of its usefulness. A pair of sandals worn down to the barest strip of scrap leather. Soon to be dropped into the fire or thrown away for pigs to eat.

I feel myself accelerating again. The sooner to meet Her there. I have to believe that She is waiting for me. Perhaps She will be more vivid when

She is replenished. Perhaps Her golden eyes will turn upon me more often. To see, truly see me, as I see Her.

But what if She is tiring of me? What if nothing changes when I pour myself into Her bowl, but that I am diminished, and She asks yet more? Then why not go faster, and faster, and faster still? Why not bait Her into cries of laughter and rage? Why not drive this car into the trees? Fatal and immovable, they whizz through my peripheral vision. Momentary blurs of motion, the passing prick of fright. That's all I have. That's all I will be left without Her. That's all we are to Her.

Why not?

"Slow down," comes Her upset murmur. "You're making me sick."

Not Her voice. Only Lenora's. Sleepy and displeased. Utterly human. I relent and lift my toes, allowing the panting engine to relax a little. It does me no good to think this way. She needs these things. I must remain with Her. There is still a long way to go.

5 HER

THE SKY TURNS the colour of fire while he stands in the grave up to his knees, his forearms streaked with black earth. He is strangely confined. When he shifts his weight, his soles lift from the mire with a soft wet 'pop.' The sea hisses so close to us here. The soil itself is filled with it. I am sure that if I took his arm and ran my tongue along it, I would taste sea salt. Perhaps She has. Any moment, now, where my focus lapses, I am given to wonder.

"Do you have the bandages ready?" he asks.

"I can get them," I say. "Is it time?"

He shakes his head, leaning on the shovel.

"No," he says. "But are they ready?"

Tired, I lean on a moss-covered stone and run my fingertips along it. The stone is not natural. It has been cut, carved, carried from somewhere else. The corners have been smoothed down, long before time began to wear at it. Nor is it alone. They rest in piles around us, a huddled remnant of some ancient fastness. Most of the structure is now underground, signalled only by the strangely unnatural ridges and bumps that disturb the earth. You would not see the line of a *ráth,* a ringfort, unless you knew to look for it. Perhaps, I think, that is how a thing such as this can survive. It has not been picked away at by scavengers, by millennia of bog-stained hands seeking stones for their constructions. By burying itself, it has only to outlast the eroding tide.

"Here She comes," he grunts, twisting the handle.

I repeat him to myself. I puzzle over the tone he used. Tired, I decide. Or perhaps resigned? I wonder that She is not in his ear, hissing Her displeasure. But perhaps it would sting Her to do so. I know chiefly that She loves adoration, and for that adoration to come naturally.

He spills a shovelful of slick stones to the side. There is little enough to adore about the smell that comes out from under them. I am curious, though I have been here before, to see Her. I wish to imagine Her emaciated frame slipping beneath my skin, Her barely flesh-wrapped bones taking the place of my skeleton while She walks within me.

This is where I imagine I take Her place. This pit, the earth pungent with preserved malice, should be as familiar to me as a childhood bedroom. Crawling my sleeves through wet soil, I peer over into the hole.

There She is.

That beautiful, magisterial form. How the thousands of years have wrapped and preserved Her. I see the patiently feeble stirring of finger bones, brown as though tea-stained. The swell of earthen juices as She turns Her narrow throat. Here She is, rendered down by aeons into a delicate doll of waxed leather. A crisped dead earthworm clings to Her slight strands of wispy hair. There is no feast for maggots here. There is no decay to writhe in. There is only life, stubborn and insistent.

I hear Her in my head.

"Blood," She says.

He must have heard the voice, too. He sighs and stands down into the grave, his booted feet carefully planted either side of Her. He retrieves from his kit the scalpel, the rubber pipe, and the spout. He holds his forearms up into the pale sunlight and seeks a vein. I look away as he touches the blade to his flesh and starts the bleeding.

"After this," he grunts, "back to the city. Come and go."

But Her jaundiced eyes, hardened 'til they can barely turn, hold to me.

"*Blood,*" She repeats.

My hand reaches for one of the disturbed stones.

I feel Her pushing inside me. The curtains are closing around the cliff-side. Before I am swallowed up, I see him turn in surprise as the underside of the painted stone splits his scalp. He, in falling, exposes the barest flash of yellow bone. It is like the peeking of a moon behind clouds. Reclining into the buried repose, I imagine that I—this once— can see the sky.

6 US

THERE HAVE BEEN so many bodies since I was laid down to rest beneath the earth.

Some were my plaything for a summer or two. Some I pulled off the main roads, sent wandering through the wilderness with me in their heads, 'til they found themselves at my grave and opened up their veins. Some I even took and threw into the water, for the same simple amusement that children seek in throwing leaves into streams. There is a thrill in feeling the wind pulling against one's face. Even in the white-heat pain of obliterated bones on the rocks below.

It is nice, in truth, to feel.

Never has a body felt like my own, though. His did not. This girl, Lenora, hers does not. They drape around me like an ill-fitting robe. I have never yet felt the skin with the back of our hand and known it was mine. I have been tall, and felt myself outsized, though I was tall in my day. And our faces—though I have looked into polished glass and seen these faces wear my expressions, they have always felt like masks of sewn leather. There is always a space between myself and the skin which I am conscious of.

I cannot remember now if I was always thus.

I can feel him atop me. Below, in the soil. He is not yet sleeping. Not yet cold. He is twitching, writhing, like the worms which sometimes cross my breast. What neater fate? What closer embrace? He loved me once. She, too, is writhing. Within. She knows, though sleeping, that there will be blood under her nails when she wakes. That is not the main thing that makes her restless.

She knows that she will now step into his place. She will become a keeper of my shrine, like a gardener who feeds a rare flower. It will be her blood that nourishes me. And if she seeks the oblivion, the dreamless sleep which once I gave her, she will have it in time.

There are always more.

I walk in her to the cliff-side. It is a shorter walk now than it once was. Every time a generation falls away, like leaves shedding in the winter, and I exalt in my permanence, this headland crumbles a little more to strike fear back into my pickled heart. In my day, I could stand upon the walls and see a field of tufted grass running before me. The sea, patient and irresistible, had had its say. Now the first of the rings have already fallen away. I lie buried at the heart. It will be many strange aeons before I feel the sea-air. But I will feel it.

I let our legs swing from the cliff's edge.

He has stopped twitching. He will become a blanket of soil to keep me in comfort.

He sleeps, and I can neither touch him nor recall him any further. She sleeps, yet will wake, but will sleep again. I will forget them both in time. I walk here 'til the sea comes for me. I know no other way.

THE BOUQUET

Ron Perovich

I did not tell her from or where
The flowers that I offered came.
It was a gift, and that's what counts,
If bought would they not smell the same?
She needn't know my thrifty eye,
When cutting through that misty wood,
Was pleasantly inspired there,
By lively color just as good.
There growing wild and out of place,
Tucked in roots, within the shadow,
Shocking red among the lichen
Underneath a leafless willow.
Fine lilies of that rarest hue,
Of which I hoped would stoke her fire,
And paired with clever compliments
In hinting at our shared desire.

Indeed, her parlor rang with joy,
For as she cradled them so tight,
Her ruby smile, it blossomed like
The blooms against her dress's white.
Her mother brought a vessel then
To douse the stems and set them out,
By contrast to my love's delight,
Her gaze still looked on me with doubt.
Same her father, ever present, And hardly even had to speak;

Just sternly glared and cleared his throat,
As when she leaned to kiss my cheek.
"Oh, I will set these close to me,
There in my chambers every night,"
As she professed to their alarm,
A minor scandal in their sight.

I was hastened shortly after,
Off to depart before too late,
More to satisfy decorum,
And stay our reputation's fate.
So back to working in the town,
And waiting out the proper days,
Before I could call once again
Upon the home of Liza Mae's.
I did my job and made my rounds
In labor of a better name,
And pay for all I would require
To play, at length, the courting game.
Upon the week,
I ventured out,
My shoes and hat all freshly brushed.
This time deciding on a cab,
To try and not to seem too rushed.

With care, the horseman drew the reins
To slow the giant wheels and halt,
To finally walk the gravel path
That crunched beneath like so much salt.
Out here, upon the edge of town,
Just past the long-neglected wood
That gifted me last week's bouquet,
Is where the family manor stood.
Well, maybe not a manor, true,
But more than I had ever known.
And all for just the three of them,
With all her brothers left and grown.
I approached in admiration

Of all that brought them such acclaim,
'Til then I spied the upper sill
Where sat the flowers, still the same.

For peeking past the pale lace shade,
The crimson petals beckoned, come,
Here may dawn first find and wake her
In her private sleeping sanctum.
Do they thrive by her affection?
For time had yet to leave a mark,
And in their vase, they stayed in bloom,
Their color holding, rich and dark.
I thought it best to not appear
As some unseemly rake who'd stare,
And locked my eyes to forward then
At just the time to meet his glare.
The father stood there, like a dam,
Astride the porch with planted feet.
I tipped my hat and dipped my head,
And in my best, politely greet.

Now presently, my Liza Mae
Was heard to call beyond the screen,
"Papa, may we stroll and visit,
Enjoying here our garden green?"
A muffled grunt was all I heard
Then gruffly turned and passed inside,
And out there came the family star,
Whose spirit was too bright to hide.
We walked at hand, but not too close,
And slowly toured the well-kept grounds,
In conversation always kept
Within the sight of genteel bounds.
'Til slowing in the cool of shade,
She proffered then, somewhat contrite,
Regrets upon her wearied state,
For she had found no rest last night.

"I could have sworn I was awake,
But at the cusp of sleep I find
So oft the crossing into dreams
Is left unclear within my mind."
Beyond the bedside scene she set,
My curiosity was drawn,
And so with prudent vestal tact,
I sympathized and bid go on.
"The moon's pale light was all I had,
But 'twas enough to see him there.
A boy of maybe ten years old,
Unkempt and looking lost... or scared."
Her bonnet jerked then with a shake
As a shiver rippled through her,
For clearly this fresh memory
Was as welcome as the stranger.

An insight then occurred to me
To proffer then a milder line.
"Perhaps this was a vision then,
And could it be a hopeful sign?"
At this, she paused to look at me,
Just briefly pulled from her distress,
"Imagine, he could be our own,
A glimpse of one day being blessed!"
This only tinged her tired eyes
With disappointment left unsaid.
"Alas, that is unlike to be
Because his hair was fiery red.
And not at all alike to mine
Or even your own chestnut locks."
I fear I played a clumsy hand,
And may have tainted further talks.

"He spoke," she said, now quietly,
"Just like the flutter of a moth."
I thought I saw a teardrop fall
And offered her my pocket cloth.
"So soft and frail,
I wasn't sure I had truly even heard it.
And after, frozen in the dark,
Losing sleep to make the words fit."
Then in the pause, across the lawn,
Came her mother, stalking toward us.
So, knowing that our time was short,
I whispered, "And his message was?"
But she, too, saw the chaperon,
Turning in to speak discretely
Her mouth hung open for a breath
Then in whispers, "Will you catch me?"

I skipped the cab to save the coin
And once again those dark woods roam,
Pondering her constitution
To slowly make my way back home.
Her story's echo filled my mind,
For the details did entrance me.
But in the end, I moved along,
Chalked it up to girlish fancy.
I happened by the willow tree
From whence my bold red flowers grew,
And sad I was to see that still
No buds had risen there anew.
I hoped I did not kill the plant,
Denying someone else their sight,
Alas, I could not linger long,
To make it home by fall of night.

Again there passed a fortnight more
'Til I could find the time to call
Upon the house of Liza Mae,
Where hung there once again a pall.
And not just in her bloodshot eyes
But now her own forebears' as well,
So much that when I greeted her,
I saw the tears begin to swell.
It was that slowly cracking glass
That tempered now their old disdain,
Too tired to be just guardians,
Now sharing in their daughter's strain.
"Oh, darling Tom," she managed then,
"I fear I look a dreadful sight."
And we three shook our worried heads
To dare not think that she was right.

Her father with his blunter edge,
Spoke, "We have woken to her screams
On each of three long sleepless nights,
When she's been visited by dreams..."
"They do not feel like dreams at all!"
My Liza blurted over him,
Before she caught the reins again,
Pretending not to be so grim.
"Or rather," now with prim restraint,
"Pray let us quit such heavy air."
And with the tact I oft admire,
She steered our hearts to kinder fare.
Then we were lent the sitting room,
All dim and cozy, to our own,
When she remarked she was too tired
To stroll among the grass and stone.

We chatted near the humble hearth,
Whose embers warmed the hardwood halls,
Our gossip hid in crack of logs,
Another murmur in the walls.
But even in this idle trade
I heard the shadow shake her lip
A quavered tone that gave away
What figure still maintained its grip.
"The boy," I broached at last to her,
"Has he returned when you cried out?"
An answer in a downcast nod,
Just after nervous looks about.
She whispered like the rising smoke,
"He has, but it has grown more clear.
For now I wake to his cold hand,
Him pulling at my arm in fear."

Her gaze was thrown into the coals
To burn away the thought once more,
Until I broke the silence, asked,
"And were his words just as before?"
Others caught on to our quiet,
For then, the matron thought to see,
Abruptly unannounced she came
Into our space to offer tea.
Of course I stood as I'd been taught,
To thereby graciously decline,
I caught my lover's weary eye
As well her silent answer sign.
A shaking chin as her head fell,
And losing briefly in the fire
Her mask of brave, untroubled grace,
And hence I guessed her true desire.

"Please, you must rest," I stated plain,
To this no argument was made,
For though I wished to see her more,
I winced within to see her fade.
Then parting kindness all around,
I saw myself out to the door.
Then to the gate, and to the road,
But not the route I took before.
Still more parting I required,
Of silver spared but for a beer.
"The Bird and Branch" was down the road,
Proprietor of ale house cheer.
I warmed a stool for several pints,
And bent the ear of tired keeps,
Uncorking my fermenting words
Upon the subject of lost sleep.

 Alas, they were no help to me,
The keep or any patron there,
Although I could not help but see
That some points did illicit stares.
I swear, I even spied a cheek
Grow wet upon an old man's face,
When I described the woods, the tree,
The flower in that solemn place.
By dark, my worries stoutly drowned,
I'd barely coin to catch the coach,
To speed me to my seedy room,
Too small for even rat or roach.
Just like a slurring little mouse,
Past my landlord's door I creep,
To crash into my empty bed
And within half a heartbeat, sleep.

The veil of night was no more clear,
No truth or revelation came.
And even through the cloud of drink,
The barbs of conscience stung the same.
Such shame, at this, my middling life,
Saving slowly but impatient.
Such guilt, to reach, to seek a wife,
Far above my stalling station.
Fear, that I am all illusion
Like some ghostly social climber,
And thus assume that's all I am,
Doomed when love will fail to blind her.
It was a squall that grew inside,
Its torrents twisting sheets and bowels,
When voice I'd never heard but knew,
Came screeching "catch me!" through the howls.

Up from the deep, I gasping woke
All tangled in my bedding shroud,
With sightless eyes I cast about
Into the dark, who spoke aloud?
My reason waking just behind,
'Twas just the boarders down the hall,
So often heard through walls and doors,
I told myself, *and that is all!*
But still, I could not calm the storm,
For some hook would not let me free.
And even in the conscious world,
My soul was tossed and lost at sea.
No glow of dawn yet crossed the lanes
To light on any sleeping guest,
And yet a beast I could not tame
Remained, determined, none may rest.

Once mind and heart and will aligned,
I rose and dressed with maddened speed,
To follow what I can't explain
Was both a fear as much as need.
That voice I could not dream away,
To hear it was to share her dread!
Overcome with worry for her,
I quickly down the stairwell fled.
From behind I heard the landlord,
Him shouting after as I ran, But I did not turn to answer,
Now past the door, still with no plan.
How could I cross the space between
And then what could I even do?
For none of this made sense at all,
But something told me, *she needs you.*

Suddenly I spied a hansom,
Its yawning driver standing near.
Moaning of his shift not started,
Of how my plight he would not hear.
Wretched luck, no funds were on me,
And so I weighed what love may cost,
Producing then my father's watch,
To be the night's first treasure lost.
So fine a trinket over paid
The horseman at least spared no whip,
Just as my own premonition
Gave spur and drove this frantic trip.
As twilight shattered by our race,
We reached the house, still shy of dawn.
But there my heart was chilled anew,
To see that all the lamps were on.

I scrambled from the skidding cab
Before it even came to rest,
And running up the moonlit path,
I saw again that crimson guest.
In silhouette against the light,
Clearly now the lily dying,
And midst the clamor flooding out,
Sounds of Liza's mother crying.
Her name they shouted, room to room,
As trespassed I their entry hall,
The father and a neighbor's voice,
Now interrupted by my gall.
"It's you!" the elder snarled at me,
"I know you did this! Where is she?!"
The mother, in her nightgown, wept,
Bereft of even words to plea.

I thought he may then strike me there,
When in his grip my collar caught,
But all had prayed for any help,
So my arrival went unfought.
Dearest Liza Mae was missing,
Found absent from her resting place,
Discovered when they checked upon
No timely screams, nor any trace
Of the unknown nightly terror,
Of which their daughter would not speak.
And now the nightmare passed to them,
Just when it seemed she'd broke the streak.
We searched the house and searched the grounds,
From fence to paddock, to the lane.
More neighbors came to comb the fields,
And wade the creek down by the cane.

Some time before the sun broke loose,
The desperate man took me aside,
"Did my daughter have a secret,
Or any clue she did confide?"
By now, I was as scared as them,
And so I told him all I knew,
How her dreams had grown more vivid,
And how I heard the boy now, too.
But when I spoke aloud those words,
Within that final twilight hour,
His face went white and still as snow,
"Where'd you say you plucked that flower?"
The careless details dripped from me,
As nothing seemed too strange or dire,
I saw no meaning in that tale,
But I would soon witness a fire.

"The tree," he breathed, and brought to mind
A specter of the sleepless child.
"The tree," he spoke to no one then,
The whisper waking something wild.
He pushed his way past all of us,
To stumbling lurch across the lawn,
Regardless of his sleeping robe,
Off toward the woods, the tree, and dawn.
We trailed behind, right after him,
And did our best to match his stride,
But only I knew where he went,
(Although I kept that hid inside)
Beyond and through the gnarly gloom,
To seek a place I knew not then
Could be of such significance
To him before and soon again.

Breaking then into a clearing
And any light the sky allows,
There stood Liza, gently balanced,
So high up in the willow's boughs.
The dawn reached through the twisted trees
In shafts of half-light, parallel,
And through her silken shift she glowed,
I froze, enraptured by her spell.
Her mother screamed and many gasped
As her father sprinted closer,
Begging with a fearful tremble,
"Please come down," he tried to coax her.
By then we all were calling out,
But she was fixed on something else.
Her eyes were wide and terrified,
But not for danger to herself.

"We have to save him," she cried down,
While crawling out onto a branch,
"We have to catch him, swear you will!"
But no one else there was to catch.
Hopeful men were dashing forward
To risk their necks to scale the height,
But standing in the back I glimpsed
The tearful elder from last night.
Here once again, his eyes were red,
He muttered, lost in some lament,
About the sorrow come again,
I briefly wondered what he meant.
But all those thoughts would fall away
When to our horror, came the sound
Like firing lines, a string of cracks,
As splintered logs and bark rained down.

Turning, stumbling, arms above me,
As if my bones could block the swat
Of this angry, withered giant
That chose this night to shed its rot.
Rescuers now ran for cover,
Myself among them, through the fray,
But not before I heard those words
Not from the ghost, but Liza Mae.
Above the noise, I heard her scream,
"Catch me!" faint but unmistaken,
The words that had so haunted her,
Just as what bade me awaken.
Once again I found they roused me,
And for a moment, broke through fear,
To crane my view to look behind
And stumbling, stop, just barely clear.

Where hope had promised there a sight
Of gentle gossamer descent,
My eyes instead will ever hold
The knowledge how her soul was rent.
There was no grace in how she flayed
Those splintered rungs with whipping head.
There was no lust beneath the slip
That tore apart, 'til she was dead.
The dust still hung like morning mist,
In silence, once the chaos stopped
As we approached her somberly,
When to his knees, her father dropped.
He cradled in his mighty arms
His only daughter, holding tight,
Her ruby smile that blossomed like
The bloom against her dress's white.

As the clearing slowly brightened,
The new day rising, waking up,
I heard poor Liza's father moan
In anguish as the tears erupt.
What fate this was, this tragedy,
That seemed to echo in reverse.
How did Liza see it coming?
And just with whom did she converse?
The elder stranger from the bar
Placed a pale hand on my shoulder.
"And now he knows," he quiet said,
Speaking with a grief much older.
"My son thought they were all his friends,
Back when these woods saw them as boys,
But to those bullies..." here he sighed,
"His fear was just another toy."

We watched as they took Liza Mae
Departing as a broken pair.
"They had a game they liked to play,"
His words a fog in morning air,
"They'd throw a rope around the top,
And lift each other up and down.
When they teased my boy into it...
Their knot work proved to be unsound."
My tear-filled eyes took in the tree,
A height until today ignored,
And saw among its reaching hands,
Some aging strands of rotten cord.
Below them now, on shattered arms,
The glinted shreds of bone-white skirt
Snagged upon the broken branches,
Still high above the dampened dirt.

The old man limped up to the tree,
And peering down among its roots,
"That oldest boy who held the coil,
When questioned, he shook in his boots."
There was anger in his whisper,
Or so I heard it, as he knelt.
"Said he didn't know the danger,
And didn't know how my son felt."
Then he pulled out from his pocket
A flower bulb of ruddy wax.
He buried it among the blood
Then stood to begin walking back.
Still in shock, I was planted,
But there within the wind that blows
I caught his parting final words:
"But now he knows. Oh, now he knows."

WOOD FOR THE TREES

AM Sutter

SHE SAW THE first hiker just as her campfire started to blaze. The boy appeared at the edge of her vision, the forest dark and creaking behind him, and leaned his head into the halo of light. She couldn't make out more than the idea of his body—scrawny, like a sapling—but his face was all too visible.

Red and blistered skin pulled tight against his cheekbones. His eyebrows had been singed off, his lips charred. The boy didn't seem to notice. He stared at the flaming logs of her growing fire.

Mari startled to her feet, a choked *hey* slipping past strained vocal cords, and let her cooking iron fall to the dirt by her boots. The child looked up briefly, but his attention returned right back to the flames as they hungrily licked and drooled against the dry wood. He shouldn't have been so focused on something so small, not on burning twigs, not when she thought his hair might still be smoldering. Though maybe it was a trick of the dark.

"Are you alright?" She stepped around the fire pit. The heat tickled against her shin and made her wince. The burns had caused the skin of his cheeks to tear, revealing dehydrated fat and muscle underneath. How wasn't he reacting? How was he even *alive?*

But that didn't matter right now. What was important was the burned child, alone in the forest, staring at the edges of the timber in her fire as it turned to ash, even as the boy's lips and button nose blackened to cinders before her.

"Hey," she tried again, fighting to hide her growing panic. "Where are your parents?" She took another step forward.

The fire popped, cracking open a log, and the child spit out a tooth, loosened in a blistered gum. A strangled noise erupted from Mari before she could stop it, and the boy whirled. Finding her too close, his teary, red eyes widened, and he vanished into the darkness.

For a moment, she teetered on the edge of the light, trying to listen for footfalls in the underbrush. She heard nothing, and though it felt indescribably wrong, she knew better than to flounder into the forest at night after the child. That was how people got lost. That was how people died.

So instead, she stumbled back to her tent and grabbed her phone. Service out there was poor, but it was just enough for the dispatcher to hear her.

Two hours later, her fire slumbered: only embers, but she didn't need it. The rangers and police had spotlights and floodlights and flashlights. The darkness fled from the forest under the onslaught, and Mari had to squint against the glare as an officer asked her questions.

No, she didn't know the child, and no, she didn't know where he'd gone. If she'd known where he went, they wouldn't be having this conversation, would they?

The policeman frowned but didn't otherwise react to her sarcasm. Instead, he asked her if she was sure she saw what she thought she saw. Mari glanced around at the crew of Search and Rescue with their maps and flashlights and walkie talkies. Maybe he should have asked that question first.

"I'm sure," she said, barely holding back from telling him she'd been solo camping and free climbing for ten years and that *he* might not know the difference between a child and a bear, but she sure as hell did. (And her family said she had little restraint.)

The officer smiled and thanked her. "I'll pass around the description. There aren't any reports of a missing child yet, but we're still spreading it around to other counties."

"Any families have camping permits out?" she asked, worried that something terrible had befallen an entire group and there was no one left to report that the boy was gone. The officer shook his head.

Mari wasn't satisfied with the answer, but she also wasn't sure how she expected him to manifest a different one for her. Instead, she asked if she needed to pack up her site, gesturing at the dying fire and the tent. He motioned a 'no' once again.

"We'll be moving operations to the ranger station once the groups head out. Obviously, just let us know if you see him again. Try to get him to stay, if possible."

By the time they cleared out from her small campground, her fire's light was only a narrow ring around her feet. Tent half-cast in shadows, she paused above the logs and waited, hoping to see the child on the edge of darkness. The other side of the fire remained empty, so she poured sand over the embers, smothering them, and climbed into her tent by feel. She tried not to think about a child out in those black woods, the roots of his hair glowing in the dark as he smoldered. The smell of cooked flesh invaded her nose every time she closed her eyes.

Mari didn't sleep much, kept up by the alien sounds of the search parties and the dogs panting as they hunted for an unknown scent, the trampling of booted feet as they crushed the fallen tree limbs in their path. They drowned out the rustling of leaves and the low, mournful calls of nocturnal birds. They gave her nightmares, and she dreamed of screaming trees and burning children.

SHE SAW THE second hiker the next morning, two miles into her hike along the canyon trail where the trees grew tall and thick. The dawn air was still chilly, though threatening to burn off in the face of the growing humidity, and it helped wake her up in a way the bitter campfire coffee hadn't. Mari savored how her hot breath fogged and how the sweat cooled into goosebumps along her arms.

On a ledge above the creek, she noticed the roots of the pines exposed and blackened, fuzzy with some unknown fungus. She wasn't sure what the mold was, but it was eating away at the toes of the thick trunks. A strangled gasp, the universal sign of pain, drifted up to where she crouched examining the decaying blood vessels of the trees. Mari stood and cautiously peered over the edge.

A woman leaned against a boulder by the water, blankly staring at the nearby tree as she held all her weight on one foot. Even from a distance, Mari could see the rot of the tree root. It tore jagged marks across the wood, turned the pulp soft and sunken like a decaying cadaver. She could smell the tree from where she stood, several yards away—a mix of sopping books and old dirt. The woman didn't seem to notice anything but the bark she studied so intently.

Nor did she seem aware of the gangrene creeping up her own leg, though she held it several inches above the ground.

From where Mari stood, she couldn't tell how bad the woman's injury was, but she swore she saw the yellowing of bone and withered tendon through the woman's ripped jeans. The skin itself was ulcerated and nearly black, reminding Mari of the mummies she saw as a child on school trips.

Did this woman belong with the burned boy? Had they both become lost and hurt in some terrible accident? *This is why people shouldn't hike alone if they don't know what they're doing,* Mari thought. Guilt immediately bubbled up around the growing dread. The wind bent wooden limbs against each other, and something groaned. Mari couldn't tell if it was the boughs of the rotten tree or the woman.

"Are you okay?" she called. As if there was any way the woman could have been, and yet she wouldn't stop studying the damn bark long enough to acknowledge Mari's existence.

But it was all right; Mari had found her. Mari would help her—and maybe, with any luck, it would lead her back to the boy, as well. Maybe she'd be able to close her eyes without remembering what cooked flesh looked like as it disappeared into the shadows of the forest.

Hiking her pack up on her shoulders, Mari gripped the spindly trunk of the nearest evergreen and hauled herself over the earthen shelf. Her boots scraped against loose soil as she tried to gauge the drop to the creek bed. Five feet, maybe six. If she bent her knees and slid down the incline, she could…

The timber under her hand shrieked as it snapped along weak bark and dropped her, laying her out on her back. Pain flared between her shoulder blades. For a moment, she could only stare at the swaying canopy above her, could only wait for the burn of bruised muscles to dissipate. She exhaled and pushed herself upright.

The woman was gone.

"Hey!" She splashed through the shallow creek to get to the tree and boulder. She placed a palm against the trunk, leaning against it as she peered behind the large rock. Her hand sunk into the moist bark. The rotten smell was overwhelming this close—a mix of mushrooms and dead bodies—and she pulled it out with a sickening pop. Her skin tingled with the cold rot. The only sign of the woman was a black smear across the boulder and base of the tree.

THE SET OF rangers stared as Mari tried to estimate the woman's last location on the trail map spread out before her. To her embarrassment, her hand shook, creating a stippling of false trails as the pen tip jolted against the paper. Five years of camping in this forest and never any issues. Now two people injured and lost, and—though she refused to say it aloud—likely dead.

"I'm not sure if she's related to the boy I saw last night," she said.

One ranger had deep bags under his eyes, and Mari thought she recognized him from the search party last night. She was sure there were still parties searching the thick woods; there would probably be even more sent out soon. The rangers knew she was experienced, each one having seen her in the forest at some point over the years, but she watched deepening wrinkles as they strived to create a story in which she was crazy, freaked out and overwhelmed by the loneliness of the forest. If they dared to think about the alternative, all they would find was a worsening disaster.

"We'll let the police know," the tired ranger finally said. "Get the search radius expanded."

"I'm going back to my campsite," Mari said.

"Try not to find anyone else," one of the other rangers stated. It was said as a joke but reeked of desperate grief.

Mari headed back to where her tent still lay pitched. She would collect firewood, prepare her fire, sit by it, and not move until morning. She would bow her head, stare into the flames, and try not to think about how easily a dead limb could snap off like a branch.

WHEN SHE SAW the third hiker, she finally understood.

The snag stood tall and lean and dead before her. The hollow, rotten wood shone white like a tombstone among the green leaves of the surrounding trees. Mari moved toward it, hopeful to break off and claim some of the decomposing bark for her armful of campfire wood. A woodpecker tapped a sharp pattern high in the trunk. The dry timber would burn well.

Maybe even as quickly as the boy had.

Mari swallowed against the intrusive thought, her mood quickly ruined, and tried instead to consider the fire that waited for her in the encroaching evening. She stepped to the base of the decomposing behemoth and tilted her head, studying the leafless, crooked limbs of the dead tree. There was no way for her to get to them, but she was sure that some of the old branches must have fallen to the mossy undergrowth by now. After all, she could trace the scars of former amputations. Shifting the weight of kindling under her arm, she circled around the wide base, stopping in the back where the trunk had rotted and split in half.

A man lay prone in the hollow corpse of the trunk.

She didn't know how long he had been there; she did know he was dead.

In spite of the obvious, he did not seem aware that he was deceased. He moved his eyes in sunken sockets as she approached, following her dread as she leaned over to get a better look at him.

His ribs were a half-eaten mess of scaffolding, exposing a sunken chest and abdomen of organs too far gone to look like anything but thick soup. One leg was fully missing, while his other limbs bent and curled under the desiccation of his skin and muscle. Mari gripped the outer ridge of the splintered trunk and dropped her body down inside the dank pit of wood as she tried to reason with what she was seeing.

He reached one gnarled hand up and grabbed her fingers. His skin felt rough like bark and smelled of pungent peat. The odor came up from him and from the wood under her hand, and she attempted to tear her palm out of his grip. He squeezed tighter, and his fingers grew longer, wrapping around her knuckles and grinding bone against bone.

Without thinking, she planted a foot against the trunk and pushed, snapping her hand free at the same time her boot crashed through the weak wood and into his pelvis. The sole stopped in the mess of his intestines, and Mari quickly yanked her foot out and took two strides away from the man. Her toes felt damp, and she gagged at the thought of what must be on the bottom of her shoe. With the man just watching her, head barely lifted off his bark pillow, she stood on one foot and brought the offending shoe over her knee. The fluid was sweet, sticky, and yellow—the honeydew of insect waste and sap, not the coppery tang of human remains.

That doesn't make sense.

Because if he was a corpse, then he was a corpse, and if he was a ghost, then he was a ghost. But nothing explained why she was covered in the remains of the snag's cadaver.

A fat spider with thin, jointed legs climbed down the man's face and began to build a web in the remains of his ribcage. Its twin appeared in the hollowed tree trunk and constructed its own gossamer labyrinth between the wood, a refractory halo above his sinking brow. The webs were dizzying and beautiful and terrifying in their symmetry.

Mari had never considered what the ghosts of other things might look like.

The woodpecker unleashed a tremendous percussive, showering the ground below with sawdust. The man groaned under the symphony, and Mari watched as splinters of bone erupted from his face, exploding from underground detonations with each stab of the bird's beak into the bark.

Mari backed away from the dead tree. The woodpecker pounded against the bark again, and the top of the tree splintered and began to fall. The man shrieked, fault lines appearing across his face, and Mari turned, unwilling to watch any further.

She stumbled away from the snag and its ghost and didn't stop until she found herself out of the state forest, tripping over into the logging camps that smelled of burnt wood and sweat.

The logging station had shut down for the day, but it still stank of diesel machinery and fresh wood pulp; the air boiled with the heat escaping engines and saw blades.

She turned around and faced rows and rows of freshly cut tree stumps. Fellers and delimbers sat quietly, ready for orders on a new workday. In the approaching darkness, their silhouettes appeared colossal, frozen in time but waiting eagerly, dwarfing the loggers standing silently by the fallen trees. And why were there people still at the site, when it seemed the machinery had been off for some time?

The workers sat slumped over or against most of the stumps. Though their backs were to her, they seemed a little too tall, a little too thin, for most of the lumbermen she was used to seeing around the woods. Maybe it was just the growing grayness of the evening. Hadn't her mother told Mari she was going night blind?

Still, no one moved, no one was packing up, preparing to leave.

She didn't like it, and took a cautious step backward. If she corrected course, she could bypass the ghost of the snag and get back to her camp.

Mari set her foot down in the undergrowth and snapped a twig in half.

The sound echoed like a gunshot through the open air, and dozens of heads tilted upward in search of its source. She couldn't see any faces, but there was definitely something wrong with the shape of their skulls. They were elongated, thin and sharp like tree crowns. They wore the flannels of the logging company, but they hadn't gotten the shape of the humans that wore them quite right. Mari picked her boot up off the broken branch as slowly as possible, desperate to move as she was to not make another sound. The bark squealed as her weight disappeared off of it.

The worker seated on the stump closest to her pushed himself up and faced her.

He stood seven feet tall, easily, and was split from chin to groin. It looked like the bite of her father's old table saw as it slashed a rip through fresh wood. He opened his mouth, and only the groan of tree branches rubbing against each other came out. As his bowels leaked out from the canyon of his belly, his jerky movements drew the attention of the ghosts beside him. They lurched themselves upward, limbs and heads and chests splitting and sliding to the ground to land beside the fallen logs cut at similar angles. The ghost in front lifted out his arm toward Mari, and it cracked at sharp angles as he reached. He grew taller all the while, sprouting like a redwood, pulling at his own loose seam as he stretched even higher.

When he towered over her, easily ten feet of curled, emaciated specter, he dragged a long arm through the sawdust and dry dirt to where she stood, frozen. Mari bit the gasp that threatened to break from her, chewed it back to sit half-digested and acidic in her stomach. The other ghosts were evolving into a throng, packing tightly around him as they each tried to break through.

Something hit him, and he swayed. His long, long body couldn't maintain its balance, even as more of him fell from the hole in his chest to feed the ground below. He crashed down among the other ghosts and didn't move again.

Had he landed beside his own cut body of bark and heartwood? The other ghosts were crowding around too quickly for her to see. While reluctant to move too far from their stumps, they creeped elongating arms and fingers along the ground toward her, trying to sense her pulse through the beating of the dirt.

Timber, she thought, and the morbid humor was enough to shake her out of her shock.

A wooden hand brushed her knuckle, then tried to claw it. Mari kicked it and retreated, and she ran back to the tree line and into the reserve.

Through sheer luck and ingrained directions, she found her campsite just as night fell heavy and humid over the forest. She tore her tent down into an ugly mess and shoved it into her pack. She wrapped the sleeping bag and made sure she had her car keys, left the cooking iron and the foldout chair by the half-built ruins of her campfire. Those could be replaced and would only slow her down. With one dismissive look around, she abandoned the site and took off into the woods, lantern bouncing against her hip.

It wasn't the best idea to leave in the pitch of the night. That was how people became irrevocably lost, but she wouldn't stay one more moment in this forest.

So she didn't pause. The electric beam of her light and the glow of the moon gave her flashes of the dark forest. Of milky eyes and long limbs. Their gazes followed her as she passed, and sometimes, a hand of ant-eaten bark would snake out of the darkness to grasp at her clothes and hair. She pressed on, but there were always more appearing in the arc of her light just before it swung back around, allowing shadows to crowd in.

Mari had never considered until now how the forest left its dead among its living, with nothing to bury the corpses. She had never had to contemplate how much deadwood was out there. Knobbed tree-branch fingers clawed her hair, tugging hard and yanking her back a step or two. She grabbed her own hair with a tight fist and pulled, breaking the thick strands and freeing herself. She ducked another limb and avoided a marching, twelve-foot-tall specter that seemed oblivious to her. When she sprinted out onto the main trail road, where the trees were trimmed and stumps pulled by maintenance, she allowed herself to slow her pace but didn't dare stop. On either side, her swinging lantern would occasionally pick up blank eyes, sometimes a twisted hand made of bark, wet with sap. The stalking ghosts left silhouettes around the edge of her light, and they were growing taller, some starting to press up against the roof of the canopy.

She watched the ground, trying to avoid eye contact with the great gray ghosts now towering in the forest, and continued her flight. She just needed to reach the ranger station, get back on the road, get to her house. She'd lock her door and never go camping again.

She just needed to get home.

Mari's thoughts faltered, but her feet never stopped. She pushed her legs to move faster because she didn't know what else to do and thought about her home because she didn't dare consider anything else.

Mari thought of her house and its sturdy plank framework of sanded two-by-fours, her polished oak rocking chair, her mother's maple table that sat in her dining room. She pictured the crisp pine paper pages of books on the teak shelves and the walnut flooring. She considered the birch bed frame, the cherry TV stand, the mahogany grandfather clock, the pulp paper grocery bags, the bamboo cutting boards, the acacia serving spoons, the—

How many corpses would be waiting for her?

Behind her, the ghosts grew taller, their arms stretched longer, and their branches trailed across her back, all the way home.

RAGE AND REDEMPTION

Michael Barron

I**T'S AFTER MIDNIGHT.** Gretchen stands outside Dresden High School's principal's office, staring down the dark hallway. Rows of lockers and classroom doors lead into shadows. She can't see the basement entrance, but she knows it's waiting for her.

Attempting her breathing exercises, she inhales the sickeningly sweet citrus-scented floor cleaner. One whiff evaporates the past thirteen years. She hears the crackle of the police radio and feels the gurney pressing against her back as she's carried to the ambulance. That was the last time she left her high school.

Something brushes her arm. Adrenaline floods her body. She leaps to the side, crashing into the wall.

"It's just me," Fennec whispers, taking her hand. "You okay?"

"Peachy." She dumps a bucket of cheer into her voice. "Ready whenever you are."

They work by flashlight, spray painting a red circle beneath a bulletin board that declares "Go Wildcats!" Gretchen focuses on the cold metal can in her hands, but memories wriggle in. She has gotten better. She can use underground parking garages now and sleeps with only the hallway lights on. However, even if she was here in broad daylight, sweat would still drip down her back.

Fennec rings the circle with intricate symbols that resemble bare branches merging into a labyrinth. Back when they were kids, Fennec used her artistic talents to create homemade comics featuring psychotic bunnies and nihilistic superheroes.

After Gretchen left Dresden, she cut ties with everyone in their small Maryland town, but she never threw away those ragged, poorly-Xeroxed comics. Then, three days ago, Fennec texted her out of the blue, never explaining how she got her number. She arrived at Gretchen's studio apartment dressed as if addressing a conference room full of old men very concerned about their stock portfolios. However, her black suit didn't hide the symbols tattooed along her neck and arms. When she caught Gretchen glancing at the crimson ink, she'd said, "I've joined the family business."

Many of those tattoos match the markings she's spraying along the floor now.

Fennec removes a leather satchel from her backpack and places it in the circle's heart. "This contains some of Marissa's childhood possessions. They'll encourage her to appear." She faces Gretchen. "We'll start with you describing the incident. When I sense her approaching, I'll light these." She removes a bundle of leafy branches from her backpack. "Don't worry. I disabled the fire alarm this afternoon."

"You disabled a school's fire alarm?"

"Once you begin, you might see things that are…unexpected. Keep talking. She can't hurt you anymore."

That's as reassuring as Gretchen's mother saying that if she ignored bullies, they'd go away.

"Whatever happens, keep talking. It'll draw her into the circle, which will trap her."

"Then you'll send her back to the afterlife?"

Her friend gives the patient smile of a teacher repeating something an inattentive student should have already learned. Gretchen saw plenty of those smiles in this building.

"Remember what I said in the car? Ghosts aren't spirits of the undead. There are places that absorb emotions. When something traumatic happens, the hatred, misery and rage linger, developing personalities and agendas of their own. What we're facing tonight is emotional residue, nothing more."

Gretchen turns from the bundle of branches to the circle haloed by symbols. The whole setup looks like an eighth grader's idea of a druid ceremony.

"Are you sure Marissa's still here?"

"Of course. She's watching us right now."

She turns in time to spot a figure staring at them. The figure steps backward—toward the basement entrance—and vanishes.

"What…?" An invisible weight presses against her chest. There's nothing supernatural about it. This is her all too real anxiety. "Was that…?" She returns to her breathing exercises, but all that does is summon more of the school's vomit-sweet stench.

Fennec takes her hand. "I know you're out of your depth, but you can do this. Remember your screenplay."

Gretchen shuts her eyes. Back in her apartment, Fennec showed her the check she would hand over when the "job" was complete. It wouldn't provide her with a Greta Gerwig-level budget for her movie, but combined with the amount she'd already scraped together, it would be enough to tell the story that's stirred inside her for years.

Taking her arm, Fennec guides her toward the circle. Gretchen stares at the floor so she won't have to look down that hallway. Her shadow is smaller than it should be, but it's also darker, as if it's a bottomless pit, and all she has to do is step to her right and she'll fall out of her life forever.

Fennec positions her on the circle's edge. "You must cross the threshold yourself. Once you do, start talking about your relationship with Marissa."

Gretchen snorts at the word *relationship*. "You already know all that."

"But you need to tell *her*." She points down the hall.

Gretchen takes one more citrus-saturated breath, considering if there is any other way she could fund her movie. Coming up short, she enters the circle.

"How did she treat you before the incident?" Fennec prompts.

"Terribly."

"Be specific. Give an example of something she did to you."

"She made pig sounds whenever she saw me." Even now, she hears Marissa and her gang snorting at her in this very hallway. The teachers didn't even bother to pretend they didn't notice. Some even laughed.

"Excellent! What else did she do?"

The next example comes a little easier. "She'd make up fake accounts and attack me on Facebook. I still get anxious whenever I post anything online."

"And?"

"She called me *Gretch*-ann, turning my name into the sound you make when you throw up. She did it for years. It got so bad I heard puking every time someone said my name."

"And?"

"She convinced a bunch of the other kids to toss my science fair poster into the river. She wrote 'Bible selling virgin slut' across my math textbook. She spread a rumor that I gave Coach Stevens hand jobs for lunch money."

"And how did all this affect you?"

"Every Sunday I was sick just thinking about surviving another week with her. I don't even know how many times I was late to class because I avoided her in the hall. The teachers knew what was happening, but they didn't care. Some even believed Marissa's rumors. People in this town are so bored they'll believe anything."

Fennec stares down the hall as if she can see something Gretchen can't. "Let's transition to the incident. Talk about the day it happened."

Gretchen closes her eyes. She hasn't even started, and she's already crying. "It was the last day of Junior year. I was walking to my American Lit final when Marissa ran up, sobbing. She said she'd spotted a calico kitten in the basement, limping like she'd broken her leg. She'd tried to get her friends to help, but they'd just laughed. 'I know you love animals, though,' she'd said. 'Please help me catch her.'

"I was desperate to get on her good side. Even after everything she put me through, I thought that maybe if I helped, she'd leave me alone. So I followed her into the basement like a naïve little lamb. Twice while we were searching, Marissa told me we should turn back. 'You have a final to get to.' But I kept looking. She really had me believing there was a kitten. Say what you want about her, she was a talented actress.

"We squeezed behind a stack of boxes, into a room even the janitors forgot was there. It was less a room than a flight of stairs to nowhere. Later I learned it used to go outside, but they blocked it off when they built the new gym. Now the steps stopped at a cement ceiling. I don't know how Marissa found it, but when she did, I bet her first thought was, 'What a great place to pull a trick on ugly, stupid Gretchen.'"

The air catches in her lungs. It's as if her body refuses to share what came next.

"Please," Fennec says. "We're so close."

Staring into her flashlight beam, Gretchen imagines her chocolate lab, Clara, pressing her warm, heavy body against her leg. Somehow, the words start to flow again. She describes what came next, following the script she always uses when sharing this part of her life.

"The room was pitch black when she slammed the door. Mama didn't let me have a phone. I couldn't call anyone. There was no way out. I shouted and pounded on the door. The walls were so thick no one heard me."

She had heard *them*, though, the final bell and the stampede for freedom. Down in that cement cage, she slammed her fists on the door, shouting until her throat ached.

Her throat aches now, like she's spent the past thirteen years shouting.

"That first night stretched on forever. I walked back and forth, promising God I'd never do anything bad again if He let me out. I forced myself to stay awake in case someone came around."

But the dreams found her anyway. She heard whispers outside the room. When she called for them, begging to be let out, they laughed. Her eyes were so desperate to fill the darkness they created images of Marissa and her mother. She even saw the kitten. She tried to grab her, just to have something soft and warm, but the cat evaporated in her fingers.

"Just to have something to do, I counted the dimensions of the room. Four paces wide… Twelve steps up… Sixteen bricks to the ceiling… I know those numbers better than I know the date of my birthday."

Darkness presses against her skin. There's a physical weight to it, just like in the basement.

"I didn't have a watch. The only way I could tell time was passing was I kept getting hungrier. I ate dead bugs off the floor, pretending they were French Fries from the Corner Diner. I licked water from the pipes. My stomach shriveled, like I was being hollowed out. The room was so silent I could hear my heart beating. I heard it slowing, struggling to push blood through my body."

Long after she abandoned hope, she'd continued making as much noise as possible to remind herself she was still alive.

Now, beneath her feet, deep in the school's guts, she hears fists beating a metal door.

Someone is still trapped down there.

"After what felt like weeks, I started to hope for death." She lay on the steps, eager for any kind of escape, but death took its time, like a predator drawing out starvation. "I tried to speed things along by bashing my head against the wall, but I couldn't stand the pain. Then I began to wonder if I was already dead. Was this the afterlife? No white light. No grandparents. Just hunger and darkness."

The pounding of flesh against metal is closer now, just out of sight down the hallway.

"When I first heard the footsteps, I assumed my ears were filling the silence. It wasn't until the door screeched open and I was blinded by a flashlight that I allowed myself to believe I was saved. Then I saw who it was."

Feet scrape in the darkness.

Marissa's voice echoes inside her head. *"You sick freak! It's been five days. What're you still doing down here? I'm not getting in trouble because you're too stupid to get out."*

Gretchen forces herself to go on. "I staggered for the door, screaming for help. Marissa lunged, driving me up the stairs until my back pressed against the wall. She grabbed my neck…"

Her throat tightens.

"I was half-dead, but somehow I got ahold of her flashlight. I struck her across the face. She tumbled down the stairs, cracking her head against the…"

A figure appears at the end of the hall.

Every muscle in Gretchen's body screams at her to run.

The figure steps forward and vanishes.

After three deep breaths, she continues. "Marissa cracked her head against the door, slamming it shut, sealing us both inside."

There's more to the story, a section she's never told friends, therapists, or her journal. She skips it now.

"Marissa brought her phone, but there was no reception. The battery died within a couple of hours. I clung to hope, though. Even if they wouldn't bother with me, Marissa was the princess of Dresden. She made half the town cry when she played Juliet in the winter play. She won an environmental award for cleaning up the park. The town would rally together to find her. The world remained silent, though. Nothingness had swallowed us both."

Gretchen's body quivers. She can barely stand. "We were trapped under that school together for three more days. At last, a janitor came down to investigate the smell. He burst into tears when he saw what was left of Marissa."

Fennec lights the bundle of branches and hands them to her. "Keep talking."

Raising the fire over her head, Gretchen says, "Sometimes I wake in the middle of the night, and I'm still down there. I turn on all the lights in my apartment to convince myself I got out." The burning leaves don't smell of smoke. Instead, she catches the whiff of her childhood bedroom and new books. "I live with what happened every day. Sometimes I'm laughing with friends in a restaurant, glance into a dark corner and I see—"

A girl steps into the firelight. Blood cakes her mousy brown hair and tattered plaid skirt. It isn't Marissa.

Gretchen steps back. "What?"

The lockers on either side rattle, as if each contains a starving prisoner giving one last struggle for freedom. The sound they make isn't the rattling of thin metal. It's the familiar pounding of broken hands against a rusty steel door.

"Don't stop," Fennec says. "Whatever happens, keep talking."

The girl walks forward, shrunken and shriveled. Up and down the hallway, lockers lengthen, transforming into the teeth of a beast ready to swallow her whole.

The girl's bare feet are two steps from the circle's edge. Her eyes bulge with rage and terror, like a demon woken from a nightmare. Her gaze cuts into the back of Gretchen's skull, transforming her thoughts into a bonfire.

"I think about that…room… I…Who are you?"

The girl raises her foot and is about to cross into the circle when she glances down and steps back, shaking her head with a smile that says, *Nice try.*

White-hot pain lightning bolts up Gretchen's arms. She's back on the staircase to nowhere. Blood trickles down her arm from hitting the door.

She never escaped.

She's been under the school this whole time.

Her friends, dog, screenplay, every one of her successes have been illusions. The school is her tomb. There's only one way out.

She faces the wall, pulls her head back as far as it will go and thrusts forward, toward the merciless bricks.

Something knocks her off her feet. She crashes to the floor, slamming back to reality. Fennec holds her to the ground.

"Get off me!" Gretchen scrambles out from under her.

The ghost is gone.

Fennec stomps on the still-burning branches, scattered across the floor. "I have more. We can try again. Ghosts can be—"

"That wasn't Marissa." Gretchen stands. "What the hell's going on?"

Head swimming, she rips open the leather satchel lying in the circle's heart. It's meant to contain Marissa's most prized possessions. Instead Gretchen finds her own high school journal, a tattered copy of *A Wrinkle In Time*, and the stuffed cat she slept with until she was seventeen. She left them all at her mother's house the day she escaped Dresden.

Ghosts aren't wandering souls or lost spirits. When something traumatic happens, the hatred, misery and rage lingers, developing personalities and agendas of their own.

Her sweat turns ice cold.

"She's the ghost of me."

Without looking at her, Fennec nods. "In every other haunting my family has investigated, the lingering emotions belong to the person who passed on. But what happened to you was so... Gretchen!"

Gretchen pushes through the school's front entrance and sprints down the steps. She'll run the seven hundred miles back to her apartment if it means never seeing this town again.

Fennec catches up, running with her backpack tucked under her arm. "If you leave now, your ghost will keep haunting the school."

"I don't care." Gretchen charges toward the street.

"You'll spend the rest of your life knowing a part of you is still trapped in that basement."

"I already told you, I don't care."

"And more girls will get hurt." Fennec pulls an open folder from her backpack, shoving it into Gretchen's face.

She freezes.

The orange glow from the streetlight illuminates the yearbook photos of four girls. She can tell by their clothes, acne, and awkward smiles that they were lost in high school, just like her.

"Four girls in nine years, all found half-dead in the basement, showing signs of self-mutilation. One will never walk again. The administration has done everything they can to keep kids from going down there, but it keeps happening." She hands Gretchen the folder. "All the victims fit the same profile. Not even the rejects let them sit at their table. At least two ate lunch in the library to hide from their own Marissas."

Gretchen shakes her head. "Why would my ghost go after them?"

Fennec lowers her eyes. "Ghosts lash out at the people they blame."

Gretchen stares at the photographs until her vision blurs. The other kids would've pegged these girls as weak from the moment they entered kindergarten. They would've huddled under their blankets on Sunday nights, dreading the following day, not because of tests or lectures, but because they went to school with predators, and most adults figured cruelty was just "kids being kids."

She stares back at the school. "I shouldn't even be here. I should be at home with my dog, worrying about my stupid job."

"You're absolutely right." Fennec lays a hand on her shoulder. "And I'll take you back if you want. Hell, I'll even give you the money to fund your movie. You've already done more than I should have asked for. But even if you go back, even if you make your movie and find success, you'll still know what's in that basement."

Gretchen shuts her eyes, but she hears Fennec say, "You didn't deserve what happened to you, but neither did these girls. Marissa was a monster, and the adults who allowed her to torment you were weak. But now is your chance to be an adult who steps in."

In the darkness behind her eyelids, she sees their English teacher smile as Marissa makes snorting noises.

She turns back toward Fennec. "Stay here."

"What're you—"

"Just stay here." She walks back across the parking lot and climbs the steps. When she reaches the top, she yanks the door open and peers down the empty hall. The girl is gone. The lockers are no longer fangs. However, from deep within the building's guts, she hears a broken fist pounding on a metal door.

Picking up her flashlight from where she dropped it, Gretchen calls, "It's just me."

Only silence.

She walks down the hall. "I know you're angry. I'm angry too."

Her flashlight catches a figure standing by the basement's entrance. Gretchen cannot see her eyes, but she knows they're locked on her. "We're the only ones who know what really happened down there. It's time we talk about it."

Far too soon, she arrives at the end of the hall. The basement door waits for her, standing wide open. As she crosses the threshold, she catches the wisp of a shadow waiting for her at the bottom of the stairs. At last, Gretchen shares the part of the story she never told anyone.

"The autopsy showed that Marissa was still alive after she fell. I told everyone I was certain she died instantly. She attacked—the bruises on my throat proved that—I defended myself, she fell, and she never woke."

She reaches the bottom of the stairs. Her flashlight illuminates rusty pipes and walls stained with black mold. The shadow walks up ahead, leading the way.

"What I didn't tell them is that she *did* wake up. She couldn't move, but she wailed and begged, calling for help. I didn't respond. I huddled at the top of the stairs, letting her think she was alone, until, at last, she was silent. I told myself I needed to stay hidden, in case she attacked again, but I saw what the fall did to her. I knew she was bleeding out. I stayed at the top of the steps because I hated her. The last thing she said was our name. For the first time since sixth grade, she didn't say it with mockery. She was terrified of me. That filled me with so much joyful rage I thought I would burst. I felt something tear out of me when she said our name. You were born down here, and you've been here ever since."

Her flashlight lands on the staircase to nowhere. The room is just the way she remembered it, except they removed the metal door. A girl waits for her at the foot of the steps, quaking with rage.

Gretchen enters the room. "I've told myself Marissa deserved what happened. She tormented me for six years before she even brought me down here, and it's a cold, hard fact that I owed her nothing. But not a day goes by that I don't hear her saying our name that last time. It haunts me." Gretchen reaches toward the ghost. "But I didn't comfort her. I didn't even let her know I was there. I can't change that now."

A door that didn't exist an instant earlier slams shut, nearly taking her leg off. The girl has sealed them in together. Gretchen's mouth goes dry. Every inch of her skin tightens.

"So much has happened since I escaped. Mama homeschooled me my senior year, and yeah, that sucked, but I survived. I met other survivors and realized I wasn't alone."

A hand clamps around her neck, turning her to face the wall.

The words continue to pour out. "Two years and three months after I climbed out of this hole, I left for college. It was terrifying, but I made some wonderful friends. I even had my first kiss. People will tell you that having your first kiss when you're twenty-one is pathetic. What do they know?"

Her flashlight flickers. When it returns to life, she finds herself dressed in rags. Her throat is raw from screaming. False memories flood in, telling her she never left this room. The basement has been her home for years.

"Stop that." She shakes the illusions away. "I did escape. I did get out. I've written an amazing screenplay that I'll turn into an even more amazing movie."

The girl squeezes her neck. Strength drains from Gretchen's muscles. Her stomach withers to a husk. The ghost tells her body it's already too late. She's moments from starvation.

But she turns enough to face her. "I've surrounded myself with people who love me and cut off everyone who treated me like shit."

The girl bares her broken teeth.

"Leave with me tonight. Things won't get better immediately, but you can still have a future."

The ghost yanks Gretchen's head back. All it would take is one blow to dash her thoughts, memories, and dreams across the bricks.

Gretchen pictures her dog, Clara. She pictures her friends laughing in her apartment. She pictures the screenplay that will amount to nothing more than a file on her desktop unless she does something about it. "I will not die down here."

The ghost rises over her, releasing a snarl that shakes the school's foundations.

"I'm leaving this room, and I'm never coming back. I want you to come with me, join me in this amazing, terrifying, wonderful life we're about to have."

The ghost releases another stone-cracking roar. Blood burbles up from deep within her throat. Gretchen tastes it on her own lips.

She doesn't flinch. "You're safe now."

The ghost leans over her, clogging her mind with images. The word "slut" written across her textbook. Boys throwing food into her hair. Marissa tripping her in the locker room.

Marissa dying at the foot of the stairs.

She wants to run, abandon the girl, never think of her again, but she embraces her. "You're safe now. It's over. I know it hurt, but it's over." It becomes a chant. "You're safe now. You're safe now. You're safe now…"

Sometime around dawn, they leave the school together. At first, Fennec assumes Gretchen is alone. Then she realizes what she's done.

The girl from the basement stays with her all the way home. She's with her when she goes on dates, when she meets Fennec for coffee, when she takes Clara for runs in the park. She's there at her movie's premier and when she takes home the trophy for best director.

There are days when she's impossible to live with. Gretchen's car breaks down, or she makes a scheduling error on her second film, and she wonders if she's cut out for this life. Sometimes she's certain the ghost will swallow her whole.

She makes it through those days, and with every day that passes, the girl from the basement calms a little more. Sometimes she even takes pleasure in life. She helps Gretchen share what really happened with Fennec and her therapist, and slowly—sometimes so slowly it hurts— they find their way out.

Last Will and Testam

THE WILL OF
LADY PENELOPE GRANT

C.R. Kane

MY HUSBAND IS getting married today.

The bride's name is Heloise Glassing, soon to be Heloise Bishop. His name, of course, will remain Dr. Huxley Bishop. Hux to friends and lovers. And *Her.*

I cannot reduce Her in thought or print. No, She remains Herself, Her will be done.

She invited me to the wedding. Even asked if I would play the maid of honor, daring the scandal of Heloise's gawping audience, still clustering around the affair. The card came a day after Hux's letter. Did She know he sent it? Was it a little allowance on Her part or was he punished? There's no guessing. But the letter made it out to me either way, and it *is* his handwriting. Irony of ironies that She never managed forgery of all things.

I have found myself going back to Hux's pages with the same hateful impulse that brings me to the memories of that manor, the sickish urge of one who tears over and over at a wound before it can heal. He sends his apologies. He sends his love. He sends his pain. He sends his farewell. He sends his prayer.

Hux, Hux.

He smuggled out a photograph with the letter. The only one I have of him now, after the exodus. After the divorce and the handsome sum he was allowed to send me away with. The photo is only a year and a half old, taken on our wedding day. He'd been afraid to touch the money then, fearful that the bubble of the fairytale blessing would burst if it was leaped on too soon. He was prepared for us to stand before the altar in our original second-hand suit and gown. But the note with the will convinced him into the tailored ensembles. Yet another loving gift from *Her.* One of many doting little insistences she'd tucked away for Hux's eyes once the corpse was buried. How could we say no? As kind as Bluebeard on the honeymoon.

But this is going around and around. You, reading this, do not know Her. You cannot guess at what She is, what She has done to us. At best, you have swallowed the swill of the newspapers surrounding the pending wedding of Heloise Glassing and all the guesswork of how she snatched my husband out from under me. Anything known about Hux is canted at the angle of the latest beau stolen, only this time with the shock of the metropolitan "Heloise of Troy" actually landing on him as the Paris to the stunned Menelaus of her former most-preferred suitor. Hux's face is in ink now along with hers. History has been dug up concerning her past tries at him and how they were met with placid rejection for months on end.

He was with me even then, you see. My face is not as frequent an appearance except in pieces that alternately pity or applaud me. It is rare to see a woman make off so tidily with a separation as I have. My new home, the pretty island adrift on the other side of the city, is joined by a padding of wealth that has left some joking that Heloise wishes to wed Hux in order to receive the same apologetic courtesy upon some inevitable split. Investing in heartbreak.

They do not know about Her.

Not counting the abstract knowledge of how Dr. Huxley Bishop received his inheritance of bloated coffers and the regal estate, the parting gifts of Lady Penelope Grant.

Lady Penelope Grant, widow to Lord Caldwell Grant of far more infamous notoriety. The man of a hundred mistresses, according to the gossip in and out of print, dying at last to one of them while his wife was half-dead in their marriage bed. According to her witnesses, Lady Penelope Grant seemed to die for a moment just as her husband was surprised by his latest girl—one of the household's own maids—turning on him with a letter opener in bed. She gasped awake as Lord Grant died.

"My husband," came the purported wheeze, "my husband is gone…"

The girl did not plead insanity. She was only destined for the madhouse because she pled that it was not her that wielded the blade.

"Something else wanted him dead," her only published quote ran. "Not me. Why would I want to be rid of him? It makes no sense."

No more than it had made sense when she was later found in her cell, hung by her bed sheets the night after the hearing. Such was the full breadth of the Lady's fame. A side note in a cheap horror. Her remaining time alive was quiet, comfortable, and spent in a steady decline.

With Hux at her side.

First as a physician's apprentice, then as the physician himself. I remember Hux came home shamefaced early on in that stage. His new arrangement had not come without a stain on his former mentor's name. The Lady had suffered another near-death spell and in it someone had made off with some rather precious items from the vanity. When She came back around with the mentor's aid, She claimed to have found his manner suspiciously anxious, followed by noting how there was a new jingling weight in his coat pocket. The man had been red-faced according to multiple witnesses in the manor and, at their Lady's hesitant suggestion, asked if the doctor might turn out his pockets.

There were the nabbed jewels, a gilded compact, and a few nice pens. All sorts of magpie flotsam that had been left in the open. As if his first priority upon seeing his patient at death's door was to snatch up whatever was in reach before bothering with upholding the Hippocratic Oath. Things turned messy very fast. The Lady, though disappointed, had not had it in her to charge the man outright, only to dismiss him. Talk did the rest from there. Not long after the talk came the discovery of the doctor's cooling corpse in his office, the killing syringe still pinned in his arm.

"I don't understand it, Lotte," Hux had muttered over his plate, his appetite knocked out with shock. "Dr. Danford was already well-off and one of the most upstanding men in the field. He was on call for half a dozen noble houses. Why would he throw it away on a handful of baubles and risking a dead patient? Why would he turn so hideously on himself?"

I'd had no answer for him. Nothing beyond the trite and true reality:

"Opportunity and our own devils strip sense away more often than not. The gambling houses would go out of business otherwise."

"I must wonder at Lady Grant's sense, then," Hux had rebutted, picking at his bread. "It's a wonder she would reach out to me when my predecessor's shadow has barely faded from her door. I am fresh from the university and so hardly the most endowed option she has."

"That depends on what endowments you refer to, Dr. Bishop." I'd batted my lashes while he turned pink. This, while speaking with Heloise's own lilt. If we'd not been eating in public, I think he would have thrown his napkin at me. Or perhaps tried to hide in it. It was difficult to play oblivious to his budding popularity among a specific demographic of patients. He'd been approached by two different husbands already demanding to know if he was "treating for hysteria" among other aches and ailments Hux was called on for. He wasn't. No more than he had been anything other than a fair doctor to Her.

A more than fair doctor. One who found himself receiving urgent summons at all hours for everything ranging from palpitations to sprains to a twinge of headache as the weather turned. As the months fattened into a year, he ceased to call Her by title at all.

"Penny again," he would sigh in apology over the latest beckoning. Penny again and again and again. Until that autumn evening when Penny called for the last time. A call we would find out was made after a visit with certain legal parties and witnesses.

"I just wanted to see you one last time, Hux," She'd told him as he made it to Her bedside. "I have put things off long enough." Hux had tried to glean more from her, to ask after pains and symptoms and anything else that might point to her frailty coming to its fatal conclusion. She'd not budged on the topic beyond stating, "It will be time soon. That's all. I'd rather not dwell on it. Give me something to look forward to instead. You and Charlotte have your wedding plans made for the spring, yes? Where do you mean to have it?"

Hux had told her. He talked through afternoon and night and the first creeping moments of morning. As if She would stay alive just to keep the conversation going. Oh, how he had worried for Her. Fretting like a son for his mother. But once dawn came, She had sent him out of the room—

"So sorry I kept you out this long, dear. Your Charlotte will think terribly of me, I know. You are free to go. But before you leave, do bother someone for me, will you? I think I would like a chocolate before I nod off."

—and he had told one of the maids her request. He almost made it out the door when he heard the same maid scream. A noise mingled with the tinny clattering of dropped silver and broken porcelain, echoing down the highest hall in the house. Hux almost collided with the butler on his way back up the stairs, the man having come running to stop his exit.

"Why'd she do it as I came in?" the maid is purported to have sobbed after Hux gave her a dose of liquid calm. "Why make me watch?"

The answer: Proof. Undeniable evidence against foul play. Lady Penelope Grant had sent Hux away and lured the maid to the door where, in full light of dawn, She had smiled and pulled the letter opener out from under Her pillow. The same one that had been slotted into her husband's face and heart once upon a time. She had gone on smiling as the steel went through Her throat.

I did not learn of this until well past noon of that day, when Hux was finally freed from the mire of questioning. He had told the authorities all he could, all that was true. Yes, She was frail, but in no worse way than anyone else of Her age. There was no sign of painful deterioration. No hacking of blood or wasting away from some fresh malady. She had simply decided She was done. Though he was aghast to hear from the staff how much She had kept under wraps as far as Her latest interests went.

The Lady was a quietly devoted spiritualist, which Hux had known. What She had not told him, and had instructed Her staff against hinting, was that She was of that sort who not only put faith in the tangibility of the afterlife and its wandering tenants but was actively looking forward to all that awaited Her after shrugging off Her living body. Stutteringly, the staff had admitted this fascination had come to a boil around the time Her husband had been murdered. They claimed to assume it was only something She chased as a balm, as though She might make up with the caddish Lord Grant in the realm of the spirits. Hux had stopped short of sedating himself to keep from erupting on the spot.

"She didn't need *me* there! She needed a proper rotation of people on watch! A psychiatrist! A hypnotist! Someone who understood the ways of walking a mind back from such an edge! Damn them for nailing down their tongues! Damn me for…" He had wilted in my arms, fatigue and ire melting his coherence down to slush as he cursed himself for not staying another minute in the room, for not suspecting, for not simply reading Her mind. I held him for most of the day, trying to find the right words to scrub the guilt out of him like a stain on a sheet.

It was still there, shadowing his eyes by the time of the funeral. I saw Her for the first and only time there. I'd thought the embalmer must have been a fine artist to set Her in a way that made a lightly impish smile form on the frozen lips. She might have been someone's wizened grandmother leaving behind a legacy of storytelling and canny tricks that only elders seem to know. How were we meant to guess at the reality She'd left stamped on the withered face like a parting wink?

We mourned Her as though She really were departed family. She had little enough of genuine kin in attendance to fill the role. They were a number who attended more for duty's sake and the prelude to the will's reading than anything like sentiment. Hux had recognized not a single face in their gilded crowd. Though that would change in time to come. They and their lawyers each became memorized countenances in the following months as we reeled from the effect of Lady Penelope Grant's will.

For She had left everything—every possession, every inch of property, every penny of Penny's in simple bequest or maintained investments—to Dr. Huxley Bishop.

God, what an ugly stint that was. Accusations of mesmerism, of deviant behavior, of any and every possible method of coercion or confusion a man or devil might inflict was laid at Hux's feet. This, when Hux himself had sat dumbstruck in the room and asked if the man behind the desk had been sure? Truly? He'd only had his patient's acquaintance for a little more than a year; perhaps there was some mistake…?

No, he and the whole rioting family had been informed by the gentleman brandishing the paperwork like a rapier. No mistake. The will was what it was. Including its notable caveats. Which were, in their own way, a posthumous leveling of a pistol at Hux's head. For if he deigned not to accept his patient's parting gifts—especially if, hypothetically, he were to try to leave them for hers or Lord Grant's relatives to squabble over—they were to be donated in their entirety to the beautification and expansion of a list of pre-selected cemeteries with the house to be converted into a museum of morbid curiosities, leaving the staff to draw straws on who would be held on as employees. All of these falling swords being accompanied by Her note left directly to Hux.

Dearest Hux,

My ending was not the last of the surprises I have arranged for you. The will is as sound as my own mind as I write this. I am in earnest that you will accept all I have to give you. You have made my final year the gladdest scene of a long and rotting life. Yes, rotting, good doctor. No medicine or regimen exists that will undo the waste of all that came before. But you did do your best for me, dear. What pills and potions could not help, your company mended in ways that morphia only dreams of.

And so, I leave you all that I am able. If you find yourself struggling to accept what I have left you, even knowing what would become of it if left alone, then do these things for me at least.

First, you and Charlotte must—must!—walk the entire house and its grounds. At least once. You have not been able to appreciate all that is waiting there, busy as you were doting on me. And she, the bride to be, deserves to have her viewing and her say in the matter.

Second, whatever you decide, there is one token alone that I insist you take away for yourself. For you and your fiancée, I insist that every expense for the wedding is to come from my purse. Attire, environs, and aftermath. All of it. I have had no children to bless with such spoiling, so you must do me this kindness at the very least.

Third, do not blame yourself for any of this. If you are guilty of anything, it is making me a very happy woman at the zenith of this stage of life. I am on to better things and am delighted to do so while departing on a joyous note. Thank you, dear. For more than you know.

All my love,

Penny

Turbulence and tears abounded.

We visited the Grant estate a week later. It was beautiful. It was grand. It was undeniable in the sheer miraculous bounty of Her charity. Lady Penelope Grant, here to grant wishes we had never dared to make. Cinderella could ask for no better godmother.

Despite this, Hux was sheepish upon arrival. It was one thing to weather the gnashing of teeth from cagey relations and in-laws. Quite another to face the Lady's own staff, who had tended her more thoroughly than he ever did, and who he feared would raise their hackles at his potential new station.

They hadn't. Instead, they welcomed us with a glassy-eyed fervor that made me wonder if they hadn't been at Her vintages before opening the doors. I think back on that day now and do not know whether to curse or pity them. Knowing what they had been living with. Knowing what became of her husband's mistress-murderess. Knowing who it was that actually screamed and upended the hot chocolate with such a theatrical clamor to bring the household's witnesses running.

But I did not know then. They could not have convinced us even if they'd tried.

Not that they dared.

No, they were too busy herding us over the threshold and wrenching us apart. The butler rattled off some pretense about showing Hux old Lord Grant's abandoned rooms, untouched since his death. *They have been put right for your perusal, if you would care to take a look, Doctor.* The maids flurried and steered me to the Lady's quarters, *Oh, so sadly under-used of late! Fit for a princess but forsaken out of their departed Lady's infirmity! Come, come, see for yourself…*

Hux and I had exchanged a glance of confusion and a half-joking plea for rescue before vanishing out of sight of the other.

"Fit for a princess," the girls said. Was Poe's loathsome Ligeia royalty? Was three-faced Hecate? I looked on what was described as Her personal chambers and wondered. Here was the stuff of mausoleums and mystics, mediums and the macabre. One room stood as a little library, its shelves bloated with topics that ranged from Scripture to sacrilege to sorcery. Rather, as near as one could get to it outside of fairy stories. All detailing some view of death and what might come after.

The girls were drifting off as we went. Inventing excuses to depart, *Madam, terribly sorry, but do call or ring the bells if you need us.* Away, away. Walking down a corridor until they could turn a corner and run. The last of them was, I think, the screaming maid. She of the spilled chocolate and shed tears for her Lady. Her lip quivered as we approached the Lady's bedroom.

"Is something wrong?"

Her mouth opened…and snapped shut so forcefully her teeth clicked. Then, without unlocking her jaw, she murmured, "No, Mrs. Bishop." She donned a smile as the dew on her lashes spilled. "Everything is perfect."

Before I could say anything more, even to correct her—I wore the ring, but our wedding day was yet to come—the girl retreated out of the room. She paused only a moment to look at me. Wet tracks on her cheeks, the rictus smile gone.

Sorry, said her eyes. *So sorry.*

But then she was gone, hustling after the others.

And then?

What do I put here that adequately describes the sensation? For it *was* only sensation. No visions of transparent wraiths. No slamming and locking of the door. Not even a chill to warn me with a spread of gooseflesh. All I can say is that I became certain that I had company. I turned. Searched. No one. Only myself and my reflection staring bewildered from Her vanity glass. Which froze me, naturally.

How could they not have covered Her mirror? Their beloved Lady was not even a month in the ground, and they would leave this glass unshrouded? It shocked more than frightened me in the moment; so I wanted to believe. Yes, Lotte, just a little surprise. They were all simply too adamant on showing the property in full, as if they were only solicitors flaunting the place's wares. That was all.

So I had almost convinced myself when I felt Her seep in.

That is the word for it. *Seep. Leach. Ooze.* An essence settling into the sponge of flesh and bone. Fear fired through me, but not as fast as a desperate rationale. I was having some sort of seizure. A spasm. Some medical rattling of the nervous system that just happened to feel like alien hands roaming and shifting and adjusting things in the bowl of my skull. A new tenant arranging the furniture. I know I tried to scream.

But in the mirror, the look of terror had already come and gone. My face was placid, then smiling, then almost dreamy. I watched and felt my own hands examine my face, observed as I twirled for the glass. Picture of a girl in a new dress. An extra pause was given to examine my wedding ring. The simple band with its fleck of a diamond.

"Lotte?" I turned—She turned me—and there was Hux. Relief in his face at having found me in the small maze of the halls. "Sorry, it took some doing to get away. Anderson had me cornered." His smile was all sunlight. "How do you feel about the place so far? I know there's still the distance to consider, but if we really do go through with this, I imagine the practice will be due for some adjusting."

"Hux," my voice said through a smile that wasn't mine, "how can we not accept this? Even if it weren't a miracle in itself to be here, to never worry about a single penny spent again, how could we shrug the Lady's gift off as though it were something to dither over?"

He blinked at that. I'd been just as torn as him on the matter, fearing alongside him that dealing with the rankled family might lead to trouble. More, my voice did not have my lilt. Not exactly. We were both of us fresh from Exeter's cluttered living, not Her polished circle. Hux only furrowed his brow and asked after the sound of me, wondering if I wasn't playing some joke.

She wasn't.

More, She maneuvered well enough as time went on over days, weeks, months. How could she not? What sign could I have waved behind my own eyes that would have told him the truth? Even in sleep I was not rid of Her in that period leading up to the wedding day. Wearing the bridal gown while She wore me. The holes in Her performance were readily filled in with Her own exuberance. Her fawning. Her joy at mine and Hux's good fortune. And so, She might have lasted some while after the wedding bells and the move into the Grant estate and the stolen hours in the marriage bed if it were not for Hux's worry.

Even if he did not know it was Her, he did know me. Enough to have been keeping notes on the sudden pivot in the girl he had known for a third of his life. His love who was abruptly forgetful of all the little hobbies she once enjoyed. His love, who turned venomous over Heloise, having naturally come sniffing around upon hearing of Hux's inheritance; an act I had myself predicted before She sank into me, which he and I had laughed over. His love who became more and more pettish as he insisted on seeing to patients and arranging things for his medical practice to be maintained in absentia rather than foisting everything off on hirelings the second the money was in order. The better to spend every waking instance with me. With *Her*.

"Lotte?" A whisper into my ear on the silk of Her bed. "Have you been feeling alright?"

"Of course, dear," from Her. I had never called him 'dear' before we stepped into that damned building. She cupped his face with my hand. "I've never been happier. Why do you ask?"

"I feel as if you have not been all yourself in a while. I know I've hardly any room to talk. My mind's been scattered between the business of the practice and the wedding and Lady Grant's will—,"

"Penny," my voice bit out. The cupping hand crawled up into his hair, petting. "She told you to call her Penny, remember?"

"…Yes. So she did. But that is all past now. I'd assumed your own change was in tune with the same bedlam of juggling all the particulars that come with such things. Yet even now, you do not bother with those activities that brought you joy, or even sought out new routes for your art or your words. All you seem to do is wait for me to come home."

"And you *are* home now, Hux. Both of us." The petting hand crept down to his nape, along collarbone and heart. "Apollo can leave the medicine to his acolytes, can't he?"

"Charlotte. Please." His hand around mine. Hers. "It's more than that. You grasp at me now. Glower when I leave the room and think I do not see. What has changed to make you think I will evaporate if we do not share the same space? If you do not have hold of me at all hours?"

"Nothing, Hux. I've merely come to appreciate you properly, to love you as any woman fortunate enough to be loved by you should be. Is that so wrong?"

His face showed it was. My words did not go with my voice, with his Lotte.

"It is when you forsake your own life to while it away on glaring down random girls in the street and clutching at me like a dragon with his gold. You are not yourself. You have not been yourself for months."

I wanted to laugh as much as scream.

My face only scowled.

"And am I not better for it? You had no issue when it was Penny giving you such attention. I hardly saw you for all the hours you gave to her."

Hux frowned back.

"Lady Grant was my patient. A woman who was only ailing by dint of age, not sickness. You said yourself she was inventing maladies to call me away. Next, you'll say I'm planning to abscond with Heloise the next time she complains of a cough."

My grip hardened around his fingers.

"Of course not, dear. I know you would never. Not when you could have shrugged this tatty little thing off for a dozen other options. Heloise Glassing was but one plum of many you could have picked with your face and your bedside manner. You chose this," my hand to my heart, "out of love. As did I. But if you do grow so sick of this face, we can move on to something better."

Neither of us understood. Hux only had time to gawp at me with a look of baffled hurt before it happened. I felt the rush of Her fleeing through the sieve of my skin and will, lurching out and forward and into—

"No! No, get out of him!" A reflexive cry, and an honest one, I am proud to say. But it was reflex foremost. There was too much relief in having her out of my brain and bones for it to be otherwise. There are not words enough to define the horror of being worn as a breathing suit for another mind to walk and talk and couple in. Just as there are none to describe seeing that same mind slither into the one you love, having no handhold to drag it out with. She was vapor. She was will. She was *him*.

Hux shuddered with the occupancy of Her, his face crumpling with a flash of deepest revulsion and worse epiphany. Though only for the moment needed for Her to take control. She leapt on me with him, both hands locked around my neck like a noose. For all the stoniness She brought to his expression, She could not stop his eyes from welling up. Huge and frightened as a child's in a nightmare.

"There will be no need to fret about accusations of murder, you know," Hux's voice fell out of him. "The staff learned early on. They know what will happen to them if they go against my will." Another press at my throat, trapped air burning, "You will be ruled dead by misadventure with scads of witnesses. Or one of the servants will step forward for the credit. They know I will be kind. Others were not so lucky as my husband's last whore. There are pieces of people that have left my employ by far more creative means scattered all over the grounds. I am tempted to add her to their number, Hux. You really could have done better than this limp thing. But we all make sacrifices for love, don't we, dear?"

Hux's eyes dripped. They broke like rain on my cheeks and brow. I could barely make out his face for all the black haze crowding my vision. One of his hands lifted away, letting in another breath for me as the fingers wiped his face dry.

"Now, now, none of that. I do hate to be short with you, honest I do. But you must learn the rules of this house if we're to get on together. How's this?" His other hand came away. I sucked in air with hungry gusts as Hux's hands folded together, the right thumbing gently over the left's knuckles. Tracing the wedding band. "You can have ten minutes with her. Just to talk. Would you like that?" His eyes ran again. "Very well, fifteen. Be mindful now."

Hux let out a breathless, despairing note as he buckled forward onto hands and knees. We wasted a minute on our wheezing. Then we saw each other. As each other.

"Lotte… How long…?"

I told him. He wept. I wept. There was little enough of talk in our allotted time. We couldn't even whisper a daydream of escape, if not for Her playing warden, then for the fact of her control well outside the estate's walls. All we could do was hold each other. Waiting. At the final minute, it was not me She went back to. Hux shivered and threw me from him, sneering.

"Enjoy the reprieve while it lasts. He is in no condition to perform as-is and your soul is a tedious roost." Hux was walked away from the bed and toward the door to the toilet. "You have until we finish the tour to come up with a convincing argument on why you should not throw yourself from the window in a fit of anguish."

I did not have to ask what tour she meant. She had Hux shed his nightclothes before locking the door behind him. Half an hour later She walked him back out, red-faced and washed. His eyes were frantic marbles in their sockets. She did not have as easy a grip on him as She had me. It was just as well, for I was able to see enough of him to know that he recognized what I was saying.

"I have a proposal, Lady Grant. One to suit all parties as much as can be managed."

"Do tell," She said while picking Hux's nails.

"You say I am a limp thing. One of the lesser options Hux might have chosen. I do not disagree. But if you dispose of me by death, whether he is accused or not, you must know he will follow after me. You are in him now. See if I lie."

She was, She did.

Hux's eyes turned to me more fully. "…Which leaves you as my skin for good." She made Hux sigh with leaden disappointment. "Tragedy upon tragedy. But we all make sacrifices for love—"

"And money. Heloise Glassing's guiding mantra, I believe."

Hux stilled around Her. Listening.

I continued, "Hux was only a distraction to her once upon a time. Now he stands even with two viscounts and a coal magnate as the pending groom. Or would be, if he were unwed. Specifically, to a love he separated with peaceably. Apologetically, even. Say, with enough spectacle around his charity to the excused ex-wife to make other prospects twice as interested as they'd been when he remained a mere bachelor. A winning husband to keep or to lose."

A minute passed. Two. Three.

Then Hux's face stretched with a smile that was not his own.

"You are an enterprising thing, if nothing else." She picked again at Hux's nails. "The sooner the better, Mrs. Bishop. Glassing is a pretty prospect, but even Helen herself couldn't keep the suitors baited forever." I watched Her slip Hux's wedding band off, curling his lip as his glassy eye peered through it. "We must make our arrangements before she begins measuring for a ring."

It was endless and quick at once after that. Like a bullet tearing through the skull.

The divorce, the pay, the departure. Heloise Glassing invited to Dr. Bishop's inherited abode. Her stunning change of manner. The grand proposal and grander pomp of the aftermath. All according to plan.

Not including today.

The day I threw my invitation onto the pyre, letting it burn with the rest of the ashes.

Half an hour ago I left the Grant estate blazing against the horizon with its people inside. I could not risk warning them. Not when She had Her handholds in all of them. The people of Her property, doomed within Her threshold. Will She feel it? Will She know?

I doubt it. Her will is reserved for one body apiece. Heloise and Hux have all er attention now. Tucked away in a plush suite in the city, the news thwarted by distance and the occasion. I will be there soon, ready to wait outside the chapel doors with my wedding gift. Unseen, for the bride and the thing behind her smile must not know I have accepted Her invitation after all.

Heloise will receive the first of it, if only so I know She will feel the bullet as it bursts the shared head. Hux will look at me, I think. I hope not, but I feel he will. Will he be sad? Smiling? I don't dare guess. But I shall follow after him just the same.

As for Lady Penelope Grant, I must wonder where She will end up. No house to haunt, no host to wear. Nothing left but a will to exercise on nothing.

SMOKY JOE

Kevin M. Folliard

NINE-YEAR-OLD NOAH AND his thirteen-year-old brother Randall were staying with Great Aunt Gladys for winter break. Mom was getting a new job. They were all going to be starting a new life, in a new town, changing schools; but Mom had to find somewhere to live first. On December 26th, Mom drove the boys from their old apartment in Las Vegas, up into Utah, to Aunt Gladys's chalet at the top of a quiet mountain town which consisted mainly of a gas station, a diner, and a grocery store.

The house sat at the dead end of a long, winding mountain road. It had an open ground floor living area with a high ceiling, like a church steeple, a second-story landing that led to the bedrooms, and a modest kitchen. Her living room featured elegant bay windows with a beautiful view overlooking the mountains and the town below. A small aluminum Christmas tree adorned with gold ball ornaments sat in one corner.

Aunt Gladys had a weathered face, a semi-circular scar under one eye, and a slight limp on her right side. She had no neighbors. She didn't seem to have many friends either.

After Mom said goodbye, Aunt Gladys drove the boys down the narrow mountain road to town to pick out food and snacks for the week. Snow crumbled from crusty wooden guardrails as the car carefully maneuvered steep twists and turns. The cashier at the food mart was a spectacled white-haired man who eyed Aunt Gladys and the boys with apprehension while they paid for their food.

After that day, they remained confined to the chalet and its grounds. Every day, the mailman arrived around noon, and that was the only other person Noah saw. Aunt Gladys spent her days reading romance novels, curled up with the cushions in her bay windows, gazing over the town and sprawling mountainscape.

Randall and Noah passed the time with the video games and movies they had packed. One morning, Noah explored the wooded area behind the chalet, but there was little to see beyond snow-dusted pines and a steep precipice that led into misty white air. The chalet had no cable TV or internet, and Randall wasn't interested in playing kid's games anymore.

Noah observed his aunt flitting about her home, settling in one area or another. A haunted, distant look seemed ever present in Aunt Gladys's eyes, and Noah soon began to wonder how she could bear this life, halfway up to the clouds, with no one around. Moreover, now that she had family under her roof, why wasn't she more excited for company?

Randall spent his time drawing in his sketchbook. Noah tried to be an artist like his brother, but he wasn't very good. Whenever he attempted to draw the same characters that his brother sketched, he could picture them in his head, but they came out pale, skewed imitations.

He tried to get Randall to help him, to teach him to be a better artist, but Randall merely shrugged and said, "Some people got it. Other people don't."

Every night after dinner, Mom called to check in.

"How much longer, Mom?" Noah asked mid-week. "Doesn't school start soon?"

"We don't know what school you boys will end up in quite yet," his mom explained. "It'll depend on where we land. We'll get it figured out in a few days. I promise."

When the blizzard rolled in, a few days turned into another week.

The snow was piling high when the boys awoke that morning. And there was Aunt Gladys, perched by her bay windows, a paperback folded next to her, cradling a steaming tea cup and soaking up the cottony blur of the mountainscape into her lonely eyes. Lumpy white evergreens shook as flurries whipped and whirled. An arctic haze swallowed the spectacular view of the town.

Aunt Gladys smiled, her first true smile that Noah had seen, as if she were somehow relieved by the snow. As if nature were reassuring her, encouraging her to remain confined at home.

The blizzard raged into the afternoon.

"We're going to be trapped," Randall told Noah. "Could be all winter before the roads reopen and Mom can get here."

"That's not true," Noah said.

"That's not the worst of it." Randall lowered his voice. "We're going to run out of food. And when we do, Aunt Gladys is going to eat one of us."

Noah found a corner under the stairs and cried. Aunt Gladys found him, her eyes knit with concern. She coaxed Noah out and sat with him at the kitchen table. Outside, frost appeared in starry patterns on the sliding back door.

"What's wrong, Noah? You can tell me."

Randall's teasing spilled out of him—not just about the lie that Aunt Gladys would eat one of them, which Noah never truly believed—but also the dig about his lack of artistic talent. And about how much he missed his mom. How nervous he was about a new school, a new home.

Aunt Gladys squeezed his hand. "Change is hard. And, oh, how rotten older brothers can be sometimes." She stood and put water on to boil. "Noah, dear, there's food in my cupboard to last three winters! Nobody is eating anybody else."

Noah sniffled. "I know."

"And these roads will be clear lickety-split. You'll see." Blue fire wrapped around the tea kettle.

"When is Mom coming?" Noah asked.

"Soon. Very soon."

The kettle gave a shrill whistle. Aunt Gladys poured and stirred hot cocoa mix into a ceramic mug for Noah.

"I know it's frustrating, stuck up here with an old biddy like me."

Noah shook his head. "You're not old, Aunt Gladys."

She laughed. "You're sweet. Randall is just as frustrated as you. It's why he's teasing. That's how *he's* passing the time. Why, I remember my own brother once told me that wolves lived under our front porch. I was afraid to go down those steps for months. But one day I found my backbone. You have to stand up to bullies, Noah. Even the bullies you love."

Noah sipped his cocoa. "Do you like it up here, Aunt Gladys? So far away from people?"

"It's lonely," she admitted. "But perhaps I'm just the kind of person who prefers to be alone."

THAT NIGHT, AUNT Gladys made pizza and played Monopoly with the boys before bed. Outside, the snow thickened on the mountain ridge. The boys laid awake in their room. Noah stared at the snow-caked window and asked: "Why is Aunt Gladys so sad?"

Randall stayed quiet for some time. Then he said: "Because of *him*."

"Who?"

"Smoky Joe."

"Who's Smoky Joe?"

"Aunt Gladys's husband."

"She doesn't have a husband."

"Not anymore. He's dead."

The windowpane shuddered.

Randall continued: "They used to call him Smoky Joe because he was a chain smoker. That means he went through like three or four packs of cigarettes a day. So one night, Smoky Joe comes home after a double-shift at the auto garage; he had a few too many shots of whiskey. Aunt Gladys was sound asleep.

"Joe was exhausted. He sat in his recliner, right out there in the living room downstairs. And he went to light a cigarette. But before he finished it, he passed out."

Noah whispered, "What happened?"

"The cigarette fell out of his mouth. His oil-stained clothes ignited, and he burned alive."

"You're making this up."

"Actually…this one's true. Aunt Gladys heard Joe's screams. But he burned so hot, she couldn't get close enough to help. By the time she got a pot of water and doused the fire, Smoky Joe was dead. Charred head to toe."

Noah's heart thudded. "You're teasing."

"I wouldn't lie about this," Randall said. "I heard Mom and Grandma talking about it once. Ever wonder how Aunt Gladys afforded to keep this nice house in the mountains, even though she never really worked? Smoky Joe's life insurance policy."

"She really had a husband who died?"

"Really." Randall folded his arms behind his pillow. "And he's still here."

Wind whistled.

"You're just trying to scare me."

"I wish. Smoky Joe haunts this place. See for yourself tomorrow. There are scorch marks under that gray chair, on the floorboards in the living room." Randall yawned. "Anyway, Aunt Gladys never wants to leave this place, because she knows Joe's trapped here. That's why she won't sell it and move closer to Grandma."

After a long silence, Randall's snores droned.

Noah pulled the covers up to his chin and watched the snow stick to the window.

THE NEXT MORNING, Noah headed downstairs to find Aunt Gladys making bacon, eggs, and hash browns at the kitchen stove. Blue flame curled under sizzling iron pans as she stirred and shifted food. Aunt Gladys had opened up to him the day before and put his fears to rest; Noah was sure if he just asked, she'd assure him that Randall was teasing.

"Aunt Gladys," Noah asked. "Have you ever been married?"

She faced Noah, eyes blank. Bacon grease sputtered. "Don't ask questions about that, Noah."

"Randall said your house was haunted," Noah said. "But he was making it up. Right?"

The color drained from Aunt Gladys's face, and she stopped tending to her food. She glared out the frosty sliding door. Her eyes seemed to sink into the tundra of the backyard.

"Aunt Gladys?"

The stench of burning bacon filled the kitchen. The pan started to smoke. Aunt Gladys jerked to attention and covered the pan. She turned the stove off, and the curls of blue fire vanished.

"Help yourselves to breakfast," she whispered. "I'm not hungry."

She left the food and retreated to her spot at the bay windows overlooking the glittery white world.

Later that day, when Aunt Gladys went upstairs to nap, Noah pushed the gray armchair aside. Sure enough, black scorch marks stained the floorboards underneath.

Something grabbed Noah from behind. He shouted and twisted around to find his brother looming over him.

"Told you."

THAT NIGHT, NOAH awoke to use the bathroom. Snow-covered skylights added an extra layer of shadows to the living room. Noah's eyes turned downward to the gray chair and the bay windows. The chalet glowed blue in the moonlight. Outside, the snow had stopped. Thousands of stars twinkled.

On his way back to the bedroom, yellow light flickered against the angled ceiling. Noah's eyes were drawn down like two magnets. His muscles froze. Fire danced in the gold orbs of Aunt Gladys's Christmas tree. A blazing pillar swallowed the spot where the chair had been. A silhouette sat hunched in the middle of the flames. A dark arm reached toward Noah, blue and white ribbons of flame wrapping around a crusty, blistering hand.

Noah raced back to his room. He slammed the door shut and pressed himself against it. He panted with fear. His heart threatened to burst.

Randall stirred. "What are you doing?"

"It's him!" Noah whispered. "Down there! Smoky Joe!"

"You had a dream or something?"

"No, I'm serious!"

"Noah, jeez!" Randall sat and yawned. "Okay, look, Aunt Gladys had a husband, but there's no such thing as ghosts. Go to bed."

"He's *out* there!"

Randall paused. "Are you sure you saw someone out there? Was it Aunt Gladys?"

"It was *him*!" Noah struggled for breath. "Sitting in that chair, on fire!"

Randall climbed out of bed. He approached the door. "Move aside."

"Don't go out there!"

"Well, either there's a burglar or your eyes are playing tricks."

"They're not!"

Randall looked him up and down. "I freaked you out. Sorry. I shouldn't have let it go this far. Get up, okay. I'll show you. There's no ghost."

Noah trembled as Randall helped him to his feet. He hid behind his brother as they entered the hallway. The flickering yellow light was gone. The blue glow of the moon and the stars had returned. The gray chair was empty.

"Get some sleep. Mom will be back soon. I promise I'll stop being a jerk, okay?"

"Okay." Noah made his way back to bed. He trembled under the covers.

All too soon, his brother was fast asleep again, and an orange glow pulsed under the door. Footsteps thudded down the hallway. Noah whispered his brother's name, clutched the comforter, white-knuckled.

Licks of fire danced in the crack under the door. A deep, gravelly voice moaned in pain. The doorknob jiggled.

"Randall!" Noah whispered. "Wake up!"

The knob glowed orange, then white. Flames sprouted through the keyhole. A terrible smell washed over the bed, like spoiled meat and burned bacon.

"Randall!"

Fire shot up the door and the entire frame burst into a white-hot inferno. Embers and cinders exploded into the room as a tall, stocky figure broke through with a horrible grimace fixed to his charcoal face.

A voice grated amid crackling, popping fire.

"Tell...her..."

NOAH AWOKE, UNCLEAR about what had happened after that. He wasn't sure if he'd dreamed the entire experience of waking up and using the bathroom. If he had imagined the parts about Smoky Joe.

But when he asked, Randall confirmed that Noah had awoken him, frantic in the middle of the night. That they had toured the living room to prove there was no ghost.

His brother apologized again that morning. "Hey bud, I'm sorry. I really went too far. Yeah, Aunt Gladys was married, but her husband's not a ghost, okay? Don't worry about it."

"What if he *is*, though?" Noah said. "And you just didn't know? Did Mom and Grandma really say she stayed here to be with him?"

Randall shrugged. "Something like that."

"He told me to tell her. What if he wants us to give a message to Aunt Gladys?"

"It's not real," Randall assured him. "These are nightmares, okay? Just relax."

That day, it snowed again. Gray circles cradled Aunt Gladys's weary eyes, making the white scar on her cheek even more pronounced. She confined herself to her room and neglected to make dinner. Randall microwaved some food for them when it was obvious she wasn't coming down.

Noah's mom called again. "We've got a new place. You boys are going to love it. Just a few blocks from your new school. I'm coming to pick you up tomorrow, maybe the next day, depending on the weather. Just hold tight."

"Mom," Noah lowered his voice. "Can you tell me about Aunt Gladys's husband? What was he like?"

There was a long pause. "Who told you about him?"

"Randall."

Another long pause. "Don't bring that up to Aunt Gladys. That's why I didn't tell you, okay? She's sensitive about this."

"Okay," he said. "But just…was he a nice man? Or was he bad?"

His mom sighed. "He was…complicated, Noah."

"Aunt Gladys loved him a lot, though? That's why she stayed here after it happened?"

"We'll talk about it sometime, alright? It's not kid stuff," his mom said. "I have to go. I love you."

THAT NIGHT, NOAH lay awake again, staring at the crack under the door. As soon as Randall was deep asleep, an orange glow flickered. Licks of fire danced across the floor of their guest bedroom, but the rug, the floorboards, did not burn. The rotten stench of overcooked meat seared Noah's nostrils.

Fiery lines curved toward the crack under the door, beckoning Noah to the hallway. Noah's stomach knotted up. Cold sweat trickled down his forehead.

"*Listen*," that scratchy, smoky voice echoed. "*Listen*."

The doorknob glowed white hot. The door creaked open. Embers floated in from the hall like fireflies.

Noah cried and hid under the covers. A terrible heat filled the room. The bedding started to blaze and char. The blackened figure of Smoky Joe towered over him; a wall of fire sprouted behind him. His jaws grinned inside charcoal gums, and his eyes liquefied in smoldering sockets.

Noah held out his hands to protect himself. His own fingers lit like torches. His skin melted, cracked, and peeled.

Smoky Joe's raspy moans grew louder.

Fire crawled over Noah's pajamas. A cloud of sulfur stung his eyes. He gagged on black smoke.

"*TELL HER!*"

"*TELL HER!*"

"*TELL HER!*"

The voice drilled inside his head, like a screwdriver stripping a rusty screw. Noah struggled for breath. Wheezed.

"*TELL HER!*"

"*TELL HER!*"

NOAH'S WHOLE BODY jerked. He twisted onto the floor.

"Noah! Noah!"

The bedside light clicked on. Randall was holding him now. "Noah, wake up! You were having a nightmare. You're fine."

Noah coughed and gagged, still certain the room was teeming with smoke. Then at last he took a long breath of precious air. He checked his hands, his skin. No burns. Everything was normal.

"It was him," Noah whispered. "Smoky Joe."

"I should never have told you about him," Randall said. "He's dead. He's gone."

"You're wrong," Noah said. "He has something he needs to say. Something to tell Aunt Gladys."

"It was just a nightmare."

"What if it's not?"

Randall pressed his lips with concern. "If it's not…then…don't fight it, I guess. Just listen. Agree to listen."

Noah wasn't sure if or when he fell back asleep, but he found himself out of bed, already walking down the hallway toward the bathroom. He stopped at the second story landing and stared down at the gray armchair. Outside, snowcapped scenery sparkled in moonlight.

"Okay," Noah said. "I'm listening."

At first, nothing happened. Then Smoky Joe's voice rumbled, *"Sit with me."*

Noah descended the stairs. Sparks ignited on the armchair, swarmed the upholstery. A man took shape, mid-to-late thirties, muscular and stocky with large hands, wearing a mechanic's uniform. But before Noah could get a good look at his face, the fire claimed him. Eating up his clothes, charring his skin, melting his features.

By the time Noah approached, the armchair had been engulfed by a column of white, yellow, and orange. The figure inside was a dark husk, with crackling glowing flecks of skin. Embers swirled toward the distant ceiling.

Joe's voice scraped: "*SIT!*" His blackened finger pointed at the wooden chair across from his own.

Noah's heart thundered. He sat. His voice shook. "Just tell me what to say, okay? I'll give her the message. Then, you have to leave me alone. Please."

"Tell her...." Joe grunted in agony as he struggled to form words. "Tell her...wherever she goes...it doesn't matter. I'm waiting...and when she gets here, I will find her."

The fire died down. Smoky Joe faded until only faint traces of smog lingered. The hint of sulfur soon vanished under the cold moon.

THE NEXT MORNING, Noah screwed up his courage and approached Aunt Gladys at her spot in the bay windows. He sat with her as a distant plow rumbled up the mountain road, and he delivered Smoky Joe's message.

"He wanted you to know," Noah said, "that it doesn't matter if you stay here for the rest of your life. No matter where you go, or where you end up, he'll find you some day, when you die. And you'll be together again."

Aunt Gladys listened, wide-eyed. Tears streamed down her face. She neither thanked Noah for the message, nor reprimanded him for it. She just nodded in acknowledgement, touched his cheek, and retreated upstairs.

Outside, the gray shroud of clouds over the mountains broke, and sunlight warmed the cozy reading nook. Noah felt a tremendous weight lift from the room, and he smiled at the empty gray chair. Aunt Gladys remained upstairs for the rest of the afternoon. But when she returned, she made a delicious dinner of chicken cutlets, mashed potatoes, and gravy. She smiled, laughed, and told funny stories about their family. After dinner, Randall and Noah helped with the dishes, and Aunt Gladys played games with them until bedtime. Before she retired for the night, she told Noah how much she loved him.

THAT AFTERNOON, MOM arrived, followed by a well-dressed man with a black coat and wool cap. At first, Noah thought the man was with their mother, but then he noticed a separate car. The man spoke to Mom outside for a few minutes. Their breaths puffed in the sunny, cold air. They soon approached the door together.

When Noah let them in, their mother first hugged and kissed the two boys, but then she called for Aunt Gladys and hurried upstairs.

The man introduced himself by showing a badge. "Hello boys. I'm Detective Jeffries."

"Why are you here?" Randall asked.

"I asked him to come." Aunt Gladys appeared at the top of the stairs, a suitcase in her hand, a lonely smile on her face. "You were right, Noah. I shouldn't stay here. And there's no escaping it. Sooner or later, I'm going to meet him."

Their mother placed her hand on Aunt Gladys's shoulder.

"I confess, Detective," she said. "I killed my husband. Right there in that chair. I burned him alive to be rid of him, his drinking, his constant abuse… And for my precious solitude," Aunt Gladys glared at the empty gray armchair, "I would do it again."

ON THEIR HANDS

Amanda Cecelia Lang

Someone is weeping.

Gauzy, heart-torn cries pull me from an uneasy pit of sleep and fade into the vast corners of our new bedroom.

I squint against the too-bright daylight, still upside-down inside unfamiliar surroundings. No more cityscape, the bedroom windows on the left now instead of the right. Vast walls textured in pretentious golden silk wallpaper, and a high ceiling bedecked with flourishes of crown molding and a teardrop chandelier. I feel tiny inside this absurdly oversized estate. Even in the stillness of waking, the place practically echoes. I roll over and draw Becca into my arms, bury kisses in her tangled mane of midnight dark hair, remind her she's not alone. Coming here was never going to be easy for her.

"Hey, babe, you crying?"

"Not crying, *sleeping...*" she mumbles into her pillow.

Did I dream it? Darkness, dirt, someone weeping. Makes sense, I suppose. Strange new dreams for a strange new house. I've been worried about her, worried how she'll process this place. She's a master at bottling emotions, but eventually things are going to spill over. It's actually a little concerning that they haven't already. I pull her tighter against me.

My shoulders ache something fierce and my arms are bone-heavy— but I'm not surprised. I lost count of the boxes we lugged inside yesterday, our whole life uprooted and shoved into cardboard. Not that there was much to uproot: struggling careers, piles of bills. This house was a godsend. But after driving halfway across Louisiana and unpacking the moving van, we barely had the energy to glance around the property before showering and collapsing onto the bare mattress of a massive four-poster bed.

"Big day ahead," I say, not moving a muscle. Lots to unpack. Acres of land to explore. This place is unsettling in its opulence. Too big for just the two of us. Yesterday afternoon, when we pulled up to a rambling driveway lined with an ancient sentry of live oaks, we couldn't believe we had the right address. Spanish moss dripped from the trees like silver cobwebs, and a front lawn of centipede grass stood so vast and lush and over-green it hurt the eyes. The house grew larger and larger before us, a monster of colonial architecture, endless foggy windows, stately columns the color of old bones. Who knows what treasures Becca's grandparents left behind? She never met them—never even knew she had a family until the last of them died three weeks ago.

"We can't stay in bed all day," I whisper, giving her a sleepy nudge. "We should take a look around."

"Should we?" She nestles closer and clasps my hand in hers, letting our wedding rings click. With a sultry warm breath, she runs velvet kisses across my knuckles and—

"Oh yuck, Henry." She shakes free of me, and we both snap fully awake. "What's all over you?"

I hold my palms up to the daylight and a nameless dread shivers through me like the echo of someone weeping. I can't explain it. "The hell?"

My hands are covered in mud, and my fingertips are shredded and bloody.

"This is insane, Henry." Becca stands on the edge of the sprawling, white-washed front porch, trying to make sense of her dead grandparents' lawn. Hundreds of bucket-sized holes pock the lavish landscape. They're everywhere. Running the length of the endless driveway, spreading like cavities all across the centipede grass, all the way to the murky woodland that surrounds the property. "Why would you do this?"

"I didn't do this." Though my arms hang like shovels at my sides. My fingertips twitch, wrapped tightly in bandages. Hell, I can still feel the grit beneath my mangled fingernails—even after scrubbing with soapy, scorching water.

Suddenly the porch with its distended, shadow-casting eaves and stern sentry of Corinthian columns—like everything about this estate—looms overlarge and surreal and ready to consume me. I resist the squirming, craven urge to run, to sprint out into the pitted lawn.

"If this is some kind of joke, just tell me." Becca studies me with that sharp edge she sometimes gets. Her liquid gray eyes turn icy, and her pale cheeks suck inward and go hollow and shadowed as if to cry: *haven't I suffered enough?*

"I said I didn't do this."

Becca storms past me out onto the lawn. I follow in accused silence as she weaves through the outbreak of holes. It's as if *someone* dug up a minefield in the night. But it wasn't me—my mind scrapes and turns at the idea—how could this have possibly been me! I crouch next to a ragged hole and a sloppy mound of grass and dirt. Leaning over the tiny abyss, a chill of disappointment whispers through me. There's nothing down there.

I scoop up a handful of the rich soil, relishing the way it crumbles like coffee grounds between my fingers. I take another handful, and the humming of the local cicadas fills my ears, a thousand tiny voices chittering about buried secrets. As I stand, the lawn around me pulls into sharper focus, and I'm astounded by what I start to see. I turn in a slow circle.

"Becca, look at the ground! I think this has happened before."

All around us, the earth is scarred and lumpy where someone long ago dug holes, then filled them back in. Hundreds of them, maybe thousands. All showing varying signs of age, like how burial mounds sink into the earth over time. Some look ancient.

We follow the holes to the end of the lawn where the trees thicken to woods. Becca peers into the moss-dripping gloom beyond.

"They just keep going."

"Now do you believe this wasn't me? How could I do all this in one night?"

"This is too weird." She steps away from me, shaking her tousled sable head, gooseflesh breaking out across her slender, bare arms. "Why would anyone do this?"

"I don't know," I say. "Maybe it was some kind of burrowing animal? A gopher or a stray dog. Or a disgruntled gardener—didn't sound like your grandparents were very popular."

"Maybe." She side-eyes the bloodstained bandages wrapped around my fingers as we cross into the trees.

The massive oaks weave a filigree canopy above our heads, and the air flickers with alternating blades of light and shadow. The holes go on and on like dotted lines on a treasure map, leading us through the eerie verdant calm. Becca treads lightly, as if she's trespassing on private ground. It still hasn't sunk in that all this belongs to her now.

We come to a small meadow marked with more holes and swaying with spidery blue wildflowers.

No, not a meadow—a graveyard.

Two lonely headstones wait for us at the far end.

Austere masonry, knee high, no fancy ornamentation, not like the rest of the property. Silver-green tendrils of moss obscure the names and dates. A mist of déjà vu settles over me. The ceaseless droning of the cicadas fills my head like a dream. I can't scrape my eyes away from the familiar outline of those stones. Whoever's buried here, it isn't Becca's grandparents. Unsure of what to do with people she never knew, Becca had them cremated.

She clears the moss from the first headstone. The cheap cement is aged and crumbling, the name worn to an unreadable blur by the muggy southern elements. Filthy handprints smudge the inscription; looks like the mud is still damp. I shove my fists into my pockets. My wife doesn't seem to notice.

She drops to her knees before the second headstone. The newer one. She cements her red rosebud mouth into a stoic, bloodless line and then, almost casually, brushes the moss aside, just far enough to glimpse the name.

"This is my mother's grave." Her voice trembles on the edges, betraying the grief she swears she doesn't have. Despite the inheritance, the loss is finally setting in. Good. I squeeze her shoulder, but she stiffens and shrugs me off. I don't take it personally. With everything she's trying not to feel, being upset with me is just easier. She'll never know the grandparents who left her everything or why their daughter abandoned her at birth. The probate attorney who hunted her down only had the official paperwork to go off of. He told us her birth mother lived in this house her entire life before committing suicide over a decade ago, an apparent victim of prolonged mental illness. Of course, the harrowing details were not part of public record. The grandparents died of natural causes. No living relatives, no friends.

Nobody to explain why, with all this wealth, her mother didn't keep her.

Nobody to explain these insidious holes.

Becca pulls the remaining moss from her mother's gravestone—though somehow, I already know what the epitaph will say. And that it's wrong.

SHE SEARCHES NO LONGER

"You want me to spend the day filling holes when I should be unpacking boxes?" I say.

"I need to be alone with all this." Becca thrusts a rusty shovel at me and retreats inside. Off to wander cavernous rooms haunted by sheet-draped furniture and the photographs of dead strangers. Maybe she'll find some leftover pieces of her mother in a drawer or closet, something to occupy the hole her birth family left inside her all these years.

I sigh. The sky drips with sunshine, and the buzzing lullaby of cicadas casts a sleepy spell across the lawn. I wipe the sweat from my forehead, then get to work with the shovel.

Right away the tool feels unnatural, clunky, a blister waiting to happen. After filling a few holes, I toss it aside and drop to my knees. Much better. The soil slides like dark velvet between my hands. Humming with the cicadas, I scoop mound after mound back into the ground. Naturally, before that, I root around each tiny abyss, making sure there isn't something secret and tantalizing down there.

But no. There's nothing.

By the time I reach the woods, my bandages have disappeared and the meaty tips of my fingers are bleeding again. Mud clots the tiny cuts, but the grit is necessary. *Yes.* My heart sits like cracked earth inside my chest, a desperate, crumbling feeling. But what am I desperate for? I can't shake this dizzy, itchy urge to sink my hands back into the ground. I feel it, like I feel the expanding chasm in the gut of my soul. A dark certainty. There's something enormous buried out here.

When I'm sure Becca isn't watching from the house, I dig three fresh holes.

Nothing's down there.

I fill them in quickly.

THE SPECTRAL ECHO of my wife weeping carries through the midnight hallways of the old estate and out through the pitted landscape of my dreams.

I open my eyes to moonlit windows and roll over in bed.

A white shadow huddles at the edge of the mattress. Becca's shoulders tremble and her breath rasps with secret tears.

I slide close and pull her into an embrace. Fresh bandages conceal my raw, seeping fingers. Becca resists for a heartbeat then buries her face against my chest, hot tears welling up from a deep, untapped pit.

"Hey, babe, I'm right here." I speak softly and kiss the top of her head. "Talk to me."

"We shouldn't have come here. I don't belong."

"You belong wherever we are. You and me."

"This whole big house," she moans, "but my mother didn't have room for me. Why, Henry? Why wouldn't she want me here?"

I don't have the answers to take the edge off her past, so I rock Becca in my arms, tangle my stinging fingers deep in her hair, and hum a strange forgotten lullaby. She relaxes into me, bones loosening. Her sobs slow to hiccups, which fade into the shallow rhythm of sleep.

My mind drifts with her in the too-bright moonlight and settles like dust along the perimeter of darkness. I close my eyes.

A long, breathy sob echoes through the master suite.

"Becca, don't…" I kiss her forehead.

But her expression is smooth and tranquil. She's still asleep.

Another sob stirs the antique air around us.

But it doesn't come from Becca's lips.

It drifts in from the pocked nightscape outside our window and crawls along the back of my neck. My veins prickle with an icy skittering awe.

I lower Becca to her pillow. Then I glide like a shadow toward the window, careful not to startle whatever is out there.

Beyond the glass, the moonlit lawn is a green-and-silver dreamscape.

The holes I spent the day filling are back.

Hundreds of dark fathomless craters pit the fabric of my sanity. I grip the windowsill, dig my ruined fingernails in.

A human silhouette crouches in the centipede grass below, opening up a fresh hole.

I don't waste a heartbeat.

I told her I didn't do this!

"Becca, wake up! Someone's outside!"

I scramble for the bedroom door, not waiting to see if my wife follows. The light switch in the hallway eludes me, so I trip through a darkened corridor of gauzy dust covers and hanging photographs. The harsh faces of my wife's estranged family watch from the gilded walls as I rush past. Quickly, half-falling, I stagger down the grand spiral staircase, following the elegant half-moon curve of red-carpet steps as if the mansion itself is ushering me toward some grand and revolutionary discovery.

At the bottom, the cold marble floor is a shock against my bare feet, and I shiver as I reach the stately double doors with their frosted oval windows and moving shadows beyond.

I fumble with the brass deadbolt and the chain lock. My bandages flop loosely, and my fingertips are slippery with blood.

I throw the door open and stagger outside.

The sultry landscape beyond the darkened, majestic porch hums with a thousand midnight insects. But not a single weeping voice. The mansion stands as a glowing apparition against the verdant night. I scan the lawn and the dripping shadows beneath the mossy oaks.

But I'm alone out here.

Worse, the holes are gone. The lawn is as I left it this afternoon. I fall to my knees, adrenaline draining from me, my treasure-hunting spirit sinking into the grass.

"What the hell, Henry?" Becca says from the doorway, clutching the collar of her bathrobe. Her eyes are bloodshot and hollowed out, and her nest of midnight hair casts her in a haggard impatience.

"Someone was out here. Digging…" I hold up a handful of grass and dirt.

She stares at me like *I'm* the stranger. A tear slices down her cheek. "I told you, there's nothing for us here."

Before I can say anything more, she slams the door.

I suppose I deserve that. Though I know what I saw. Someone was out here.

As I turn to survey the night, a distant voice, a voice of sorrow and loam, whispers between my ears.

"*Shhhhh…*"

WE SPEND THE morning apart.

I scrub my bloody fingerprints off the windowsill and the front door and try to pretend last night never happened. When that's done, I catch myself wandering the yard. The sun swells higher and higher above the trees. My head buzzes. I know why I came out here, but I ignore the ground and the restless ache in my hands. I slip between the live oaks and roam the acres of tangled green property. I tell myself I'm familiarizing myself with our new home, not searching for holes or murky silhouettes or loamy disembodied voices.

The sun hangs bloated on the horizon by the time I return to the house. I poke my sweaty head into a dozen shadow-dappled rooms before I find Becca.

My wife sits like a child in the center of a bedroom floor. A little girl's bedroom, at first glance, judging by the frilly Raggedy Ann canopy bed and the collection of small antique tea sets and porcelain dolls.

But as I step closer, I realize with a start: this is Becca's mother's room.

Judging by the tangled mess of dust covers and vintage treasures strewn around her legs, my wife has been excavating the past. Outdated lace sleeves and bubblegum pink skirts hang from open drawers, picture books that haven't been read in over a decade sit spine-cracked across the rug. Everywhere, trinket boxes lie on their sides, spilling obscure mementos and girlish costume jewelry like innards.

The floorboards creak as I approach, and Becca hastily wipes her eyes.

"What am I doing here, Henry?" she says, not looking up from the framed photograph she holds in her lap. "Why am I trying to get to know someone I'm never going to know?"

"You're reclaiming your roots. It's what you've always wanted."

"Not like this. I can tear up this entire house, puzzle all this junk into a loose picture of who they were, but I still won't have my mother. I won't know what was inside her heart."

"Give it time. We've barely scraped the surface of this place."

"It's too late." She stands and trips past her mother's belongings. "I want to go home, back to the city. First thing tomorrow, I'm putting this monstrosity on the market. Then I'm going to forget I was ever here."

"You're joking."

"You said it when we got here, this place is too big for the two of us." She hesitates, and in the distance between words, I feel us breaking apart. She looks at me as if I'm a stranger, as if I don't understand her. And at this moment, I don't. "Henry, it just keeps getting bigger."

I shake my head. "Have you lost your mind? You don't just toss a house like this aside."

"Like they tossed me aside?"

"The house didn't do that." I nod my chin at the crown molding and weeping-whispering walls. "Take a step away from yourself, Becca. This place is amazing."

"What do you even care about the damn house? You've done nothing but wander the yard since we got here."

"Oh, Christ, *that* again? How many times do I have to say it? I didn't dig those holes!"

She regards me coolly. "We're leaving tomorrow."

"Running away won't heal you, Becca. We're not leaving. Not yet."

Maybe not ever.

"That isn't your call." She pauses in the doorway, glaring daggers. "Your hands are filthy, by the way."

She tosses the family photograph to the hardwood and stalks out the door, leaving me with disbelief pulsing between my temples.

I retrieve the frame and flip it over, smearing muddy dark prints across the glass.

The grandparents glower up at me, pinched smiles, severe gazes. In the photograph, they stand behind Becca's mother, a young woman in her late twenties dressed in the poofy pink dress of a child. A paralysis of youth. Their knotty, age-spotted hands clutch her arms, digging indentations into her skin, pinning her in place. She wears dainty white gloves stained at the fingertips, and her eyes are black and joyless. The resemblance to Becca is striking. Echoes of petite figure, aristocratic chin, pale dewy complexion, and sable hair, yes. But the real parallel is in their wistful expressions. The vast longing. I try to align the young woman in the photograph with the smudge of shadow I glimpsed in the yard—yet what I see is someone desperate to pull away, someone desperate to come to terms with the gaps inside her soul.

Someone who would walk beyond earth and grave to find what it is she's searching for.

I WAKE TO weeping, the window on the wrong side of the bed, and the whisper of fingernails scraping the floorboards.

My wife is there, crouched in the corner, spine arched like an animal burrowing. Her midnight hair is muddy and stringy. Her fingertips are stubs of meatless white bone. Splinters and blood and cracked fingernails smear the floor around her.

My fingers twitch and tingle, eager to join in. I sit up.

Becca snaps her head my way.

Except it isn't Becca, of course it isn't. Though, God, the family resemblance is uncanny.

"What are we searching for?" I whisper.

The dead woman's eyes glitter blackly at me from the gloom. She raises a finger bone to her lips and speaks inside my head.

"Shhhhh. You'll wake them."

Her daughter stirs beside me in bed, breathing softly, unaware. But I don't think it's Becca we're trying not to wake. This is the master suite, where the grandparents used to sleep.

"They won't let me," the woman whispers. *"They control everything. Even my dead part. They won't let me have it…"*

She reaches for me.

I take her hand.

Together, we slip through a long and jagged darkness.

When I raise my eyes to meet hers, I find myself standing in a low, rolling mist on the edge of the mossy woods, sweaty and alone.

The holes are back. Hundreds of them.

I hold my muddy hands up, and the whites of my finger bones wink at me through the ruined tips of my flesh.

I drop onto my hands and knees, keening in pain, eager to go deeper. The cicadas buzz. A shadow flits across the corner of my eye—a shadow no living creature could cast.

The dead woman crawls between the oaks, burrowing arm-deep into the ground.

My vision rolls with the fog, the night blurs. I step toward the woods and emerge in the graveyard. Ahead, the woman stoops before the abandoned headstones. She collapses atop the older of the two graves and drags her finger bones across the ruined stone inscription. Then she claws at the grave soil. Furiously, silently, dirt scattering, as if she's desperate to uncover a missing piece of herself before it stops beating.

Eagerly, I drop down and join her.

"They said it was right here," she whispers. Her voice scoops me out. Her lips move out of synch with the syllables inside my head. *"They said I wasn't allowed to see it. They said they buried it…"*

"We'll find it," I promise. Whatever *it* is.

Together, we uproot the ground, our icy fingers tangle and dance and exhume the rich fertile grave. Down and down we go until the opening is above us. But it's not deep enough.

With pits of agony elongating her eyes and mouth, the dead woman clutches her empty arms against her chest and wails at me.

"A stillborn! My baby! Please, just let me hold her! Please, please! Let me hold my baby! Where have you buried her? WHERE?"

She reaches for me with withered arms, and I clasp her hands.

Our finger bones click.

Her stolen life ricochets through me—all the lullabies, all the bedtime stories, all the cherished motherly memories that never were, every missing milestone that hollowed her out and crumbled her foundations. A flash of despair, a too-short lifetime left sheltered and unfulfilled, then, like the echo of a lonely voice weeping, she grows faint and vanishes into the dust.

I'm alone down here.

But I know what I must do.

I crawl from the empty grave and face the house where my wife sleeps.

Then I crack my knuckles and dig the final hole.

THE RISING SUNSHINE dances spades across Becca's peaceful face.

I double-check that my hands are clean, then I sit quietly on the edge of the mattress. I want everything to be perfect for her when she wakes. Our first days here were rocky, but life will be better now, fuller.

Everything will be as it should've been.

Making sure my hands are still clean, I brush a stray grain of soil from the bedsheet. Becca stirs on the edge of waking, and her mother's thin arms loosen around her. Humming a quiet lullaby, I readjust the woman's silty bones so that she cradles her daughter closely.

Then I fold my hands and wait for the joyous reunion.

THE MAN WHO BUILT GALLOWS

Terry Campbell

"**D**EACON BLACKRIDGE, YOU have been convicted of the murders of three nameless Mexican drifters and are to be hanged from this oak tree from the neck until you are dead."

Heat lightning flickered, momentarily brightening the subdued sky above the barren hill. A low growl of thunder rumbled in the distance. Sheriff Caney Rimshaw took the reins of the horse on which Deacon Blackridge sat, steadying the animal to help prevent it being spooked by the approaching storm. Beyond stood a small crowd—Deputy Higgins, the mayor, and a handful of townsfolk who had turned out for the hanging.

"I didn't do it, Sheriff," the condemned man said. Every man who ever sat on horseback under the hanging tree with a rope around his neck said the same thing. The sheriff ignored him.

Instead, he looked up at what remained of the once proud and mighty oak. *It must be over two-hundred years old*, Caney thought. Only this lone thick branch remained capable of conducting a successful hanging, and it had a sizeable crack running through it near the trunk. The tree had sustained a direct hit from a small but mean twister several years prior, taking out most of the other limbs and causing the break in this one. Since then, decay and carpenter ants had set in.

"All right, if there's nothing more to be said," Caney began.

There was the beginning of an objection from Deacon, but before the words could spill completely from his quivering lips, the sheriff shouted and slapped the hindquarters of the horse. Deacon spun through the air, kicking his feet, when everyone heard the sound.

There was a loud crack, as of bones breaking, but the noise was from the oak branch and not Deacon's scrawny neck. A spray of mealy wood chips, sawdust, and ants exploded into the air, and the would-be hanging victim struck the rocky ground hard. Sheriff Rimshaw ducked away quickly, hitting the dirt and rolling to safety. A second later, the girthy tree branch found the top of Deacon's head, simultaneously snapping the man's back and neck.

The few women in the crowd shrieked and shielded their children's eyes. A simple hanging was one thing, but this gruesome display was unexpected.

The crowd stood stunned, waiting for the dust to clear and gathering its collective breath.

"Sheriff, you got any more hangings scheduled this week?" someone asked.

Nervous laughter emanated from the townsfolk. A bit of brevity was just what the situation needed.

Caney rubbed the back of his neck and dusted off his britches. "I guess it's a good thing I don't. I'm afraid our trusty old oak has seen its last hanging."

THE CROWD HAD dispersed. Caney watched as the undertaker and his mule-driven cart rolled slowly down the hill toward the cemetery on the outskirts of town. He inhaled deeply and stared up at the remains of the once sturdy tree. They'd all known it was just a matter of time, and time was up.

"Sheriff?"

Caney jumped, startled at the voice. He thought everyone had left.

Sheriff Rimshaw turned to see a man wrapped in a dark woolen poncho, a red and yellow zigzag pattern sewn into the shoulders. A small derby sat upon his head, a similar patterned band encircling the hat just above the brim. A single owl feather protruding from the band completed the look. Caney was sure he'd never seen him before.

"I didn't see you there, stranger. Have you been here the whole time?"

"No, Sheriff. I just arrived. My name is Flint Gaston." The man in the black poncho strode forward and stopped just under what remained of the oak tree. "I build gallows."

"Gallows?" Caney said. He kicked at the broken limb with his boot and chuckled. "Well, we may be in need of your services. We just lost the last sturdy branch on our only hanging tree."

"I know," the stranger said. "That's why I'm here."

"So, you did see."

"I see that my services are needed."

The sheriff nodded. Flint Gaston was a peculiar man, short on words, but harmless, nonetheless.

"Well, Flint Gaston, let's head back into town and we can discuss business," the sheriff said. "Where's your horse?"

"I have no horse. I travel by foot."

Caney led his horse over to the stranger. The steed didn't seem too shaken by the afternoon's events. "Hottest part of the day. Hop on and you can ride back with me."

"No thank you, Sheriff. I'll meet you there," Flint said. "Like I said, I travel by foot."

Sheriff Rimshaw was surprised to see Flint Gaston shuffling up to him so soon after he had arrived back in town. *How did Gaston get here so quickly?* the sheriff pondered. It was two miles to the hanging hill. The sun was dipping low in the west, painting the streets in an orange glow.

Caney offered to buy Flint a drink, but he politely refused. They wound up sitting in front of the sheriff's office with a cool glass of water from the well. The evening air was comfortable; the storm had passed the town by. Caney eyed the odd stranger, attempting to gain some sort of reading, but could not. Flint's eyes were dark and always seemed to be shaded, no matter where the early evening sun landed on his face. His skin was cracked and ruddy. Likely from all that exposure to the weather, if he truly did walk everywhere, as he claimed.

"So, Flint Gaston, tell me your story. Where are you from?"

"Many places," the man said. Caney had not really expected a straight answer. "And nowhere." He finally looked up and directly into the sheriff's eyes for the first time. "My wife and child were taken from me. Slaughtered in their sleep by a gang of scoundrels when I was gone on business."

"I'm sorry to hear that," Caney said. "I'm sure you're out for vengeance, hunting them down. Is that why you're from 'many places'? Why do you walk everywhere?"

Flint shook his head slowly. "I'm not a violent man, Sheriff, and I'm no count with a gun. I'm certainly no gunfighter, if that's what you're getting at. I'm not the type of man who would seek vengeance in that manner."

Flint Gaston drank the last of his water and waved off another glass when offered. His attention was on the town square, as if calculating and planning the construction of the gallows.

"I'm a carpenter by trade. That is where my skills lie. The only vengeance I could seek would be through gallows built by my own hand."

Sheriff Rimshaw nodded and leaned back in his chair. "So, these killers, this gang that murdered your family. Were they ever brought to justice?"

"I don't know. I truly have no idea. But now I travel the country, building gallows wherever they're needed. The more gallows I build, the better the chance that those unholy bastards swing from one of my making. In that, I gain my vengeance."

"Certainly not your typical revenge, but I suppose it does serve a need, even if you never learn who killed your family."

"Indeed. There will always be those worthy of a hanging. There will always be others who seek the retribution a noose provides. I'll need to borrow a wagon and a couple of horses to pull it. I travel by foot, but I can't carry the heavy timbers I will need."

"Of course," Caney agreed. "We can round up a couple of strong hands to assist you."

"Thank you, but no," Flint said. "I work alone."

This struck the sheriff as strange. "Okay, whatever you say, but where will you get the lumber? Slim pickings around here for trees, as you've no doubt noticed."

"I have my sources. I have my tools. I need only the wagon and horses."

"Sure, we'll get you those. How much is this going to cost our fair town, Mr. Gaston?"

"I make no charge for my services, nor any materials used. What I do, I do for my own reasons. My only request is that I'm allowed to be present for the first hanging from the new gallows." Flint stood and thanked him for the cool water. "I will leave shortly and begin work tonight."

"Tonight? But it will be dark soon. You won't have time to—"

"Time does not press on me. I will build the gallows and then I will take my leave."

"But how will we know how to reach you if you leave before the first hanging?"

"You don't need to concern yourself with that, Sheriff," Flint answered. "When the time comes, I will know."

"I HEARD ABOUT a man who came through New Mexico a few years back and built a whole staircase overnight in a chapel. People say he was an angel," Deputy Higgins said. "Do you think Flint Gaston was an angel? Maybe even the same guy who built the stairs?"

Sheriff Rimshaw shrugged and looked up at the gallows that now loomed high in the sky in the center of the town square. How could something so macabre, something that's very existence was necessary only because of terrible, ungodly actions, be so incredibly beautiful? The craftsmanship was amazing, the materials exquisite. The wood was unlike any he had ever seen and had been finished to a rich golden hue that practically glowed in the morning sun. Dark grains ran like stripes through the wood, reminding Caney of a tiger he'd once seen on a poster for a traveling carnival. Upon closer inspection, he noticed that there were no iron nails, only wooden pegs supporting the timbers at every joint. The sheriff ascended the steps, bouncing up and down as he did, testing the structure's strength. There was nary so much as a creak. Having reached the platform, Sheriff Rimshaw pushed against one of the uprights that provided support for the heavy crossbeam. It did not move a bit. Solid work indeed.

He stepped back and removed his hat, scratched the back of his head, and peered up into the sun. *One night. How did Flint Gaston gather materials and build this all in one night?* he thought. The mysterious stranger was gone, a slinking, secretive, poncho-clad carpenter disappearing into the dark.

SIX WEEKS HAD passed since Flint Gaston's uncanny appearance in the town of Buzzard Ridge. Sheriff Rimshaw had broken up a cattle thieving ring, and an assisting lawman from the next county had lost his life in the ensuing gunfight. Today, the man who fired that fatal shot would be the first to hang from Flint Gaston's gallows.

Quite a crowd had come out for the big event. This was no ordinary tree lynching. This was big news. There was even a reporter from a newspaper in Abilene who had arrived on the morning train to cover the story. The town folk were abuzz with anticipation. Murmured voices flitted around the mass of people. The atmosphere was almost festival-like.

Sheriff Rimshaw scanned the gathering people, his eyes ever open for a glimpse of Flint Gaston. He thought he might have spotted him in the crowd on several occasions, but it turned out to be someone else. Then, standing to the right and behind the stairs that led to the gallows, was that him? Again, there was nothing. But Caney continued to catch brief flashes of black and that colorful zigzag in and amongst the throngs, but his eyes could not train on them long enough to make a definite confirmation.

The crowd grew silent as the commencement of the execution drew near. The offending criminal was led up the stairs, and it was time for Sheriff Rimshaw to focus his attention on the matter at hand.

After all, he had a job to do.

FLINT GASTON'S GALLOWS accepted its first offering. The crowd had slipped away, the day's excitement now drawn to a close. The lifeless body of the lawman-killing despot swung ever so slightly in the fading evening breeze. Lively piano music emanated from the saloon across the road. The hanging was now a fading memory to most. The undertaker had just arrived to begin his somber work.

"Sheriff Rimshaw, might I have a word with you?" It was the reporter from Abilene.

"I suppose," Caney said, "although I don't really see how anything I have to say would be of interest to your newspaper."

"Surely you jest. Everyone's heard of Sheriff Caney Rimshaw," the reporter said. "You've cleaned up this county from what I've heard, and certainly this town. Your exploits are nearly legendary, what with the lone hanging tree and the sheer number of executions from said tree. And then when word of this made it to Abilene…" He swung his hand out to the gallows. "I heard a stranger just blew into town and built it overnight. Is that true?"

Caney nodded and looked about. There was no one left. Only him and the reporter. "I was hoping to see him here. He asked for no payment to build our gallows. His only request was to be present for the first hanging." The sheriff again perused the empty city streets. "But I saw nothing of him."

"What was this kind stranger's name, Sheriff?"

"Flint Gaston," Caney answered. "His family was murdered, and the killers never found. Now he travels from town to town, building gallows to make sure outlaws everywhere are brought to justice."

He looked off into the fading sunset a long moment, expecting another rapid question from the reporter, but the newsman was silent. The sheriff turned back to him. The reporter's flesh had grown pale. His eyes stared straight ahead, blank and unblinking.

"Son, are you alright?"

The reporter's eyes moved to the sheriff's, snapping from his sudden trance. His voice shook ever so slightly.

"Sheriff, I wrote an article on Flint Gaston five years ago, just after his family was murdered. The killers were never found because the sheriff never looked for them. He laid all the blame on Flint Gaston himself."

"But surely Gaston didn't—"

The reporter nodded. "Gaston was convicted and tried for the murders, and he was executed. Flint Gaston hung from the very gallows he himself had built just days earlier."

SHERIFF CANEY RIMSHAW walked slowly back toward the gallows, pondering how a condemned man might feel, taking his final steps to his own death. The reporter had departed on the last train back to Abilene, leaving Caney alone with his thoughts.

He was tired. It had been a long, draining day.

It explained a lot. Answered a lot of questions but opened so many more.

The sheriff stopped behind the gallows, and there they were. They were unmistakable. The winds had diminished completely. The footprints were still sharply defined in the red sand. One set leading from the outskirts of town to the gallows, and one set back in the other direction, out of town.

I travel by foot, he had said.

When the time comes, I will know.

How many miles has he walked? And how many more? And would the walking go on forever?

Time does not press on me.

Sheriff Rimshaw turned away and started toward his office and the comfort of his bed. It was late, and he was ready to retire for the night.

His thoughts returned to the footprints in the sand, and Caney smiled, a bit forlornly. Perhaps he had managed to keep his end of the agreement with Flint Gaston after all.

TRACKS IN THE DUST

Re Gwaltney

FATHER KEPT MOTHER in a room those last few weeks. I thought of it often, while I whiled at the window or ran my eyes past rivers of words in the scriptures he gave me. How she must have felt in her room of eight feet by ten, all sliced to segments by a bed and a desk and a wardrobe. She had a desk, but she never used it, I think. It was covered over with a thick layer of dust the day we collected her body.

There was dust on the floor, too, though long hours of pacing had tracked witness marks through it. The bed was made. I remember marking that specifically, as the maid was never allowed to clean that particular room. Only to enter twice a day, bringing meals and emptying the chamber pot. I asked Father once why Mother wasn't allowed to the outhouse. It's only a few steps outside the home, I said, and surely she can't harm anyone on the trip. He said surely she could, and she must be kept away from all but him until she was better.

Her funeral was beautiful and somber. All of father's friends came to comfort him at the end of his great struggle.

It would have been inappropriate for me to join them, of course. So my maid took me home, and in the privacy of Father's great, silent house, I padded my way up to the room Mother occupied in her last moments. I saw the desk, the dust, and the untouched bed. I walked carefully, keeping every step to the paths she made in her pacing. To keep

Father from suspecting, I told myself. Not to keep myself close to her. Not to feel the echo of her madness, as though it were the only thing left.

There was a space in the corner of the room, between the desk and the bed, where no dust lay. Its edges had frayed as with the sweeping of a besom across ash. I kneeled, pressing my hand against the center of the circle, and felt the weight of her presence—her absence—settle in my chest. And by some illucid compulsion, I found myself sinking, curling forward and laying against the grain of the floor. A subtle pain bloomed from where it pressed against my shoulder. My head set against it at an odd angle that pulled my neck askew, one side taut, one side bunched.

I'm unsure how long I drifted. The weight in me spread through my chest, winging out through my shoulders and filling every finger. Warm. Heavy. All but my eyes, which stared and stared, my lids open fast. I acquainted myself with the dark places under the bed. I teased out every shade of shadow until I saw a shape in them.

Was it a hand? No. A handle.

Finally, the fugue released me. My own hand slid through a welcoming path in the dust, closing around a hard cold stem. When I pulled it to me, I saw it was a hand mirror, its tarnished iron frame curling into whorls of fronds that hugged the glass itself. Every inch, a gap in the design left a hole just by the rim, small enough for me to fit my delicate fingers. Cold radiated up my arm from where I touched it, but it wasn't unpleasant. It was a welcoming cold, like a cool stream after a day's labor.

Turning the glass toward me, I saw it had clouded with neglect. No image of my face stared back at me, blurred or not. I took my sleeve up in my fingers and pressed it to the glass. A heavy sound of a door closing rang from downstairs.

Father. *Drunk*, I thought, and my heart raced.

I took myself away to my room, mirror and all. Every hurried step set in the center of Mother's route, not a scuff out of line. I had barely hid the mirror beneath my mattress before Father appeared in the door.

He watched me. I stood demurely and let him gaze.

"You're still in your funeral clothes," he said in a tone I could not place.

"Yes, Father," I answered.

"You're not uncomfortable?"

Was I not? Mother was dead. He had stolen my last weeks and months with her. If he had only let me see her—speak to her—before the end, I might know what to do now.

But it was his right. Stealing her, staring at me.

I bowed my head. "I'd be more comfortable in my normal clothes, of course. You're right, Father. I'll change now."

"Good. Black has never suited you." Before he left, he added, "Perhaps the blue dress. You look sweet in it."

FATHER GAVE ME scriptures to read. Among them were notes and studies from scholars far smarter than I, whose words were dense as bricks and snarled in my thoughts. He wanted me to read them all while he was away. Once, I tried to explain how heavy they made me, but he got angry and pushed me against a wall.

I promised to read very carefully. Perhaps if I memorized the failings of Eve and all the virtues of the dutiful daughters of Lot, I could speak them back and satisfy him.

Yet every time I tried, my eyes burned with the threat of tears and my breaths came fast and heavy. It only ceased when I took myself to the window seat and thought of Mother.

One afternoon, I allowed myself a break to pace around the room. My stiff legs tottered from wall to bare wall and prickled with the blood flow. As I stretched, considering the virtues of a trip to the outhouse, my gaze ran across the subtle rise in one corner of my mattress where the hand mirror hid.

The grime-covered glass smeared when I pulled it free, making horrors of my face when I peeked at it.

"Mother, did you not care for your things?" I asked and caressed its edges. Even in this hot room, the iron was cool to the touch. By some inexplicable urge, I pressed its back against my cheek and let it seep into me.

Memories of a cool damp cloth on a sick day. Gentle hands.

The corner of my bedcover sufficed to wipe the glass clean. It gleamed in the sunlight. Yet when I turned it to my face, I saw nothing but a bunch of brown threads. Threads like hair. Hair like stringy brown clumps that should have, if washed and brushed, fallen in waves. It filled the mirror frame to frame, exactly where my face should have been.

Confused, I turned from side to side. I held the mirror before me and spun, lifted and dropped it, searching for an angle at which I could see my face. Only the stringy hair. Perhaps it was not a mirror, but a painting on glass? I touched a finger to it, testing the texture. Smooth, with that cloying friction of glass against my fingertip and nothing like any of my paintings.

I noticed a turn in the image when I angled the mirror away from me. Was this some magic? The turning image might have been the back of my own head, though my hair was washed and loosely braided for comfort—nothing like this straggly mass. Breathing deep, I held my face steady as I moved the mirror in an arc to the side. My eyes pricked and strained with the effort of keeping it in my vision.

Brown hair, tangled and long, swept in a bunch over a thinly sloped shoulder.

The side of my face coming into my view past a curve of a cheek, the whites of my eyes meeting my own in the glass, the pale shape of a hand resting on my shoulder.

A face, a familiar face, watching me. I'd stretched my vision to its periphery, and this sidelong reflection depicted myself as I was, pale and panting, with another standing before me. In the mirror, Mother's face was so close to mine. Her nose hovered a hair's breadth from my nose, her bright hazel eyes set in a ring of wasted purple skin. I imagined the candy-sweet scent of her breath across my cheeks.

I choked. My hand shook. The mirror shook. Grief had driven me to madness, surely. The endless thoughts of Mother conjured her image in her old mirror, as close as I longed for. Yet the sight didn't comfort me; it was a stone in my belly that dragged me to the floor. And when her fingers curled slowly around my shoulders, I shattered into a scream and threw the mirror away so it slid beneath the bed.

FATHER HEARD MY scream. He rushed into my room with a thunderous glower and a voice that boomed off the walls. In my panting state, I couldn't understand him. His presence only scattered the remains of my thoughts to the wind, and I babbled. His hands dug into my arms as he hauled me from my corner-hiding-place. He shouted.

I sobbed, and I sobbed.

"She's just a young girl," the maid told him, but only once I had fallen silent, and he'd calmed and guided me back to the floor.

"Not you as well," he muttered. "Sickness. Hysteria. Not you."

"She's simply a child," the maid said, but quieter. "A girl mourning her mother."

His sharp tone made me flinch. "Old enough to be married. A woman!"

The maid said nothing else.

Soon, Father kneeled before me and scooped my hands in his. His devastating harshness bled down into soft whispers and a kind hand stroking through my hair. When I didn't raise my head, he tipped my chin up.

"I'm sorry. It's fear, you see, only fear. I see you and I see the same wildness that grew in your mother. It killed her. Please, listen to me and do what I say. I couldn't bear to lose you, too."

My throat was swollen, and my breaths sucked in like boots from mud. He must be hurting so, to lose control of himself this way. His words made no sense, but the fear and love within them were real. He could see I wasn't well. A well person didn't see ghosts in mirrors.

Fresh tears fell, but I didn't allow myself to fall apart. Father let me slip my arms around him in a desperate hug. He held me back, whispering how good I was, how he would be sure I was safe and healthy, how I should listen to him.

Within an hour, I was alone. All my trinkets and toys were gone, all my paints, easel, the floral perfumes and all my pens and journals. He left the fine dresses. He left the scriptures. Neither he nor the maid noticed the mirror tucked far under the bed, so he left that, too.

THE VISION OF my mother's face in the mirror haunted me so I couldn't sleep. When the first rays of light peeked shyly past the drapes, I abandoned hope and stood. Habit and the echo of Father's voice had me laying out the sheets and coverlet to perfection, though I felt sick and sluggish after the sleepless night.

I was curled on the window seat when my father entered. It nearly startled the texts from my hands, though they were heavy and didn't shift much. He was early—very early—before even the maid had started her day's toils. And when he laid eyes on me, a visible annoyance filled him from tense shoulders to clenched jaw.

This time, contained. Neither drunk nor driven to violence by my disposition, he stood in harrowing disapproval. His brow furrowed hard and mouth set in a line. With a deep breath, he controlled himself down to a low and even tone.

"You're awake."

"I am," I said hoarsely. "I couldn't sleep."

Clearly, this was the wrong thing to say. His displeasure magnified.

"Is that as far as you've made it in your reading?" he demanded. "In all this time?"

I opened my mouth to protest, to say it was my second time through these boring words. My head swum and spun, and I only spluttered out a few syllables with none of the care necessary to calm him.

"I should have seen it sooner. Your health is already declining. Tch." Then, a pause. His glower faltered, flickering between anger and affection and some other sharp, aching something so quickly I became dizzy. He only spoke again when I turned my gaze back to the floor.

"There is something wrong with you," he concluded. "Just like your mother."

When I looked back up, Father's eyes were those of a beast, focused and heartbroken and hungry.

"I will get you some medicine," he said. "So you can rest. Perhaps you can survive what she did not."

I READ AND read until the words seemed less like words and more like snapping mutts chasing each other across the page. Reading had never been a favorite pastime. I was much more inclined to amble through gardens, collecting new tableaus to commit to my paintings later. Now my limbs clamored to toss the scriptures clear across the room.

I didn't. I feared who would answer the noise.

Evening light filtered in, highlighting floating motes of dust in the peach rays of sunset. Lamenting my lack of paints, I stood and walked through them. I fruitlessly tried to dodge them all in my quest for the most picturesque view, which I might impress so hard in my memory I could paint it later.

Later. I would be better in time, of course. Father would see me better.

My gaze fell below the bed, to the inky black where the mirror still lay. Was my mother still in it? No—of course. I was ill, just like her. Father never mentioned her seeing things in mirrors, but I couldn't grasp any other explanation. If I wanted to get better, I should leave it where it was. I should give it to the maid to dispose of.

I sat again, pulling the heavy tomes into my lap. I stared at them for several minutes.

With a great breath, I stood again and made my way to the edge of the bed.

It wasn't hard to reach the mirror. I'd thrown it, but it was heavy iron and not prone to skidding far across rough wood. At first I feared the glass might be cracked, but when I turned it over, it was clear and clean.

Two sets of matching eyes gleamed back at me: my own and my mother's.

A tremor ran through my hand, but I clamped down before my grip could fail. My bunched muscles ached, and I heard the incessant thudding of my heart in my ears. *This is magic*, I thought. And then I thought, *I am truly mad.*

My mother's lips parted, purple limned in orange sunset light. I dropped the mirror away before she could say whatever she meant to say—whatever my mind conjured her to say. Even with a short glimpse, my chest felt ripped open and exposed to the world. Unquenchable joy mixed with the horror of her appearance: dead, bruised, pale, unwashed. But her eyes were so bright. They were the same bright eyes I would always love and crave.

I moved myself to the window seat and breathed carefully, deeply. All considerations of rational thought and Father's urgings played through my mind, but they felt distant now. What was rationality in the face of seeing her again?

Steeling myself, I gazed into the mirror for a third time.

There was Mother, seated behind me with her hand raised to cradle my head. If I stayed very still, I felt pressure like a hand against me. Her eyes were on me, not the mirror, with a tearful smile so full of bitter love, it twisted my heart again. Her grief echoed my grief. And for an endless moment, we shared this painful communion in silence.

"I'm so sorry," she murmured. "I loved you with all my heart."

"I loved you too," I answered between tears. "I still love you."

"Yes. As we always will," Mother said, weaving her fingers through my hair. I could only feel the ghost of it making my strands dance in a gentle wind.

She continued, "Take care, sweet, and do not drink the medicine. Stay up with me tonight, won't you? It's been weeks, months since we've spoken, and a mother needs her daughter."

Ignoring my heavy limbs and sagging eyelids, I nodded once. There was no other answer. There was no other conceivable choice.

SLEEP STILL ELUDED me; whenever I touched my perfectly folded sheets, a strange revulsion took hold of my stomach. Something deeper than heart and bone warned me away. So I paced, and I read, and I looked in the mirror. Whenever medicine came with my meals, I poured it directly in the chamber pot where it was masked by other sights and smells.

Father continued to visit early in the mornings, when the staff were still asleep. It upset him each time, though I was sure to be at the scriptures whenever I heard his boots approach the door. He looked at me like he could see through my secrets. Like he knew that I wasn't obeying, that the call of a ghost in a mirror had wrapped itself around me. He knew, didn't he? That I was allowing myself to slip deeper and deeper for the sake of grief. Closer to death. Further from him.

Guilt wracked me. He must have loved me very much to keep looking this in the eye.

On the third day, I sat by the window and watched him leave our home. It felt like a dream. Everything felt like a dream. His form wavered in my vision. To the side, I held the mirror up so I could see myself and Mother sitting together again, and she watched him as well with a vicious tension in her jaw. Her nails scraped against my skin as she played with my hair.

I could almost feel it.

The urge to call out to him filled me. I could open the window enough to shout, or perhaps even enough to throw the mirror. If he took it away, perhaps my mind would give me rest. Perhaps I could have peace. Sleep. This weight of my mother would be gone from me.

I gripped the window's handle.

"No," Mother commanded. A single word that thrummed through me like an earthquake.

I froze. By the time I could move again, he was too far to reach.

My hand eased from the handle and fell to my lap. My eyes sagged further in defeat, and a misty fugue rolled through me. Only then did Mother switch her grasp to both my shoulders, squeezing.

"Good. You may rest now, little thing. But not in bed. You may become too comfortable and sleep too deeply. Be sure you will wake. Be sure."

I chose the corner of the room next to the door, where boots and creaking hinges would wake me from my fitful slumber.

A WEEK OF long nights and stolen naps and flavorless meals that I barely ate. My dresses began to sag off my arms and hips. I could run a finger down the ridges of my shoulders, wondering if I followed bone or muscle. Some part of me wanted to gorge on every scrap of food brought to me, but when I tried, I couldn't swallow. It all tasted like curdled milk.

My father visited. Sometimes he scolded, and sometimes he held and hugged and stroked. He sometimes looked at me with an odd look, a wanting-hurting I didn't understand. Though I hid the mirror from him, I glimpsed Mother's reactions to him every so often: tense, piercing focus. Arms and hands frozen with vestigial violence.

I paced the room. I stared at the slice of the world visible from my window, memorizing it as clear white morning, yellow day, sunset orange and twilight blue. Though I tried to read, to open the gifts Father gave me, Mother always pulled me away.

I memorized the mirror instead.

The iron was so beautiful. My mother was so beautiful.

Whenever I set the mirror down, a tremendous weight dropped on me with a high screaming ring. I dissolved into a thoughtless panic. It only ended when I saw Mother, who comforted me with hugs and gentle murmurs and made me promise not to put her down again.

I paced, gazing at the mirror. I lay on the floor, gazing at Mother. I sat hunched, all but doubled over, looking in the glass, whispering to it. It whispered back sweet things in my mother's voice. Comforts. Her scent filled the air. When I shared my hopes of getting better someday and being free again, Mother glowered and snapped in her iron tone.

I stopped speaking of—or even thinking of—leaving the room.

TRACKS IN THE dust. Thin lines drawn by shuffling feet. A clean cocoon in my sleeping corner. A thin white blanket over an untouched desk. A mirror. My mother. Those bright hazel eyes. Gentle hands sliding across my hair and shoulders, holding me still.

Perfect sheets. Disgusting sheets. The bed, frozen, mocking me. Inviting me to its warmth, repelling me from its horror. Bile rising in my throat.

I could not sleep.

ONE DAY—I DIDN'T know which day—Father visited at an unusual time. I wasn't ready for the thumps of his boots or the turn of the key in the lock, my eyes fast with Mother's as she braided my mirror hair. By the time I returned to reality, he filled the wide open doorway, eyes blazing.

"Father," I started, breathless. But I didn't know how to continue.

He stared at the mirror, his shock holding him fast, even if just for the moment. His hands closed to fists. More anger built and bubbled, swelling him to a giant stature. Turning him into a monster. It felt like an age passed that way, and yet I had no time to act before he reached the point of eruption.

In the mirror, Mother said, "Don't let me go."

I gasped, and he was on me.

He shouted words I didn't understand, words that slid over my skin and down my throat, where I would have to digest them later. His large hands clawed and grasped at me, though each jolting tug was only a means to an end: the mirror. Clasping both my hands around it, I held fast. I screeched and fought him. He dragged me this way and that by our shared anchor, knocking me against the wall, the windowsill.

But I wouldn't be dislodged.

Until, finally, he landed a stunning blow against my cheek.

"Drop it! Let go of it, you stupid girl!" he raged. He lumbered over me to where I lay dazed. "You're mad, you're sick! This piece will only make it worse. It's twisting you into something horrid, don't you see?"

Somehow, I held on. Even with the throbbing in my face, even with the fear, the sight of the mirror still in my grasp sent a thrill through me. I laughed. How had I fought Father's strength? It didn't matter. Cradling the mirror close, I protected it with my curled body.

He had stolen everything else from me; he wouldn't take Mother.

A roar of fury rent the air. His weight dropped on me with suffocating heat and his hands gripped at my arms, my legs. His breath, sharp with drink, filled my nose and mouth. Even straining every muscle, I couldn't fight him as he pried me open.

"You'll see, whether you like it or not! I do this because I love you. You are my *daughter*."

I screamed. I begged.

He cracked me apart like a bone for marrow, his brute force overwhelming. There he was at the heart of me, and all my strength amounted to twitching muscles under heavy weights. Even my breath left me. Numbness crept cold up my limbs and formed a hollowness in my stomach. I was carved out, and he did the carving.

My last scrap of self clung to the cold metal. It was the only thing I had, even as he dragged it up and away from me. The glass flashed white in my eyes. I blinked and refocused to see Mother's pale hand reaching. Palm flat against the mirror, delicate fingers reaching through the gaps in the curling iron rim.

But that wasn't in the reflection. They were there, peeking out—real fingers. As if a hand lay against the back of the mirror, holding it tight. So tight it stopped moving; Father couldn't budge it. He hauled and heaved, but it remained locked where it was, suspended in the air.

"What?" Father looked between it and me, confusion hardening to fervent hate. Releasing the mirror, he drove both hands toward my throat. "Witch. You wi—"

The mirror swung and took my hand with it. It rammed against his skull with more force than I could ever have conjured on my own, sending him sprawling. As he lay there, stunned and groaning, the mirror dragged my numb form up. To my knees, to my feet. The iron fused with my skin. My hand extended upward at an angle that shot pain in bright lances down my back.

"Mother," I whimpered, not knowing what I begged for. "Mother."

I couldn't feel anything but her. The weight of her rage had replaced the weight of Father's, equally terrifying. She didn't answer me, only dragged me along to where Father fumbled at the foot of my bed. The mirror swung again and again. It swung me, or I swung it—I didn't know anymore. And only when Father lay still did the mirror clatter to the floorboards.

I stood there, unmoving. For how long? How could I tell?

The maid screamed when she found us.

WHEN THE POLICE arrived, they gathered around me cautiously at first. Then, when they understood I would do nothing and react to no one, they ushered me to another room, to a place that lacked the musty scent of dust and glowed in bright lantern light. They gave me water and a blanket, and I obediently drank.

Finally, a man sat with me and asked me questions. What happened? Why was the room in that condition? Who killed your father?

"I couldn't sleep," I said with a shuddering breath. It was the only thing I could say. "I couldn't sleep."

COLD COMPANY

Miranda Allen

THE CHEERFUL SONGS of birds split through the hazy darkness of sleep to drag Mia into the waking world. The cold sank down to her bones, a deep chill gnawing at her core. She'd fallen asleep in the cemetery again.

The old alcohol taste in her mouth left her tongue dry and vile. Her head didn't hurt as much as she expected. Her stomach didn't roll with the need to purge whatever she'd filled it with the previous night. She was there, alive. How disappointing.

"Every night, a little death you taunt me with," she whispered. "Every morning, your cruel reminder that I am alone." Her hand slid longingly over the grave marker. Pale marble with clean perfect lines, beautiful and pristine and mocking.

ERIN WERNER
Beloved Wife and Daughter

In her head, Mia could see the teasing smile on those lovely lips, reminding her she had no right to complain. Erin was the one who'd suffered. Her hair, like gold, had looked black from all the blood.

The world stumbled. Or maybe she did. A sharp pain ignited briefly in her chest, and then it was gone, and the world went still.

"Fuck, I really screwed myself up last night."

She gazed again at the headstone, too dehydrated to cry.

"Haunt me. Haunt me, and I'll be grateful for it," Mia begged. She needed to go home, to get warm, to clean up. She probably looked like a disaster, but still her eyes lingered on the grave. "Please?"

Erin never responded, though Mia imagined her walking along the road ahead. Ever leading her on, never letting her catch up. Mia turned away as the chill gnawed at her, and she followed the phantom she wished was there.

The walk wasn't long. The house she'd bought with the settlement money was only a few blocks from the cemetery—a choice her mother had heavily criticized. It wasn't her money, though; it was Erin's. Mia needed to buy a house close to Erin.

"Jesus, Mia, did you sleep out there again?" Tom asked from the neighboring porch as she stumbled by. He stood in his bathrobe and slippers, coffee in hand. Despite Mia's worst attempts at being neighborly, Tom had always been very nice. It was likely out of pity. They might have made friends, been barbecue buddies, if Mia had been even remotely interested in socializing.

Well, that, and she'd sort of made things awkward after puking on his really nice lawn less than a month after moving in.

"Yes," Mia mumbled.

He sighed and shook his head. It'd been a year. He knew better now than to say anything more about her bad nights. "Want me to bring you some coffee?"

"Nah, I'm going to jump straight into the shower. Thanks, though." She should have liked a person like Tom. He was considerate, had a good head on his shoulders, little bit of a nerd but all green flags. In another life, she and Erin would have had him over for dinner every weekend and spent their time trying to set him up with their friends. In another life, she would have loved sitting on her porch and being so *suburban*, commiserating with him about the lady down the street who let her dog poop in everyone else's yard and the garbage truck that always knocked cans over. Instead, she avoided meeting his eyes as she passed him on her walk of shame, crossing her own overgrown dandelion-filled lawn to get home.

The porch swing swayed lightly in the breeze. Erin smiled back at her, laughing, a sparkle in her eyes. In another life, Erin would have loved that swing. It'd come with the house Mia bought with the money she only had because Erin was gone.

She hadn't locked the door when she stumbled out last night to go yell at Erin's tombstone. When she was drunk, she could let herself be angry: angry at Erin for abandoning her, angry at Erin for being too good for this world and getting herself killed, angry at Erin for not letting them die together. Anger was a balm.

When she was sober, all she felt was guilt.

A horn honked, distant, probably a street over, but the sound still made Mia's heart pound, and she clung to the doorknob, frozen.

Headlights streaking through the dark, a horn blaring, the wind knocked from her lungs…

She gasped like she hadn't taken a breath in ages.

Mia had insisted they were too drunk to drive after their monthly date night. Mia had insisted they walk home. Mia had been too impatient to wait for a ride service. The driver had been drunk too, or so the cops later told her. Mia hadn't even seen him coming, but Erin had. Erin had shoved her out of the way. The driver died instantly when he hit the large electrical box on the corner.

Erin wasn't so lucky.

Mia shook her head and leaned on the door, taking a few steadying breaths before pushing it open and quickly locking herself in the darkened interior of the house.

"You should have let me die you, stupid bitch."

She let her clothes lie wherever they might fall on the way to the bathroom. It wasn't like she ever got visitors. The frigid feeling in her bones would not leave her. She just wanted a hot shower and to wash the horrid taste from her mouth.

She left the shower to heat up while she grabbed the mouthwash. Her tongue must've still been numb from the vodka she'd been drinking, because she didn't even notice the minty burn. Her mouth still tasted ashy and sour. She spit the mouthwash into the sink and watched the blue swirl down the drain, eyed the toothbrush, and decided that was too much effort.

The bathroom mirror had its own dim lights, so she didn't bother to turn on the overhead light. The softer yellow glow was soothing for the mild headache (that, really, felt like it should have been worse), but it cast tall, long shadows in the room. She avoided looking at herself in that mirror, knowing she'd be an absolute wreck. Instead, she turned and watched her silhouette on the wall.

For a moment, the shadow wavered. Mia's chest felt wrong again. A creeping, frozen cold clung to her, squeezing. The shadow flickered a little, though the lights behind her were steady. She forced a deep breath and rubbed her eyes, pinching the bridge of her nose.

"I'm fucking tired of this."

As she moved toward the shower, she eyed the shadow while it slowly divided in two. That cold creeping through her chest solidified. Breathing around it felt unnatural. The second shadow cast was hazier, not as clear as the first.

A trick of the light. Must have been.

Still, her gaze lingered. Her heart rate picked up. She felt unusually aware of it beating in her chest.

When they'd first started dating, Erin had loved to sneak up on her, grab her hips and plant kisses on her spine. Erin had been so much shorter than her, but she loved to be the big spoon, cuddling her from behind.

"You're so warm, I just wanna soak you up," Erin's memory said.

Mia lifted her arm, watching her shadow do the same, expecting the second shadow to do so as well. Funny, she couldn't see the second shadow's arm reach. It almost, *almost* looked like it had moved differently, its edges blurring a little more.

It was almost like it was looking back at her.

If she squinted, it was almost like she wasn't alone. It was almost like Erin was right there, about to give her a hug and tell her it would all be okay in between kisses down her back.

When had she started holding her breath?

The shade darkened. It seemed to loom larger, closer. She watched as its arm slowly lifted and reached out, about to touch her shadow, about to touch *her*.

Was she still holding her breath?

Mia stepped to the side and flicked on the overhead bathroom light as an unfamiliar fear permeated her.

"I'm still drunk."

She looked at the wall, now illuminated from above and blissfully free of any shadows at all.

The now steaming shower looked inviting, though the room felt no warmer. She stepped in and diligently began to scrub all evidence of her binge from her body. Dirt and grass stains on her hands, knees, and elbows. She gargled to, again, try to get the flavor from her mouth. She cranked the temperature but couldn't get the water hot enough, irritated that the water heater was probably going out. The demands of home ownership kept building up.

"You would have known how to fix it, wouldn't you, Erin?"

She couldn't chase the chill away even as the steaming water turned her skin pink.

"Maybe I'm the problem," she muttered as she turned the shower off and got out. Her eyes looked past the fogged mirror, afraid of what she'd see in it.

She draped a towel over her shoulders to catch the water from her hair as she strode down the hall to the bedroom. Only a small desk lamp illuminated the room while she dug in her dresser for a pair of oversized flannel pajamas and thermal shirt. She preferred tank-tops and boxers, but it didn't feel warm enough today, so she dug into the winter clothes.

As she pulled the shirt over her still wet head and tossed the towel on the floor, she thought she caught a flicker of movement from the wall. She turned and her heart rate leaped again.

Just her own shadow.

Cold crawled up her arms, and a tightness gripped her chest, expanding slowly, crawling down her veins like new frost. The edges of the room seemed to darken. It was just a shadow. Still, Mia's heart pounded like she was standing face to face with a mountain lion. She wanted to run. She wanted to scream or throw something. Why did she want to flee so badly?

"What the fuck, I'm literally afraid of my own shadow now? I really need to quit drinking." Mia groaned, tearing her gaze away.

Everything in her told her to look back, to not let the threat out of her sight.

She walked to the door, each step feeling forced.

It's nothing.

Mia leaned down to turn off the desk light and glanced back at the wall.

The ice exploded through her, and she stopped breathing.

There, against the wall, exactly where it had been before, was the shadow, its edges darker, more defined. It had not moved. It hadn't changed at all.

Mia glanced rapidly down at the light, then back to the shadow, checking it and her sanity. The light was between them now; she couldn't possibly be casting that shadow.

Nothing was casting that shadow.

She stared at it, a ragged breath yanking into her deprived lungs, followed by short breaths as she fought the rising panic. Mia's hand on the lamp trembled. If she turned off the light, the room would be engulfed in darkness. What happened to shadows in the dark? Did they vanish? Or did the darkness only give them room to expand?

She left the lamp on and pulled the door shut, scrambling backward to the living room and throwing on every light switch along the way. Then she ran to the curtains and threw them open wide to let in the sun. Light filled her living room. Warm, clear sunshine illuminated the messy couch covered in laundry and the coffee table decorated in old takeout containers. No unnatural shadows anywhere.

"This isn't real. I'm still drunk. Did I…did I hit my head? Shit, am I actually going insane?"

She took slow breaths, in and out, forcing each one through frozen lungs. Her eyes darted to the well-lit hall and the bedroom door. Nothing.

Mia cautiously went into the kitchen. Still nothing. The fear receded as she convinced herself that it wasn't real.

"I'm hallucinating. I… I have a problem, and I'm hallucinating."

Clumsy fingers dropped a pod into the coffee machine. Her phone still sat where it had been charging all night next to the two open bottles of vodka and the remains of last night's drinks. Mia grabbed it and began searching the internet. Were hallucinations a normal part of alcohol poisoning? The resounding answer was, yes, it could happen, but it wasn't exactly common. The search engine kept telling her *help is available.*

She glanced at the bottles on the counter. "Fuck, maybe I do need help." She opened her contacts and scrolled, stopping at the therapist her mother had referred her to. Payments for the texting plan came out of her account every month, though she never used it. The option to message if in crisis and regular check-ins were available to her, but she never used either.

Mia

Hi, it's been a while, but I think I need help.

Mia typed it out, staring at the send button but not hitting it. She didn't want to talk to someone. She didn't want them to tell her it would all be okay. She didn't want it to all be okay.

She wanted Erin.

Erin's memory smiled at her from the light by the window where she stood holding her favorite coffee cup, hair caught in some breeze that wasn't there.

Mia bit her lip and shook the tears from her eyes.

"Why couldn't you just be here? Why'd you have to save me?"

The sound of her coffee maker sputtering as it spat the last of her coffee into the cup caused her to set the phone down without hitting send. She dumped a pack of sugar-free sweetener in the cup and moved to the fridge for the creamer. Mia liked her coffee sweet and mostly dairy. Erin drank hers black.

As she turned, she caught it from the corner of her eye. There, in the living room, cast on the far wall, just next to the hall, was the shadow.

"*Fuck*," she gasped in a barely audible whisper. "Fuck, fuck, fuck. What are you?"

The creamer fell forgotten to the floor. Mia staggered back against the counter, grabbing for a kitchen knife and thrusting it out in front of her.

The shadow did not move. It did not follow. It was just…there.

She stared at it. It existed against that wall doing nothing.

It was so hard to breathe. The hairs on her arm stood straight up, and her teeth started to chatter. She let out a sob as her arm finally fell to her side, and tears welled in her eyes.

"What *are* you? What do you want from me?"

Tears flowing freely, she sank to the floor, losing sight. She blinked and rubbed her eyes. When her vision cleared, she yelped and lifted the knife again.

Cast across the lower cabinet where she kept pots and pans…was the shadow, sitting like she was, a silhouette from which she could discern no details. A humanoid shape lacking definition or dimension. Mirroring her position, yet not cast by her. The harder she looked, the less clear its edges became, and the more her vision tunneled.

She felt like prey, like something about to be eaten. The longer she stared at it, the colder she got. The sour alcohol from her binge drinking the night before surfaced. She could still feel the wet grass felt under her hands, the cold marble of the grave marker pressed to her face.

That was how she had woken up, and the chill still hadn't lifted.

The shadow loomed larger, darker, though its dimensions hadn't changed at all. Slowly, definitively in a way no shadow could possibly do, it tipped its head to the side all on its own.

Mia swallowed.

"Fuck this, fuck you. I'm not going out like this."

She pushed herself to her feet, ready to stab the cabinet if she had to.

But, in the space of a blink, the shadow was gone again.

She looked frantically around the room but saw nothing. The sun continued to shine outside. The lights in all the rooms continued to illuminate her home. She was alone.

The unease lingered as Mia walked around the living room and even boldly went down the hall to her bedroom and the bathroom, still finding nothing. Her unease didn't settle as suddenly as the vision had, though with every passing moment, Mia was more convinced that she had imagined it.

"Honestly, Mia, a fucking shadow? You're out of your damned mind."

She grabbed the rest of the vodka and tossed it into the bin, then started picking up laundry and trash.

"This is it. This is your wake-up call. Get your life together, Mia. You can't mourn the dead forever, and you're clearly doing brain damage at this point."

She eyed the phone, the screen still open to the unsent text to her therapist. A few quick taps deleted the message. She'd be fine.

Mia spent the rest of the day cleaning the house. There were three entire bags of trash in the now overfull can and she was considering what to do with the fourth in her hand.

Tom was out front again, meticulously picking every weed out of his golf course-like-lawn with some special tool just for pulling weeds.

"You doing some housekeeping?" His voice was lightly skeptical, though still friendly.

Mia sighed as she gave up on pushing the bag down into her overburdened can. "Ya know, I might have finally fucked up hard enough to think I need to make some life changes."

His look of surprise was justified. He'd seen a lot of shit from her since she moved in. "That's, I mean, that's great, Mia. I…" A little too obvious a hesitation. They weren't friends, really; loose acquaintances, but Tom was a decent guy. "Are you…are you okay?"

Mia smiled slightly. "I think I might have had way too much last night, Tom. Enough that I scared myself this morning with how messed up I've been."

His awkward attempt to be nice shifted to concern. "Shit, really? Do you need anything? Should I call someone?"

She shook her head. "Nah, I'm okay. Or at least, I think I might be okay. With time."

Tom nodded. "Just let me know if I can help."

"Will do." She headed back into the house as Tom went back to his assault on dandelions.

She lingered on the porch, staring at the swing. Erin's memory tugged at her. A pretty smile as she'd read a book, the little snort when she giggled. Mia swallowed hard as a lump formed in her throat. What was she playing at? She'd never be able to get her shit together because Erin wasn't there. Erin was her reason. Without her, what was the point?

Back inside, she wandered from room to room. Cleaning made it feel emptier. She'd never hung pictures on the walls, because Erin was in all of them and reminders of when they were happy hurt too much.

"Haunt me, I'll be grateful for your company," Mia whispered to the room. "Haunt me or let me join you."

Her gaze shifted to the sky out the window, just beginning to go deeper blue as the sun set.

A horrifying, beautiful, wretched thought occurred to her.

She wandered back to the bedroom. The table lamp was still on, though there were no unnatural shadows now. She crossed in front of the lamp, casting her own shadow onto the blank wall, and walked toward it. Her shadow sharpened as she got closer until she stood just in front of it.

"Are you here somewhere?" she called softly as the chill she hadn't been able to shake today bloomed again across her senses like a strange caress.

There was no answer, of course, just a shadow on the wall. A different kind of fear started low in her gut. Not the new, primal fear she'd felt when she saw the shadow, but something achingly familiar. The fear of loneliness and longing.

"Erin?" she said quietly. "Erin, is it you?"

She waited, and waited. The sky grew darker and her own silhouette more pronounced as the little desk lamp became the only light source.

Nothing answered. The shadows didn't move in any unnatural way. She didn't feel anything. She was alone in her own room. Somehow that hurt more.

"I'm such an idiot. You aren't here. You're dead and it's my fault and I don't deserve to be here. I don't want to be here anymore!" She spun to leave the room but stilled at a feather soft touch at her hips, cold.

It wasn't the almost ticklish squeeze of affection she remembered as Erin would grab her and plant kisses on her spine between the shoulders. It was soft, almost intangible. More like a very targeted breeze than anyone actually touching her, right at the curve of her hips, just below her natural waist. Against her back, it almost felt like breath, only too cold.

Fear like she had never known permeated her body. Each joint locked up, stiff with an ache she could not fight. Her breath was too heavy in her lungs. A cold that burned ran through her veins, numbing her to all but the oppressive fear that ruled her in that moment. Yet through the pain, her heart screamed hope.

"Erin?" Mia whispered through a sob. "Gods, Erin, is that really you?" She squashed the wild terror in her chest and dropped a hand behind her, feeling for something, anything.

The impossible touch of the shadow crept up her arms. It lacked the strength to move her but seemed to urge her backward.

"Baby, I'm so sorry. I'm sorry you died. I'm sorry I didn't. I'm so sorry I said we should walk home. It's my fault. It's all my fault." She sobbed even as her hand found the wall she was backed into. The bitter touch fluttered over her arm and at the nape of her neck, so close to memories of Erin, so close, but not quite.

She could see it all in her head again. The car had hit Erin across her lower body as she shoved Mia out of the way. The force had dragged her, but she ended up sprawled in the street. Mia hadn't even been able to hold her. She had crawled over to where Erin lay crying.

"Mia," Erin had gasped.

Mia had wanted to help, but there was no helping. Erin's skull was the wrong shape, and things were missing below her waist. There was so much blood.

"I'm so sorry. Baby, I love you. Please, don't leave me. I'm so sorry."

"Mia, open your eyes," Erin begged.

"It was my fault." That soft breeze became a little stronger, more tangible. She wanted to be with Erin again. She wanted to hold her for just a few more minutes in this memory. "Erin, please. Just don't leave me alone."

The image of Erin's face as the light faded from her eyes was burned into Mia's memories.

"Mia, please. Love, I need you to open your eyes."

Mia hesitated. The touch behind her felt more firm, almost real, and so much colder. Erin hadn't asked her to look. Erin had been in too much pain; she'd been fuzzy with blood loss and trauma. She hadn't understood what was happening.

"Mia, open your eyes!" Erin shouted.

Erin's last words had been confused nonsense. Unintelligible syllables uttered by a damaged brain. The doctors said she likely hadn't been aware enough to feel the pain.

The grip on Mia's arms turned solid, freezing to the point of burning.

"Mia! Look out!" Erin screamed as she shoved Mia forward.

Wait. That was the wrong order, she'd said that first.

Mia's eyes flew open as she lurched away from the wall and spun to look, Erin's scream echoing in her head and mingling with her own.

Pulling itself from the wall was a dark, nearly humanoid shape, half shadow, half indescribable horror. It writhed in a soundless scream, reaching for her with half-formed arms of swirling darkness. She glanced at her arms, realizing they hurt. Her skin was bruised and throbbed everywhere the shade had touched, like frost-burn.

The thing was caught between being a shadow cast upon the wall and being real. Above the waist, it was a horrid darkness, reaching out for her with monstrous hands. At the waist, it was stuck to the wall, and everything below was just a shadow, flat and intangible. It was a horrifying half-thing, there and not there, real and not real. It reached out with one semi-formed hand and dragged its two-dimensional form across the floor toward her.

As it pulled itself closer, reaching out with hideous malformed limbs, Mia scrambled backward. The lamp shattered as she crashed into the nightstand before she turned to sprint down the hall. She looked back in time to see the thing shut the light off in the hall as Mia burst into the living room. Suddenly it was there at the edge of the light. It moved faster in the dark.

What happens to shadows in the dark?

She sprinted out the front door as it reached for the living room switch. The last remnants of light from the sun were fading, but the streetlights had kicked on and they couldn't just be turned off.

The shade appeared in her doorway, dragging itself toward the long shadows cast by the streetlights.

Mia ran for Tom's house, his garage motion lights kicked on, bathing the area in an ultra-bright spotlight. Mia stopped in the spotlight, panting, watching the thing seethe and writhe in the shadows of the dimmer streetlight, still edging closer.

"Mia?" Tom stepped onto his porch with a look of confusion.

"Tom! I…" She hesitated, not sure what to say. How was she supposed to explain whatever this was?

He squinted, and his gaze drifted past her.

"What the hell is *that?*"

Even as he said it, the timer on the garage spotlight clicked over, and the lights went out.

Oppressive cold wrapped around Mia's arm in the shape of a hand. Fingers bit into her; she could almost hear her skin pop and sizzle. It had her. The pain spread, crawling up her elbow and down her fingers.

She couldn't breathe. A solid smooth surface against her cheek. The grass, sharp and itching. It smelled of old flowers and sick.

There were headlights and a horn.

The garage light kicked back on, and Tom was there, his metal weed pulling stick in hand, and he swung it like a bat at the shade. It hit the creature then pulled through it, like fighting water or smoke, but heavier. The shade recoiled, releasing her.

Tom grabbed her other wrist and dragged her into the house, slamming the door behind him.

"What the hell?"

Mia panted in pain and held her arm to her chest. It was real. It wasn't a dream or a hallucination or a nightmare. This thing was real. A panicked little laugh escaped her, and she had trouble stifling it.

"Why are you laughing? What's going on?!" Tom yelled with an understandable amount of fear and exasperation.

"Until you hit that thing, I thought I was having a psychotic break." Mia sighed. "I am, actually, exceedingly happy you could see it."

After a brief consideration, he laughed nervously too. "That's fair. I did see it, but what *is* it?"

Mia looked at her arm and the imprint of a blackened handprint with veins of darkness bleeding off of it. It didn't hurt anymore. She couldn't feel it at all. "Well, this morning it was a shadow that could move on its own. Now, I have no idea. I thought I was drinking too much and hallucinating until it tried to get me, or whatever it was doing."

"You do drink too much, but you're not hallucinating." He disappeared into his office and returned with a long white stick with a metal handle.

Mia did a double-take. "You can't be serious."

He shrugged. "You said it was a shadow and how many chances am I going to get to actually use this thing?"

"Isn't that just a prop?" Mia asked skeptically.

Tom smirked. "Hey, I'm a grown man with adult money." He pressed a button, and the white tube began to glow with a whooshing laser sound. "And this is the combat ready model made for dueling."

She wanted to call him a nerd but didn't. He'd been a decent guy to her. He'd been a decent neighbor. She didn't have any right to tease him. She'd been a shitty neighbor, and he was still helping her.

The front door rattled loudly.

"Fuck."

Tom held his lightsaber in front of him. "Can it get in?"

"I don't know, I really don't know." She glanced around for a weapon, grabbing a flashlight hanging on a hook by the door next to a couple of coats. She looked at the door as it shook, then over at Tom.

He was in danger because of her. This sweet guy who deserved a hot partner and a gaggle of kids was here trying to help her fight off literal darkness just because he was unlucky enough to be nice to her. He didn't deserve this. She should just go; it wasn't after him.

As if in answer to her fears, the shadows beneath the door seemed to grow longer. From them, the semi-tangible parts of the shade's upper body peeled upward, reaching for her.

Before it could fully form, Tom swung his lightsaber at it. Shockingly, it hit fully, knocking the thing to the side. That surprised Tom, too, but he pulled back and swung again.

"The garage! Get in my truck!"

He urged her down the hall and hit the shadow one more time before turning to follow. They sprinted into the garage, illuminated by overhead fluorescent bulbs. The shadow followed with its inhuman shrieks, flailing limbs knocking over furniture in an enraged pursuit.

"I think your glowstick pissed it off, Tom," Mia yelled as she jumped into the truck and hit the button for his garage door.

Tom jumped in right behind her. "I literally fought the darkness with a lightsaber, Mia, don't take this moment from me." He slammed on the gas. They tore out of the garage just as the shade appeared in the doorway.

They drove a few moments in silence, searching the night for moving shadows.

Tom sighed deeply. "Where are we going?"

Mia had no idea. Her thoughts swam with how to keep it away. Bright areas like the mall or a grocery store where others could see it? The police? A hospital? Drive until dawn?

Headlights and a horn, but it was just another car passing by.

Cold marble and grass.

Her thoughts returned to the moment in her room. She'd been pushed away from that thing. *Erin* had pushed her away from it.

"Go to the cemetery."

"Is…is this like a hallowed ground thing?" Tom asked with way more seriousness than should have been possible in this situation.

Mia shook her head. "How much of a nerd are you?"

"I am a tremendous nerd. I invited you to my Galactic Barbeque in May. How have you not figured that out?" He actually sounded annoyed, or possibly nervous, as he turned to head to the cemetery. It wasn't far.

"I never showed up. I'm sort of a shitty neighbor, aren't I?" She saw the edge of the cemetery come into view.

"Not a shitty neighbor, except for that time you puked on my lawn. That was foul." He laughed, but it sounded uncomfortable. "And the jury is out on that time you brought a shadow monster over. I'm literally next door though, if you wanted a fucking friend in this neighborhood. I'm mean, I have to be better than Karen, right?"

"Why are you so nice to me?" she asked as they pulled into the dark graveyard.

"Well, at first I thought I had a chance. Not a lot of single homeowners our age." His face fell as he took the slow, careful turns through the graveyard. "Don't worry, it took about ten seconds to figure out that wasn't going to happen." He frowned, shot a sideways glance at her for a second, then looked back at the narrow paths. "About a month after you moved in, I saw your mom at the house. You weren't home but…has anyone ever told you your mom is really nosey?"

Mia had an idea of how that conversation had gone. "How humiliated should I be?"

"It wasn't that bad, but she did let me know about your wife. She gave me her number and wanted me to call her if…" he trailed off.

"If what, Tom?" Mia demanded.

"Your mom was worried you'd hurt yourself," he said quietly. "She just wanted me to call if I noticed anything or thought you needed real help."

Of course her mother meddled. Mia'd never had to have that conversation with Tom, so maybe it wasn't so bad. Still, it wasn't great.

Mia pointed down one of the paths. "Go that way. Park in the little lot over there."

They pulled into the guest lot closest to Erin's grave.

"Did you ever call her?"

He parked and met her gaze for a long silent moment, the car still running. "No, but I probably should have a few times."

The honesty should have hurt, but he was still sugar-coating it. He should have called a bunch of times.

"You're not wrong." She looked out at the cemetery. Maybe this wasn't a good idea. "Why didn't you?"

"You always recovered before I could figure out if I was crossing lines." He looked away, uncomfortable, as though he'd failed at something that was never his responsibility. "What are we doing here?"

Mia searched the darkness for any signs of the shade but saw nothing. "I need to get to Erin. I think she's trying to help."

Tom's eyes snapped to her like she'd just sprouted an extra head. "Seriously?"

Mia bit her lip and turned the flashlight on. "Yeah."

"Alright." He adjusted his grip on the lightsaber. "Let's do this."

They left the truck's headlights on and walked in the beams, carefully inching towards Erin's tombstone. Tom kept the lightsaber held up like a lantern. Fear crept in, pervasive and aching. The closer they got, the more it sank into Mia's bones. The air felt like it weighed too much again. She had to force it into her lungs. Her vision narrowed to the place where she knew Erin's pale marble headstone was.

A shape came into view—a dark form motionless upon the ground.

Lying across the tombstone was a body.

Tom stopped walking, eyes wide and disbelieving. "Mia?"

There was no air. The cold crushed in on her. Mia's vision narrowed to only the body on the tombstone. She wanted to scream, but it came out as barely a breath.

There it was, clawing toward her at the edge of the light.

Tom swung at the monster, knocking it back into the dark. "Mia?" He was there, holding it off, eyes questioning. He didn't understand, but he was there anyway, protecting her even though he had no obligation to do so.

Mia should have helped him; she should have fought back, but she couldn't. She couldn't look away from the body on the ground.

She stared at it.

She stared at herself.

Mia sank to her knees beside her body, still reeking of alcohol. It had been here all day. No one had noticed her curled up beside Erin's grave. No one had cared.

"Mia?" Tom huffed as he beat the thing back into the darkness. "Mia, talk to me!"

There was nothing she could say. She reached out and touched her own skin, expecting cold.

But it was warm, the first real warmth she'd felt all day.

Time stopped.

Tom froze, lightsaber pulled back like a baseball bat. The shadow monster looked as though it was recoiling from him and the light. It was like someone had pressed pause on the tv.

"Hello, love." A quiet voice right in front of her, but she couldn't see it through the blur of tears.

Mia squinted and blinked her vision clear. Erin sat there on the grass beside her.

"Erin?"

"You really screwed this one up," Erin laughed.

Mia's tears poured. She was here, really here.

"What's happening? Am I dead?"

Erin reached out and touched her cheek, a cold touch, so cold. "Not yet. You do know I was joking when I said you were hopeless without me, right?"

"I don't understand." Mia immediately lifted her own hand to cover Erin's, to hold it there. She didn't care that the cold burned, that it felt like her skin was sizzling. It was *Erin*.

"Remember that time you screwed up our flight reservations, and we ended up stuck in Hawaii for a few extra days on our first anniversary?" Erin smiled. "We called it our bonus vacation."

"You were mad 'cause you hadn't taken the extra time off work, and it was really expensive to get the extra night's stay on the island." Mia laughed. "I loved it, and you hated it."

"This is a little like that," Erin said, leaning in to rest her forehead against Mia's. The cold burned there too. "You missed your death and took an extra day. You're not alive, but you're not dead either."

"But I was there today. I cleaned," Mia whispered.

"You didn't eat. You didn't drink. You didn't sleep. You're neither hungry, nor tired, nor thirsty. You only breathe when you remember to. You're dead, but you didn't remember dying, so you just kept living." Erin's face was a sad kind of happy, a contradiction. "It's a very you sort of screw up."

"Then what do I do?" Mia asked, wanting only for Erin to never leave her side. "Can I go with you?"

"You could, but," Erin pulled her hand away, "I want you to stay here, love. You have a second chance."

Mia's tears blurred her vision again. "But what about us?"

"I love you, Mia. I will always love you, but I can wait."

"What about the monster?" Mia asked, looking at the frozen image of Tom and the shade.

Erin continued to pull away. "That is your death. It's waiting to claim you, and it will always be there."

"Always?" Mia was horrified. "I can't live running from it."

"You don't have to. It's not evil, Mia. It's chasing you because you want to die." Her eyes became so sad then. "It scares you because you're afraid to die. It only tried to take you when you started to feel guilty about me, when you lost your will to live." She frowned deeper. "I need you to let go of that, Mia. It wasn't your fault. It was an accident. I made a choice and none of that was on you."

Mia sobbed. "I don't want to leave you."

Erin kissed her, a small, loving, frigid goodbye kiss. "I know, but I want you to go, for me, for us. I died for you, my choice, because I love you and I want you to live. I need you to do that, okay? I need you to want to live, talk to our friends, talk to Mom, make friends with that sweet, well-intentioned nerd. Make other new friends. Live your life, and when you've lived it all the way and you're done, you won't be scared anymore."

"But I don't want to be alone," Mia cried.

"You aren't. You never have been." Erin stood and moved away, gently stepping around Tom.

"Wait, not yet!" Mia tried to get up but couldn't. She felt herself being pulled sideways.

"We're out of time." Erin then sank into the shadows, her form going fuzzy, then dark, then the thing that'd been chasing Mia blurred. "I'm always with you."

For a moment there was only Erin, then a shadow, and then both were gone, and everything went dark.

Mia dragged in an agonizing, ragged breath as she realized she was lying on the grass. Her muscles screamed at her as she tried picking herself up off the ground. Her mouth tasted of day-old alcohol, her body hurt worse than she could recall it ever hurting, and her stomach actively rolled. She heaved, but there was nothing in her stomach to throw up.

Tom swung at air where the shade had been. "Mia?" He looked around, confused. "What…what just happened?"

Mia wobbled, and he rushed over to help her stand. "This is hard to explain, but can you take me to a hospital? I think I might be mostly dead right now."

He looked at her then, really seriously *looked*, and there was something haunted in his gaze. "Jesus, you do look like shit. Let's get you to the car."

Mia leaned on him heavily, feeling feverish and chilled at the same time. Everything hurt.

"Maybe, when we get there, just tell them you found me here. You know how I am on my benders and because of what my mom said, you came to check."

"You wouldn't know that I'd talked to your mom if the last day hadn't happened." He pulled her arm over his shoulder and started walking toward the car.

"Yeah, I know." Her vision swam, and she swallowed the urge to heave again.

"You *have* been here the whole time, haven't you? You're still in the clothes from this morning, but you'd changed."

"It's true. I wonder if my thermal is still in the dresser at home. Shit, was all that cleaning undone?" Was there even a way to make sense of the last day?

"I'm not going to be able to explain this, am I?" Tom looked a little pale.

"No. Might be best not to think too hard on it." She squeezed his shoulder and pulled away, slumping against the truck for a minute to take a few deep breaths. "But thanks for being here."

He smiled tightly. "I guess nobody will believe me when I say I fought the darkness with this thing." He showed his lightsaber as he shoved it into the truck.

"I'll know," Mia reassured as she climbed into the passenger seat. "I promise not to puke in your truck, but can you roll the window down?"

There was a touch of horror in his eyes as he slammed the button to bring the window down. "Don't you dare, Mia. I'll make you ride in the back."

She leaned out the window a little and felt the cool night air on her face as he drove. The smell of streets and cars hit her. The smell of everything. She hadn't noticed how dull her senses had been over the last day.

"Hey, can you call my mom after you get me to the hospital, like she wanted you to?"

His face registered surprise, but then settled into a smile. "Yeah, yeah, I can call her."

THREE DAYS, FOUR different doctors, and so many tests later, the hospital cleared Mia to go home. Weekly appointments with her therapist were prescheduled. Her mom was going to check on her daily for a while. Tom had put a bouquet of recovery snacks on her kitchen counter with a get-well card. He'd also taken it upon himself to groom her poorly maintained lawn. It didn't look as good as his, but he'd mowed it and ripped out every dandelion and filled the holes with some sort of seed patch.

The shade had been there the entire time at the hospital, and it was there now in her home, its hazy outline never very distinct, but Mia could tell it was always watching her. It would always be there, waiting.

"Not today." Mia raised her coffee toward the shadow across the room with a slight nod of acknowledgment before heading out the door.

She was grateful for the company.

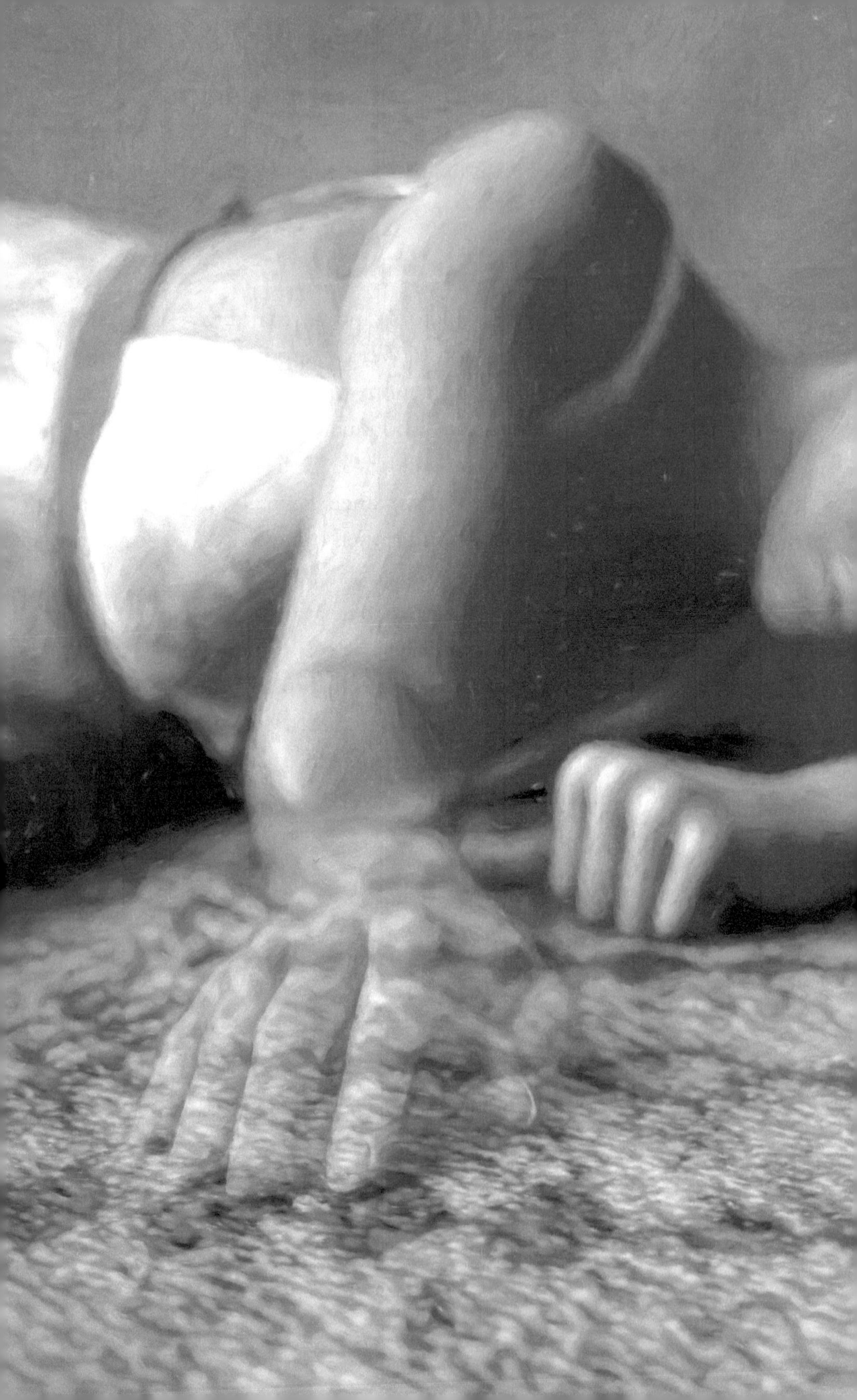

WHAT IS DONE

Michael Vance

THE *WRITING DOWN* of all this is my last defence. Already, so much is lost, and I know that the rest will soon vanish if I don't hurry. Even now, my head pounds as I try to recall even the most unimportant details. Morphine alone relieves it but leaves me stupid for days. Written notes on scraps of paper disappear. The house rearranges itself around me, like some accommodating region of hell, and I become lost for hours in my own kitchen. Work is out of the question.

For weeks, I have endeavoured to get it written—just the beginnings of it. I have sat for hours, pen in hand, accomplishing nothing at all, until I break down in pathetic sobbing; a pitiful, shattered wretch. But I will end that part now: I will finish this before it is all lost.

There are flickering figures all around me as I write. Always maddeningly at the edges of my vision, watching and muttering. At night I hear them tapping at windows in the other rooms—tapping from the *inside*—refusing to be forgotten. It has left me withered and wasted and defeated.

And what is it I am trying to accomplish? Is this to free her, and let her go forever? Or to trap her, so that I can keep what is left of poor Lily? I do feel that this decision should be mine, but obviously that is the whole question. But I know now: I need to hurry.

I WON'T SAY I knew something was wrong. What I do remember is a sense of something pending, some darkness looming, an ending approaching. I awoke agitated and angry one night, not knowing why, and sat at the edge of the bed, head in hands, knowing I had to do something. *What* I had to do was unclear, but there it was. Eventually I rose, and I drank, and that settled me. When I came back to bed, all I could do was stare at her, sleeping there. She was very beautiful, my Lilith, and that only made me feel worse. I wanted to wake her, to tell her something, but I had nothing to say.

I didn't wake her, of course, and I'm not sure what held me back, but I recall that I was staring at the fine lace of her hair across the pillow when I first noticed the arm. She was lying on her side, curled up like a child, with her left arm extended as if reaching for something that should have been there. For *me*, I realised, but *the arm was not there.*

Something was there, some part of it—an outline, a ghost—but I could see right through her arm to the bedsheets below. It was like staring through water or glass, and despite myself I reached out and extended a finger, and watched with horror as it sank right through the faded flesh. Something gave way to my touch, but reformed when I removed my hand. Like a sponge, if I had to describe it.

Trembling, trying not to scream, I touched her neck, her chest, and was relieved when my hand did not pass through her flesh. But something was wrong besides the arm, and when I tried to shake her awake, nothing happened. I staggered back and crashed against the wall, pushing myself out of the room, unsure of where I was going.

Downstairs I ran, and then out into the night, into the pitch black without a coat or shoes. I saddled the old horse and urged him out onto the dirt road, begging him for speed. I barely remember riding into Old Highbury or pounding on the door of the ridiculously named Dr. Love until he came cursing down to meet me. He returned with me to the old house, although I'm certain he understood nothing of what I told him. But I did not have—back then, at least—the reputation of being a madman, and he could see that something was clearly wrong.

At the house, he told me to wait in the kitchen and said he would examine me separately, which struck me as odd, though I can't say I was sorry to send him into the bedroom alone. When he returned, his face was grim, and he refused a drink. At first, he would not speak, and made a show of looking into my eyeballs and listening to my heart, until I became angry and put a stop to it. This was necessary, he explained, because sometimes the patient was not the one we assumed it to be. He was a doctor, he reminded me, and he assured me that he had seen this before: the victim might not be vanishing, but rather it might be the people around them losing their ability to *see*.

Could *he* see her, I asked. Yes, he said, but the arm was definitely gone; we stared at one another, both of us realising this made a mess of his theory.

And was I certain this had just begun tonight? Of course, I replied, annoyed by the ridiculous question. Was it even possible, I thought, that we can lose the ones we love, and never even notice it happening? And not see what was missing until it had gone so far?

None of that conversation made sense.

What was to be done? I asked finally. Nothing, he said. It was outside of his purview—medical science had no answer for me. Would she continue to fade? I wanted to know. Could she still see me? Would she wake again? Dr. Love had answers for none of this. He could send away to the university for a second opinion perhaps, but their opinions wouldn't be worth a damn, he said. It was likely she would fade away until nothing remained, but he couldn't say how much time I had left with her. It was up to me to discover if she was still aware, and if *she* could see *me*.

Eventually he left, and Lily and I were alone in the house again. I tiptoed back into the bedroom, terrified. She appeared peaceful, and I struggled not to wake her as I climbed into the bed, avoiding the arm. I did not want to lie on it, I decided, in case it happened to return in the night. I wanted to give it that chance, at least.

I was a long time falling asleep, and lay stiff and straight, staring up at the ceiling until morning.

THE NEXT DAY I sent a letter to her mother in Aldwych, explaining things as best I could, and asking her to come at once. Then I returned to the bedroom and settled in beside Lily, determined to wake her.

At first, I merely held her hand. (And I mean the one that was still there, of course, and not the other one, which had now thoroughly disappeared.) Though I never saw her move, her position had altered, and I liked to think that she was comfortable as she lay there in repose. The missing arm seemed to rest across her midsection, or at least that is how my mind completed the picture as I sat there with her. She was relaxed, breathing steadily, and she smiled occasionally as she slept, and I could only assume she was dreaming of better times we'd had together.

It troubled me to see that the arm was missing entirely now, right up to the shoulder. The sleeve of her nightdress lay limp, removing all doubt. For a while I talked to her, and by the end of that day I had spoken more to her than in all the previous seven years of marriage combined. When night came, I fed her—soup only, and she woke at least enough to swallow several mouthfuls of broth, though her eyes never opened, and she made no sound. Before sleeping, I checked her over very carefully, to see if her disappearing had spread, but only her arm was affected.

I started the following day by reading aloud from her diary. I had not made it far when I came to the first blank pages. On some, I could see the faint imprint of the pen, but the ink had vanished. Thinking that the words themselves might provide a clue as to *why* they had vanished, I at first attempted to read from the impressions on the page. This proved pointless, and after an hour or so I flipped through the rest of the diary and found that perhaps one page in ten was now blank. Not knowing what to make of this, or how it connected to Lily's condition, I closed the book up and went outside to walk.

While the feel of sunlight on my face did serve to temporarily lift my spirits, I could not help remembering all the times that Lily and I had walked those peaceful woods *together*, and I soon returned home painfully aware of something already missing.

Thinking I might dress her properly, and so anchor her more firmly in this world, I rooted briefly through her things when I returned home, but I was disturbed to find that some familiar items had gone missing. I did not have a clear idea of what exactly she owned, but some items of clothing I could recall clearly. For instance, a blue and white-checked dress, which she'd had for years, was nowhere to be found. I could picture her clearly in that dress, insisting that I go into the attic and examine a leak she had found there, and patch it up immediately. How long ago was that—?

Unsettled, I dug deeper with shaking hands. There was a certain bonnet she had worn, and I recalled a conversation with her perhaps a week before. She had reminded me that there was a gap in the fence around one of the pens and told me that now some of the animals had succeeded in wandering off, and she had suggested forcefully that I retrieve them. That bonnet was gone. How?

A pale blue apron was another item I could picture clearly. Just this spring, Lily had worn it when she told me that a garden did not plant itself, and when she walked off, she had added gently that there was a leak in the attic, which I might consider. This also had disappeared—the apron, I mean; not the leak, alas, which was still there—and I felt deeply troubled when I returned to the bedside.

But it was not only the bonnet, or the dress, or the apron, I discovered with horror, but Lily's feet: they were gone. With trembling hands, I lifted the sheets away to check, and her legs now ended slightly above where the ankles would have been. Hastily, I dropped the sheets back in place and collapsed into a chair. They had been there that morning, I knew. (Or had they? Could I *not* have noticed such a thing?)

Sobbing uncontrollably, I went to the kitchen and drank myself senseless before collapsing into a chair to sleep.

WHEN HER MOTHER arrived, I thought I might gain a respite. By then I was half-mad from a lack of sleep and was wandering the house like a ghost at all hours of the day and night. Sometimes I would become lost in the little house, walking into rooms that I felt I had never seen before, looking for things that were nowhere to be found. I cried once or twice, I must admit, sitting alone by the fireplace, confused to the point of insanity.

The old lady, for her part, took it with stony silence, although I admit I had not adequately prepared her beforehand. Lily was half gone by then. Her legs had disappeared up to the knees, and the right side of her chest was missing entirely. You could see that the lack was travelling up her neck. I dreaded what would happen when it reached her head, her heart. I gibbered a useless explanation to her mother, and then together we covered Lily again. Her mother muttered the lines of some verse or poem and then returned to the kitchen to make tea.

The situation, she told me, reminded her of Lily's father. For an instant, hope flared, and I felt myself on the brink of sanity: an explanation at last. Did this run in the family then, I asked her. She cast a baleful eye in my direction, then went about arranging her teacup before answering. Her husband, she explained, had never really been there for her, had never really been present. And over the years, he had grown more and more distant and withdrawn, until one day she simply lost him entirely.

Unsure if this was a parable meant to explain things in some fashion,

I waited, grinding my teeth. Lily had never mentioned her father to me, which in light of this story seemed to make sense. Lily's mother picked up a stuffed lamb that Lily had knitted and admired it sadly. Lily had been a delicate child, she said, more as if talking to herself than to me. A sad and beautiful thing, seeming misplaced in a world like this one. She had never really fit. Perhaps the world had become too much for her to bear, and she felt like she had to leave, to let go.

Rage bubbled in me then—exactly why, I do not know—and I stood up, prepared to unleash my fury on the old woman. But then I saw the way she was looking down at the little lamb in her lap, the tears in her eyes, and my anger crumbled. I stumbled back into the bedroom and took Lily's hand in mine. I even said a prayer. Then I picked up her diary, prepared to read to her again.

When I opened it, *all* of the pages were blank.

THE FOLLOWING DAY, I left Lily in the care of her mother and went to town to see Dr. Love. He had not returned to the house since that first day, and I don't know how I thought he could help me now, but I knew I needed to get away from the house for a time.

Lily's mother's remarks from the day before haunted me all the way into town—the idea that Lily might leave on purpose was simply too much for me to bear. It implied that somehow this might be my fault. It was my *job* to make her happy, in a way, as she had made me happy. So was I to blame? Even Dr. Love had hinted at something like this, I remembered, with his comment about how sometimes things vanish because we refuse to see them. Had something been absent in *me* all that time then? Or looked at another way: if she was leaving now, had I pushed her? There had to be two sides, of course, and I knew that I had not clearly examined my own role in this thing. There had been *something* I was going to say on the night when the arm had first vanished. What had it been, though? I realised I had no idea.

I felt like I was walking in a dream as I stumbled through town, and I can imagine what I must have looked like when I arrived at Dr. Love's office. They might logically have assumed that I was the emergency. The doctor, they said, could not see me at the moment. He *could* see me, I replied, and I told them I would wait. There was muttering, and frightened looks from the other patients, who sidled away from me, but eventually the doctor arrived to speak to me. He looked blank and slightly irritated, as I told him he had to come to the house immediately, that Lily was almost gone. He told me to slow down, to start over, and I hastily updated him on her deterioration since his last visit. His last visit? He seemed surprised. Yes, I replied, not even a week ago. And her condition was—what? Disappearing still, I said, and almost entirely vanished. Baffled, he looked at his assistants, and had them try to look up Lily's name in his records. He knew me, I could see, but apparently, he had forgotten the house call the week before. I waited in anguish as they fumbled papers and snuck glances at one another.

Until finally: we have no record of the appointment, and no record of ever having seen your wife at all.

I don't recall leaving the office and Old Highbury. Much of that day remains unclear to me. But I do know I made it back to the house to find Lily's mother packing her things in eerie silence. I pleaded with her not to leave, to which she replied that it was too late, that we both had to let go, and that Lily was, in fact, already gone. I ran into the other bedroom to see that Lily was *not* gone (although she was close to it). I returned to the other room and railed at the old woman, telling her we needed her, that she had some responsibility to her daughter. But she ignored me, and I ran out of steam quickly and sagged against the door. Only then did I notice that she wore a glove—over one hand only—but I was too exhausted to remark on it.

Finally, I limped from the room and collapsed in front of the fireplace. Only distantly did I note that the little knitted lamb, which always sat on the table there, was missing.

WHEN I WOKE the next day, I was alone. I tore all the sheets from the bed to make sure, and even checked underneath it, but there was nothing left of Lily. I wandered for a time, rifling through the closet, paging through the empty diary, cursing Lily's mother for the theft of the knitted lamb. That day is a blur, but the night remains clear in my mind.

Sometime in the middle of the night, I woke to the sound of a door closing gently down the hall, followed by the tread of soft footsteps approaching the bedroom. They stopped just outside the door, and as I lay there terrified, I could clearly hear the sound of someone breathing right outside the bedroom.

Paralysed at first, I just listened. Eventually I could stand it no longer and called out in a trembling voice, saying simply, "Hello?" Whoever it was chose not to answer, so I tried again, this time with, "Lily?" But if it was her, she was not cooperating. Gathering all my courage, I finally pushed off the bedsheets and mounted a mad charge out into the hallway, yelling as loudly as I could. There was nothing there. Quickly I rooted for a candle in the kitchen, lit it, and scoured the entire house, knowing that sleep would be impossible until this mystery was solved. But though I checked every inch of the place, including in the drawers where no person could possibly fit, I found nothing. The house was still empty.

I returned to bed eventually and left the candle lit, then lay with my eyes wide open for many hours. At one point I heard voices murmuring in the kitchen, and cold terror nailed me to the bed. My breathing became hoarse, and I believe that whoever or whatever was in the house heard me panting, and the whispering stopped. Would they come to investigate now, I wondered, as I had gone searching when I first heard them? Would I be killed? But nothing happened, and for the rest of that night the house was quiet, and I believe I did sleep at some point.

You would think that these things—these phantoms—would use the daylight hours to rest, since they were so persistent throughout the night.

But there was always something there, just at the edge of my awareness in one way or another. I might turn my head at a breeze and catch just the back of a figure as they stepped into another room—and when I entered that room, it was empty. I soon stopped chasing them, whoever they were. Someone who did not want to be seen, I thought, and naturally I could imagine who that was. Had she chosen this, I wondered? Was this, for her, a better way to live with me in our little house?

Perhaps she hadn't left me after all. The idea was comforting. She had hurt no one in life, and if I had to live with a ghost, it should be hers. I took to speaking to her in a way that invited her to reply but did not demand it. I am going to make tea now, I might say. Or: it looks like rain.

In Old Highbury, she had been forgotten entirely. I mentioned her name to neighbours and saw confusion on their faces, and inquired of people who I knew had seen her a hundred times. Did they remember Lily? No, they did not. I wrote to her mother, remembering my anger at her before she left, and said that I apologised and hoped that she was well, and that her daughter was all gone now. Weeks later, a neighbour replied, saying that the old lady was not well, and did not recall a daughter. Perhaps it was memory, and age, they said, because the old woman 'was fading'.

One day, I returned home and looked at a painting that had hung over the fireplace for years. It showed the fields outside the window, the little house tucked among the trees. There was a sort of smudge in the foreground that I stared at for hours with some concern because something was wrong with it. Something was *missing*, and it tormented me because I could not say exactly *what* was missing.

But what the smudge was, I was certain, was me. A small blur without features, evidently looking out over the property. Who had painted this? I wondered, this picture with me in it. There had been a signature on the painting once, but I could not find it, though I took the whole thing down from the wall and looked on the back as well. What was more, I was sure that I had not always been alone in that painting, and this disturbed me in a way I cannot even describe. There had been someone beside me. It was only hours later, when I heard someone enter at the front door and remove their coat and shoes, that I was able to calm down and recall.

I called out to her, telling Lily that I was in the kitchen, then I slumped in my chair to think. I could not allow her to be forgotten completely—not by me. That was too much. I felt a dim pain in my skull as I tried to think what to do, how to hang on to her, and finally I rose and went to the bedroom. Her empty diary was still there, and I stared at it for a long while, noting how the pages were so pristine, as if they had never been marked.

I will write it down, I muttered.

Yes, Lily, I will write it down.

Your diary, the story of your life, it will be restored. Stay with me, and try to help if you can, because it is like grasping at a dream as you start to wake, so I need to get it all down quickly.

I returned to the chair by the fireplace, energised, trying to think of where to start. A log tumbled in the grate, and sparks scattered, but I hardly noticed. The memories receded like shadows, but they were there—I simply had to crawl back into the past, and it would all still be there. And at last, I put pen to paper to write, comforted by the quiet sound of somebody unseen making tea in the kitchen behind me.

VESSEL 401

Relvin Gonzalez

LIGHT IS A gamble, and in the end, darkness takes all. That's what my grandfather used to say to us, his little ghosts. We were born above water, absorbing daylight and turning it into divine energy.

Our parents didn't consider our energy divine. To them we were an uninvited laughter, a silence-interrupting yell, a nuisance. One day, our father and mother, John and Annie, held us close, and it was warm, very warm indeed. Then it was cold, then very bright, then dark, and then dark forever.

My name was George, that one there was Stella, and the other was called Elizabeth. Elizabeth watched over us most of the time while my parents floated off into the darkness. I asked her why we needed watching after, on account of there being no dangers apparent to us. She shushed me and sent me floating back to my chamber to taste the rusty waters that had invaded the insides of the ship. My parents returned looking worse than when they left, but at least they always came back.

I was not supposed to ask about Douglas, Dorothy, Constance, or Thomas. All I needed to know was they were not here, and that was that. Other than some faint shapes and colors, I rarely saw anything around me. I was used to it now. My sisters, too. But my father was always looking for ways to change his surroundings and would drift off toward the slimmest beacon of light.

Elizabeth said our parents were too old to mold reality and bend it at their will. She said it happened at one point in life, and no one knows when. One day you're building sandcastles and making up stories, the next day you're walking all stiff wearing a suit and holding a briefcase, just like that. It was the most terrifying thing.

It had been so long; I couldn't recall colors. My chamber was full of floating objects, sharp objects, rusty objects, and I knew this because I had touched them all in the dark. Stella liked to follow me around, touching all the objects I just touched a second ago. I told her to find her own chamber. She said mine was the best; a big lie, since I had been to other chambers and had touched the same things. They were all identical.

Elizabeth enjoyed sitting by the hole in the glass window. I sensed the waves she created when she shifted her body; the water undulating and crashing onto me. She used to be a dancer but now has the slightest moves, as if any sudden jerk could break her entire body apart. We were on our way to a farm my father had bought, where she dreamed about meeting and falling in love with an American farm boy. Ever since the crash, she rarely moved more than what was necessary.

"Elizabeth, I'm scared," I said.

She laughed. "Silly. What do you have to fear?"

I stayed silent. I didn't know, I just was. "It's…cold."

The water undulated. She was shifting toward me. "Here, take my hand."

"Can I take your hand, too?" Stella always followed in my footsteps.

Then my parents' voices approached.

"Annie, we must go farther out. I can feel it. We're close."

"No, John! I'm done with you and your never-ending getting-close-to-places-but-never-reaching-them excuses. I'm done following you around, waiting for you to figure things out. I'm done with this, the darkness, the waiting. Why can't we just die like everybody else? I'll tell you why. It's because of *you*. Because you won't learn the lesson, even at your dumb old age, you're still as stubborn as ever."

"What are you talking about?"

Mother exhaled. "Forget it."

"Nothing?" Elizabeth said.

"Nothing, sweetie. Let's get you guys to bed."

We swam down a hatch and into the lower chambers of the cruise ship. Whenever we swam that way, the water made a gurgle sound as our bodies passed through the hatch. One gurgle, Elizabeth. Another, Stella. And one more, Mother. I always waited in vain for the fourth one, but Father liked to pace by himself outside the ship, to scream wordless, awful screams into the ocean's void, to light up the world with wonder and scheming, his energy devoted to get us out of this or that, from one hole to another, to dodge one bullet only to get us killed by an axe, and in the darkness outside, I could almost hear him choke, asphyxiating forever in the unsolvable equation of our death.

I OPENED MY eyes first. My family floated, dreaming beside me, and I made my way up to the deck and outside the ship. There, swimming toward us, I saw a beautiful whale. Its body was shiny against a light beaming from its mouth. When it came close, its bright eyes illuminated the ship, and I saw it in spotlit patches, and I remembered.

Everyone had been celebrating until the crash rocked the ship and turned our world upside down. Some drowned, loud, coming in and out of the water, kicking, screaming, reaching out for salvation, hoping to live their unlived chunk of their lives, while others departed quietly with the cold, their breathing slowed and slowed until they froze up, motionless as a horrific death portrait.

The whale hovered and hummed, flashing lights at the ship. Satisfied, it whirred away into the blackness it had come from. I jolted, sending schools of fish escaping in every which way, and rushed to wake up my parents.

"A whale! I saw it, a whale! It was bright as day. I remember it all," I said.

"George, is everything all right?" Mother said, her voice tired.

"Your boy has lost his marbles." That was Father.

"Outside, it was a shiny whale."

Elizabeth said she believed me and accompanied me outside, Stella behind us.

"Maybe she'll come back later," Elizabeth said in that condescending voice. I hated that voice.

My anger came out all sad. "I know what I saw."

"I'm sure."

Back inside, I pleaded with my parents to let me stay up all night on the balcony to watch for the whale.

"Why do you care about a stupid whale?" Stella said.

"I don't care about the whale," I said, looking out into the dark ocean and feeling Father pacing the waters.

I SNUCK OUT to the deck a few nights after. I turned around, encircled by a complete and lonely darkness. I moved my hand from side to side and felt the weight of my transparent hand moving the water with it. I kept myself entertained, waiting for the whale by imagining my hands and water, a dance between the live and the dead. No one else believed me, so I had to make them believe. I had to trap the proof and bring it to my family.

Before the ship had crashed and sunk, some adults drank and talked about their jobs back on the mainland. One talked about how to sell to his clients. He must first study them, their routines, their wants, their unaccomplished desires, and package all that into a pretty little box, wrapped in the fear of regret should they pass the opportunity up, and once they got close to the box, they released the stick holding the structure together and trap their clients within. It was a lovely metaphor, and I observed the adults drinking and cheering, and having a toast for such a funny way of describing it, but I recorded it deep inside. It was quite a thought. Humans as nothing but mice addicted to cheese, and oneself as the sole owner of all the cheese factories in the world. If I wanted to catch this whale, I first had to learn its routine, study its desires, and package it neatly under a trap of my making.

There was also a marine biologist on the ship who, mostly, sat in front of a glass window and mumbled the secrets of the ocean life to anyone who sat close to him. When my father told me to go away, on account of an adult conversation about to start, I explored the ship and found the marine biologist. He told me all about the hydrothermal vent mussels and how they could tell time by using clock genes as timekeepers. It was now a Friday; I knew because I watched and studied the mussels from the moment we morphed from flesh and bones to the atomic particles of the undead.

The whale visited again that Friday. This time, I didn't rush to my parents. I hid, instead, and observed its routines, figured its desires. I watched the whale move from window to window with its mouth full of light, and at one broken glass window I saw the most marvelous thing. For all his knowledge, I'm sure the marine biologist would have never seen a whale like this, with a thin protrusion that extended from its belly six feet out into the ship's glass window. And from the chamber beyond the glass, it pulled the thin extension back into its belly, holding a shiny golden object—a necklace. Stella had found that necklace and asked me many times to put it on her when she was playing make-believe queen of the sea. Once the whale had its extension folded into its body, it turned and disappeared into the void, and I watched its light shrinking, and I smiled. I smiled because I had nothing in one second, and now I had it all.

The whale came on a Friday, looking for gold.

I SPENT THE next six days floating from chamber to chamber in secret—a difficult thing when I had Stella following me around asking what I was up to—hunting for gold and accruing all of its shiny gleam into one box. On Friday, I laced the box with a string of gems and pearls, and waited until nightfall when everyone was asleep to carry the heavy box out of the ship and place it on the highest rock I found. I put a fancy caftan from one chamber over it, leaving enough of the box exposed, then pulled a fishing net from the ship's cargo and hid it in the rock above the box and waited. The darkness of my dreams had almost replaced the darkness of the ocean when the whale appeared, leaving a trail of light in its wake. It came slowly, scanning the ship and flashing a thunderstorm at it.

"What's going on?" my father said from inside the ship.

The rest of my family woke up to the whale's light, and I smiled.

When the whale turned my way, I brought forth a large silver coin and moved it up, down, sideways, just right for the whale's light to bounce off of it. I knew it had worked when the whale purred and whirred and hurried toward me with a desperation I had never seen. It angled slightly down toward the box and approached it. It released its extension arm and slid the caftan off the box with it. The arm had digits like fingers at the end. It wrapped its digits around the lid and opened it, the whale's light illuminating the treasure inside.

"What is this?" Father said.

"The whale, Father, is our ticket out of here," I whispered.

And when the whale was within the boundaries of my trap, I released the net from its hiding hole and let it fall over the whale. It purred again, making a whining noise. It moved back but got stuck inside the net.

I saw Father's eyes in the darkness. "This is our chance, Annie!" he said.

My family rushed to the whale.

"Now it's our chance, it has stopped for us!" Father said. "Let us all get on the whale. Thank you, Whale. Kids, thank the whale for its service!"

My father had never displayed such vitality, and my mother welled with pride and relief. Such relief. It was infectious.

"Thank you, Whale. I love you, Whale." I hugged the whale's glassy face. I couldn't believe our luck.

Mother, Elizabeth, Stella, and I covered the whale in our embrace while Father swam up to its back, studying its majestic body. I rested my cheek on its eye, its cold, transparent eye. I had closed mine from all the joy. Between blinks, the whale's hollowness became apparent. Inside the whale were four men and one younger man, their faces pointed at us, stricken with absolute terror.

The whale purred and whirred more. It moved sideways, crashing its tail against rocks and reefs, and shaking us with its flail. We held tighter onto its cold, rigid body.

"George, hurry! Help me over here," Father said, and I swam with such ferocity, with such speed to heed his call, to be of service, that I made it to him in no time at all. "There, grab that wheel and, on the count of three, turn it as hard as you can."

I gripped the hard circle on the whale's back and waited for the signal. "One…two…three!"

We turned the steering-wheel-like circle with all of our strength. The whale's glassy eyes extended to its top, and inside, the people living in the whale threw their necks up frantically and covered the pouring stream of water with their hands while a man in a suit embraced a younger version of himself. The younger boy, about my age, had been frightened about something. I turned the wheel more, eager to calm him down, to offer him a game to play. Another man pulled and pushed on a black stick and the whale whirred, no match for the wide net I had cast over it. The whale's insides made hungry, muffled screaming sounds.

"One more turn, son!" Father said, his eyes wide and happy. Wide and happy. Wide and happy.

I turned the circle with all of my might, my aching arms just about to snap off my body, but I didn't care. I simply stared into my father's eyes. Wide and happy. Wide and happy. Wide and happy. We turned until the circle wouldn't budge. The hatch opened and the entire ocean poured in.

I turned to a whistling sound coming from the ship. The majestic ship in front of the whale, now illuminated in all its past indestructible glory, lay on its side, once crushed by ice and now buried by water. It opened its cells and loosened its shackles, and in one last exhale, released its prisoners. A thousand souls had materialized and were now rushing toward the whale. Toward us.

"Annie, grab the kids, we must go!" Father said while cutting the net with a golden knife from the treasure box.

Mother did so and swam into the hatch while the people inside the whale grabbed at their throats and coughed and pounded at the whale's eyes from the inside, then spasmed and convulsed until they floated lifelessly. Father was the last one to enter the whale. From the whale's insides we watched the dormant souls of the ship rush toward the whale and crash on its eye, and pound at the glass, and stare at us, and begged to be let in.

"Away!" Father said. "Find your own!"

"What now, John?" Mother said, huddling us close to her, her body twitching with every slam against the glass.

Father looked at the whale's belly filled with water, its black sticks, and lighted squares that were blinking and going dark and not coming back on, and he sat on the floor in surrender. "I don't know."

"You don't know? What do you mean you don't know? Figure something out!" Although Mother sounded enraged, in her face I found fear.

The devilish phantoms opened their mouths as wide as the whale, their fangs biting down its glass. A crack formed at the top, then one in the middle.

"John!"

"I'm sorry," Father said. "I can't."

My father had never said those words. *I can't.* But it didn't scare me. He was at peace at last. His shoulders relaxed, the lines on his brow vanished. Mother huddled Elizabeth and Stella closer, and offered Father and me an opening. We curled up inside her arm. They closed their eyes, but I watched until the last moment. The shattering of glass, the spirits and their undead protest, their ghost claws at our throats, their despair to escape the darkness and get into the whale.

After a hundred years of purgatory, our release was full of light. It was a gift to die forevermore.

Light is a gamble, and in the end, darkness takes all.

QUIET LAKE

Patrick Herald

Y OU CAN ALMOST see the cold in the air here, Anna thought as she looked out over Lake Mjøsa. She had never expected to move to Norway, one of the most peaceful countries on earth. She and Will couldn't believe their luck when he got the job offer. No more school shooting drills for Connor. No more trying to figure out the difference between a deductible and maximum out of pocket on a hospital bill. No more fear.

This was, of course, before Will was murdered in Hamar, their quiet new town by the lake, a mere three months after they arrived. Not by a gun, but a crossbow. The victims: an eighty-four-year-old woman who nearly lost an arm to the man, who ducked from building to building in the early northern darkness, shooting almost silently. A teenaged boy who was shot in the leg. And Will, who was shot in the chest by the crouched figure, his takeaway pizza—he'd walked out to get them dinner—splattered on the snow like an obscene echo of the fatal wound hidden beneath his jacket.

There were no answers. The killer was a local and offered no explanation for his actions. There was nothing remarkable about him: thirty years old, a maintenance worker for farm equipment, wasn't known to cause trouble. He grew up in Hamar, attending the same schools Connor would. He surrendered immediately when the police arrived.

After the initial torrent of shock and grief, Will's father started talking about Anna and Connor moving back to the States. He'd made a halfhearted attempt at it immediately after the murder, when he and Anna's parents came to see her and Connor. Anna, who was in no state to think of the future yet, brushed it off; the only decision they came to was that they felt Will would have wanted his father and his old friends to spread some of his ashes around his favorite places in Grand Rapids. Anna would bring them on her next trip home. She wasn't willing to part with any of him yet.

It was around the time that Will's father brought up a move back to America more seriously that Anna started seeing things.

LAKE MJØSA WAS far and away the biggest lake in Norway, even if small when compared to the Great Lakes back in the States. It was, of course, like so much in this country, breathtakingly beautiful: ringed by trees, rocks, and pleasant towns. Will excitedly showed her pictures from locals and tourists leading up to the move, and they'd talked about taking walks along it as a family.

Anna was glad that they'd had a chance to do that a few times before Will died. She recalled the three of them walking west and north from the city center, stopping at the railway museum before going further up the coast to Furuberget, a nature reserve. There, they looked across the lake toward the peninsula, where tiny Holstad and Nes lay. Someday soon, they decided—before Connor's complaints forced them back— they would go from Nes to the island of Helgøya and walk its perimeter together. She didn't say it, but Anna was less excited about this prospect than Will, whose enthusiasm could sometimes be overbearing.

It was this moment that lingered in Anna's mind today, while she tried to keep out the cold. The chill was amazing, considering there was no wind at all. Standing there on the wintery beach, looking out over

Mjøsa, which looked more like a tremendous field than a lake under all the snow. Or a cloud. She didn't enjoy walking out onto the lake, though she knew—even in late winter with the weather they'd had—that the ice was so thick she couldn't fall if she tried to break through it deliberately. It felt ethereal, somehow. She didn't let Connor onto it either, holding his hand tightly whenever they approached. Soon she would walk to his school to pick him up. But not yet. She wanted a few more moments to look across that expanse.

Thinking back, Anna regretted her lack of excitement. She was as relieved as Will to move to this country. But in hindsight, her relative apathy when it came to the leisurely times Will planned felt like a betrayal. While trying not to show it, did she make his final days somehow less perfect than they might have been? Did he think she was unhappy?

Foolishness. Neither of them had adjusted yet, and nobody expected perfection anyway; it was nonsense.

Lost in these thoughts, Anna was only now realizing that something had formed in her field of vision, in the blank expanse ahead of her. Some kind of gray out there in the white. She hadn't seen anyone on the lake today, but when she had in the past, they remained clear, like little crabs scuttling across white sand. This was something else. It was… fuzzier somehow, it—

"Anna?"

She jumped at the sound of her name.

"Sorry," the woman continued as Anna turned. "It's Karoline—my daughter's in school with your son. Are you alright?"

"*Hei*, Karoline," Anna replied, suddenly conscious of a freezing tear on her cheek. She brushed it away. "I'm okay."

"I just wanted to say, if you'd like some company sometime, I'm willing. If you'd like to practice your Norwegian or walk to the school. Maybe Connor and Maja could play together while we have a coffee?" Karoline was really defying the stereotype of Nordic reticence, and in the moment, Anna was grateful.

She looked back at the lake. Whatever she had been seeing was gone; she hadn't noticed the tears forming until Karoline found her, and they must have affected her vision.

"How about now?" Anna said. She pictured the two of them stopping for coffee, the takeaway cup warming their hands as vapors rose from them like little volcanoes. A happy image. She could use that.

LIKE SO MANY large lakes, Mjøsa is full of shipwrecks. They're usually found somewhat near the shore, where they can be spotted more easily. Peering into the depths is not a possibility without deploying some serious technology. Lately, that had been happening more often: less than a year before Anna and Will moved there, researchers found a ship more than 400 meters deep—and likely more than 400 years old, as well.

But there was no big moment, certainly not recently. No event that made the lake famous. Periodic flooding, a chance drowning, the usual things to be expected from any large body of water. The truth is: it is a quiet lake.

HE MEANS WELL, Anna thought, *but he needs to cut this shit out before I lose my mind.*

Will's father was talking again about her moving back to America with Connor. The implication: Norway wasn't actually any safer, Anna and Will didn't *really* know what they were doing in researching it as a new place to live, and really all that mattered now was being close to the rest of the family, so, "Come to Grand Rapids." Logically, Anna knew this was wrong, but it still added another layer to a miserable day.

Connor was in bed, and she needed this time to herself, even though she had it while he was in school as well. This afternoon and evening had what must have been a new record of heartbreaking "I miss daddy" comments. She felt perpetually recovering.

"Okay. I'll keep thinking about it," she was saying, before being distracted by a sound. Their second-floor flat was very exposed to the wind coming off the lake, which had picked up during the evening. Curiously, the noise often picked up after a gust died down. There must have been some technical term for what she was hearing, but Anna thought of it as the frost settling.

After hanging up, Anna moved to lower the blinds, which she'd forgotten while managing Connor.

She immediately cried out.

There was a figure in the window. Impossible. There was nowhere to stand out there, as the window was on a flat exterior wall with no balcony. But Anna clearly saw a silhouette from the shoulders up. She stood, frozen after her brief exclamation, facing it.

The shape changed. The frost settling: was this how it looked? It shifted yet again as Anna took a step back. But the shift was just her shadow. All of it was just her shadow, her reflection—it had to be. She stared at it for a moment. It seemed less clear now, hazier. In fact, she thought, it must be nothing at all. Just a transitory shape in the cold.

With an eye on the window, she sat down on the sofa. There was no movement, and she could no longer make out a figure. She flicked the TV on, saw Will's killer's face next to an impossibly regal-looking newscaster, and flicked it back off.

THAT MORNING, ANNA felt only anger. She let it in, let it warm her blood. For a few hours, at least. A family, minding their own business, looking only for a better life in a new place, destroyed by the whims of some bastard. Some piece of shit.

The police had found incriminating materials, the papers said. Anna really didn't care what they were. She'd avoided the TV news, mostly successfully, since the talk with Will's father. But she spotted the headline in a shop window, the paper splayed in a manner that made her think of old-time newsagents in films. She'd found it charming when they moved; less so lately when she was greeted with things like *"Hamar Morder"* whenever she saw them. She appreciated her infirm grasp on Norwegian at times like these: no accidentally catching details. The man had offered no explanation to the police, and that was that, wasn't it? There was nothing that could possibly justify it—nothing to *really* explain why someone would commit such an act. It was called senseless murder for a reason.

She hated him.

ANNA LIGHTLY INHALED the bittersweet aroma of her Americano. She liked the way hot drinks let off so much steam on these frozen days, even indoors.

Karoline looked across the table at her, waiting for her to speak. Their meetings had become an almost weekly occurrence.

"I'm still angry," Anna started.

"Of course you are. Fuck him," Karoline said. "'Unaccountable.' I don't believe in it. He was fit for a crossbow license. He was fit to live among us for years and years. Now after this one act he's suddenly incapable, unfit for trial?"

"Let's not dwell on it."

"Of course."

Anna sighed. She needed something to take her mind off this. "Will the paddle steamer open soon?"

"In a few months. June, I think."

"Connor will like that."

"Oh, yes. The children always do. We can go together, the three of us and Maja, the day it opens. Shall we?"

Anna had spent yesterday afternoon trying to explain to Connor that he shouldn't react so negatively to things that happened at school. He let another boy borrow his pencil, and he wouldn't return it. Catastrophic, to a child that age. But he'd forget about it quickly, and maybe even be friends with the other boy soon, she thought. The advantages of youthful whims.

"We shall," said Anna, with the ghost of a smile. More socializing would do Connor good.

"Have you had any more sightings? In your window?"

Anna froze for a moment with her mug half raised. She hadn't expected that to come up and had only mentioned it to Karoline half-jokingly the day after it happened. She had mostly decided that it was nothing at that time. But that was many weeks ago now, and things had changed. She hesitated before responding.

"To be honest, it's happened twice more."

"You're joking. Tell me about it."

"Most recently," Anna began, running a finger along the rim of her mug, "I woke up around three or three thirty in the morning—"

"The witching hour," Karoline said.

"What's that?"

"Supposedly when devils and spirits are active. Witches."

"Is that a Norse mythology thing?" Anna asked.

"I don't think so. I think it's just a human thing. More general. I'm sorry, go on."

"Well, I woke up during the witching hour," Anna said, trying and failing to force a smile. "And I went out to the kitchen for a glass of water. I had a few sips. Nothing special happened. But then when I turned off the light to leave the room, something made me look over at the window above the sink."

"And?"

"There was a figure in the window. It must have been there the whole time," Anna said, prickles of anxiety running up her shoulders at the memory. "I couldn't see out with the light on, but once it was off, it was backlit by the streetlamps outside. An outline of a person, from the shoulders up, like the first time."

"*Helvete*," Karoline said. "Was it moving?"

"No, I don't think so. I couldn't see a face, either. It was just dark. And blank. But it felt like I was being watched, you know?"

"Mm," Karoline said. Anna had been afraid to bring this up to anyone, now that it had happened more than once. But Karoline had asked, and still appeared to be listening with no judgment. And so she continued.

"The strangest part was the way it left."

"Left?"

"Yes. It didn't stay for long. It sort of flickered away, bit by bit, or piece by piece. And it took time for it to disappear. It almost looked like a pattern."

"What kind of pattern?"

"I have no idea. I think I need more coffee." Something—the absurdity of the conversation, perhaps—finally made Anna laugh.

THE LAKE REMINDED Anna of her coffee today; it was steaming. What would it look like in the spring, she wondered? She watched the light cloud of her breath puff forward and dissipate. Spring wasn't too far away now. Who was the Norse goddess of spring she'd read about in Karoline's book? Idun, that was it. She was supposed to set things right after they'd been thrown into disarray. *Maybe she'll fix my life*, Anna thought, smiling wryly to herself.

Not likely. Every time she felt a moment of peace, it was quickly crushed. News of the killer—she didn't see him on NRK much anymore, but the papers continued to cover it—or Connor would have another episode. She'd managed to keep her own breakdowns on a fairly set schedule: about once a week, always when Connor was asleep or in school. Less predictably, Will would appear in her dreams, acting normally while blood flowed in a straight line from a hole in his chest, sometimes with a crossbow bolt still protruding from it.

Last night, she woke from a new one: Will sitting at the table in their old apartment in Wichita, eating breakfast. His allergies were acting up again, and he put down the crossbow bolt, which he'd been using as a fork to spear bits of pancake, to blow his nose. He kept blowing, his eyes widening. Then he turned to her with a look of disgust on his face, showing her his now bright red napkin.

When she snapped awake, it was 3:22. The witching hour, she remembered, which didn't make her feel any better. But she'd had no nighttime visits in a while, and as the last stretches of winter plodded on, the darkness began to feel less intense, less defiant.

Anna walked across the hall to check on Connor. The room was quiet and dimly lit by the soft glow from the window. She leaned over to see his tiny face, half-buried under blankets. Her shadow lay over him. Then, almost imperceptibly, another shadow rose up softly to the left of hers, within the same light from outside.

She gasped and whirled around, heart already racing, just in time to see the wisp of a figure finish sliding away from the window. After five or six machine gun heartbeats, she rushed to the window and looked out. Somehow, she expected to see a figure standing down below, under the streetlight. But there was nothing other than scattered snowflakes gently coasting on the breeze.

THERE WAS ONE part of old Norse culture she couldn't get out of her head once she learned about it. The *nidstang*, or *nithing pole*. As

Anna understood it, the nidstang involved taking the head of a horse—Godfather style—but instead of leaving it as a warning, you mounted it on a pole inscribed with a curse before pointing it in the direction of the person you were targeting. The person you wished ill, the person who had wronged you. The person you hated. Had there ever been a nidstang on Lake Mjøsa?

"But what do *you* believe, Karoline?"

They'd been meeting weekly for some time now, and Anna enjoyed both Karoline's company and the familiarity she felt with the staff at this cafe. The cafe itself, with its cozy wood floors and view of Mjøsa through clouded front-facing windows. In some small sense, she was beginning to feel at home. Some small bit of normalcy.

Anna was not religious but considered herself open-minded. And she felt something had awakened in her these recent months, something brought about by the great tragedy she had suffered, and by experiencing the stark beauty of Norway. *Or maybe I'm just losing my mind*, she thought.

"Karoline?" she asked again, as her friend sat silently behind the haze of her coffee.

"I'm thinking," Karoline said. "I want to say it carefully. And I don't want you to think I'm mad."

"It's okay. I won't. Take your time," Anna said.

Karoline was silent for what felt like a full minute before responding.

"I believe," Karoline said, "that there are such things as spirits. *Vættir*. Wights. That they inhabit the land. I believe they are displeased, or hurt, by modern humanity. I believe, Anna, that they have been drawn to you, and that is why you have been seeing shapes and figures around your home."

Anna didn't respond, though she nodded along as Karoline spoke. She would have taken this for some kind of new age ranting in the past, but after these past few months, she found herself wondering if there wasn't at least a grain of truth to what Karoline was telling her. She thought back to the pattern she saw as the figure disappeared from her window. It was almost like it was trying to tell her something. Or, again, perhaps she was losing it.

"I also believe," Karoline continued, "that there is a reason you've taken an interest in nithing poles."

"What's the reason?"

"Revenge."

Anna laughed.

"You think I am going to cast a hex?"

"I'm not joking, Anna."

"But that's—sure, I wish the worst for this guy. I do. But beyond not really believing in this kind of thing—sorry—I wouldn't even know where to begin if I did believe. I'm not exactly qualified."

"That's just it," Karoline said, taking a slow sip. "Did you read about how a nidstang works?"

"Yeah, basically. Um, you put a horse's head—"

"I don't mean that way, not how you *build* it," Karoline cut her off. "I mean how the curse itself works."

"No."

"It's the spirits. The nidstang disturbs the spirits, it drives them. Your nithing pole riles them up and directs them. In this case, to our man, the murderer." She paused again. "Shall I continue?"

"Yes."

"I believe that the figures in your window are vættir."

"So you think *I'm* being cursed?"

"No, I don't. You didn't see them until after the murder, correct?"

"Correct."

"I believe these are the spirits of this area, and they are upset on your behalf. What happened is an affront and a stain on the land. I believe they are waiting to act—waiting for your signal."

Anna looked outside through the slightly steam-obscured glass; it made the park across the street look veiled in fog.

"Anna the witch." Anna chuckled, though she was disturbed by Karoline's description, which made the phantom visits seem real. She'd continually told herself she was imagining things, that they were a figment of her grief-stricken imagination. Yet until this point, she'd found some comfort in telling Karoline about it (she certainly wouldn't speak a word of it to Will's father). On the question of her nighttime visitors, Anna remained skillfully agnostic.

"Not a witch. A person with human motivation. Revenge isn't unnatural," said Karoline.

Anna felt on the defensive, suddenly self-conscious about her lighthearted dismissal of something cultural, something she likely didn't understand.

"Sorry. Though it's not exactly how I was raised, either. Turn the other cheek and all, you know?"

"Do you really believe that?"

"I don't know. Not really."

"So, what *do* you believe?"

ANNA PUT WILL'S ashes back on the shelf. While she didn't have a clear answer for Karoline regarding her beliefs, there was still some small comfort in this. It was concrete, something that wouldn't fade or evaporate. It had been four days since she had cried.

She pulled down her tools and went back to the living room where she had laid down newspapers. She picked up the carving where she'd left off last night.

Spring was coming soon.

WHEN SHE SEARCHED online for the prison, Anna had seen an image of a cell. As she expected. While nobody would likely choose to go to prison anywhere, the cell looked more like a moderately upscale college dorm room back in the States. Nothing like a US prison cell. This was another thing they had admired about Norway. But not for him. Not for him. He didn't deserve it.

She stumbled and caught herself. Adjusted the backpack and her grip on the wooden walking stick. It had taken her hours to get here: a lengthy bus ride around the lake to arrive at the island, Helgøya, then a hike to the eastern edge. To get roughly where she wanted, she'd had to take her time and be patient with herself and her lack of formal navigation training. It was less heavily wooded than she'd expected, and rocky as she neared the water. This made finding the right spot, where nobody was likely to stumble across it for some time, more difficult. But after a bit, she could see it—she could *feel* it—the right place was about one hundred feet ahead of her.

"This is the craziest shit I've ever done," she said aloud. Despite the strangeness of her activity today, she had her mind on dinner for Connor after she picked him up from Karoline's. Karoline would feed him if Anna ran late, but she didn't want to be a burden.

She looked down at the hiking stick, holding it with both hands like a serving tray. It was beautiful, in a way: it was carved from beech wood, and further carved with a number of inscriptions. Runes. Karoline had also helped her with this step.

She was interrupted by a vibration in her left pocket. Switching the stick to her right hand, she pulled her phone out with the other. Anna wasn't sure what was more amazing: that she had reception out here, or that Will's father was awake this early back in Michigan. She put the phone back in her pocket.

She took off her backpack and pulled out another important item she'd brought. Crude, ugly, but carved with just enough skill to be recognizable. The wooden horse head she'd been making for the past two weeks was about the same size as the one on the hobby horse Connor had at home. It was her second try, the first being a throwaway disaster. She turned it over, inspecting the shallow depression at the base of the neck. That's where the end of the stick would go, secured by the straps she had attached to the neck with screws, which matched two notches in the walking stick. More than anything, Anna was relieved that she wasn't required to use a real horse's head (how would she even transport it?) or even a real lamb's head. She'd never done well with blood or dead things.

Next, she dug, using a small trowel. The wooden head wasn't heavy, but she aimed to bury the stick about a foot and a half deep, hoping that would be enough to keep it from toppling in the coming days.

Finally, she placed a compass near the digging spot, so she could ensure she aimed the pole in the right direction: Northeast, toward Hamar Prison. Planting the pole went swimmingly, easier than she imagined. With the dirt filled back in and stomped down a bit, it was impressively stable, even once she'd attached the head.

Now it was time for the most difficult part, for Anna. She brought Will's small folding knife out. Gingerly, her hands trembling a bit, she ran the blade along her left middle finger. Nothing. Damn it. She instead took the point and drove it in a bit, aiming the blade away from her and flicking it, hoping she wasn't doing something that would lead to her needing stitches.

"Fuck!"

It was more painful than any small cut had a right to be. But it was necessary. She took the finger and began smearing the blood onto the horse's head, which was almost more painful than using the knife on herself. It didn't take much, she'd been assured. She wasn't sure if it had to go anywhere special on the head, but she tried to get some around the eyes and mouth. A few small streaks and splotches. It would have to do. Then, reading from her paper, she said the *mid*, the curse, the last part

Karoline had helped her with. She didn't understand it, and probably pronounced much of it incorrectly, but she poured every ounce of negative energy she felt into it. She still had her doubts, but it felt like an inversion of a desperate, faithless prayer: just in case.

After she bandaged her finger and packed everything away, Anna stood next to the nidstang and gazed out over the lake to Hamar. She stood for ten minutes, waiting for something to happen, some sign. She felt no release. The water shone brightly on this sunny day, the panorama so impartial to her anguish and anger.

FLASHING LIGHTS AS the bus approached Hamar. It stopped in a backup of traffic the small town rarely saw. She felt a needle of anxiety that parents are often so helpless to ward off: *there's an emergency, my child is in the area, and I'm not with them.* She phoned Karoline to reassure herself, letting her know she would be late. Connor and Maja were playing, and all was well.

The emergency lights were due to a road accident. A bad one, from the looks of it. A tractor, something she found so quaint to see on the roads here, pulled out in front of a speeding car. The tractor didn't look too bad, but the car was in terrible shape. Anna was horrified to see stretchers with prone, bloody figures, as the road cleared enough for the traffic to go by.

ANNA DREAMT OF birds that night. She was in the town center, and there was a cacophony of birds, all shapes and sizes, plunging and pecking and ripping feathers from one another. Feathers littered the ground to such a degree that it looked like a dirty snow had fallen over Hamar.

A large gray sea bird landed next to her and looked up quizzically.

"What are you doing here?" it asked.

"I'm trying to see what all this commotion is about," Anna found herself saying.

"One of us drowned," the bird said.

"So, you're all fighting and plucking each other's feathers out? Why would you do that?"

"What else would we do?" the bird responded.

"NOTHING YET." KAROLINE pushed the paper back toward Anna.

They sat together at the cafe after school drop off, inspecting the morning paper for any news from the prison. The deadly crash Anna rode past was the top local headline, of course, and another story covered the first paddle steamer journey of the season, to take place in three days. Mercifully, the papers had mostly forgotten Will by now, but Anna hoped to see the story reappear in the form of the murderer suffering some kind of accident or deterioration. Dark thoughts as summer approached.

Despite everything she'd done, though, Anna still didn't truly expect the nidstang to do anything. She'd felt genuine emotion when she recited the nid, but nothing had changed. All she'd felt since was a loose sense of unease. Perhaps that she'd done a bad thing, even if it was ineffective. Or perhaps it was seeing the aftermath of that accident, being reminded of the thin curtain between life and death.

THE NEXT NIGHT, Anna woke to settle Connor down. He'd had a bad dream. One inspired, it seemed, by the stories the other kids were telling at school. Several of them were claiming to have seen and heard things at home. Typical creepy, fantastical children's stories of strange figures, of voices. Anna herself still occasionally saw the shape in her windows, but she felt certain the tales being told at

Connor's school were imaginative children's fads; she remembered a frenzy of fear running through her own school as stories of seeing Bloody Mary in bathroom mirrors circulated. She'd suffered from nightmares for weeks before it was forgotten. It took an hour of gently stroking Connor's forehead before he fell asleep again.

Early that morning, Anna had another dream. Or a vision. It was so vivid that she couldn't be certain of her state of consciousness. But she was floating above Hamar, and she could hear a sound ringing out, a nearly verbal sound: *done, dumb, don't*. She continued to float on, much like the drone footage of the town she and Will had looked at before they moved, and the sound grew louder. She recognized the ruins of the cathedral, preserved within its greenhouse-like glass structure. The sound was coming from it. *A bell*, she thought. Only there was no bell there, certainly not in the present.

She passed over the ruins and then she was above Lake Mjøsa, scrolling across its royal blue depths toward Helgøya. It was calm, peaceful. So much so that Anna had no trouble spotting the object in the lake, heading in the opposite direction she was: an enormous, dark fish. No, there were no fins… A snake. It was a gigantic snakelike creature, swimming lazily toward Hamar, traveling in a perfectly straight line. It must have been two hundred feet long or more.

She descended as she neared the snake. The bell stopped, and she could now only hear, or feel, a reverberation, a low thrum that intensified. As she approached the surface of the water, there was a crackling sound, as though she were staring directly into a tremendous bonfire. The snake was almost at the surface, and she was about to submerge and meet it head on when she came out of the dream, thrashing in her bed as the early morning sun leaked into her room from behind the curtains.

She lay there for several minutes, allowing the intensity to subside. After a time, she replied to Karoline's text to confirm when and where they would meet for the paddle steamer trip. She made coffee and pulled up the curtains of the living room window. The steam rising from her mug mirrored the mist rising in the distance.

No. Not mist. It was too dark, too localized. It was smoke rising from several streets over. Was a building on fire? Then she heard the sirens.

Anna put down her mug. She thought of the lake monster in her dream. She thought of the bell ringing out. And the crackling sound. She thought of the nidstang, and the crash, and the missing hiker in the news, and even the things Connor's classmates had told him, which suddenly seemed like something more than the output of overactive imaginations. She thought of the paddle steamer. And then she began to move.

KAROLINE HAD BEEN confused when she dropped Connor off, but Anna knew she wouldn't understand. She hadn't bothered to explain, but Connor should not come with her. She warned Karoline to be careful and mentioned the fire to her. Told her not to take the steamer without her. That too seemed to cause only confusion, but there was nothing more she could do to explain herself.

She was already out of breath. She'd paid up for the taxi, and had far less distance to travel on foot than last time. But she wasn't entirely confident she could find the place. She just knew she had to get there before the first steamer journey started, and she ran.

The nidstang, she had realized.

It wasn't pointing toward Hamar Prison alone.

It was pointed at *Hamar.*

It was directed at them all: at Karoline, at Maja, at the innocent people of their quiet town by the lake. At herself. At Connor. She'd riled the spirits of the land, she thought, profaned the environment. She had spread hatred almost blindly. The accident, the missing hiker. The fire…

Anna stopped to vomit coffee and bile, then continued. Looking up, she recognized where she was.

When she finished throwing the last of the nidstang's broken pieces into the lake, some small sense of clarity settled over her. Maybe it truly had been nothing, that Hamar's ills were coincidental. Or perhaps it really was her fault. She was taking no chances. Yet she hadn't acted alone. Karoline had carved the runes, had spelled out the nid for her. She played a role as well, and Anna wanted answers. But that would come later.

THEY STOOD ON a promontory. Not the spot where she'd planted the nidstang. That wouldn't do. Instead, Anna had let Connor pick the location.

"Daddy would have liked this spot," he said with uncomplicated certainty.

Anna agreed. The steamer had been running for weeks now, with no trouble to speak of. Hamar itself had been peaceful, as it was before. Anna's darkest thought these past weeks had been that Hamar's problems had begun not with the nidstang, but with Will's death. And that Karoline—who very suddenly moved to Bodø after Anna smashed the nidstang—could have somehow had something to do with it. She then thought of the murderer, though. And she felt nothing. He was nothing to her, not worthy of revenge, of time or energy or further thought. She closed the book on him. And she closed the book on Karoline.

"Shall we spread it together?" she asked.

"Mhm," Connor said.

Anna produced the last of Will's ashes.

She suddenly thought back to the sound of the bell in her dream. Was it *done*, or was it *don't*? There was no answer. She chose to provide herself with one, the one that felt right to her. She would spread no hatred, direct nothing. The rest of Will's ashes would not go back to America. His father would be enraged, but it was out of his hands. It wasn't about him. Will loved it here. He wanted to stay here. And now he would.

But it wasn't just about Will, either. They'd made their home here, all three of them. She and Connor would stay. Not for Will, no. But *with* him.

She found herself blinded by tears, but she could feel Connor's little hands helping her, and together they cast the ashes out as far as they could, toward Lake Mjøsa and Hamar.

"Mama! Look!" Connor yelled.

She couldn't clear her eyes quickly.

"What is it?" she asked.

"Daddy!" Connor said. "His ashes stuck in the air! They froze!"

Impossible, she thought. It was July. She finished wiping away her tears, just in time to see the last wisp of frost silently, serenely sweep out over Lake Mjøsa.

THE DUMB SUPPER

Ainsley Hawthorn

THE SIGHT OF Kitty walking backwards towards the table, heels kicking up the hem of her evening gown, was so eerie my scepticism almost wavered. She moved unevenly, in stops and starts, her hands extended stiffly behind her to grasp for her chair. The whole effect was strangely insectile. Her cocked elbows produced a peculiar downward arch in her arms so they resembled the forelegs of a mantis, and her faltering movements put me in mind of the creature's spasmodic gait. Though her eyes gazed unfixedly into the darkness whence she had come, the furrow in her brow suggested total concentration, and I had little doubt she was intent not merely on gaining her seat but on the total object of our evening's gathering.

That image of a monstrous insect, animated by an intelligence quite separate from Kitty herself, made me loathe to follow her example, but the friendship that had brought me there that evening despite my reservations was enough to overcome any hesitancy. I shuffled in reverse to my own chair and, swinging about, sat down.

Although the table was laid for eight, only four places were occupied. Kitty sat to my left, Blythe to my right, and Wilda directly opposite me, with empty chairs interposed between us so that we were cloistered and solitary despite the company. Blythe was solemn, but Wilda's eyes met mine with a gay twinkle; pursing her lips, she settled and resettled herself in her seat. The murmuration of her silk skirts as they rasped one against another seemed deadened by the still, close air.

The place settings nagged at the eye with their subtle disarrangement. The cutlery was laid out contrary to its habitual position, knives and spoons to the left and forks to the right, all of them turned upside-down so their blades and tines pointed back on us accusingly. In the midst of each setting sat a little dish of bread pudding, and, as I began to eat, the lush taste of butter warmed me against the chill air.

The gamekeeper's lodge might have been quite cheery in its day. The front room was ample enough to accommodate a sitting area between table and door, although we had commandeered its two chairs and pushed back its couch to make extra places at the board. Between spreading, fernlike stains where rain had seeped through the roof thatch, the walls were a dull orange-pink, fuzzed over with mildew like the skin of a peach. In one of the two bedrooms leading off the far wall, a pair of low bunks suggested a nursery for a gaggle of girls and boys whose antics would have amused and exasperated their mother in turns.

When in bygone days the paint had been fresh as sunset and a fire blazed in the hearth to brighten the bleak days of autumn, when activity had kept the dust from settling like a muffler over the floor and the furnishings, I could imagine laughter echoing off the ceilings and pealing cleanly through the cottage like the clap of a bell. Now, the chalky odour of disuse permeated the place, mingled with more ambiguous scents— the animal musk of neatsfoot oil or leather and, high in the nose, a brimstone tang as of gunpowder.

The lodge was on the grounds of Osridge Hall, Kitty's family estate, at some distance from the main house and almost fully concealed from it by the broad horse-chestnut and linden trees, their branches not yet bare of tawny leaves, that stood where the lawn of Osridge's park turned to woodland. To all appearances abandoned, the cottage had in fact merely been shuttered when the head gamekeeper was moved to a more capacious residence with an attached stable, and it was the place's privacy and obscurity that had recommended it to Kitty as a site for our séance.

On my right, Blythe sat like a Roman bust—as still and nearly as pale, her prominent brow overshadowing her features. She worried at her pudding with the nib of her spoon, flipping sodden lumps of dough over and back onto themselves, and I wondered whether Kitty would oblige us to clean our plates before she would be satisfied that we had fulfilled the conditions of her ritual.

"I CANNOT IMAGINE a less congenial way to spend Hallowe'en," I said.

"That betrays nothing so much as a lack of imagination," Kitty retorted. "What is in the least cordial in spending the evening at home alone, or genial in going early to bed? If we do as I propose, we will, at the worst, spend a memorable evening in one another's company."

The four of us sat in Osridge's broad and airy drawing-room, playing at whist. Dinner had passed glacially in exchanges about weather, wind direction, and the local terrain with Kitty's father's gentlemen guests, who were planning a shooting party for the following day. Not a man amongst them was eligible, but perhaps the greater offence was that not a man amongst them was entertaining. Their wives, meanwhile, expressed only as much interest in their host's daughter and her provincial companions as propriety dictated before becoming engrossed in a rather closed conversation about the upcoming London season. It did not escape our notice that their subject of preference was which girls of genuinely consequential families were expected to come out this year.

After dinner, one of the men suggested cards. While the others arranged themselves for commerce, Kitty excused us from the group for a rubber of whist, on account of our being a perfect foursome. I suspect my friends were by then as eager as I to escape to a more intimate and amiable conversation, and none of us supposed Kitty might have another motive for speaking with us in confidence. We had retreated to a small table in a recess of the wall at some distance from the rest of the party. Over our heads arched a Palladian window, and the wan rays of a crescent moon, barely visible at the window's apex, refracted through the faceted pendants of the valance and flickered on the wall above the reach of the candlelight.

"How does it work, then, this dumb supper of yours?" asked Wilda, absently laying a card. Wilda was petite, with a youthful plumpness that lifted her cheeks into high apples when she smiled. She cocked her head in earnest curiosity so that her short, brassy curls fell into her eyes.

"Work?" scoffed I. "It doesn't 'work' at all. It's false hope for credulous and desperate young women."

"Oh, hush, Aggie," said Kitty dismissively. She turned to Wilda. "The meal must be conducted as wrongly as possible. We shall eat the courses in reverse, from pudding to soup, and we ought to move backwards wherever we might. But the critical element is that we must all maintain absolute silence, the silence of the very grave, from the beginning of the meal to its ending. Utter so much as a single word, and the spell will be broken."

Wilda screwed up her face at this, having no taste for quietude, but Kitty continued, "If we perform the supper correctly, at the stroke of midnight the spirits of our husbands-to-be will walk through the door and join us at the table." She laid a card and took the trick. "To my mind, that would be a reward well worth the effort. Blythe, your lead."

Blythe scanned her cards and played a low spade before asking guardedly: "And what if there are no husbands in our future?"

"Yes," Wilda nodded, following Blythe's line of reasoning, "what if we all are doomed to spinsterhood? What will happen then?"

"I cannot think that will be your fate, Wilda," Kitty replied, "but, in that case, the chairs beside us would remain empty, or there would be some other sign." There was some hurry in her voice that gave me pause, but Wilda cut in on my thoughts.

"Well, I think it's a perfectly splendid idea!" she exclaimed, tossing a card to the trick and flinging herself back into her seat. "The village is so very dull just now and the season so very dreary. I am even tired of myself. To preview the delights of the future would be a perfect antidote to the tedium of the present."

In her verve, she had made a poor play, and I claimed a cheap trick.

"Oh, for heaven's sake, Wilda!" said Kitty, tossing her cards on the table. "Do pay better attention. You've quite lost us the game."

As I took up the deck and began to shuffle, she resumed her campaign. "And what do you say to that, Aggie? How can you deny us a romantic little diversion?"

"Would we not pass a happier evening if you joined me at Clivemont instead?" I entreated. "Would our enjoyment not be the greater in conversation before a charming fire than mute in a draughty derelict?" Kitty was headstrong, and I cast about for a substitute that would capture her imagination. "If it's entertainment you want, we could stage a tableau or read from a play."

"Happier, you say! What could have more bearing on our happiness than the identities of our husbands? I do not concern myself with the transitory amusements of today but with the enduring fulfilment of our tomorrows."

Her brow shone, and she spoke breathlessly. I saw then from the fervour of her aspect and the zeal of her words that she was not to be swayed from her intentions.

"I understand you perfectly, Aggie," she declared. "You needn't belabour your point. Spirits are for winter's tales and, if not that, then for those who wish to warm themselves of a winter's night. But you can't begrudge us a bit of silliness, can you? We have our whole lives to be sensible."

Before I could make any answer, Kitty fixed on Blythe. "As it stands, we are one for and one against," she said breezily. "It's down to you, Blythe. What do you think? Shall we hold a dumb supper, or no?"

Blythe was not by her nature credulous. On the contrary, happenstance required of her a prudence that perhaps none of the rest of us could fully appreciate. Blythe's father was a gentleman, but of no great means, and she was the youngest of several daughters. For that reason, she was accustomed to thrift, and, though she accompanied us on shopping excursions to the village, she only purchased for herself at the explicit direction of her mother. Their estate, moreover, was entailed, with the effect that only judicious planning would prevent Blythe's spare lifestyle from becoming in future even more tightly constrained.

Blythe's only brother had died in infancy, so that the heir to the estate was a distant cousin, a barrister from Leicester, who was professed to be miserly by those who had reason to like him; those with reason to dislike him were even less liberal in their praise. Blythe's hopes and those of her sisters were consequently pinned on marrying well. While each had claim to a modest dowry, Blythe's prospects for a good match were rather worse than her sisters by virtue of being the youngest. By the time her elder sisters had come out and been shown sufficiently in society (in sufficiently extravagant finery) to attract suitable proposals, the family coffers might no longer have adequate means to grant her an equal opportunity. And so, if not credulous, she may be desperate indeed.

Blythe eyed me across the card table, and, when she spoke, it was at first not to Kitty but to me.

"Are you certain you have no spades, Aggie? You failed to follow suit." She was trying to save me having to revoke. I shook my head—I could not play otherwise than I had. Under the circumstances, I realised, neither could she.

"Yes, Kitty," she said. "Let's hold a dumb supper."

KITTY ROSE FROM the table, and, in the absence of direction, we took her exertion as our signal to clear the dishes, walking backwards all the time. Where Blythe's pudding had hardly been touched—a point on which Kitty thankfully showed herself to be unconcerned— Wilda had eaten with gusto, scooping out the last of her custard down to bare porcelain.

From a basket, Kitty drew a starched tablecloth secreted from the dining room at Osridge. It was bleached pristine white and was at such variance with the gloom pervading those neglected quarters that it seemed to glow with its own light. To each of us she passed a corner, and we lofted the cloth over the table so that it hung for a moment like vapour before settling upon the hoary surface an expiating lightness.

The settings remade, we sat to our second courses and our soup. Our portions were not overlarge as we had dined severally earlier in the evening, before donning our cloaks and departing our homes on pretext of "cards at Osridge" or "tea at Clivemont" as dictated by our own place of residence. The weightier challenge was Kitty's, who had taken it upon herself as architect of this mad scheme to procure the necessary accoutrements.

Over the course of the days preceding, she had smuggled small quantities of bread and milk and meat from the larder to a wood shed not far from the main house where we had played spillikins as children. Had Kitty not advanced her own candidacy for the task, we must needs have done so ourselves, for not only were the stores at Osridge best provisioned to furnish the evening's needs without arousing notice, but the estate's cook had also regarded Kitty with utmost affection since girlhood and would doubtless wink at any vacancies in her pantry if she in the least suspected it was Kitty who was responsible.

Pirating silver and china proved a rather more delicate matter. Osridge's housekeeper, while unfailingly courteous, did not share the opinion of its cook, and she gave evidence in small gestures of her eyes and mouth that Kitty was not among her darlings, nor did she consider the young lady by any means an adequate substitute for her mother, the late mistress of Osridge. The housekeeper, furthermore, was a mean accountant who kept all the hall's fittings under scrupulous supervision, but it was the maids who bore the brunt of her officiousness in place of Kitty. She had on more than one occasion upbraided a housemaid for inquisitively rifling through her master's chattels only to conduct a detailed examination of the servants' personal effects in the same evening—solely, as she maintained, to check for ill-gotten gains.

In consequence, Kitty had risked only a raid of the linen cupboard, the which, she reasoned, was unlikely to be checked before the next wash, which was not until Thursday. For the remainder of the service, we relied on what remained at the lodge and on silver conveyed, by mutual agreement, in our reticules. We had jangled like men of fortune as we made our way over the fields in the twilight.

An hour strangely spent passes swiftly, it seems. I had just touched my fowl, so it appeared to me, before Kitty was on her feet and we performed another remove for the soup. Twelve chimes of the clock should have given us the sign that our ritual was at an end, proclaiming four girls' success at maintaining an hour of silence if not heralding the arrival of our husbands-to-be. But any clock that had once stood in that place had left with the gamekeeper, and we therefore had no warning of their coming.

There was no screen between us and the biting October wind when at midnight the lodge's front door swung open, so that the gooseflesh that scaled over my skin like an armour could have been as much from cold as from terror—could have been, but was not. I felt the awe that passed over my companions, felt rather than heard how their breaths caught in their throats, felt rather than saw how their spines stiffened and their fingers clenched. I felt it because in that instant we shared an animal sympathy greater than any fellow-feeling that had previously existed between us.

Through the door walked a man. Though he was not tall, he was well proportioned with fleshy but pleasing features. A good deal may be guessed about a man from his clothing, and this fellow was dressed like a gentleman of moderate income and even temperament. His coat and waistcoat were closely tailored and, though they followed the current fashion, were tasteful and unobtrusive in both colour and texture. The knot in his cravat was restrained but sufficiently complex to suggest a valet of no mean skill.

The man had no appearance of being a spirit, no blue mist hovering about his person nor hollows in the sockets of his eyes. Yet his behaviour was wholly unnatural. Conversing with us not at all, nor indicating by the least glance, bow, or inclination of his head that he was in any way cognisant of our presence, he strode to our table as a man in a trance and took the seat at Blythe's side. Despite shrinking somewhat away from him, her right hand flying to her breast as a kind of bulwark between them, she appraised him sidelong, and I detected a faint collapse of her frame that could not be attributed solely to unease but rather bore the hallmarks of a certain relief.

We did not know then what to do or whether we could speak. I had been convinced there was no possibility of our success, were we to perform the ceremony rightly, wrongly, or standing on our heads, so my discomposure was only natural; though I had believed my friends to be at least receptive to the prospect that the procedure should work as they intended, they appeared no less astonished than myself. But the silence of the man who had joined our company seemed to admonish us to hold our tongues still, so hold them we did as a second gentleman stepped into the cottage.

Lankier than the first, his face was uncommonly handsome and his bearing courtly even in his strange, stuporous state. In his attire there was something of the dandy; he wore a blue clawhammer coat, buckskin breeches, and riding boots polished to a reflective sheen. Though it was impossible to be sure due to his catatonia, I sensed from a certain disdainful aspect in his countenance that he might prove himself, under ordinary conditions, somewhat high in the instep.

That arrogant mien was not to my liking, but it proved insufficient to dissuade either Kitty or Wilda. On the contrary, they were so quickly recovered from the strangeness of our circumstances as almost to swoon over the dashing newcomer, and by coquettish smiles and demure expressions each seemed to undertake to lure him to her, although he gave no sign of seeing them.

When he took the place beside Kitty—to Wilda's consternation—the flush of delight that suffused Kitty's features was almost on the instant overcast by a fearful pallor. In sitting, the stranger had laid his hands upon the table, and in his right fist was loosely gripped a ferocious hunting knife with a haft of horn. The unsteady beams of our candle flames caused the steely teeth of the knife's serrated edge to jab and withdraw and jab again, as though animated by an innate violence. Forsaking in her agitation both decorum and self-preservation, Kitty grabbed at the man's hand and, with normally agile digits grown numb in the extremity of her distress, fumblingly drew the blade from his grasp.

For a suspended moment, she held it lightly between her fingertips, and, when finally she dropped it to the floor with a clatter, a chilling blast of autumn air announced our third caller. Where the two previous apparitions had given no proof as to their otherworldly origin, this visitant was preceded by the whiff of the tomb: rot, swampy vegetation, mothballs, and the incongruous tang of summer berries. It crossed the threshold in a billow of yellowed linen that wound about its body and trailed in mouldering fragments at its feet. As it walked—or, more precisely, hobbled, its gait hampered by its tightly twisted mantle—the layers of sallow cloth rasped one against another and discharged wisps of some fine grey powder into the air.

The foetor of decay was by now almost unbearable, and I could scarcely breathe for want of pure air. Extending a lean and weathered arm out from under its shroud, the figure clasped the chair adjacent to Wilda's and lowered its body tortuously into the seat. As it did so, its cerements caught beneath its slight frame and fell back from where they had hooded its head in sagging folds, blackened at the edges of the face from the effluvia of decomposition.

Its visage—oh, its obscene countenance the very mockery of the living! Skin as crisp and membranous as vellum, pulled taut over its bones where the corrosion of the tissue had deprived it of that forgiving artifice which, in the living, conceals the fragile and impermanent stuff of which we are made. Lipless and perhaps, in the echoing cavern of its jaw, tongueless, this spectre was subject to an enforced speechlessness that cast our silence in a dreadful new light. Its eyes, or the chambers where its eyes should have been, dissolved into the blackness of its empty skull, and in that rancid cavity I believed I could distinguish convulsive, writhing movement. Wilda, in the great mercy of providence, had long since fainted.

Only one seat remained to be occupied, and, before the door could reopen, before I could face my future as had the others, I filled my lungs to bursting with rank air and screamed. I screamed as I had never screamed before. I screamed as if to redeem our silence with sound.

Blythe was the first to receive and accept an offer of marriage from a reserved young gentleman with fleshy but in no way displeasing features whom she met at a ball in the neighbouring quarter. He had only recently taken up permanent residence in the district after the death of his father, and the affinity between them was immediate, revealing itself in chaste flirtations that made staid Blythe seem girlish and bashful.

Though Blythe discouraged us with admonitory scowls, Kitty, Wilda, and I could not help probing by veiled comments and indirect queries whether he recollected the events of that All Hallow's evening, whether he had perhaps been having fun at our expense or, if not that, whether he had been whisked from his apartments in the city and been compelled to attend our occult gathering by some obscure supernatural force. Yet he betrayed neither a hint of recognition nor even the sleepy bemusement of one who strains to summon up the memory of a dream.

When, some time later, Kitty was introduced to her husband through the machinations of her aunt, who had arranged for both families to join her at her country house in the interest of making a match, we no longer asked questions, cowed perhaps by what two prophecies fulfilled might imply for the third. Wilda, who had been spared the full horror of her Hallowtide visitor by her lapse into insensibility, seemed remarkably unperturbed and looked to Kitty's pending nuptials with considerable anticipation. The only one of the bride's attendants who was not a relation, she spent a great deal of time with the happy couple, penning invitations and planning the celebration.

I, however, could never expunge from my mind the events of that evening. Walking by the river, I would catch a vegetal scent of putrefaction and take fright. I struggled to dress, for my linen chemise seemed to wind about my legs and immobilise me. Thus, as soon as I saw Kitty married, I left Clivemont for an extended series of visits with friends and family.

And so it was that the news reached me by means of the evening papers before ever I received word from home: Wilda was dead. In the guise of friendship, she had insinuated herself into the company of Kitty's husband, and that contemptuous rake had broken faith with his wife of so many months to conduct a secret affair. Their mistake was to underestimate Kitty's powers of discernment, for by the brief glances they exchanged and the innocent words that intimated deeper meanings, her suspicions were raised and, eventually, by the interception of an indiscreet letter from Wilda, confirmed.

Kitty had, according to the account published in the dailies, invited Wilda for a morning visit on a day when her husband was managing his affairs in London, giving in her invitation no suggestion that she was in any way conscious of their intimacy, and when ingenuous little Wilda arrived Kitty had accosted her with proofs and recriminations. Wilda had at first wailed tearful apologies but, finding Kitty in no way moved to forgiveness, had let fly her own remonstrances against her once dear friend, imputing the liaison to a frigidity and self-absorption on Kitty's part that had so frustrated and dispirited her husband as to cause him to seek comfort elsewhere. Incensed, Kitty had traced Wilda's retreat through her husband's study and, coming upon a horn-handled knife that had been left atop the desk, in a fit of rage, had stabbed Wilda through the heart.

Kitty was tried as a murderess, convicted, and hanged at Newgate. Her faithless husband, meanwhile, enlarged his estate with astute investment of Kitty's dowry and has since bestowed it on a new wife—no less pretty nor less wealthy, but significantly more biddable. I understand they have been blessed with a number of children.

I am now in my twenty-ninth year and not yet married. I have entertained suitors, of course, and they me, but there is something in my demeanour that seems always to drive them away before an offer is made. Perhaps I will die an old maid at Clivemont with my brother and my nephews; yet I can never find it within myself to regret my solitude, nor to long for its abatement. Sometimes I think on the vacant seat at the table, that persistent absence that contained within itself every possible future, and I wonder at the potential of emptiness before it is occupied and of silence before it is broken.

ABOUT THE AUTHORS

Miranda Allen – Cold Company

Miranda Allen is a writer and artist living on the Northern Coast of CA. While her days are mostly spent working a day job to support her family, her leisure time is generally filled with her children, partner, pets, and the many creative pursuits she enjoys. authorcmallen.wixsite.com/cmallen

Michael Barron – Rage and Redemption

Michael's fiction has appeared in *Uncharted Magazine* and *NewMyths. com* as well as other publications. His comic *The Secret Lives of Demon Hunters* is currently being illustrated. Michael is a member of the neurodivergent community. When he is not writing, he is either training for a marathon with his wife or searching for the world's greatest hot sauce. michaeljbarron.com

Warren Benedetto – Blame

Warren Benedetto writes dark fiction about horrible people, horrible places, and horrible things. He is an award-winning author and a full member of the SFWA. warrenbenedetto.com

Hannah Birss – Manifestation

Hannah Birss is a writer and aspiring magpie based out of Ontario, Canada. She lives with her partner, children, and multiple animals. She can usually be found in a nest constructed of books, writing journals, and shiny trinkets. hannahbirsswrites.carrd.co

Christopher Allen Bond – Barefoot in the Bleach Water

Christopher Bond is a writer, husband, father, thrift store archaeologist, and a bookstore explorer. His short fiction has been included in multiple magazines and anthologies. His debut novella, *The Devil Came Down the Mountain*, was released earlier this year via Horrorsmith Publishing. christopherbondauthor.com

Terry Campbell – The Man Who Built Gallows

Terry Campbell lives and writes in a tiny house in TX with his lovely wife and two hairless dogs, but with an eye towards AZ. His story was a top 5 finalist for the inaugural Longhorn Prize presented by Saddlebag Dispatches and was the first piece of fiction he had written in 20 years. His self-published first novel, *Kindred Feather*, is available on Amazon.

Pablo Lacalle Castillo – From Darkness to Promote Me

Pablo Lacalle Castillo is a twenty-two-year-old Spanish postgraduate student from the University of Edinburgh. He lives in Madrid, Spain. Other work by Pablo has been published in *The Foundationalist* literary journal and *The Broad Online* student-magazine. When not writing, he can be found walking his dog, spending time with his family and fellow triplet siblings, and adding books to the ever-increasing tower beside his bed.

Anastasia Dziekan – Kid Sister

Anastasia Dziekan is an emerging queer American horror author. Anastasia's work can also be found in anthologies such as *Moonflowers & Nightshade* and *Scissor Sisters*. Outside of her own writing, Anastasia teaches English, watches scary movies, and spends time with her dogs.

Kevin M. Folliard – Smoky Joe

Kevin M. Folliard is a Chicagoland writer whose fiction has been collected by The Horror Tree, The Dread Machine, Demain Publishing, and more. His recent publications include his horror anthology *The Misery King's Country* and his sci-fi dinosaur adventure series *Tales from New Pangea* from Dark Owl Publishing. Kevin currently resides in the western suburbs of Chicago, IL, where he enjoys his day job in academia and membership in the La Grange Writers Group. kevinfolliard.com

Relvin Gonzalez – Vessel 401

Relvin Gonzalez is a Puerto Rican fiction author. His stories include his first novel, *The Void Beyond the Walls*, a dark literary fiction written from the point of view of a Texan serial killer who becomes part of a crew to terraform Mars, the *444* mythological science fiction series, including the titles *Hefnd*, *Path of the Hybrids*, and *Messengers Rising*, and the psychedelic journey into madness, *Glia*, among others. Relvin lives in Austin, Texas, with his wife, son, and dog. relvingonzalez.com

Re Gwaltney – Tracks in the Dust

A lifelong writer of fantasy and horror, Re Gwaltney loves to dig into the darker things in life and pull out both the painful and beautiful in their inescapable Venn diagram. They seek to fill the world with nuanced and powerful representations of LBGT+ and disabled experiences one story at a time. When not writing, Re can be found snuggling their dog, practicing witchcraft, and gaming way too much. regwaltney.com

Patrick Herald – Quiet Lake

Patrick Herald was born and raised in Michigan. A former writing instructor, he now lives with his family in England. When he isn't working or writing, he enjoys countryside walks and training in Brazilian jiu-jitsu.

Ken Farrell – Kin

Originally from Colorado, Ken Farrell lives and writes in Texas, his work appearing in various anthologies and journals such as *Pilgrimage*, *Coffin Bell*, and *Watershed Review*. Ken holds an MFA from Texas State University, an MA from Salisbury University, and has earned as an adjunct, cage fighter, pizzaiolo, and warehouseman.

Ainsley Hawthorn – The Dumb Supper

Ainsley Hawthorn, PhD, is an author and cultural historian who writes about forgotten events, curious folklore, and the surprising connections between past and present. She has contributed to *National Geographic*, *The Washington Post*, *Psychology Today*, *CBC*, and more and edited the nonfiction anthology *Land of Many Shores: Perspectives from a Diverse Newfoundland and Labrador*. ainsleyhawthorn.com

C.R. Kane – The Will of Lady Penelope Grant

A scribbler of the sinister and enthusiast of the eerie, C.R. Kane has published multiple short stories. They have recently debuted their first novella, *The Vampyres*, as of March 2024, and is currently chipping at a number of other gothic horrors-in-progress. When not writing, they can be found hoarding excess amounts of novelty mugs and trying to convince the cat to please let them have the desk chair back. seearcanescribbles.com

Amanda Cecelia Lang – On Their Hands

Amanda Cecelia Lang is a horror author and aspiring ghost whisperer from Colorado. Her stories haunt the dark corners of many popular podcasts, magazines, and anthologies, including *Gamut*, *Ghoulish Tales*, *Cast of Wonders*, *Uncharted*, *Dark Matter*, and Flame Tree's *Darkness Beckons*. Her short story collection *Saturday Fright at the Movies* will debut in October 2024 (Dark Matter INK). amandacecelialang.com

Felicia Lee – Every Day is Thursday

Felicia Lee is a Florida-based writer and editor. Her fiction has appeared in anthologies, including *Borderlands 7* from Borderlands Press and *Bodies in the Library* from Flame Tree Press. Her non-fiction work has appeared in publications, including the *Los Angeles Times* and Salon.com. tardigrademedia.com

Nicola Lombardi – Desire & Sons
(translated by J. Weintraub)

Nicola Lombardi has published six novels and seven collections of stories as well as translating works by Jack Ketchum, Seabury Quinn, Charlee Jacob, F.B. Long and many others for the Italian market. In 2021 Tartarus Press published in English his collection *The Gypsy Spiders and Other Tales of Italian Horror.* nicolalombardi.com

J. Weintraub has published fiction, essays, and poetry in many literary places, and his plays have been produced throughout the USA and internationally. As a translator, he has introduced the Italian and Swiss horror writers, Nicola Lombardi and Davide Staffiero, to the English-speaking world, and his annotated translation of Eugène Briffault's *Paris à table: 1846* was published by Oxford UP in 2018. jweintraub.weebly.com

Marshall J. Moore – Fudakaeshi

Marshall J. Moore is the award-winning author of the *Rites of Resurrection* trilogy of high fantasy novels from Shadow Alley Press, the pirate cozy fantasy duology *Son of a Sailor* and *Prisoners of a Pirate Queen*, and over thirty short stories appearing in publications such as *CatsCast, Mysterion, Flame Tree,* and many others.

Ron Perovich – The Bouquet

Ron Perovich is an American artist, musician, and poet, currently crafting elaborate nonsense from a sweltering and/or freezing Texas apartment. He is gently tolerated by his belly dancing accountant wife and their very spooky cats.

AM Sutter – Wood for the Trees

AM Sutter currently works as a zoo and exotic animal veterinarian and has been fascinated with storytelling ever since she snuck downstairs as a child to watch *The Twilight Zone* with her father. Whenever she's not arm's deep in tiger guts or elephant poop, she enjoys playing the French horn, reading, and hiking with her Shih Tzu, who fully believes he is a wolf. amsutter.com

Michael Vance – What is Done

Michael Vance is a resident of Ontario, Canada. He has previously published fiction in the *Tesseracts* anthology series, On Spec magazine, and BFS Horizons. He has been writing since the age of ten.

R. Wren – Graves in Different Places

R. Wren (they/she) is an Irish writer of weird tales. They write because they don't believe in ghosts, but wish that they could. R. Wren's story *Becoming* appeared in *Beyond the Veil: Queer Tales of Supernatural Love*, *Zoey* appeared in *Dread Imaginings*, *To Mirror Lake* appeared in *Tower Magazine Volume 2*, and *Carrigan* appeared in *InterZone #299* .

CONTENT WARNINGS

Please note that because this is a horror anthology, it should be assumed that the basic horror tropes will apply. These include death, gore, and violence.

Barefoot in the Bleach Water – mutilation, bodily experimentations (off-page)

Blame – references to sexual assault, suicide

Cold Company – loss of partner, substance abuse, suicidal ideation

Desire & Sons – n/a

Every Day is Thursday – child death (off-page), abusive parent

From Darkness to Promote Me – child death (off-page), self-mutilation

Fudakaeshi – n/a

Graves in Different Places – mind/body possession and control, dubious consent

Kid Sister – n/a

Kin – confederate soldiers, animal abuse

Manifestation – child death

On Their Hands – mother/child separation

Quiet Lake – loss of partner, mild self-harm

Rage and Redemption – bullying

Smoky Joe – implied spousal abuse

The Bouquet – child death

The Dumb Supper – n/a

The Man Who Built Gallows – loss of partner and child (off-page)

The Will of Lady Penelope Grant – mind/body possession and control, suicide

Tracks in the Dust – abusive parent, death of a parent

Vessel 401 – child death (off-page)

What is Done – loss of partner

Wood for the Trees – n/a